Beat of the Heart

Beat of the Heart

Katie Ashley

Beat of the Heart

ISBN-13: 978-1493511457

ISBN-10: 1493511459

Image Copyright Eric Battershell, 2013

Image Model:
Assad-Lawrence Hadi Shalhoub

Cover Design by:
RBA Designs | Letitia Hasser

Book Design by:
Indie Pixel Studio | www.indiepixelstudio.com

To the Ladies of the Ledge: Marilyn Medina, Marion Archer, Cris Hadarly, Michelle Eck, Kim Bias, Lisa Kane, and Karen Lawson

Without these fabulous women, dear readers, you would not receive my books. They have supported me by holding my hand during the blood, sweat, and tears of the writing process as well as talking me down from the ledge we crazy writers put ourselves out on. Most of all, their keen eyes have helped to make my books the best they can be through editing, revising, and brainstorming.

"You and I travel to the beat of a different drum. Oh, can't you tell by the way I run every time you make eyes at me?"—Mike Nesmith

"One good thing about music, when it hits you, you feel no pain"—Bob Marley

"If music be the food of love, play on"—William Shakespeare

Chapter One

AJ

With my foot pumping steady on the bass drum, my arms flew in a frenzied flourish over the toms and cymbals, sending a deafening thunder throughout the auditorium. As stinging sweat threatened to blind my eyes, I quickly swiped my arm across my forehead and then focused on the song's encore and my third solo of the evening. Jake and Brayden's echoing harmonies had ended only moments before, and now it was a battle between the metal and drums on our most hardcore song to date, *Ride the Pale Horse*. Their guitars screeched to a halt, and then it was me, and only me, pounding out the rhythm. As the house lights flickered in a mosaic of colors, I felt the beat echoing deep within my chest. Although I loved any excuse to show off, I knew the importance of solos to my band mates—we were only as good as our last show or our last album. Even though I was in a stadium with twenty thousand people, moments like these always took me back to when I was a kid and was learning how to master the drums from my Tio Diego.

Just as I finished the last beat of the crescendo, everything went black in the auditorium. It took only a millisecond for the audience's approval to begin as a resounding roar. For a full minute, we remained in the pitch black until the house lights slowly came back up. As I took off my headset, whistles, cat-calls, and applause stung my ears. I rose off my stool and made my way out of the drum set to join the guys at the front of the stage. During the blackout, roadies had taken Jake, Brayden, and Rhys's guitars. I, on the other hand, stood twirling one of my drumsticks between my fingers.

Standing toe to toe with each other, we waved to the crowd before doing a united bow. Jake passed each of us the microphone so we could say our individual goodbyes. Once Brayden returned it to him, Jake grinned. "Good night, Oklahoma City! Keep it rockin' til next time!" he bellowed, his voice echoing throughout the auditorium. With a final wave, we started jogging off the stage. When I got to the edge, I turned back. I kissed each of my sticks before chucking them out into the crowd. It was a wonder, after all the times of doing it, I hadn't managed to poke someone's eye out or inflict some other heinous injury with them. The

potential liability and lawsuits were something that 'legal-eagle', Rhys, loved to remind me of constantly.

Security quickly escorted us into one of the backstage rooms where we'd gotten ready earlier in the evening. The members of Jacob's Ladder—Jake's fiancée, Abby Renard, and her twin brothers, Gabe and Eli, lounged on the over-stuffed couches, awaiting our arrival. With sweat pouring off of me, I gladly took an ice-cold water bottle, along with a towel, from one of the roadies. As I guzzled down the water, another guy thrust a clean shirt in my face. It was t-minus five minutes till Meet and Greet time with lucky fans.

"Ew, Jake!" Abby squealed. I glanced over my shoulder to see that Jake hadn't bothered to towel off or change shirts. Instead, he was rubbing his sweat-soaked body over Abby's glittering stage dress. When he nuzzled his face against her neck and whispered something in her ear, she grinned and didn't seem to mind that her appearance to meet fans was getting shot to hell.

"Get a room," I teased, as I whipped my old shirt over my head.

"We may have to call the room on your bus tonight," Abby said with a giggle.

I groaned as I pulled on the clean, skin-tight, black Runaway Train T-shirt. "I thought the whole point of you two buying a separate bus was so you could keep it rockin' without us having to know."

Wrinkling her nose at my description of their activities, Abby replied, "Yes, but since Lily is with us for the next three shows, we want to give up the bed to her and Bray."

Jake rolled his eyes. "Let's rephrase that, babe. *You* want to give the bed up, not *me*."

Abby smacked his arm playfully. "But the roosts can be awfully fun too, you know."

A wicked grin curved on Jake's face as if some elicit memory had just been rekindled in his mind. "That's true."

Just as they started to engage in some serious lip-lock, a knock came at the door, signaling it was time to start the Meet and Greet. Running a hand through my sweat-soaked hair, I tried to steady myself. Don't get me wrong, I loved the hell out of our fans—they made us what we were, but I preferred pre-show Meet and Greets. With the pre-performance energy adrenaline pumping, you really could give to your fans what they deserved.

But the suits and event planners never quite understood that. So, after days of touring and hours spent playing your heart out has sent exhaustion prickling over your body like nicks from a razor blade, it was hard finding the energy after a show to give your all to each and every person who came by—especially the over-eager women who wanted more than you were willing to give. You're too tired, and you let your guard down, which results in having your ass and junk unwillingly grabbed.

A flurry of movement came from the doorway indicating the eager fans had arrived. Abby and Jake quickly rose off the couch and then went their separate ways with their respective bands. The line remained steady, and my face felt frozen in a smile as I posed with different fans. I signed so many shirts, CD's, and body parts that my hand cramped up so bad that I thought it would never recover to play in tomorrow night's show. Rhys and I were now the only guys who signed breasts. Brayden had been out of that game practically since we started, and now that Jake was engaged to Abby, he was refusing too. In his absence, I was happy to oblige.

We only had about ten fans left when Kylie, Lily's younger sister and sometimes nanny, poked her dark head in the door. Before she could open her mouth, Melody's high decibel scream echoed throughout the room. "DADDY! I WANT MY DADDY!"

With one hand signing a program, Brayden used the other to beckon Kylie. She hurried into the room, trying to muffle Melody's cries by cradling the fifteen month old to her rack. But Melody pulled away and reached out for Bray. The moment he took her, Melody quieted, wrapping her arms around Brayden's neck.

He gave an apologetic smile to the fans. "Excuse me, but it seems my daughter needs her daddy. I hope you all won't mind if I duck out?"

Since it was only women left, they practically melted into a freaking puddle in the floor at Brayden's words and actions. A chorus of "Aw's" coupled with "What a good father you are" rang through the room. As Bray left with one of our jacked-up security guards, Kylie didn't follow him. Instead, she hung around, talking to Abby, while cutting her blue eyes over at me.

"Trouble, bro," Rhys said, as he handed a hat back to the last fan left.

Glancing up at Kylie, I winked, causing her to grin. "Nothing we haven't already done before."

"Yeah, I know." Rhys turned his back to everyone else and eased up beside me, so no one else could hear us. "You're all about the game and the freakin' chase. Once you caught Kylie, she threw *you* for a loop by not being heart-broken when she went back home for spring semester." Rhys grimaced. "Dude, you got shit-faced for a week."

I shrugged. "So I got a little attached. It doesn't mean it will happen again."

Rhys huffed out a frustrated breath. "Whatever man. Just don't come to my roost drunk and crying over her."

"Whatever," I grumbled. With the last fan exiting the door, Jake began tugging Abby out of the room. I hoped for their sake, Bray had managed to get Melody to sleep so it wouldn't

interrupt the rated R plans I imagined Jake had for himself and Abby.

I gave Kylie my best 'you will be screaming my name in an hour' smirk. "Hey stranger."

With a smile, she tossed some of her chestnut brown hair over her shoulder. "Hey yourself."

"Good to see you back."

"Thanks."

"How long are you along for the ride?"

She cocked her head, as if surmising whether there was some loaded innuendo in my question. "Just for the week. I'm off for Spring Break."

"Ah, I see." I rubbed the stubble along my chin, trying to decide the best way to approach getting her naked in my bed as soon as possible.

"I'm not seeing anyone now," Kylie said softly.

"Good to know."

She brushed up against me. "I missed you."

"I've missed you, too."

"With your hoard of female admirers, I highly doubt that."

I gave her a reassuring smile. "It's the truth." Glancing over my shoulder, I saw the room was starting to thin out. "What would you say about coming back to my bus tonight, instead of Jake and Bray's?"

"I think I would like that."

Pinning my hands against the wall on either side of her head, I leaned in, my lips inches from hers. "From what I remember you used to like it a lot, especially when I gave you multiple orgasms. All. Night. Long."

A flush tinged her cheeks as I ground my pelvis into hers, eliciting a slight gasp that stroked my ego. "AJ," she murmured, closing her eyes in anticipation. After a quick kiss, that was harder to control than I had originally thought, Kylie groaned in disappointment. I almost did the same

thing. Instead, I pushed back off the wall and wrapped an arm around her waist. "Come on, let's take this to the bus."

She bobbed her head and let me lead her out of the room. We started weaving our way through the hustle and bustle of roadies breaking down the show's equipment and loading the trucks. Ahead of us, Frank, our head roadie and father figure, joined up with Jake and Abby. We were only a few feet from Jake's bus when Frank stumbled on the pavement. Jake and Abby stopped, but when he didn't continue walking, Jake reached out for him. But before he

could catch him, Frank slumped to the ground.

"Oh shit!" I cried, as I sprinted away from Kylie.

Ashen faced, Frank clutched his chest. "My heart."

"Somebody get the paramedics!" Jake shouted.

Roadies scrambled around, grabbing for their phones. An ambulance was always on stand-by during a show, and I hoped to God it hadn't left yet.

Instead of kneeling down beside Frank, Abby raced to the bus. The driver saw her coming and hurried to have the door open. She disappeared inside for a minute before running back with the first aid kit. Brayden was right on her heels, obviously sensing something had happened.

When she got back to us, Abby fumbled in the bag before digging a bottle of aspirin out. She then knelt down beside Frank and popped a pill. "Here. Swallow this," she commanded.

As Frank took the pill, the wail of an ambulance's siren pierced the silence. It was only seconds later that it came screeching around the corner. Slamming on its brakes only a few feet away, it stop with the paramedics rushing out of the doors. I backed away so they could get to Frank. That's when I glanced over at Jake. He stood frozen, unblinking and unmoving—pure horror etched on his face. "Jake?" I questioned. But he didn't respond.

After getting an oxygen mask over Frank's face, the paramedics worked on putting in an IV and loading him onto the stretcher. "He's stable, so someone can ride with us," one of them said.

Abby glanced over her shoulder. "Jake, do you want to ride to the hospital with Frank?"

He ignored her question. Instead, he murmured absentmindedly, "You were crumpled on the ground."

Rising to her feet, Abby's blonde brow lined in confusion. "What?"

"Your white dress was stained with blood...Then, she was on the ground at the stables when she had the last seizure." Jake shuddered. "She never got out of bed again after that."

Tears sparkled in Abby's bright blue eyes as she crossed the distance between them to put her hands on Jake's face. "Baby, I'm here. Don't go back there," she crooned softly.

One of the paramedics poked his head out the door. "Okay, we're ready to go."

Abby threw a panicked glance over at me. I knew she wanted to go, but she couldn't bear leaving Jake in the state he was in. "Don't worry. I'll go."

"Thank you," she replied, before wrapping Jake in her arms.

I hopped in the back of the ambulance and slid across the

bench. Reaching out, I grabbed Frank's hand, which was already wrapped in IV tubing, in mine. He squeezed it back. The doors closed behind us just as the wailing siren started up. I glanced out of the window to watch Jake and Abby's retreating forms. Kylie threw up her hand, and I felt a pang of remorse that I hadn't even said good-bye. As I waved back to her, it was almost like my dick felt an intense pang of

frustration that there would be no getting busy tonight. Glancing down at Frank's ashen face, I felt like a gigantic ass for even thinking about a missed hook-up. The dude was like a father to me and the guys for fuck's sake.

As we started down the road, Frank tugged me closer to him. "This means a bypass," he croaked.

"You don't know that. Could be they just need to put another one of those stent thingies in those old, crusty arteries of yours."

He shook his head. "Doc said so last time."

With a shrug, I replied, "So you'll have a bypass or two. It's not the end of the world. People have them all the time. My abuelo in San Antonio had one a month ago. Good as new."

Frank seemed to be weighing my words. The heart problems he'd dealt with in the last two years weren't a secret to anyone on the crew or in the band. He'd had two separate angioplasties while during our down time not on tour. We hadn't given it much thought since he had bounced back so easily both times.

"I just want to get it done back in Atlanta, okay? I want it to be with my doctor and where my boys can be with me."

"You got it, man. We'll get you back there ASAP, even if we have to call the label's jet."

"Thanks, son."

With a wink, I squeezed his hand. "No problem."

Chapter Two

Mia

"Hey stronzo, why don't you learn to use a fucking turning signal!" I shouted at the car that had just cut in front of me, causing me to slam on my brakes and almost drop the bagel I was balancing on my thigh. Just like every morning as I battled Atlanta rush-hour traffic, I cursed like a sailor, or probably more like the hot-blooded Sicilian men I'd been raised around. I also pondered why I thought it was necessary to continue living in the burbs, rather than closer to the city and St. Joe's—aka St. Joseph's hospital—where I was a charge nurse on the Cardiac Care Floor.

Traffic edged along at a snail's pace while I ate my bagel and cream cheese. I didn't dare glance at the clock on the dashboard because I knew it would only piss me off more at how late I was going to be. Finally after a small eternity, I whipped into the parking deck. Once I eased the car into a parking spot, I reached for the hair clip on the strap of my purse. I wound my long, dark hair into a tight twist and clipped it into place. After throwing a glance in the rearview mirror to make sure I didn't have bagel crumbs or cream cheese in my teeth, I grabbed my purse and threw open the car door.

When I pressed the lock on the key fob, I was once again reminded of the sting of grief that always accompanied that beep. A subtle grief trigger, as my therapist had called it. It certainly felt like a trigger had been pulled on a gun, lodging a bullet into my heart. The Mercedes convertible, SLK250, which was way out of my usual budget, had been Mama Sofia's, my late grandmother.

After she died unexpectedly of a heart attack nine months ago, I found she had left implicit instructions in her will that I should have the car. Regardless of her slew of other grandchildren, she reasoned, that since it had originally been a gift from my father, it was mine outright. Considering her feisty personality and status as family matriarch, no one dared to question her motives. Whatever Mama Sofia said, you did. She was the youngest acting eighty-five-year old you would ever see. With a decorative scarf wrapped around her perfectly coiffed, bouffant hair, she always had the top down—even on her daily trip to mass.

Shifting my cup of coffee into my other hand, I rubbed my chest over my aching heart. After my mother had bailed on my dad when I was just a baby, Mama Sofia had been the only mother I'd ever known. She'd left her home in Jersey to come to Atlanta to help my father raise me. Her loss had shattered me to the core. As I made my way out of the parking deck, I shook my head, trying desperately to shake myself of the cloak of dark, smothering grief that seemed to hang tight around me.

Just a few minutes before seven, the hospital slowly stirred awake from the evening shift. I smiled and bobbed my head at the stream of bleary and beleaguered looking doctors and nurses heading out to their cars. I remembered all too well what it was like to pull the night shift—I'd gotten that experience years ago during my clinicals.

As I lurched off the elevator, I ran into my nursing partner and best friend, Derwin, or Dee, as he preferred to be known as. "Hey boss lady, settin' a nice example being late. *Again*."

"Bite me."

A wide grin curved across his caramel colored skin. "Hmm, maybe if you were six feet of broad shouldered-muscled man, I might be tempted."

I rolled my eyes. "You know how much it pisses me off to be late." I set my cup of coffee down on the desk with a little more force than I intended, sending steaming liquid

sloshing out. "Figlio di puttana!" I cried, before bringing my burning finger to my mouth.

Dee clutched his heart and staggered back a little. "Oh lawd, she's already cussing in Italian. It's gonna be a helluva a day."

"Do me a huge favor and clean that up, please?"

He gave me a mock salute. "Yes ma'am."

"Thanks, smartass." Hustling into the break room, I shoved my purse into my locker. I slammed the door shut before returning to the front room to Dee. He had just finished tossing the soaked paper towel in the trash.

I gave my coffee a wary eye before picking it back up. "How's it looking this morning?"

"Well, I was doing a little scan of the charts, and it seems one of the dudes we're getting post-bypass is sorta famous."

"Really?"

Dee bobbed his head, causing his tightly woven dreads to bounce slightly. "I guess you'd say famous by association. He's the head roadie for Runaway Train."

I slurped down another scorching gulp of coffee. "Who?"

With a frustrated grunt, Dee threw up his hand. "Girl, don't tell me you don't know who Runaway Train is?"

"Excuse me for not knowing every random band out there."

Dee sank down into one of the station chairs. "They aren't random—they were nominated for Best New Artist at the Grammys last year."

I shrugged. "So?"

Reaching to gather up some charts, he replied, "And the band is made up of four incredibly hot dudes."

"So that fact alone is supposed to make them worthy of my time?"

"Hell to the yes!"

"Just because they have dicks doesn't make them worthy of my time or knowledge," I huffed. Grabbing a chart from him, I cocked my brow. "So what kind of music do they play?"

"Light metal mixed with pop. Kinda like Maroon Five, Matchbox Twenty, or One Republic."

I wrinkled my nose. "That's why I don't know them. You know I only listen to country, the classic Italian crooners, or...rap," I replied, as I dug my stethoscope out of a drawer.

Dee gave a contemptuous snort. "You only listened to rap because of Dev."

A wave of nausea overtook me at the mere mention of my ex fiancé. With my legs feeling wobbly, I flopped down into the nearest chair. Wrapping the stethoscope around my neck, I fought not to hurl the bagel and cream cheese I'd

just scarfed down. "Did you have to bring him up?" I whispered.

"Mimi," Dee said softly, using his nickname for me. "It's been six months. You gotta let go."

"I'm trying." At Dee's 'You gotta be shittin' me look', I threw up my hands. "Give me a fucking break, okay? I have a reason for being completely on edge about Dev."

"Oh really?"

I huffed out a breath that was coupled with both frustration and grief. "I got in last night to a fuckload of Facebook notifications alerting me that he and the slutbag were living it up in Fiji—the same place *we* were supposed to go on our honeymoon."

Dee grunted. "Only you would have the screwed up luck to have your ex-fiancé not only cheat on you, but the bastard had to do it with one of your friends, which means you're forever stuck seeing and hearing about them from the rest of your circle."

"I'd call it more of a curse than luck—I am Sicilian after all." I gave a mirthless laugh as I pulled out another chart. "Let's face it. My whole fucking love life has been a curse from start to finish."

"Seriously, Mimi, a curse? Quit being such a drama queen." He mimed playing a violin—a small one at that. In a sing-song voice, he said, "Oh, poor pitiful me of the sucktastic love life."

"Asshole," I snapped. When he chuckled, I crossed my arms over my shoulder. "Don't make me play the Jason card this morning...it won't be pretty."

Dee's comical expression faded. Scooting his chair closer to mine, Dee leaned forward to place his palms on my knees. He rubbed them tenderly. "You know that Jason is in a whole other realm than Dev."

"Still a curse."

"As for Dev, he didn't deserve you, Mimi."

Although I fought like hell and wanted to slap my own face for being weak, tears still stung my eyes, making Dee's appearance before me wavy. Dev had burst into my life three years ago—a bright beacon of light that had been impossible to turn away from. I thought we had the perfect relationship, right down to the glittering diamond on my left hand and the wedding dress being altered at the designers. But the shining façade had shattered when I discovered he'd

been sleeping with one of my close friends. And once again, I was left to pick up the pieces...*and* fight the urge not to inflict bodily harm on him and the skank he ran off with.

It was more than just the betrayal of the man I loved and the girl who I'd thought was my friend. It was the fact it had happened a mere three months after Mama Sofia's death—

the truly darkest period I've ever known, and I'd seen some pretty bad ones. Dev's betrayal kicked up a shit-storm of emotions that wounded my pride to my very core. It had done a number on my self-esteem that I had yet to overcome.

After swiping my eyes with the back of my hand, it took me a moment to meet Dee's intense gaze. I sighed. "Deep down somewhere inside, I believe that. But unfortunately, it's hard to get it through my thick skull."

"The right one is out there for you—I have no doubt of that. Just because it wasn't Dev, the epic dickhead, it doesn't mean it won't happen."

I gave a bark of a laugh at his summation, but then the mention of the elusive Mr. Right caused a different pang of regret in my chest. "You sound like Mama Sofia."

"That makes sense."

"Let me guess. Because you're both wise, know-it-alls?"

Dee shook his head. "No, because she always loved you and wanted you to have the happiness that you deserve, and I feel the exact same way."

"Stop it, or I'm going to cry again," I moaned.

He grinned. "Can't help speaking the truth, baby girl." He gave me a smack on both my thighs. "Come out dancing with me and the boys tonight to get your mind off things."

"Um, I'm not sure how hitting up ATL's finest gay nightclubs is going to make me feel better about myself." When Dee started to protest, I reached over and patted his cheek. "It's a sweet thought, Dee, but it would just be a constant reminder that all the good guys are gay."

"You gotta get back in the game."

"Someday...just not...now."

Dee gave a grunt of frustration before rising out of his chair. "Whatever. Guess it's time we hit it, huh?"

I grinned. "Hey, who is the shift supervisor here?"

Making praying hands, Dee bowed deep at the waist. "You, oh great and powerful one."

"That's right."

As I started out of the station, Dee smacked me on the ass. I couldn't help the snort of laugher that escaped my lips at his antics. He was one of a kind, and I couldn't have had a better friend and nursing partner. He'd stood by me through

the last year when a lot of friends would have bailed. His friendship, along with working with him, kept the fragile pieces of my sanity intact.

Chapter Three

AJ

Rhys and I stepped off the fourth floor elevator of St. Joseph's Hospital armed with gifts for Frank. Although it felt like an eternity had passed, it had been just a week since Frank's collapse at the Oklahoma City concert. Once he had arrived at the hospital, he had received both good and bad news. He would need a bypass, but his condition was stable enough for him to return home for the surgery. With a nurse at his side, he'd flown home the next day to meet his sons at the airport.

As for the guys and me, we felt like shit doing it, but we had to keep up with the next few stops on the tour. Frank's oldest son, Rob, kept us updated on his condition during the surgery and while he was in CCU. Fortunately, we had two days off in a row where his second family, the band, could come back home to check on him.

"Which room is it again?" I asked.

Flipping out his phone, Rhys scrolled through his messages. "405."

I glanced at the sign across from the elevator doors, reading off the room numbers. "Okay, it's that way," I replied, pointing to the left.

When we got to 405, I rapped lightly on the door. "Come in," Frank called.

I poked my head in the door. "Hello, hello. You gotta little room for two wickedly handsome and charming men?"

Frank's face lit up. "Look who is here!" he exclaimed, pushing himself up in the bed.

Holding the door open for Rhys, we stepped inside. The room could have doubled for a florists with all the *Get Well Soon* flowers and balloons. I knew Abby and Lily had gone a little overboard on sending daily reminders to Frank about how much he was loved and missed.

I stepped over to the bed. "Hey old man, how you holding up?" I questioned, leaning over to hug Frank's neck.

Wagging a finger at me, he replied, "Almost good enough to smack you upside the head for calling me 'old man'!"

I chuckled as I pulled away. "You look a helluva lot better than the last time we saw you."

"I know. I feel a lot better too."

Rhys stepped forward to hug Frank. "Bray, Lily, and Abby are coming by to see you in a little while, but Jake…" Rhys grimaced.

Frank smiled knowingly. "I understand. He's gun-shy between what happened with Abby's attack and poor Susan's illness. It's only been six months, so it makes total sense that hospitals and illness spook him." He waved his IV-clad hand dismissively. "Besides, he doesn't need to come by and see me. Hell, he called Rob three or four times a day when I was in the CCU, and I've talked to him several times."

My brows rose in surprise. "Really?"

"Yep."

"He didn't tell us that," Rhys replied.

"He probably didn't tell you that he put me on three months paid leave either, did he?"

Rhys and I exchanged a glance before shaking our heads in unison.

Frank smiled. "He wants me to rest completely and be in the best shape possible to take my old job back."

"Jackass coulda told us all this," I grumbled.

"You know Jake well enough by now not to assume that."

"True."

Frank sniffed the air appreciatively while a curious grin spread on his lips. "Is that the Varsity I smell?"

Rhys laughed. "It sure as hell is. We figured they were starving you to death with shitty hospital food, so AJ and I decided to get you some of your favorites." Digging in the bag, Rhys produced the Varsity's familiar red box with a football player on the front.

Closing his eyes in bliss, Frank said, "Chili dogs, fries, and onion rings, right?"

"Oh yeah." Taking the box from Rhys, I added with my best French accent, "And for the Pièce de résistance—a fried peach pie."

I set the food box on the standard hospital table in front of Frank. He lifted the lid and inhaled the deliciously greasy aroma. "Mmm, mmm, you boys are amazing."

Holding up a finger, I said, "Ah, but we're not done yet. Show him, Rhys."

He nodded before his hand disappeared into the bag. "Your favorite drink—a Frosted Orange."

"We kept it in a cooler so it wouldn't melt," I added.

Frank shook his head with a grin. "You two thought of everything."

"Beats flowers, doesn't it?" I questioned.

"Sure as hell does." A look of shame flickered on his face. "But don't tell Abby and Lily that I said that. For some reason, those two gals think a gruff, old widower like myself needs daily flowers and balloons. Not even my daughters-in-law do that shit."

Rhys and I laughed. "It'll be our little secret," I replied.

As Frank went to work devouring a chili dog, Rhys jumped up on the ledge in front of the window, swinging his legs back and forth, while I plopped down into the heinously uncomfortable chair next to Frank's bed. We were just shooting the shit on all that had happened while he had been gone when the door swung open. Immediately, I got a swift kick in the pants of the most delicious kind. A tall, dark-haired, dark-eyed goddess of a nurse strode into the room. Through her standard blue scrubs, I detected she possessed every attribute that gave me instant wood—wide, curvy hips, thick thighs, a voluptuous ass, and a full, natural rack.

"Oh shit!" Frank exclaimed. His panicked gaze swept right and then left, as if he were trying to think of a speedy getaway. I couldn't imagine from the way his Angel of Mercy nurse looked, not to mention her genuinely caring expression, that she could possibly be worthy of such fear. He was acting like she was Nurse Ratched out of *One Flew over the Cuckoo's Nest* or something.

She only smiled at his reaction. "Now Mr. Patterson, that's not your usual greeting. You're always so happy to see me."

"I can see why," Rhys muttered under his breath.

"No shit," I replied.

"Er, uh...I'm sorry, Mia." Frank gave her a reassuring smile.

"I promise I'm very grateful for the care you have been giving me. It's just, well, you kinda took me by surprise. That's all."

"I'm glad to hear you approve of my care, and I'm sorry if I gave you a shock. I'll be more careful since that isn't good for your ticker." Her gaze flicked over to Rhys and me. "You must be Frank's grandsons. He said you were coming in from out of town."

Frank chuckled. "Actually, those knuckleheads are my bosses."

Mia's dark brows popped up in surprise. "Really?"

With a nod, Frank said, "Yep, that's AJ Resendiz and Rhys McGowan." He gazed over at us. "Boys, this is the most amazing nurse any man could ever hope for, Mia Martinelli."

"You're such a flatterer, Mr. Patterson," Mia replied, before giving Rhys and me a wave. "Oh wait, now I remember. You're the guys my nursing partner was telling me about. The ones in the band."

Pursing my lips into my signature smirk, I replied, "Well, we're not just in *any* band. We're in Runaway Train."

"I'm sorry, but I hadn't heard of you before," she replied, appearing genuinely apologetic.

Ouch. That statement was a different kick in the pants. I couldn't remember the last time a chick hadn't instantly recognized us or at least been utterly star-struck by being in our presence. I leaned forward in my chair. "Maybe you'll give us a listen?"

She smiled. "Of course I will. It's not every day I come into contact with a Grammy nominated band."

"Thank you," Rhys replied, giving Mia his own seductive smile. I fought the urge to knock it off his face.

"Maybe you could sign something for me?" she suggested.

My gaze honed in on her breasts, and I knew exactly where I wanted to sign. "Sure, I'd love to."

Mia cleared her throat, and I snapped my gaze to hers. The expression on her face told me she knew exactly where my one-track mind had gone. "Actually, would it be too much to ask for a CD or—"Mia sniffed the air suspiciously. Her dark eyes bulged at the sight of the opened Varsity containers in front of Frank. "Mr. Patterson, please tell me that just three days after you underwent a triple bypass that I am hallucinating the artery clogging food in front of you?"

Frank's face turned the color of an overripe tomato at her admonishment. "Maybe," he replied weakly.

Crossing her arms over her ample cleavage, Mia shook her head back and forth so fast I figured she would get whiplash. "How many times have we been over your diet since you were discharged from CCU?"

Cowering a little, Frank replied, "Several."

"I'm so disappointed in you," Mia admonished. Her wrathful gaze turned on Rhys and me. "Since this food didn't materialize out of thin air, I suppose you two are to blame?"

"We just wanted to bring him his favorite food," Rhys replied.

Mia's eyes narrowed. "He just had by-pass surgery! He can't eat stuff like this."

I shrugged. "We didn't know that."

"Did you leave your brain in your guitar case?"

"I play the drums," I corrected.

"Whatever," Mia snapped. She grabbed Frank's box of chili dogs and fries and slammed them into the trash. "I suppose you would think it was a good idea to take a bottle of champagne to someone just discharged from rehab, huh?" She started to swipe the drink off as well, but it bounced off the trash can lid and landed straight into my lap. Busting on impact, the ice-cold orange soda coated my crotch, stinging like tiny daggers over my skin. "Fuck!" I shouted, leaping to my feet.

"Oh my God, I'm sorry," Mia apologized.

What happened next could only be expressed as something out of a warped fantasy. With a wad of napkins in hand, Mia dropped to her knees before me—my dick eye-level with her gorgeous face. She began furiously toweling off the front of my jeans. It took all of two seconds for the visual, along with her ministrations, to have me at half-mast.

"Umm," I began.

"Sorry, but this will stain if we don't get it off."

When I dared glancing over at Rhys, his hand covered his mouth, smothering the laughter that caused his whole body to shake. Frank wore an expression of amused horror. Okay, so Florence Nightingale couldn't take a hint. I guess I was going to have to make it as plain as I could. Leaning over, I whispered into Mia's ear. "Cariño, as much as it kills me to ask you to stop this rubdown, if you don't, you're going to make another mess to clean up. *Inside* my pants."

She jerked her head up and stared into my eyes. I watched as the realization of my words, along with what she had been doing, washed over her. My breath hitched as I waited for the usual signs of extreme mortification to follow—reddened cheeks, stammering speech, avoiding making eye contact. All the things that would make it easy for me to move in for the kill.

But I got none of those. Oh no, not from this chick.

Instead, Mia rose up and smacked the soggy napkins against my chest. As I fumbled to grasp them, she replied, "I'm so terribly sorry. I don't know what came over me." She then proceeded to give me a sickeningly, sweet smile—one that reminded me of Abby right before she gave one of us a verbal smack-down. When she edged closer to me, I knew I was in for it and then some. She cocked one brown brow. "How terribly embarrassing and inconvenient it must be for you to have such a sensitivity problem down there. I mean, chicks expect a night of passion with Mr. Latin Lover, and they get mere seconds." She made a tsking sound in the back of her throat. "Pity."

My mouth gaped open, and instead of a witty, maybe even scathing, come-back, I could only open and close it, like a dying fish out of water. I couldn't remember the last time I'd been rendered completely speechless by a female outside of my mother and abuela.

Mia eyed me one final time before turning to Frank. "Mr. Patterson, I'll be back to check on you on the hour," she replied before quickly side-stepping me and stomping out of the room.

When the door closed behind her, Rhys and Frank howled with laugher. "Holy shit, dude! I can't believe what she just said to you!" Rhys exclaimed, wiping the tears from his eyes.

I stared momentarily at the closed door before a smile spread across my cheeks. "Now, that gentlemen, is the future Mrs. Resendiz, right there."

Chapter Four

Mia

As soon as I slammed the door shut behind me, my thinly veiled composure evaporated and mortification replaced it. At the sound of muffled laughter from Mr. Patterson's room, I hustled down the hallway, wanting to put as much distance as I could between myself and what had just happened. But as hard as I tried, AJ's words, coupled with the image of me giving him a rubdown, kept playing over and over in my head. "Jesus," I grumbled. Rubbing my eyes, I wished more than anything I could bleach those images out of my mind forever.

I skidded into the nurse's station, mowing into Dee. "Oomph," he muttered, as multi-colored paperwork scattered through the air like confetti. "Damn girl, where's the fire?"

"In AJ's pants," I muttered.

"Huh?"

I shook my head. "Nothing. I'm sorry. Lemme pick these up

for you."

"Why is your face so red?"

"I said, it's *nothing*. Just drop it, okay?" I bent over and started sorting the papers.

Dee harrumphed before crossing his arms over his chest. "Don't tell me Mr. Gordon in 409 asked you for another sponge bath? Cause you know I'll go down there and tell him *I'll* take care of whatever he needs. I'm sure that'll shut his perverted, old ass up!"

I rose up off the floor. "That's not it."

With a skeptical look, Dee took the paperwork and tossed it onto the desk. "Well, something sure has you riled, Mimi."

"Okay, fine. You want it, so here it is. I'm totally mortified because I knocked a drink onto one of Mr. Patterson's visitors."

Dee shrugged. "What's so embarrassing about that?"

"Well, I panicked and started cleaning him up—"

"Once again, not a crime considering our profession is to help people."

I rolled my eyes. "Would you let me finish?"

"Fine, fine."

"Anyway, of all places, the drink fell in the guy's lap and—"

Dee gave me a contemptuous snort. "Mia Martinelli, how

many times have I told you not to molest the guests of hospital patients?"

"Wait, what?" I questioned, trying to process his response.

"You know your little drink spill routine is just a ploy to get to rub up on some hot dude."

My eyes widened. "Dee, what the hell is wrong with you? I just told you I was mortified, and now you're acting like I'm some crotch grabbing pervert?"

A throat cleared behind me, and I whirled around. "Oh shit," I muttered, before I could stop myself. With an 'I can melt your panties at twenty paces' smirk, AJ stood at the door with his hands shoved in the pockets of his holey jeans. While the front was still damp, they were no longer tented like when I left him. From his expression, I could tell my little tirade hadn't had a lasting effect on him at all.

Pointing at Dee, I said, "Just for the record, he is being a total ass right now."

AJ chuckled. "Yeah, I know." He took a tentative step forward. "I wondered if I could talk to you for a minute?"

Grabbing a chart, Dee batted his eyelashes at AJ. "I'll just duck in the medicine room real quick, Mimi, and let you and sweet cheeks have some privacy."

As he sashayed away from us, AJ's brows furrowed, and he blinked a few times in disbelief. "Is it just me or does he remind you of—"

"Lafayette on *True Blood*?"

AJ's dark eyes widened. "Holy shit, yes!"

"Yeah, he gets it all the time." With a laugh, I added, "Most of the time, he uses it to scam free drinks or get closer to a guy he's scoping out. People never seem to be disappointed that it's not really the actor—I mean, that guy doesn't act like LaFayette in real life anyway." When I realized I was rambling, I pinched my lips shut. It had been a long time since any guy had gotten me rattled enough to run my mouth like an idiot.

"You a fan of the show?" AJ asked.

"Oh, yeah, I adored it—well, until the whole sixth season and Billith."

AJ snickered. "I couldn't agree more. I used to be pretty much obsessed with it, but yeah, I couldn't get it up for the last two seasons. Now I'm more a *Walking Dead* and *Sons of Anarchy* fan myself."

"Oh my God, those are awesome shows, too." I stared at AJ in disbelief for a moment. Was I actually making small talk with the guy I'd just accidentally molested? I hadn't talked to any guy—or I guess I should say straight guy—since Dev had left me shattered. Shaking my head, I snapped out of my daze. "So what is it exactly that you wanted to talk to me about?"

"Oh yeah, that. I wanted to see if you'd like to have dinner with me sometime?"

My brows shot into my hairline. "After I just verbally berated you like that? Not to mention the physical thing." When AJ nodded, I snorted. "I must've made one hell of an impression cleaning you up."

He grinned. "Your talents are quite impressive, but I'd like to experience the full range of your...napkin abilities."

"I think you're getting a little presumptuous, don't you think? You only asked me to dinner."

"That's true." AJ scratched the stubble on his chin. "But to prove my intentions are honorable, I'm still offering dinner—*just* dinner." With a pointed look, he added, "And maybe some third base action if the mood strikes us."

I laughed in spite of myself. "Tempting, very tempting. But, no thanks."

"You drive a hard bargain, Ms. Martinelli, but I'm willing to take the third base action off the table for dinner and maybe a good night kiss—with or without tongue."

"No."

Crossing his arms over his broad chest, he tilted his head

to one side, surmising me quizzically. "Fine then. No dinner with its somewhat provocative undertones. How about just a drink after you get off?"

"Sorry, but I'm not interested in dating at the moment."

AJ's dark brows furrowed in confusion, and I could tell he wasn't used to getting rejection from a female. Undaunted, he pursed his lips in a smirk. "I get it. You're a little gun-shy about dating a musician, or you're career minded, or some other shit is telling you to say no. But I can work with that." He snapped his fingers. "Coffee it is!"

"AJ, really—"

He held up a hand. "Yeah, I get it. I now can see where coffee might be a little loaded for an outing. You know, with caffeine being an illicit, addictive substance, so maybe I should switch gears. Ice cream's pretty innocent. How about that?" His gaze honed in on my mouth as he closed the distance between us. "After all, who can say no to some sugary sweetness? Maybe add some smooth whipped cream topped off with a ripe cherry?"

His voice had taken on a deeper edge, a more seductive tone, which caused my resolve to momentarily fade. Instead of being focused on giving him the brush-off, I suddenly envisioned him lying buck naked on a bed while I licked ice cream off what I imagined were his perfect abs. Beads of sweat broke out along the base of my neck. I fought the urge to fan myself. *Get a grip, Mia.* "Um, no."

"How about I take you to the party in my pants?"

"Look, I...wait, did you seriously just use a line from *Anchorman* on me?"

AJ gave me a teasing wink. "I just wanted to make sure you were paying attention."

I huffed out a frustrated breath, blowing away a few errant strands of hair from my face. At his earnest expression, I held up my hands. "Listen, I'm really flattered by all your offers, but I'm just not ready to date again."

"Again?" AJ questioned.

Dammit. How could I have let that slip? Glancing away from him, I stared over at the desk. "It's just this year hasn't been the best for me in a lot of ways."

"So, let me make it better by taking you out and showing you a really good time."

Dee sidestepped us on his way out of the medicine closet. "Trust me, sweet cheeks, baby girl needs a good time in the worst way possible." He paused to run his gaze from AJ's head down to his feet. "And you look like just the hot ticket she needs to clear away the vajayjay cobwebs."

AJ busted out laughing while I screeched, "Dee, you faccia di merda!" I smacked him on the arm. Hard.

Pursing his full lips, Dee ignored my rant and bodily harm. "You can curse at me all you want in Italian, but the truth is the truth." He eased closer to AJ, lowering his voice. "You see, our girl has closed up shop ever since she caught her dickhead fiancé banging one of her friends."

It was at that moment that if looks could kill, Dee would be toe up in the floor, writhing in agony with a slow death. I could not believe he had just told my most intimate details to a perfect stranger, especially someone like AJ.

While I debated making a run for it, AJ's amused expression turned sympathetic. "Damn, I'm sorry, Mia. I had no idea. That fucking blows."

I shrugged, trying desperately to play off my heartache. "What can you do? Shit happens." My voice cracked betraying my emotions. Oh yes, I was going to kill Dee for dredging up my past in front of AJ. Yes, maybe slow torture would better serve him.

With his eyes boring into mine, AJ stepped forward. He swept a strand of hair out of my face. Tenderly, he ran his fingers over it before tucking it behind my ear. "Mia, he must have been fucking blind, not to mention stupid as hell, to have had you in his life, most of all in his bed, and then gone looking somewhere else." He gave a quick shake of his head. "His loss, cariño."

The intensity of his stare, along with his husky tone, caused my breath to come in rapid pants. Okay, he was having way too much of an effect on me in such a short amount of time. It was time to send him packing. "That's a very sweet sentiment, but now can you see why I'm not able to take you up on your offer?"

"Actually, I think that's all the more reason for you to go out with me."

With a sigh, I shook my head. "I'm sorry. Now, if you'll excuse me, I have to get back to my patients." Side-stepping him, I grabbed a chart and powerwalked away from him. The whole way down the hall until I disappeared into room 410, I could feel his heated gaze searing into my back. Part of me wanted to whirl around and tell him I'd love nothing more than to go out with him. But the more dominant side of me—the one who was still licking its bloodied and beaten wounds—wouldn't let me.

After putting more distance between us and making a few rounds, I returned to the station to find Dee waiting for me. By his expression, I knew exactly what he was going to say, so I held my hand up. "Please, don't go there."

"Oh girl, I'm *so* going there."

"Dee, he is the last thing I need right now."

"Bullshit. He is exactly what you need and then some." When I stared down at my shoes, he gently pulled my chin up so I would be forced to look at him. "Mimi, he was a hot piece of male flesh who was totally and completely jonesing for you. He just worked harder for a chance at your snatch than I've ever seen a guy—straight or gay."

I smacked Dee's hand off my chin. "*Snatch*? You know I hate that word. And I don't think gay dudes are working hard for the....," I gulped before whispering, "*snatch*."

"You are such a difficult, stubborn ass!"

"Guys like him...they don't date women like me."

"Oh, and just whom do they date?"

"Stick figures with no souls—you know the type, size zeroes with fake tits who make great looking arm candy."

"Please, lawd in Heaven, tell me you just didn't turn that guy down because of your damn self-esteem issues? Must you make a stop in negative town, rather than booty town?"

"Dee—"

He wagged his finger in my face. "Uh, uh. Don't pull that one on me. I know AJ wanted you in all your thick, junk in the trunk glory."

"Whatever," I grumbled.

"Mimi, you need something—better yet, someone—to get you out of this funk."

"You call the aftermath of having your entire world implode around you, leaving you symbolically bloody and barely breathing 'a funk'?" I demanded.

Dee's shoulders sagged a bit. "That was six months ago. Dev's moved on, and it's time for you to move on, too."

"It all makes sense up here," I said, tapping my head. "But it just doesn't seem to get here." I then covered my heart, which ached beneath my fingertips.

"Hell, I'm not saying you need to marry the dude and pop out ten children. I'm just saying he could be a good distraction—a way to help you see you're a beautiful, amazing woman that any man would be thrilled to get to bang."

Although I tried fighting it, the corners of my lips curved up at Dee's final words. "Thanks for the compliment that was in there...somewhere."

"You're welcome."

"We should probably get back to work now, don't you think?"

"Oh, I think you've definitely got some work cut out for you."

"What are you talking about?"

Dee stared past me with a curious expression. "He's baaaack," he said, mimicking the little girl from *Poltergeist*.

I whirled around to see AJ striding down the hall with a giant bouquet of colorful wild flowers and roses in his arms—a determined expression etched across his handsome features. When he ambled up to me, I shook my head in disbelief. "You seriously never get turned down, do you?"

"No, I don't." He grinned and shifted the flowers in his arms. "But there's another reason why I came back."

"Oh?"

He bobbed his head. "Listen, I figured that we got off on the wrong foot with you drying my junk, and I thought maybe for you to truly consider going out with me, we needed a do-over."

"Wow," I murmured. Holy shit, was this guy for real? I fought the urge to glance around to see if there were some hidden cameras, and I was totally being Punked. He wanted me to go out with him enough that he'd not only come back, but he'd brought me flowers. I had a weakness for men bearing flowers.

A beaming smile lit up his face. "So, Mia Martinelli, I'm Alejandro Joaquin Resendiz aka AJ, and it's a pleasure meeting you." He then handed me the bouquet.

"Thank you." I brought the flowers to my nose and inhaled the sweet fragrance. "These are beautiful." My eye caught the card poking out, so I reached for it.

"Um, wait!" AJ cried, but I had already jerked it out.

"Get Well Soon," I read aloud. When I glanced from the card with its smiley face beaming loud and proud over to AJ, I couldn't help laughing. "Nice."

For the first time ever, AJ's swagger receded a bit. He ducked his head and rubbed the back of his neck furiously. Finally, he peered up at me with a sheepish expression, which made him even hotter than before. "Okay, I'm busted. I bought them downstairs in the gift shop."

I opened my mouth to respond, but Dee beat me to the punch. "I don't know what Mimi's problem is if she doesn't appreciate the fact you went all the way downstairs to get her some flowers."

"I didn't say I'm not appreciative," I countered.

"Then maybe don't bust my balls so hard by giving me shit about some gift shop flowers?" AJ suggested with a small smile.

"Okay, I won't."

"Thanks."

"And I did mean it when I said they were beautiful. I haven't had a man bring me flowers in a very long time."

"It was a nice gesture, huh?"

I smiled. "A very nice one."

Dee's neck had been bobbing back and forth between AJ and me like he was watching a tennis match. "I think it's time I leave you two to talk." As he started off, he glanced at me over his shoulder. "Don't worry about your patients. I'll cover for you."

"Yeah, make sure the boss lady doesn't find out."

Dee snickered and gave me a wink before heading down the hallway. I glanced at AJ, trying desperately not to let the anxiety bubbling within me show through. I knew he was the type of guy who could smell fear and use it to his advantage. I shifted uncomfortably on my feet in the awkward silence. "So, how old are you?"

His brows shot up in surprise. "Wow, that came out of nowhere."

With a shrug, I replied, "I thought we should get to know each other a little. Age is pretty basic."

"Fine then. I'm twenty-five. How old are you?"

My nose wrinkled a little. "I'm twenty-eight. I don't usually date younger men."

AJ rubbed his palms together. "Then let me take your cougar virginity."

I laughed. "You're not letting this go, are you?"

"Nope. I'm going to keep on and on until I wear you down, and you finally go out with me."

"Seriously?"

"Mia, Mia, Mia, what am I going to do with you?"

"I'm sure you have several NC-17 rated scenarios running through your mind at this moment."

Throwing his head back, AJ laughed heartily. "Yep, I do actually. But all joking aside, do I really need to continue pleading my case? I just brought you gift shop flowers for Christ sake!"

"That's true."

"Can I shoot straight with you?"

Tilting my head thoughtfully, I replied, "I think after I gave your junk a rubdown, we can be pretty honest with each other."

AJ groaned. "Don't remind me of that." When I opened my mouth, he wagged a finger in my face. "And before you can demean it, I did enjoy it."

"Fabulous."

"Anyway. Here's how I see it. We're both young, single people needing a 'date'—be it a romantic interlude or hot, sweaty sex."

I turned a strangled cry into a cough. "That's certainly not beating around the bush."

"The time for subtlety has gone, Mia."

"I see."

AJ closed the gap between us. I stepped away from him until my back banged against the wall. Looming over me, AJ's dark eyes twinkled with intensity. "You were totally shit-on by a major dickhead and need to get back in the game. The easiest way to do that is no-holds bar, uncomplicated sex. Don't you agree?"

That statement got my blood up and thrumming through my veins. "Yes," I whispered.

"Finally we see eye to eye on something. It's a win-win situation for both of us. You get to fuck that douchebag of an ex-fiancé out of your system, and I get laid in the process."

"How generous of you."

AJ laughed. "I'm a very giving person—of myself, my time...of *orgasms*."

"I'm sure you are."

"Then it's a date?"

"It's a maybe right now because I have a few conditions."

"Such as?"

"Being a famous musician, I would wager you've gotten around a lot."

AJ's lips curved up into his signature smirk. "Regardless of your comment back in Frank's room, you don't have to worry about my stamina, cariño. I'll give you a night you'll never forget."

I couldn't help rolling my eyes. "Yeah, that's not what I was talking about."

"Then what?"

Leaning closer to him, I said, "If I were to take you up on your offer, I would want you to get tested before I slept with you."

AJ's jaw dropped to his chest. "Are you serious?"

"Dead serious. You wanted to know if I was free this weekend, and the major tests only take forty-eight hours to come back." When he didn't respond, I replied, "I'll be happy to do the same."

A curious expression replaced the scowl on AJ's face. "Does that mean I'll be riding bareback if my tests come back clean?"

My brows furrowed in confusion. "Huh?"

"You know, sex without a condom."

"Um, no, I don't think so."

"And why the hell not?"

"Well, if you must know, I can't take birth control because of the migraines I have. So we would need the protection."

"Ah, I see. Bummer."

"Take it or leave it, big boy."

AJ grinned. "I'll take it."

"Good."

"So we're on for Friday night?"

My heartbeat accelerated in my chest while I fought to catch my breath. Was I actually going down this road? Sex with a stranger? Well, a man who was basically a stranger to me but well known to everyone else—lots of females included. I thought of Mama Sofia and how dead inside I'd been since her passing. That coupled with Dev's infidelity had crippled me. I wanted—no I needed—to feel alive again.

"Yes," I finally replied.

AJ clapped his hands together. "All right then. How about I pick you up for dinner around seven?"

My brows furrowed. "Oh, you actually want to go out?"

He snickered. "You really think I'm a 'wham, bam, thank you ma'am' kinda guy, huh?"

I lifted one of my shoulders. "I just figured since this date was about sex—"

"First of all, I'd never take you straight to bed—only assholes with no game do that. Second, for you, this is about experiencing life again."

"And that includes dinner?"

"Yes, ma'am it does, along with something else thrown in just for kicks."

I found myself smiling. "Okay, then. That sounds nice."

"Gotta pen?"

"Sure." I reached into my pocket and handed him one. He took the Get Well Soon card from my other hand. "What's your number?" Once I gave it to him, he grinned. "I'll text you for the directions to pick you up, okay?"

"Okay," I replied as he handed me back the pen.

"Mia, I'm glad you finally decided to take me up on my offer."

"Me too," I replied honestly. Of course, I sounded a lot more sure of myself than I felt. Inside, I was on a Merry-Go-Round of emotions.

When AJ leaned closer to me, an intense fire burning in his eyes, I jerked back. He grinned at my reaction. "Easy girl. Just a chaste good-bye kiss," he whispered, his breath fanning over my cheek.

"Sorry."

His warm lips pressed a tender kiss on my cheek, rather than my lips. When he pulled away, he winked. "I'll make sure to ply you with a little alcohol on Friday night to make sure you're not so skittish."

Shaking my head, I pushed him playfully. "Whatever."

"I'll be back to see Frank, so maybe I'll see you before then."

"Maybe so."

Walking backwards down the hall to Frank's room, he wiggled his fingers at me. "Bye Mia."

Shifting the flowers, I waved back. "Bye AJ." Once he disappeared back into Frank's room, I exhaled the breath I'd been holding. As I walked into the station, Dee greeted me with a grin that stretched from cheek to cheek.

"Hellz to the yes! Mama Mia's gettin' back in the game!" he exclaimed, before doing a little happy dance.

"Yeah, nothing like extreme peer pressure from your bestie along with an overly persistent guy to make it happen."

"This is going to be epic!" Dee gyrated his hips as he danced over to me. "You need to make an appointment for hair and nails ASAP." His gaze dropped below my waist. "And I'm thinking a bikini wax as well. Don't wanna be welcoming Mr. Latin Lover to the jungle."

"You ass!" I cried before smacking his shoulder. My outrage only fueled him on, and two of our other shift partners broke into hysterics when he started twerking in front of me.

"Thanks. I think I need some bleach for my eyes now," I groaned.

Slinging an arm around my shoulder, Dee gave my cheek a smacking kiss. "I'm proud of you, baby girl. I think this is exactly what you need...and more."

"We'll see about that."

"You gotta have faith," he mused.

I wagged a finger at him. "So help me God if you start doing a George Michael ass swish in front of me like in the *Faith* video, I'm going to request a transfer for you."

He pursed his lips. "Don't be hatin' on my mad dancing skills."

"Let's get back to work, shall we?" I prompted before grabbing a chart.

Chapter Five

Mia

Friday night found me wine glass in hand, stomach twisted in knots, and pacing back and forth in my bedroom. Standing in front of Mama Sofia's antique mirror, I once again gazed at my reflection. Dee, along with my best girlfriend, Shannon, had insisted on taking me shopping at Lennox earlier in the day. Everything in my closet that was dressy or sexy had too many Dev memories attached to them. I needed a whole new ensemble for my big splash back into the dating world.

After a few stores and a few close calls, we'd finally found something we all could agree on. Well, sort of. Although they'd insisted the dress was to die for and I was going to take AJ's breath away, I was still unsure, as I turned left and right in front of the mirror. Red had always been my color, and tonight's tight little number was ruby red with tiny spaghetti straps that made a crisscrossing pattern across my lower back.

While I thought I should have gone up a size, Dee insisted that it hugged my body to the point it was like a second skin. "Trust me, baby girl. Latino men love a woman with curves."

I took his word for it and bought the dress along with some killer red heels that had a patent leather strap. Shannon had insisted on taking me to have my hair and make-up done. For a sure fire sexcapade, I thought I was going to a little too much trouble, but I decided to bite my tongue and go along for the ride. Don't get me wrong. I was all about dressing to impress and feeling sexy. I didn't get a lot of chances to do it during the week in my scrubs. At the same time, I knew AJ wanted to screw my brains out whether I was wearing a Hefty bag or couture. In the end, I was so grateful for letting Dee talk me into the shoes and dress as well as Shannon with the hair and makeup. For the first time since Dev left, I felt truly sexy and desirable.

So I was all decked out at five until seven, waiting on my Prince Charming to arrive and begin this Cinderellaesque fantasy night. All the while, I fought the urge not to throw up or refuse to answer the door when AJ arrived. The doorbell rang, and I jumped a mile, sloshing wine onto the

floor. "Shit!" I exclaimed. I sprinted into the bathroom and grabbed a towel. I threw it on the puddle and quickly wiped it up. I'd just made it into the hallway when the doorbell rang again. "Coming!" I shouted.

When I finally flung open the door, AJ's appearance took what breath I had left away. He wore khaki pants, a crisp white shirt with an electric blue tie, along with a navy blazer. It was quite a difference from the jeans and T-shirt from the other day. "Hi," I murmured.

"Hello there, sexy." His gaze drank me in from head to toe. "You in that dress is testing my firm resolve to make this a true date and not just sex."

I fought against the tiny fluttering of my heart at his words. "Thank you. You're looking pretty amazing yourself."

"Thanks. I do clean up nice, don't I?"

Oh hell yes, you do. Now let's get you out of that tie and out of those pants and into my bed. I shook my head to free me of my naughty thoughts. "Yes, you do." I eyed the bouquet of flowers in his arms—they were my favorite pink roses.

"Flowers again?"

"Hey, I'm a firm believer in romance." He handed the bouquet to me.

With the Baby's Breath tickling my nose, I inhaled of the sweet smell. "But how did you know pink roses were my favorite?"

"Dee gave me a little head's up."

"Ah, I see."

He motioned to the card. "Aren't you going to read it?"

"Is it *With Deepest Sympathy* this time?" I teased.

"No smartass."

"Fine then." I balanced the flowers in the crook of my arm while I took the paper in my fingers. When I opened the envelope, I saw that there was a folded letter inside. After I unwrapped it, I saw that it was AJ's test results. When I glanced up at him, he grinned.

"All clear and ready to roll."

I laughed. "I'm glad to see that. Mine are in my purse."

"Good to know. So are you ready?"

"As I'll ever be," I said softly. I closed the front door and then locked it.

Once I was out on the porch, AJ grinned. "When you took so long, I was beginning to think you'd decided to bail on me."

"Sorry. I had a little wine spillage." At his puzzled expression, I shook my head. "It's a long story."

When AJ stepped aside to lead me down the porch steps, I gasped. A shiny black, stretch Hummer limousine sat in my driveway. Glancing over my shoulder, I cocked a brow at him. "A limo? Seriously?"

"My Hummer's in the shop."

"Are you sure you didn't do this just to impress me?"

AJ snorted. "Since when would I need a limo to be impressive?"

I laughed. "You're such a cacasodo."

He gave me a mischievous grin. "Ooh, I like it when you speak dirty Italian to me."

Cocking my brows at him, I asked, "How do you know it was dirty?"

"By the expression on your face." He scratched his chin. "If I had to guess, I think it means something along the line of arrogant ass?"

"Yep, pretty much."

A chauffer, outfitted with a black suit and cap, waited with the door opened for us. "Thank you," I said, as I hopped inside.

"You're welcome, ma'am."

As I slid across the plush leather seats, I took in the twinkling interior lights and stocked mini bar. AJ got in behind me. "Benny, we're going to 5505 Marietta Street."

"Yes, sir."

Once Benny closed us in, I turned to AJ. "Is that the address of the hotel you're taking me to?"

He shook his head, making a tsking noise. "What did I say before about this date?"

"That it's not straight to bed, and you're at least going to feed me first."

AJ chuckled. "That's right. I also had a little something in mind before our dinner reservations."

"And?" I pressed.

"Nope. You're just going to have to wait to find out." He scooted forward on the seat to dig into the mini bar. "How about a little champagne to start off our *date* night?"

"Plying me early with alcohol?" I teased.

"Whatever I have to do." AJ handed me a crystal flute before pulling out a bottle that had been chilling on ice. He popped the top and then filled my glass with champagne. As he poured himself one, I gazed out the tinted window and sipped on my bubbly. We'd gotten off the interstate and were traveling along some side streets downtown. "Do you live around here?" I asked.

"No, I'm over at The Buckhead Grand."

I made a low whistle. "Pretty posh."

He waggled his eyebrows. "The penthouse."

"Why am I not surprised?"

He grinned. "It's not like I spend a whole lot of time there. Once our first big checks from the label started coming in, my parents were on my ass to invest in something like real estate. So I bought the condo." He gulped down the rest of his champagne. "I'd love to show you my views sometime."

"Nice line, Rico Suave."

AJ rolled his eyes. "That's not what I meant." When I cocked my brows, he laughed. "I'm serious. There are some killer views of the city."

"Then I'd like to see them."

"It's a deal."

The limo shuddered to a stop. It seemed like only a second before the door opened, and Benny held out his hand for me. As I stepped onto the pavement, I glanced left and right, surmising my surroundings. "A dark alley? What exactly do you have in mind for this evening?"

AJ chuckled as he hopped out of the limo. "It's nothing shady, I promise. I just wanted us to be let out at the back of the dance studio, rather than the front. You know, less chance of being seen."

"Dance studio?" I questioned.

"Yes, the first stop on our evening of romance—and a little more—is for us to get to know each other better through dancing."

I straightened my purse strap on my shoulder. "You're serious?"

"Totally."

"Hmm," I murmured.

AJ's hand came to rest on the small of my back as he led me through the door. A tall, lithe woman stood waiting for us. "Good evening, Mr. Resendiz."

"Hello, Molly." He thrust out his hand to pump hers. "Please call me AJ." When she bobbed her head in agreement, he added, "Thank you so much for helping me out."

She smiled. "I'm more than happy to do it. Won't you follow me?" She beckoned us with her hand. AJ motioned for me to go first, so I fell in step behind Molly. "I've made sure everything was very private and secure. Although, at the moment, our evening classes are going on, no one will know the two of you are here."

"I appreciate that."

Molly stopped at the first door on the left. From up ahead, I could hear a cacophony of different genres of music from far down the hallway, along with the sounds of tap shoes clicking on the floor. After she unlocked it, she flipped on the light. "This is one of our older instructional rooms. I hope it will be okay."

AJ gazed around the room, sizing it up. "Looks great."

When Molly turned to me, I bobbed my head in

agreement, although I would have had no idea whether it was really all right or not. The room was outfitted with a ballet barre, wall-to-wall mirrors, and a stereo system in the far right corner.

"Well, I'll leave you to it. If you need me for anything else, please feel free to ask."

AJ nodded. "Thank you." After Molly closed the door behind her, he rubbed his palms together. "All right. Let the lesson begin!"

I eyed him warily. "I don't know if this is such a good idea."

"Why not?"

"I've never been the dancer girl type."

"And exactly what type are you?" AJ asked, leaning back against the barre.

"The athletic type. I lettered in soccer and volleyball in high school—I wasn't too bad in basketball either."

"Hmm, I never imagined you being all Sporty Spice."

I laughed. "Sorry, but that's me. My late grandmother never liked me playing sports. She didn't think it was lady-like, so she started me out in ballet when I was five. But I seriously sucked. I think it was after my first recital that she decided maybe I wasn't going to become a ballerina." Catching AJ's amused expression, I pinched my lips shut. For some reason, my brain and mouth didn't seem to be communicating with each other when I was around AJ. I couldn't help speaking more freely with him than I have done with a member of the opposite sex for a long, long time. Well, excluding Dee and the male members of my family. Everything about AJ screamed that I should be uber uncomfortable around him—considering the whole fame, fortune, and good-looking thing. I couldn't imagine why in the hell I felt so comfortable around him to do that.

"It doesn't matter if you were a dance school dropout. There's no plies or leaps involved with the waltz, so I think we're safe."

"Famous last words," I grumbled.

AJ walked over to the stereo system and grabbed a remote. After flicking through a few choices, he decided on one. Taking the remote with him, he made his way back over to me. Grabbing my hand, he dragged me closer to the wall of mirrors. "First, I'll show you how to do the steps on your own, and then we'll put it together, okay?"

"Whatever you say, Master."

"Ooh, I kinda like you calling me that. Very kinky."

I rolled my eyes. "Get on with it."

"Okay, so here's what you're going to do. First, go back with your left foot." Once I stepped back, AJ commanded,

"Now bring your right foot to the side." "Now bring the left one together." He motioned to my image in the mirror. "Okay, try it, and let me see."

Trying not to break a sweat with my concentration, I repeated the steps AJ had taught me. "Good. You're a fast learner."

"Thank you."

"Ready to try it together?"

"Sure."

AJ clasped one of my hands in his, bringing our arms out straight out. Then he brought his other hand to rest to the side of my shoulder blade. When my gaze locked with his, he winked. "As much as I'd like to get extra close and personal with you right now, you're just going to put your other arm on my shoulder."

"Oh, you mean we're not going to be doing the Down and Dirty Waltz?"

"That's for later."

I grinned. "Whatever."

"All right. Let's do this."

The moment AJ brought his foot forward, I forgot about stepping back, and instead, I brought the heel of my pump down on his toes. "Fuck!" he cried, breaking our embrace.

"Oh God, I'm sorry."

With a grimace, he shook his head. "It's okay."

"You sure?"

"Mia, I'd be a real pussy if a little high heel to toe action took me out, don't you think?"

I laughed. "I guess."

"Let's go again." His arms came around me, and I clasped my palm in his. "Remember, step back."

"Got it."

The next time I managed to execute the entire step perfectly. "Nice job, cariño," he complimented.

"Thanks."

"Think we can try it with music now?" When I bobbed my head, AJ took the remote out of his pocket and reset the song. "Ready. Five, six, seven, eight...Slow, quick, quick slow." I managed to keep up with him, even when he turned us side to side as we waltzed around the room.

"See, you've got it in the bag."

"Miraculously," I replied, still concentrating on steps that seemed so effortless to AJ.

"I am a good teacher." When I glanced up at him, he wagged his eyebrows.

"Do you ever stop?"

"Nope." He leaned in closer to me. "And trust me, once I get started, you'll be begging me not to."

A burning fire rippled through my lower-half, but I quickly played it off. "We'll see about that."

"Okay, now, I want to teach you the rumba."

I grimaced. "You mean the whole waltzing shit wasn't painful enough?"

AJ shook his head with a smile. "The waltz is the stepping stone—a traditional and formal dance, but the rumba is more a dance of passion and desire." At my hesitation, AJ added, "I'm just going to show you the American style for tonight. I don't want to make it too complicated for you."

"I think we passed complicated the minute you suggested it," I groaned.

Grasping my chin in his fingers, he replied, "Quit whining and let me teach you."

"Fine."

"Like before, I'm going to show you the steps first." AJ stepped closer to the mirror. "So you step out on one foot, and then when you bring the other together, you're going to kinda pump around on your feet and then slide the other foot away again to repeat the process."

As he moved, my eyes honed in on the flourishing movements of his hips. With his blazer off, I could see his back muscles flexing through his shirt. Moist heat burned between my legs from watching the way the rhythm moved so effortlessly through every inch of him. My mind couldn't help wandering from the dance steps to what those hips and shoulders might feel like moving above me, my hands running up and down his corded back muscles as he thrust in and out of me...

AJ's voice brought me out of my fantasy. "Got it?"

"Huh?"

He laughed. "Come on, Mia. This is the easiest part I could show you without blowing your mind with the complications."

"It wouldn't take much."

"Let's try it together." Once again, he took the remote out of his pocket. He flipped through several songs. When a sultry, Latin beat came from the speakers, he shoved the remote back inside his pocket. He then slid his arm around my back while the other went to clasp my hand. He waited for the music to pick up at the right place. "Slow. Quick, quick, slow," he instructed, his breath fanning across my cheek.

While the rhythm rippled easily through AJ's body, I wasn't quite getting the upper body flow or the swishing of the hips.

"Keep your frame locked, don't slouch."

I rolled my eyes. "Jesus, I feel like I stepped into *Dirty Dancing*."

AJ laughed. "I don't think I've ever been likened to Patrick Swayze, but hey, I'll take it. The man had some serious moves."

As I looked at AJ's body, so built and muscular with its fluid movements, my stomach rolled with nervous energy. I glanced at my reflection in the mirror and shuddered. I couldn't do this. My head was starting to swim with old insecurities rapidly taking over my pretense of sexy and strong. There was no way in hell I looked graceful. Beads of perspiration had started to pop out on my face and chest from both my exertions and anxiety. Dancing, or attempting to dance, was so not me. This was a huge fucking mistake to even attempt it with someone like AJ.

"AJ, I can't do this. I'm completely robotic compared to you!"

"No, you're not."

"I tried to tell you before that I just don't have it in me." I dropped my arm from his shoulder and started to stalk off, but AJ tightened his grip on my hand before whirling me back against him.

"Yes, you do have it in you, Mia. And I'm going to show you." He turned me to face the mirror before sliding behind me. His hands came to rest on my shoulders. "First of all, you're way too tense. You need to loosen up. You have to let the music flow through you." His deft fingers began massaging my neck and shoulders. His dark eyes locked on mine. "That's it. Let the tension go. It's only you and me here. No one is judging you."

"But you—"

He shook his head. "You're the one doubting yourself, not me."

AJ's fingers slid down, teasing along my clavicle. I felt the muscles in my neck and shoulders go limp. My eyelids started fluttering closed as he continued massaging me. "Mia, when will you get it through your thick, stubborn, Sicilian skull that your body is made for dancing...and for fucking?"

I popped my eyes open to stare open-mouthed at his reflection. He winked at me before leaning down to kiss my cheek. "Turn your head, and give me your mouth, Mia."

Although I wasn't one for commands of the non-dancing kind, I obliged. AJ's warm lips crushed against mine. As he deepened the kiss, I felt my tension releasing as I melted into him.

He pulled away, and I had to fight not to whine in protest. "Now for the lower half." His hands slid down the side of my body, slightly catching the sides of my breasts, before coming to grip my hips. His hands rose up and down on my flesh, causing my hips to roll forward and backward. "That's right."

When he eased up on his grip, I kept up the same pace of undulating my hips. "Very nice." He met my gaze in the mirror and grinned. "See, you don't suck." Keeping his eyes locked on mine, he slid his hands slowly back up my torso. My breath hitched when they paused above my ribcage to tease the underside of my boobs. Surveying my reaction, he then splayed out his fingers to fully cup my breasts.

I raised my brows at him. "And when did groping second base get added to the rumba?" I questioned breathlessly.

His head dipped to nuzzle my neck. "It's all part of *my* rumba."

"I see."

"Do you like it?" he asked, as his thumb and forefinger pebbled my nipple over the dress's fabric.

"It's not bad," I managed to croak out, despite my rapidly fluttering heart, not to mention my jittery, rubbery legs. I had reached a new level of Heaven. AJ's fingers were divine.

"Hmm, 'not bad'? That's not exactly good, is it? Guess I better work on my moves." His right hand released my breast and trailed down my side before coming to rest between my legs. "Think I might be able to sell you on third base better?"

A shudder rippled over me as he cupped and stroked me over my dress. Even through the fabric, I could feel the heat of his fingers. "Pretty good."

"That's what I like to hear." When his hand left me, I moaned at the loss of sensation. In a flash, AJ was tugging at my hemline. My eyes widened when I watched his hand trail up my bare thigh.

Trying to steady my erratic heartbeat, I sucked in a breath when his hand delved into my panties. "AJ—"

"Don't fight it. Just feel." His fingers stroked my clit, causing me to whimper. My gaze darted over to the door, fearing that at any moment the instructor was going to walk in on us. As if he could read my mind, AJ said, "Don't think about her. Just think about what my fingers feel like against your warm, wet pussy."

I opened my mouth to protest, but AJ silenced me by sliding two fingers deep inside me. "Oh God," I murmured. A little whimper escaped my lips at the delicious way he felt pumping his fingers while thumbing my clit. My eyes locked on AJ's hooded gaze in the mirror. No matter how hard I tried, I couldn't tear myself away from looking at what he was doing to me.

"Do you like watching me touch you?"

"Yes," I panted.

"I like watching you react to me—the way your eyes widen, the way your chest rises and falls, the way your hips move." He dipped his head to where his breath burned fiery against my ear. "I can't wait until it's my dick, not my fingers, that's inside you."

"Me too," I murmured. With my first male induced orgasm in six months within reach, I no longer cared that we were standing in a public place or that AJ had a thing for dirty talk unlike any of my other lovers. All I cared about in that moment was getting off. My arms went behind me to grasp onto his hips that were moving against my ass. "Mmm, I'm close. Make me come, AJ," I commanded.

His fingers quickened to a lightning fast speed. Holy shit, those fingers were like magic. More parts of me tingled and had been set on fire more than I ever had before. And then a warm rush filled me from head to toe. As I went over the edge, my head fell back against AJ's shoulder. I bit down on my lip to stifle my cries, but they still echoed through the room. AJ kept on stroking me as I pulsed around his fingers. When I finally came back to myself, I met his gaze in the mirror.

"Fucking hell, that was hot." He then jerked his hand out of my panties. With my eyes still hooded from a post-orgasm haze, I watched as he brought his index and middle finger to his mouth and sucked them inside. "Mmm, you taste amazing."

His words and actions, along with the fact he continued to rub his erection against my ass, almost caused me to come again.

"I gotta get you out of here."

Still coming down from my high, I blindly let him drag me behind him while trying to smooth down my dress. "Wait, why are we leaving so fast?"

"Because if I don't get you out of here, I'm going to fuck you right in the middle of the dance studio, which I'm pretty sure would get us arrested."

A giggle escaped my lips at his summation. Wait, was I actually giggling like a vapid teenage girl? What was happening to me? When we got to the door, I tugged on his hand. "Shouldn't we at least tell Molly thank you?"

His lips curled up into that signature cocky smirk of his. "If she took one look at you right now all sexed up, she'd know we weren't doing much dancing in there."

I smacked his arm. "Yeah, well, whose fault is that?"

"Mine." He winked at me. "I'm not one bit sorry either." His lips grazed mine before kissing a trail across to my ear. As he breathed in my ear, he whispered, 'Nor am I gonna regret sliding my hands back up under that sexy dress of yours, jerking down your sexy panties, and getting right up close with your gorgeous pussy." I shivered as AJ thrust his tongue against my ear, swirling it around my earlobe. "I'll tease you. Taste you. Make you come again, but this time, on my face. And just when you think you won't be able to come again, I will not regret fucking you senseless, right there, in that limo where Benny will be able to hear every moan and every cry of intense pleasure I give you. No, I will not regret that. At. All. Beautiful carina."

A tremor of excitement went through me at his words, and I had to press my thighs together to alleviate some of the pressure building between them. "I guess I'll let you," I teased breathlessly, as we stumbled out of the door and into the evening heat.

"Oh you'll more than let me," he growled.

At the sight of us on the street, Benny hopped out of the limo. "Sorry sir, I didn't know when you would be coming out."

"No problem, man." As Benny stepped forward to open the door, AJ asked, "Can you let me know when we're ten minutes from the restaurant?" He glanced over at me and winked.

A flush entered Benny's face, but he managed to bob his head. "Yes, sir."

When I started into the limo, AJ gently pushed me forward onto my knees on the floor. I glanced back at him in surprise. "So this is how we're playing it?"

He shot me a wicked grin. "This time, yes. I've waited all night to see that fabulous ass of yours."

I planted my palms firmly onto the limo floor while AJ nudged my thighs apart with his knee. He then jerked the hemline of my dress up, shoving it over my hips. Just when I expected him to grab the waistband of my thong, he grasped the lacy scrap of cloth covering my core and jerked it to the side. I waited for those delicious fingers he'd used in the dance studio to reenter me, but instead I got a warm, wet surprise that caused my toes to curl. AJ's tongue slid agonizingly slow up my slit. "AJ! Oh yes...YES!" I cried, digging my fingertips into the carpeting. He continued lapping and sucking at my center. "Oh God, I'm close again...so close."

Just as I felt myself tense up to go over the edge, AJ suddenly pulled back. Throwing my hair out of my face, I peered over my shoulder in desperation. "No, don't stop," I pleaded, shoving my hips back against his face.

He shot me a wicked grin. "Oh, I'm just getting started."

When I felt AJ's fingers spreading me apart, my neck loosened, and I almost smacked my face onto the limo floor. But I could have cared less. I wanted and needed this orgasm so much I would have endured face-planting onto the carpet to ensure I was going to get it. As AJ's tongue thrust inside me, the curtain of my hair pooled around me, thankfully muffling my scream. Down on my elbows, I rhythmically rocked my hips against his face as his tongue swirled around and around inside of me, darting deeper each time. When his thumb slid down from one of my lips to circle and then rub my clit, I went over the edge.

Jerking my head up, I clenched my fingers into the carpeting so tight my knuckles turned white. "AJ! OH GOD! YES!" I knew from the high octave of my voice that there was no doubt that the driver heard me. Hell, anyone driving within a five mile radius probably did. I hadn't come so hard in years. *Bless AJ and his magic fingers and tongue*, I thought silently as I continued thrusting my hips toward him as I rode the pulsing wave.

A voice crackling over the intercom brought me out of my sex haze. "Uh, sir?"

"Yeah?" AJ questioned, his deep voice vibrating against my still convulsing core.

"Um, there's not much traffic, so I, uh, I believe that we're about ten minutes from the restaurant."

"Thanks, Benny," AJ called, as he pulled himself back on his heels. When I started to move, he playfully swatted my backside. "Don't move that fabulous ass one inch." He dug his wallet from the back of his dress pants and ripped a condom out. In a dizzying flurry, he managed within seconds to undo his pants, shove them and his boxers down, and slide on the condom.

I quirked my brows at him. "Wow, minute man. I'm impressed."

AJ grinned as he took his erection in his hand. Mesmerized, I couldn't help but watch as he pumped his hand up and down his length. I was going to have the worst crick in my neck tomorrow, not to mention my knees probably would take a week to recover. But being taken from behind was my favorite position, and after my lengthy sex drought, I was thrilled to be using it to get back in the saddle.

"Once again, this is only round one. I plan to properly fuck you when we get back to my place, but for now, this will have to do."

I laughed. "Okay then. I'll try not to judge you too harshly then if it doesn't live up to my expectations."

AJ winked. "I think I'll blow that challenge out of the water." And with one harsh thrust he drove himself all the way inside me, sending us both crying out. "Oh fuck me, you're tight as hell."

I bit my lip in pleasure when he slowly withdrew every delicious inch before slamming back inside me. Once I could speak, I muttered, "Why thank you. I think."

AJ chuckled as he rotated his hips, causing me to whimper. "You don't like my compliment?"

"Sure, but I like what you're *doing* at the moment, rather

than what you're *saying*," I rasped. I wanted more than anything for him to keep doing that sexy move, his dick plunging even further within me.

His hands came to grip my thighs, jerking me back against his thrusts. He drew in a ragged breath. "I would have thought you would have appreciated my sincere words about your hot, incredibly tight pussy."

My fingers tried to wrap even further into the tightly woven fibers of the limo carpet. I felt myself already careening towards the edge again. Even though I would never admit it to AJ, he really was a sex god. It usually took me a long time to come through penetration, and here he was barely five thrusts in, and I was starting to feel the tell-tale fluttering. Just as I prepared to let go and give into the intense orgasm that awaited me, AJ withdrew all the way. "W-wait, w-hat are—"

"You didn't answer my question."

"Seriously?" I huffed in a frustrated pant.

"Umm, hmm," he murmured, as one of his hands left my thigh to dip between my legs, grazing my clit. Wiggling my ass, I hoped to somehow slide him back inside me. I could feel his hot, wet tip only inches from my entrance. But AJ anticipated me and eased back, teasingly stalling my pleasure as he waited for my response.

Panting, I fought to catch my breath. Glancing over my

shoulder at him, I replied, "I thought it was the chick who was the cock-tease, not the dude?"

He chuckled. "Maybe. And then maybe I'm trying to drive home the fact that I'm in control here—I'm the one who can make you come or make you beg for more."

When he continued to pause at my opening, I growled in sexual frustration. Oh, I was going to make him pay for this little machismo act later. "Thank you so very, very much, AJ, for your compliment about my...how did you say it? 'Incredibly hot, tight pussy'?"

"That's right." He rewarded me by sliding the tip of his cock inside me, and I shivered in anticipation.

"Okay, now can we cease the talking and just screw, please? I mean, my knees are starting to go numb here."

AJ grinned. "I thought every woman loved a little dirty talk."

"Yeah, well, here's the deal. I've never really had a guy take the time to compliment my alleged 'hot and tight pussy'. I've sorta only read shit like that in romance novels."

Massaging the exposed globe of one of my ass cheeks, AJ shook his head. "Then that's a pity. More men should have told you how amazing you feel when thrusting balls deep into your tight walls."

"Oh Jesus," I muttered as his words started to have the

same effect his actions did.

He smacked my ass cheek, and it sent a tingle up my spine. "You need to know it's like you're made to fit my dick, and I could practically come just staying still inside you." And with that, he pounded into me so hard I skidded forward. After three more deliciously jarring thrusts, I came with a loud shout. But as my pleasure started to fade, my knees screamed in pain from the carpet burns AJ's thrusts were causing. I had to get up, or I was going to look like I'd been in a bicycle accident. It was a hell of a way to kill a third orgasm buzz.

Craning my neck, I momentarily forgot my train of thought at the mere sight of AJ's sex-hazed face. Beads of sweat trickled down his tan cheeks, while his eyelids fluttered shut in ecstasy. His perfect white teeth nibbled his plump bottom lip as he concentrated on thrusting in and out of me. But when I felt more stinging, I gasped, "AJ, wait."

His dark eyes flew open, and concern quickly caused the desire to evaporate from them. "What's wrong? Was I too rough?"

"No, it's just we gotta change positions. I'm getting carpet burns."

"Oh shit, I'm sorry."

I giggled. "It's not your fault. I'd say it's more of a sexual hazard from screwing on a limo floor."

AJ grinned as he pulled out of me. He pushed himself up and then flopped onto the backseat. His dress pants and boxers appeared comical as they bunched around his ankles while his proud cock jutted forward. "Come here, baby," he beckoned.

When I rocked back on my heels to sit up, all my weight rested on my knees, and I screeched in agony. Before I could turn around to hoist myself out of the floor, AJ's strong hands splayed into my waist, gripping me tight. I gasped as he effortlessly lifted me up and onto his lap. "Better?"

I threw a glance over my shoulder at him. "Yes, thank you."

He placed a gentle kiss on my shoulder. "Good."

"You ready to finish?" I asked, as I teasingly rolled my wet core over his lap.

A low growl erupted from deep in his throat. "Oh yeah, I'll finish. And so will you at least another time—maybe two."

"Hmm, bring it on, big boy." I grabbed his erection, causing him to suck in a harsh breath, before I guided it back inside me. Leaning forward, I gripped the sides of the leather seat as I worked myself on and off AJ's cock. Heavy breathing and skin slapping together echoed through the close quarters. Closing my eyes, I focused on the intense sensations ricocheting through my body.

AJ's deft fingers sought out the zipper on the back of my dress. He eased it down slowly, causing cool air to rush at my inflamed skin. Once he finished with the zipper, he then eased the spaghetti straps over my arms, pushing the top of the dress down until he bunched it around my stomach.

His hands slid around my ribcage, brushing momentarily against my exposed flesh before he cupped my aching breasts. "Umm," I murmured.

"You like it when I touch your tits like this?"

"Yes, oh yes," I panted.

"I bet your nipples are rock hard for me."

"Why don't you find out?" I dared.

Without a reply, his hands dipped inside the cups of the strapless bra. His hot breath scorched against my back as he whispered, "Just as I thought." His fingers then went to work tweaking and pinching my nipples.

"Mmm, yes. Just like that," I cried, letting my head fall back against his shoulder.

"I'm getting close," AJ groaned.

"Me too."

Instead of pushing me harder against him, AJ surprised me by stilling our movements. His warm breath singed the tender flesh of my earlobe. "I'm gonna slowly turn you around, baby, because I wanna be looking into your eyes when we both come."

A shudder rippled through me as I loosened the grip of my thighs against his, so I could slide around to face him. I'd never gone from reverse to regular cowgirl while a guy was inside me. "Oh God," I moaned at the delicious way it felt to rotate around on AJ's cock.

Once I faced him, AJ brought his lips to mine. "I've missed these," he murmured against my mouth. Tasting myself on him, I thrust my tongue inside to dance along with his.

As I started riding him hard and fast again, AJ's fingers raked through the strands of my hair. His mouth never left mine, and our tongues fought and tangled against each other. Gripping his shoulders tight, I felt the first wave of my orgasm start. I cried out as I stilled my movements as my head fell back.

With a slight jerk at my hair, he pulled me back to stare into his eyes. The intensity of his lust-filled gaze held me captive as I rode out the last delicious tremors. AJ's hands then left my hair to rest on my hips, working me even harder against him. Only a few moments passed before his body tensed. "Mia, oh God, Mia!" he exclaimed as he came hard and fast inside me. Never once did his eyes stray from mine.

After he finished, he brought his lips to mine again, giving me a tender kiss. When he pulled away, a lazy, satiated smile formed on his face. "That was pretty fucking amazing."

Thoroughly wiped out from the sex and the orgasms, I nuzzled my head into the crook of his shoulder. With what energy I had left, I softly dragged my fingers through his hair, smoothing down the places where I'd mussed it earlier. "Yeah, it was," I replied hoarsely. Between my cries of pleasure, I'd practically lost my voice. Cupping his face in my hands, I said, "That was everything I needed to get back into the game and more. You lived up to all my expectations, Mr. Latin Lover."

His smile widened. "Thank you."

"No, thank you."

I leaned over to kiss him again when Benny's voice crackled over the intercom. "Sir?" he asked hesitantly.

"Yeah?" AJ croaked.

"We've, uh, been here at the restaurant about fifteen minutes. I was letting you...um, finish."

Glancing down at our still joined bodies, AJ laughed. "Thanks, Benny. But we're still going to need a minute or two."

As I slid off of him, a delicious soreness filled my lower half—one I hadn't experienced in a long, long time. "Can you zip me up?"

"With pleasure."

"One sec." I quickly adjusted my breasts back into the cups of the bodice before I turned slightly. Just as AJ's fingers started pulling up the zipper, they stopped. "What's wrong?"

"Just admiring your ink," he said, feeling along my shoulder blade.

I tensed as he touched the puckered skin beneath the Italian script words of the tattoo. "Thanks," I murmured. Suddenly all the languid, post orgasmic bliss was snatched away.

"Did you get in an accident or something?"

My eyes pinched shut as a horrific memory assaulted my mind. "Something like that," I finally replied.

AJ must've sensed I didn't want to talk about it because he finished raising the zipper up my back. Once he was finished, I leaned forward to try and find my crumpled panties. Feeling blindly along the floor, I sighed.

"What's wrong?"

"Finding black panties on a black limo floor is harder than I thought."

"Shit, I'd turn the lights on, but..." I glanced over my shoulder. Although he'd gotten rid of the condom, he still hadn't gotten his pants back up yet.

At the feel of lace, I shook my head. "Got them." I collapsed back on the seat before shimmying them back up my thighs. AJ watched my every move. After I readjusted my dress, I cocked my brows at him. "Quit eye-balling me and fix your shirt."

He responded with a bark of a laugh. Grabbing my purse, I dug out my brush, lipstick and body spray. As AJ readjusted his tie and tucked his shirt in his pants, I went about trying to make my appearance a little less 'I just screwed my eyes out in the back of a Hummer limo'. After spritzing my thighs and arms with the body spray, I reached over and sprayed AJ.

"What the fuck?" He sniffed his shirt. "I smell like a chick."

"Better than smelling like sex."

A smirk curved on his lips. "That happens to be one of my favorite scents."

Out of my purse, I produced some hand sanitizer. As he eyed me suspiciously, I patted one of my hands over his mouth and cheeks like aftershave. "Ow! That burns like hell," he whined.

"Yeah, well, I know sex is one of your favorite smells, but I'm not going in a restaurant with you if you're smelling like sex and..." I trailed off, not wanting to say the word.

"Pussy?" he questioned.

With a grimace, I replied. "Yes."

"Whatever."

Cocking my head at him, I asked, "So sex isn't your top scent, huh?"

He shrugged. "Nah, probably Top Five. I gotta give props to some others like my drum set and my abuela's tamales."

"Speaking of tamales, are we eating Mexican tonight?"

"Actually, we're eating at my favorite Italian restaurant. I figured with you being Sicilian, you'd probably like that."

"I do."

"Then for dessert, we're going down the block to my favorite Mexican café. They make Flan that melts in your mouth. It's fucking fabulous."

I shuddered as an eerie feeling came over me. No, it couldn't be. Out of all the restaurants in the entire city, it couldn't be possible that AJ had picked my family's restaurant to eat at. But then again what were the odds of an Italian and Mexican place on the same street? "Where are we eating?"

"Mama Sofia's. You know it?"

I gulped down the rising bile in my throat. "Yeah, it's my dad's."

Chapter Six

AJ

My eyes widened at Mia's revelation. "You're shitting me."

"Sadly, I'm not."

Glancing from her to the building, I shook my head. "Why do you look so upset? Mama Sofia's is nothing to be ashamed of. It's one helluva gold mine for your family I bet."

"Yes, it is," she replied modestly.

"Seriously, Mia, this place is awesome—I mean, not only is the food amazing, but everyone who works there is fabulous. You come from good people."

"Thanks."

Then it hit me. "Wait a minute. You're Duke's daughter?"

Mia paled a little further. "Yes."

"Fuck me, this is intense."

"I guess this means besides being a connoisseur of Italian food, you're also a traitor to your culture by liking American football?"

I laughed. "Yeah, I guess you could say it like that. But come on, your dad's a legend around these parts."

With a shadow of a smile, Mia replied, "Not to mention his face is plastered all over the back wall of the restaurant."

"And for good reason." Enzo aka 'Duke' Martinelli had been one of the best wide receivers the Atlanta Falcons had back in the late 70's and early 80's. An injury had taken him out of the professional football arena, so after spending a few years teaching and coaching, he'd started a restaurant on the side with his parents. That had grown into what was now Mama Sofia's. I'd gotten the lowdown one night when after casually asking to meet Duke, he came out and had dinner with me. "Your dad is amazing."

"Wait, you know, *know* him?"

"Oh yeah."

Bringing her hand to her forehead, Mia leaned back against the seat. "This is a nightmare."

"It shouldn't be. He really likes me."

Mia closed her eyes. "Even worse," she said in a whisper.

Benny interrupted us by knocking on the door. "Ready sir?"

After I nudged her, I gave Mia an encouraging smile. "Come on, I'm starving. You made me work up one helluva an appetite."

I hopped out first before turning back to offer Mia my hand. As she slipped her hand in mine, her complexion had turned positively green. Her first steps out onto the pavement were

92

wobbly, and I wondered if they were from our previous activities or from nerves? Bringing her hand to my lips, I kissed her fingers. "Look, cariño, if you're going to be this uncomfortable being seen with me around your family, we can eat somewhere else."

"Everywhere else will be slammed at this time." She gave a slight shake of her head before swallowing hard. "We might as well go in." She sounded like someone headed off for an execution, rather than dinner.

"Alrighty then." I turned back to Benny. "I'll have them send out a menu for you. Get whatever you like."

His eyes widened. "Oh, that's not necessary."

I grinned. "With what I've put you through, I think you've more than earned yourself a dinner."

He chuckled. "Thank you, sir."

Placing my hand on the small of Mia's back, I led her to the front of the restaurant. When I held the door open for her, she refused to step inside. Instead, it was like she preferred to hide behind me. With a sigh, I ducked inside and let her follow me. Looming over the hostess stand was my buddy, Angelo. At the sight of me, a grin spread on his

cheeks. "Hey stranger, long time no see. I thought I saw your name on the books tonight."

We gave each other an enthusiastic handshake. "Good to see you, man."

"I gotta say that the new album is fucking kickass." At his

cursing, he quickly glanced around. When he saw no one had caught him, he added, "Seriously."

"Thanks. I'd like to take credit, but that always goes to Jake and Brayden for their songwriting skills—well, and this time Abby."

"Yeah, that duet is killer." Peering over my shoulder, he asked, "Ah, you have a lucky lady with you tonight. I'm used to you flying solo with us."

"Um, yeah," I murmured, rubbing my neck furiously while trying to figure how to play this off. When Mia continued hiding behind me, I laughed. "She's a little shy."

Recognition flooded Angelo's face. "Mia?"

"Yeah," she squeaked.

Angelo's almost unibrow furrowed. "*You're* with AJ?"

"Sort of."

It took a moment before a beaming smile lit up his face. "Holy shit, you two are dating?"

I started to open my mouth, but Mia surprised me by stepping in front of me. Plastering on a smile, she said, "Actually, I was hoping to fix him up with Dee, but he got called in to take someone's shift."

Angelo's tan face paled considerably as he glanced back and forth between Mia and me. "AJ, I didn't know you were..." He appeared to be struggling with the words. "Um...out."

"Me either," I hissed through clenched teeth. When I shot Mia a death glare, she cowered a little. "How about that table, huh?"

"Yeah, yeah, sorry." Angelo fumbled with two menus before handing them over to the seating hostess. "Have a good dinner."

"Thanks," I grumbled. I could feel his heated gaze on me as we made our way through the packed restaurant. Boisterous conversations and clanging silverware assaulted my ears. The hostess escorted us over to a secluded corner booth. Candles burned in the red votive candles, giving off the highest romantic vibe. "Enjoy your meal," she smiled at Mia before glancing over at me.

"Thank you, Gabriella."

Once we were alone, I motioned for Mia to sit. After she slid across the leather booth seat, I also sat. "AJ, I—" She nibbled her bottom lip nervously.

"Look, for the record, I have nothing against gay people— hell, my brother, Antonio, has been out since he was fifteen. What I do have a problem with is you skewing my image for your benefit."

"I know, I know. And I'm truly sorry. But you have to know what it's like to a have a big family all up in your business, right?"

"Yeah, try having the world all up in your business."

She nodded. "Since Dev and I broke up, everyone, from my father to my uncles to the freakin' bus boys, have been on me to date. Think of it like Dee's behavior but on Italian steroids."

Even though I was still pissed, my lips turned up in amusement at her description. I didn't expect her to reach across the table for my hand. "I just wanted to try to enjoy tonight without all the other bullshit hassle, okay?"

"Whatever. I still don't like it," I replied glumly, before glancing down at the menu.

When she tugged my hand, I met her mischievous gaze. "I could promise to make it up to you later," she suggested coyly.

My brows rose in surprise. "Just what did you have in mind?"

Tilting her head, she tapped her finger on her chin. "Maybe some special attention...of the oral kind?"

I opened my mouth but a waiter, who couldn't have been more than twenty, appeared at the table. "Hiya, Mia, sorry to interrupt."

Pink tinged Mia's cheeks. "Hi Pauley."

Glancing between them, I said, "Lemme guess. He's one of your cousins?"

Pauley bobbed his head as he sat down two glasses of water. "First cousins. My dad and Duke are brothers." He eyed me suspiciously for a moment. "Hey, I know you—you're the guy in the band. Uncle Duke calls you Drummer Boy, always tells us to give you the best cut of meat."

I laughed. "Yep, that's me."

With a grin, Pauley held out his hand. "Pauley Martinelli."

"AJ Resendiz." I paused before adding, "Mia's gay friend."

Mia had just taken a sip of water, and my comment sent her hacking and sputtering. "Sorry," she replied in a strangled voice as she mopped up the water.

Rubbing her back, Pauley asked, "You okay, cuz?"

"Fine."

"Good. Thanks."

When he was sure Mia was okay, he took out his envelope. "Since you both are regulars, I'm guessing I don't need to go through all the house specials and stuff, huh?"

"No, that won't be necessary," I replied.

"So the usual for you Mia—the Sicilian Special along with a glass of Prosecco?" Pauley questioned.

Shifting uncomfortably in her seat, Mia replied, "Erm, no, I'll have the Prosecco, but give me the Chicken Caesar Salad instead."

As Pauley's brows rose in surprise, I cleared my throat. "Give her what she usually has." Mia opened her mouth to protest, but I held up a hand to silence her. "Please do not be one of those chicks who thinks she can't eat around a guy. I like a girl with a hearty appetite."

Mia glanced from me to Pauley and gave a quick bob of her head. He grinned. "All right then. And you, AJ?"

"Sirloin, medium rare with pasta."

"Got it. I'll bring out your wine and bread in just a sec."

"Thank you."

Once Pauley was out of earshot, Mia narrowed her eyes at

me. "It wouldn't have killed me to have a salad, you know."

I shook my head. "I don't want you to ever change who you are or what you like for me." At her skeptical expression, I added, "I like you just the way you are—physically and personality wise."

"Really?"

"Hell yeah. But you wanna know what I like the most about you?"

"The fact I'll let you bang me on a limo floor?"

I snickered. "That's a good one but no. What I like the most about you is how real you are—inside and out. The business I'm in—it's nothing but fake people twenty-four-seven, who will say and do anything to impress you or get you to do what they want."

Mia tilted her head, taking in my words. "I see now why you like this place so much. If my family is one thing, it's completely and totally real."

"Exactly."

As we fell into silence, Mia stood up. "I think after our limo exertions, I better go freshen up."

I gave her a wicked grin. "I should do the same."

I followed her to the restrooms. I finished before she did and returned to the table. She was just coming back when Pauley returned with our drinks and a basket of garlic knots. With my stomach grumbling, I quickly snatched one up and scarfed it down. "So," I began after I finished chewing.

"So?"

"Tell me about yourself."

Swirling the wine around in her glass, Mia shrugged. "Not much to tell."

I cocked my brows suspiciously at her. "Yeah, right. Don't make me start in with some lame-ass get to know you questions."

She grinned. "And what would those be?"

Even though I knew it would probably irk a woman like Mia—one who was refined and cared about class and style, I leaned in on the table with my elbows. "What do you like to do when you're not mending hearts?" I asked, my tone serious like a newscaster.

"Hmm," she murmured, closing her eyes to think. After a few seconds, she popped them open and replied, "I like piña coladas and walks in the rain."

It was my turn to tsk at her. "Not getting off that easy, Miss Martinelli."

"Fine then. What I enjoy doing is probably a huge bore to you, but you asked for it."

"Yep, hit me with it."

"I like the usual stuff like books, movies, and TV. I like traveling. And..." A little flush filled her cheeks.

"And what?"

After a hearty gulp of wine, she replied, "I like to knit."

I couldn't help laughing. "You're shitting me."

She narrowed her black eyes. "No, I'm not. My late grandmother taught me how to knit *and* crotchet."

At her still seething anger and embarrassment, I held up my hands. "I'm sorry I found it so shocking that a smoking hot woman like yourself did something so old-school and nerdy as knit."

She shrugged. "You asked, so I was honest."

"You're right, I did." Grabbing another garlic knot out of the basket, I grinned at her. "You think you would ever make me something?"

"Hmm, like a dick cozy for those cold nights when no woman wants to put up with your relentless cockiness?" she asked, with fake sweetness.

Choking, I fumbled for my wine before taking a long swig. When I recovered, I couldn't help laughing at her fiery response. "I would be honored if you would make me a dick cozy. I would wear it with pride and think fondly of you."

"Oh you would, would you?" she asked, her lips curving upward.

"Yes, I would." With a wink, I added, "But make it extra-large because I want it to fit."

Mia snickered. "I'll keep that in mind."

Pauley returned to the table with our dinner. "Here ya go. Watch the plates, cause they're hot. Lemme know if you need anything else."

"Thanks, cuz," Mia replied, with a smile.

"No problemo."

Once Pauley left us, I eyed Mia before I started cutting my steak and pasta. "At least we know we have something in common. We both like to read."

"Seriously?"

I slurped a strand of pasta into my mouth. "Yeah, I read all the time when we're on the road."

"I'm not sure the articles in *Playboy* count."

I snorted. "I have more varied tastes than that, thank you very much."

Mia chewed thoughtfully on her lasagna. Once she swallowed, she asked, "So tell me what's your favorite kind of book?"

"I'm going to sound like a total freak, but I love fantasy— *Game of Thrones*, *Lord of the Rings*, you know, shit like that."

"Interesting."

"What? You're not going to give me shit for that?"

She shook her head. "I think it's wonderful you read, period, so I'm not going to knock you for liking high fantasy books."

"But for you, it's all about romance novels."

"Yes and no. I like to read non-fiction stuff too." She finished off a bite of chicken parmesan from her Italian sampler. "I'm kind of a royalty nerd. Love the Tudors."

"I liked the show."

Mia rolled her eyes. "Of course you did. The historical

inaccuracies were off the charts, and it was basically a thinly veiled excuse for porn."

I grinned. "Sounds good to me."

"I would figure as much from you," she replied with a smile.

"Speaking of romance novels, I have a question for you."

Eyeing me warily, she took a sip of wine. "Okay."

"Why is it that during the sex scenes the guy always says, 'Come for me, baby', and the chick comes?" I snapped my fingers. "Just like that. I mean, on command like she's a dog or something. What the hell is up with that?"

Mia laughed. "I don't know why they do that. It's certainly never happened to me in real life before."

"Like, I could just look at you right now and say 'Come for me', and you'd come."

Pursing her lips in thought, Mia replied, "Maybe it's all about the timing of the command—like it has to be in the heat of the moment. You'd have to be pretty amazing to pull it off across the booth from me in a restaurant."

"So it's all in the delivery, huh?"

"I would think so."

"Something like this?" I leaned forward, taking her hands in mine. Using my thumbs, I rubbed circles over the tops of her hand. I licked my lips and stared intently into her eyes. "Mmm, what you do to me, Mia," I whispered. "How hard you make me. What I'd like to do to your body...buried deep inside you, pounding away while your tight-as-hell walls clench around me." I brought her hand to my lips and licked along her fingers. Transfixed, she stared back at me. "Come for me, baby."

A little tremor ran through her body. "Definitely the delivery," she murmured.

Grinning, I pulled away. "I still call bullshit but whatever. I needed to ask."

"I think the better question is how do you even know that goes on in romance novels?"

"Research."

"Really?"

I bobbed my head. "When you hear a bunch of chicks raving about this book or that one because the sex is hot or what the dude says is sexy, you take notice."

"So you can always be in tune with what women want?"

"Hell yes." I winked. "I've picked up a few things along the way. Being a stud like me takes practice and cultivation."

Mia stared at me for a moment before throwing her head back and laughing heartily. After she wiped her eyes, an amused look twinkled in them. "Oh my God, AJ. You crack me up. Will I be benefiting from any more of your learned expertise tonight?"

I gave her my signature smirk. "You never know."

Chapter Seven

Mia

Throughout dinner, conversation flowed effortlessly between AJ and me. There was none of the usual first date awkwardness. Just like he craved realness with me, I felt like I could be myself with him, which was something I hadn't experienced in so long.

"So you're a real smart cookie, huh?" AJ questioned with a smile, as he sopped up some of his remaining tomato sauce with a garlic knot.

"What makes you say that?"

He smiled knowingly. "Duke told me a lot about you."

"Oh shit," I muttered, covering my eyes with my hands.

"Hey, it was all good. Like how you had your Master's degree in Nursing, you'd already made shift supervisor—that's impressive at your age."

"My ripe old age?" I asked with a grin.

"Don't be a smartass."

I opened my mouth to protest when I was interrupted by the screech of a microphone. "Good evening ladies and gentlemen. I'm Vince—your band-leader here at Mama Sofia's. I'm joined by Rico and Joey on the violins and accordion. First off tonight, we want to welcome a very special couple to the floor—Mr. and Mrs. Michael and Dorothea Castorini, who are celebrating their Fiftieth Wedding Anniversary with their friends and family." A round of applause went up over the restaurant as a silver haired couple teetered onto the wooden floor before the band's riser.

Vince smiled. "So for the happy couple, here's their favorite song, *Anema e Core*."

As the familiar opening chords echoed from the violin, it felt like a knife speared my heart. A searing ache spread throughout my chest, sending tears to sting my eyes.

"Mia?" AJ questioned.

Embarrassment at my out-of-control emotions sent warmth into my cheeks. "I'm sorry." I swept the napkin from my lap and dabbed my eyes.

"Old couples make you weepy?" AJ asked.

I hiccupped a laugh. "Not exactly."

"Then what is it?"

With a wave of my hand, I replied, "Nothing I need to bother you with."

AJ reached over and grabbed one of my hands. "You know,

most people think I'm just this goofball who never takes anything seriously and lacks any emotional depth or sensitivity.

But that's not true at all." He squeezed my hand. "I can feel your pain all the way across the table. If it's about a guy, I can handle it."

I stared into his dark eyes that pooled with empathy. Although I couldn't fathom why, I drew in a deep breath. "*Anema e Core* was my late grandparent's song. When I was growing up, they used to dance to it all the time. Even at their Fiftieth Wedding Anniversary party, when my grandfather was on oxygen and was walking with a cane, they danced to this song. He always called her his anema e core—my soul and heart."

"That's really beautiful," AJ said softly.

For some reason, I felt compelled to keep talking to AJ. "I never knew my real mother—she was some sports groupie who basically hooked up with my dad because he was Duke Martinelli. She wanted to trap him into marrying her, so she got pregnant. Four months after I was born, Dad blew out his knee. She figured her meal ticket had dried up and she didn't want to be saddled with a kid, so she left us both. My grandparents moved down here from Jersey to help my dad with me, and they never left. My grandfather died when I was fifteen, and that was gut-wrenching. But my grandmother—she was my mother. And when she died nine months ago…a

little bit of me died as well." I didn't bother stopping the tear that escaped and trickled down my cheek. "She was my anema

e core."

Without a word, AJ left his seat to come sit by me in the booth. Before I knew it, he had an arm around my shoulder. "I'm

so sorry, Mia."

The room began to spin in a dizzying flurry. I'd let my guard down and let him see more than I should have. "No, I'm sorry. I shouldn't have brought this up. I—" I started to edge away from him, but he gripped me tighter.

"Don't pull away because you think showing some emotion is going to turn me off. Because that's the farthest thing from the truth." He gripped my chin, tipping my head up to meet his gaze. "Remember what I said about wanting people to be real?"

"Yes," I whispered.

"I know for you to be letting your guard down, showing this emotion—it's about as real as it gets for you, right?" When I bobbed my head, he gave me a reassuring smile. "I'm right here, right now. I'm not going anywhere because I want to be here for you."

His tender words and the comfort of his embrace caused all reason to leave me. Instead, I let myself snuggle closer into him.

With my face pressed against his chest, I finally murmured, "Thank you...for listening to me and for being here."

"No problem." His lips brushed against my temple. "I wish I could say I understood the pain and what grief feels like, but I've never really experienced overwhelming loss. My mother's parents died before I was five, so I really didn't get the chance to know them. Six months ago, my buddy, Jake's, mom died, and that hurt like hell. But I can't imagine losing your whole world like he did...or you did with Mama Sofia."

I gazed up at him. "You're a really decent guy, you know that?"

He chuckled. "You're just now realizing that?"

"I'm serious. I mean, you're a famous musician with money and good looks. You could be a real asshole."

"But I'm not."

I shook my head. "As much as I would like for you to be, you're not."

AJ's brow creased in confusion. "What's that supposed to mean?"

Even though I could've avoided the question, I wanted to be real for him. "You being decent will just make it harder for me in the end."

He stared intently into my eyes, searching them for the answers I wasn't ready to give him. It would take a pretty strong blast of dynamite to get past the walls I'd erected around me to protect from the pain previous men had inflicted.

When AJ abruptly pulled away, I felt bereft of his comforting embrace. "What—"

He held out his hand. "Dance with me."

I started to protest, but at the insistent gleam burning in his eyes, I thought better of it. Instead, I rose up and put my hand in his. He then led me across the restaurant to the dance floor. We sidestepped through the other couples, edging over to the bandstand.

As the music grew louder around us, I teased, "Do you wanna be deaf by the end of the night?"

He glanced over his shoulder and winked at me. As the last chords of the song wound down, applause and whistles rang throughout the room. The elderly couple smiled and waved before starting to make their way off the dance floor. The guys shuffled their music, preparing to play something else when AJ called, "Play it again, boys." At Vince's surprised look, AJ added, "Please."

Vince must've met AJ before because a wide grin stretched on his face. "You heard him boys. *Anema e Core* it is,"

As the opening chords started up, AJ quirked his brows at me. "You wanna show-off what you learned tonight?"

I grinned up at him. "I'm not sure everything we did back at the dance studio is appropriate."

AJ returned my grin. "That's true." His arms snaked around my waist, drawing me flush against him. Instinctively, I wrapped my arms around his neck. One of his hands splayed across my back, his thumb rubbing back and forth across the exposed skin above my dress. I shivered under his touch, causing him to tighten his arms around me. "How about we try this instead?" he questioned, his breath fanning across my cheek.

I fought to catch my breath. When I could finally speak, I replied, "I think...this is nice."

He snorted. "You and your usage of *nice.*"

Pressed tightly together, we swayed as the passionate words of the love song echoed through the room. I closed my eyes and rested my head against AJ's chest. Tuning out the sounds around me, I focused on the gentle beat of his heart, thrumming through his shirt. "I can see why your grandparents liked this so much," AJ said, breaking the silence.

"Really?" I murmured.

"Yeah, it really speaks to the beauty of true love. Kinda reminds me of one of the first songs I learned to play on the drums, *Amorcito Mio*. My Tio Diego he's the one who got me started playing music. He used to have a band back in Guadalajara. His song with my Tia Anita was *Amorcito Mio*, and he used to play it all the time."

"That means, 'my love', in Spanish right?"

AJ nodded. "Yeah, but sorta more affectionate like 'my baby' kinda usage, too." He stared down at me. "Like I would want to call you, amorcito mio."

"You would?" I questioned softly.

"Yeah, I would." He then brought his lips to mine. In that moment, I didn't care we were on display in front of the entire restaurant. All I wanted in that moment was AJ's lips on mine and his hands on my body. Wanting him to deepen the kiss, I opened my mouth. He obliged me by flicking his tongue against mine. I moaned as I slid my hand up to tangle in his hair. I got so lost in him and what we were doing I didn't realize the song had ended. It wasn't until a more upbeat tune blared around us that I jerked away.

"Fuck me, that was intense," AJ murmured.

I couldn't help laughing. "You have such a way with words."

He grinned. "I try. Now come on, let's show these stiffs how it's done."

Widening my eyes in horror, I shook my head furiously. "But I don't know what to do."

"Just follow my lead."

"Easier said than done," I shouted, over the music.

"Piece of cake." AJ then quick-stepped me over the floor while several times spinning me back and then out. When the music came to a close, he dipped me. My chest rose and fell in harsh pants as I tried catching my breath.

"Wanna go again?"

"Um, maybe?"

AJ laughed and drew me back up. Once again, the music was fast paced, and I fought to keep up with AJ's manic movements. When the song ended, I tugged his arm. "I need something to drink."

"Yes, I should be plying you with more wine, shouldn't I?"

I giggled. "I think you do just fine without it."

Just before we got back to our booth, my dad stepped into our path. "Emiliana, what a surprise." He grabbed me in his muscular arms and hugged me tight against his broad chest. For a man pushing sixty, he was in great shape. With his salt and pepper hair, bright smile, and rugged good looks, he was quite the prize around these parts. Of course, after one marriage before my mom and one brief one after, he was quite content as a confirmed bachelor.

"Hi Daddy." I leaned back to kiss his cheek.

His eyes, that were the same onyx color as mine, glittered with excitement. "You should have told me you were coming out tonight, and I would have had dinner with you and your..." He glanced between me and AJ before his mouth gaped open. "Drummer Boy? Don't tell me you're here with *my* little Mia?"

AJ grinned before he and my dad hugged and smacked backs. "Yes sir. Of course, I didn't know she was your daughter until after I'd made the reservation."

Daddy smiled. "I kept telling you I had a daughter you should meet."

"Oh please, tell me you didn't," I moaned.

AJ laughed. "Actually, he did."

"You didn't tell me that earlier."

"Well, you were freaked out enough about this being your family's place. I didn't think adding in that little tidbit would help."

Daddy cleared his throat. "You know what Mama Sofia would say about this?"

"What?" AJ asked.

"She would say it was truly meant to be because fate and destiny decided to intercede." Daddy took my hand to plant a kiss on it. "I think I would have to agree, mia cara."

"We'll have to see about that," I replied, nervously shifting on my feet. My head spun in a dizzying flurry at the mere fact that AJ and my dad not only knew each other, but apparently liked each other. A lot. It had taken Daddy weeks to come around about Dev. Now he seemed like he was practically ready to marry AJ and me off. Of course, his words about Mama Sofia and fate sent me tail-spinning even further.

Eyeing our table, Daddy said, "You weren't about to leave, were you?"

"Not until we finish our wine."

"I'll send over another bottle along with some dessert."

"No, you don't need to do that."

Daddy smiled. "Of course, I do." He turned to AJ. "Have you ever sampled some of Mia's Mousse?"

I held my breath, hoping to God and all that was holy that AJ would refrain from making any smart ass innuendo remarks or getting that sexy little smirk on his face.

Thankfully, he behaved. "I've had some of the gelato and the tiramisu, but not any of the mousse." A look of revelation flickered on his face. "Wait, is that the one spelled like the animal, moose, on the menu?"

With a chuckle, Daddy replied, "My father named it for Mia. She loved being in the kitchen with my parents when they were cooking. One day when my mother mentioned using a new recipe for the chocolate mousse, Mia got all excited because she thought there was going to be a real moose in the kitchen. Pop and Ma loved it, so they introduced the new mousse as 'Mia's Moose', and it's been that way on the menu ever since."

Warmth flooded my cheeks. "Thanks for the embarrassing

story, Daddy. Why don't you take AJ back to your office and show him some of my baby pictures next?"

AJ nudged me playfully. "I loved that story. And I bet you were a real cutie when you were little."

Daddy grinned. "She could certainly be a precocious little handful."

"I don't think that has changed," AJ teased.

Reaching over, Daddy cupped my cheek. "But most of all, she's been the greatest achievement and blessing of my life."

I swallowed the lump that formed in my throat at his words. Willingly myself not to cry, I wrapped my arms around him again. "Thank you. I love you so very, very much."

He kissed my cheek. "Go on and have a seat. I'll get Pauley to bring out the wine and dessert."

"Thanks, Duke," AJ replied, thrusting out his hand to shake Daddy's again.

"You take care of my little girl now," Daddy replied.

"Would you stop? I am twenty-eight, not twelve."

AJ winked at me. "It'll be my pleasure taking care of her."

I narrowed my eyes at his innuendo while Daddy reached over to give him another hug. "I'm happy to hear that." He then glanced over at me. "See you Sunday night?"

"Of course."

"Bye sweetie."

As I watched my dad's form retreat down the hallway to his office, AJ motioned for me to have a seat. Instead of sitting across from me, AJ slid in next to me in the booth. "Nothing like having you and my dad sharing the same air for a few minutes on a first date," I groaned, as I smoothed down my dress.

"Hey, you should be thrilled that he likes me so much."

"Yeah, I'm not so sure if that's a good thing or not."

We were interrupted by Pauley returning with the wine and mousse. As he set down the plates, he smirked at AJ and me. "Gay friend my ass."

I grimaced. "Sorry, but I was trying to keep you guys off my back."

"Then next time try not to make-out on the dance floor. We're running late on dinner plates because half of the kitchen and wait-staff were watching you two."

"Oh God," I muttered, cupping my head in my hands.

"Quit your bitching, cuz. You looked good out there." When I peeked at him through my fingers, he was smiling genuinely at me. "It's been a long time since we saw you looking so happy."

"Thanks, Pauley."

"You're welcome."

After Pauley left us, AJ eyed the mousse before smirking at me. "Hmm, can't wait to get a taste of Mia's Moose."

"You're an ass," I replied.

"If I remember correctly from earlier this evening, it was mighty tasty."

I smacked his arm. Hard. As he grimaced, I replied, "Just shut up and eat."

On my command, AJ took a hearty spoonful. "It's kinda rich," I warned, but he shoved it in his mouth anyway.

He closed his eyes in exaggerated bliss. "Damn, that's good." He grinned at me. "Orgasmically good."

"Whatever," I mused. After such a big bite, he had a glob stuck on the corner of his mouth. Using my thumb, I reached over and swiped it off. Before I could get my napkin, AJ grabbed my hand and brought it closer to his mouth. With his eyes locked on mine, his tongue reached out and licked my thumb. I held my breath as he sucked my whole thumb into his mouth, suctioning off the chocolate. I instantly had a heated flashback of what that tongue had felt like on me earlier in the limo. Blood rushed to both my cheeks and lower half.

"You want some?" he asked, his voice taking on a lower, husky tone.

I bobbed my head. Instead of using the spoon, AJ dipped his finger into the chocolate and brought it to my lips. Leaning forward, I sucked his finger into my mouth, never taking my eyes off of his. As I pulled harder against his finger, swirling my tongue around it, a lustful gleam burned in his that caused me to shudder.

"We should go. *Now*."

I was having a weird déjà vu moment from earlier in the dance studio when AJ was ready to leave in a hurry so he could ravish me in the limo. A delicious tingle of anticipation ran down

my spine. I still couldn't help questioning, "Don't you want to finish the wine and mousse?"

"I just wanna finish you off a time or two...maybe more."

"Oh, Jesus," I muttered as my panties instantly moistened.

AJ chuckled. Pulling away from me, he searched the restaurant for Pauley. When he saw him, he waved him over. "We're going to need the check. ASAP."

Pauley ducked his head, trying to suppress his laughter. "Uncle Duke said it was on the house."

"He didn't need to do that, but tell him thank you for both Mia and me."

"I will."

AJ reached in his pocket. I watched him slide a crisp hundred bill over to Pauley. "For your excellent service."

Pauley's dark eyes widened. "Holy shit! Thank you, man."

"You're welcome." Pauley stepped aside to let AJ rise out of the booth. He held out his hand for me. "Coming?"

Pauley snickered at the loaded innuendo. I rolled my eyes, feeling like I was surrounded by teenage boys.

"Goodnight, Pauley. And do me a favor?"

His brows rose. "Anything for you, cuz."

"Wipe that shit-eating grin off your face."

He nodded. "Will do."

"Thank you. I appreciate it."

Leaning over, he gave me a kiss. "Have fun, cuz."

"I'll try."

AJ and Pauley shook hands. "Can we go out the back? That's where our driver is waiting."

"Sure thing. You know the way?"

AJ nodded. "It's usually how I come and go when I'm here."

"Night," I called as I strode through the kitchen door.

The moment I entered the room a shouted chorus of "Emiliana!" went up all around me.

"Hi Louie, Petey, Carmine, Carmilla!" I shouted over the sound of clanking plates and silverware scraping food preparation bowls. I would have stopped to talk, but AJ's insistent hand was against my lower back, pushing me along. As soon as we were out the door, his hot mouth was on mine in a hurried, frantic kiss. Pushing me against the brick wall, his hands started roaming over me. "Not here," I panted against his lips.

"Ready sir?" Benny called behind us. I actually felt sorry for him. He was going to need a whole lot of eye bleach to get rid of the images we'd given him in the last five hours. With my past, I never would have expected or imagined that I would be comfortable with such PDA, yet with AJ, it felt right.

"Yeah," AJ grunted, pulling away from me. My heels clicked along the pavement as I made my way to the limo. Benny stood, his head tucked to his chest, with the door open.

"Take us home, Benny," AJ instructed, as we collapsed into the limo in a wild tangle of arms and legs.

"Yes sir," came the mumbled reply, before the door was shut

tight behind us.

Once our bodies had adjusted on the bench seat, AJ crushed his mouth against mine, thrusting his warm tongue into my mouth. He tasted sweet like the chocolate and wine we'd just consumed, and I moaned into his mouth as our tongues intertwined. With one hand cupping my ass, AJ brought his other to my breast, slipping through the satin of my bodice to cup my naked flesh.

As much as I hated to, I jerked away from him. Our gazes locked, and I'm sure mine mirrored AJ's lust-filled one. It took me a full minute to find my voice. Even AJ's broad chest heaved up and down from our passionate lip-lock. "We should go to my house."

"Nuh-uh," AJ grunted, his hand kneading my breast harder.

"But you'll need to drop me off at my place anyway," I argued, trying to ignore the heat pooling below my waist at his actions.

AJ shook his head. "Mine's closer. And I don't wanna waste any time before I can be buried back inside you."

His words stoked the fire burning within me. I couldn't believe just thirty minutes ago we'd been slow dancing at my family's restaurant. Now we were mauling each other like sex-starved deviants. Of course, it was that damn chocolate mousse that had turned dessert into foreplay between the dancing and the limo.

As his thumb flicked over my pebbled nipple, his other hand
snaked up my dress to find my already damp center. When one finger slid inside my panties, I involuntarily thrust my hips up. Although I wanted nothing more than to be with him again, I smacked my palm against his chest, pushing him away. "Oh no, just a minute, big boy."

AJ's chuckle scorched against my neck as he nudged his erection against my exposed thigh. "Thanks for the compliment, babe."

"I'm serious." Grabbing the sweat-soaked strands of his hair, I jerked his head up to meet my gaze. "You've already had me once in this limo. What kind of girl do you take me for?"

A wicked gleam burned in AJ's dark eyes. "The kind who gets off on satisfying her man."

I quirked a brow at him. "Oh, but you're not *mine*, Mr. Latin Lover."

"I've *had* you, Mia. So you're *mine*,for the night."

Shaking my head, I scooted away to where I was on the opposite bench seat. AJ shot me a predatory glare, reiterating the fact he was not accustomed to females not giving him his way. "Quit playing fucking games," he growled.

"I said, no."

"Yeah, well, I call your bluff since I can smell how fucking aroused you are right now. Not to mention, you're practically soaking the seat."

He leaned over to grab me, but I nailed him in the chest with my stiletto heeled foot, thrusting him back against the leather

seat. His gaze dipped from mine to my pump and then he snorted. "Are your 'come fuck me heels' really supposed to deter me?"

When I shrugged, he dropped his head. Never breaking eye contact with me, he then ran his tongue over the strap slowly before taking it between his teeth and jerking. The wet leather smacked against my foot, and I shivered at his actions, causing him to wink at me. "These heels just make me want to throw you on your back and pound you even harder as they dig into my ass."

His tempting words caused me to press my legs tighter together to ease the tension while at the same time I crossed my arms over my chest. "Baby, your little machismo act may work for some helpless bimbos, but I've got strong Italian blood pumping through me. I fuck when *I* want to." I flashed him a defiant look. "And right now, you're *not* having me in this limo."

We stared each other down in a silent battle of wills. AJ eyed me so intently that I could almost see the wheels turning in his head, like he was sure at any moment I would relent and let him take me on all fours like he had earlier. In a firm voice, I said, "Not. Happening."

Keeping my foot firmly against his pectoral, I inched my skirt further up my thighs. His nostrils flared at the sight. "Don't. Fucking. Tease. Me."

I gave him a sweet smile. "I'm not teasing you, babe. Just giving you a preview for later."

An agonized groan escaped his lips as his hand cupped the bulge in his pants. With his gaze still locked on mine, he rubbed the length. "Mia..." His voice had taken on an almost pleading tone.

My mouth ran dry at the image before me, and I licked my lips. "You want me that bad?" I questioned in a whisper.

"Fuck yes."

"Show me," I commanded, nodding towards his crotch.

Without a moment's hesitation, AJ's fingers quickly worked the button and zipper on his khakis. Raising his hips, he eased down his pants and boxers to his mid thighs, exposing his erection to me. "Stroke it."

AJ's hand gripped his hardness before he began to slide his palm up and down. "You owe me, remember?"

"I do?" I replied, playing dumb.

"Yes," he hissed.

"Oh right, I promised you some oral attention for playing gay." Crossing my legs, I adjusted my dress and shook my head. "But the cat's out of the bag now with my family, so I don't owe you anything."

"Mia," he growled, causing a tingle to run from the top of my head down to my toes.

"Fine, but we do it on my terms." When he let his erection fall from his hand, I made a tsking noise. "I didn't tell you stop, did I?"

A lazy grin stretched across his face. "You're fighting a losing battle here, amorcito mio. You want control, and I don't give it up."

My brows rose in surprise. "Oh, I'm sorry. I was under the impression you wanted me to suck your cock."

A strangled noise came from the back of his throat. "I do," he replied hoarsely.

"Then we do it on my terms. Capisce?"

"Si."

"Glad to hear it." Easing off the seat, I knelt down before him. I knocked his knees further apart before wedging myself between them. Sliding my hands up his chest, my fingers came to rest on the bulge of his tie. I kept my eyes locked firmly on his as I undid his tie. With a jerk, I slid it off his neck and dropped it on his exposed thigh.

"Mia, everything you need is uncovered right in front of you," AJ protested.

Ignoring him, I then began undoing the buttons his shirt. Slowly I worked myself down to his waist. When I was done, I opened his shirt, exposing his bare chest and feasting my eyes on the six-pack I had fantasized about in my mind. I ran my hands up and down his chest. "Nice. You work out a lot?" I teasingly asked.

He shot me a death glare. "From time to time."

I grinned before grabbing the tie. Taking his hands, I wrapped it around them and knotted it once.

"Mia?" he questioned.

Motioning above his head, I instructed, "Put your hands up."

"What?"

"Grab hold of the bar."

"Okaaay," he replied, rolling his eyes.

Once his hands were on the bar, I rose up where I was crouching over him. I wrapped the rest of the tie around the bar and knotted it.

When AJ tugged and found he was caught, his eyes widened. "What the fuck are you doing?"

"Exactly what I told you before—I'm having *my* way with you. So sit back, shut your mouth, and enjoy it." Grabbing a small handful of ice from the minibar, I popped a few pieces into my mouth. Bringing one between my teeth, I began teasing a slow trail from the stubble on AJ's neck, over his bobbing Adam's Apple, down to one of his nipples. I then blew across the moistened skin. "Oh fuck," he muttered, bucking his hips.

I circled his left nipple, until it was hard and erect, before I moved on to the right one. AJ continued raising his hips, rubbing his erection against my stomach. I pushed myself away so he could no longer get the friction, causing him to groan in frustration. Working my way slowly down, I trailed the remaining cube over his stomach, causing his muscles to clench under my touch. As I gazed up at him, his
chest expanded in harsh pants. Bending over, my hair fell over his lap as I raked my nails up and down over the tops of his thighs. I pressed tender kisses along the taut muscles of his abdomen.

"Mia…"

"What babe?" I asked.

"Quit teasing me."

"Oh am I teasing you?" I questioned, before I blew cold air across his stomach.

All the muscles in his body went taut, and he was almost shaking with pent up desire. "Suck. My. Dick."

I snorted. "What are you, a caveman? Can't you speak in a complete sentence?"

He growled as he jerked against the tie. If he kept it up, he was going to get loose. With my fingertips still raking over his thighs, I said, "I will if you ask me nicely."

His dark eyes glittered with rage. "Would you suck my dick?"

With a tsk, I replied, "You didn't say the magic word."

A growl rumbled through his chest. "*Please*. For all that is holy, please, please suck my dick!"

I smiled. "Was that so hard?" I took his cock into my hand. "I know this is." Glancing up at him, I gave him my best doe-eyed look of innocence as I lifted up and slowly straddled him. "Open your mouth. Give me your tongue."

When he hesitantly stuck out his tongue, I sucked it into my mouth. After swirling my tongue with his, I pulled away to murmur against his lips, "Is this what you want me to do to you? Down here." I wrapped my fingers tighter around his shaft.

"Yes...please do that, Mia."

I slid off his lap and back onto my knees. Since all the ice had already melted, I put another cube into my mouth as I worked my hand over his erection. Once I swallowed the ice, I flattened my tongue against him, sliding from base to shaft.

AJ shuddered. Circling his cock, I continued licking him like a popsicle, while only letting my tongue give a teasing flick across the tip. AJ's hips jerked up, trying to wedge himself into my mouth. "Enough already. Please suck me harder, Mia."

I narrowed my eyes before letting go of his cock. "You're not calling the shots, remember?"

After grabbing another piece of ice out of the cooler, I started licking and nibbling an icy, moist trail up the inside of one of his thighs while my hand rubbed a cube along the other. When I looked up at him again, AJ's jaw was clenched, and I could see the frustrated lust burning in his eyes.

Deciding to end his suffering, I took only the tip of cock in my mouth and suctioned hard. "Finally. Fuck yes!" AJ cried, his eyes rolling back. Letting him fall free from my mouth, I then blew across the sensitive head glistening with my saliva. "Jesus, you're killing me. Don't stop sucking me off. Please."

"I've only just started, babe." With my hand, I stroked him hard and fast for a few minutes before bringing him back to my mouth. As I bobbed up and down in a frenzied pace, his groans and curses echoed through the limo. His hands tugged at his bindings while the muscles in his biceps bulged with the efforts to get free. I knew he wanted nothing more than to be able to wrap his hands in my hair and fuck my mouth with his dick. But

it wasn't happening. Each time he tried to take control of the pace, I eased back, sending him shuddering with frustration. A sheen of sweat had broken out along his bare chest. "So good...oh baby, I love your mouth."

Changing up the position, I brought my fingers to his base. Twisting my hand back and forth like I was opening a bottle, I alternated between tonguing and hard suctioning the very tip. The saliva that fell from my lips, slid down his length, allowing my fingers to give him an even smoother swirl off my hand, as I pumped up and down. As I pulled away, I said, "Doing this to you...it's making me so fucking wet."

AJ's eyes bulged at my comment. "Untie me, and I'll make you scream."

I shook my head slowly from side to side. "Nope. Not happening." I slid my free hand under my dress and into my panties. As I stroked myself, I stared up at AJ. "Mmm, I like getting you and me off at the same time."

"Fucking hell," he croaked, his hooded eyelids watching my movements.

"But this is supposed to be about you, right?" I took my hand from my panties and brought my fingers to his lips. "Lick please."

He didn't have to be told twice. His tongue darted out to lick my fingers before he sucked them into his mouth. "You still taste amazing."

"You do, too," I murmured, before I took him back into my mouth, grazing him lightly with my teeth. It wasn't long before he began tensing up. "Oh fuck...oh yes!" AJ arched his hips as I let him fall free of my mouth. Negative tests or not, I wasn't ready to go there with him yet. Rising off my knees, I quickly brought my mouth to his while I pumped my hand on his cock. Sucking on his bottom lip, I breathed against his mouth, "I'm so turned on right now." AJ let out a grunting moan as he came on his stomach. I pulled back and met his eyes, which were a combustive mix of satisfaction and pure desire. "Jesus, Mia, I can't even move. You fucking obliterated me."

"Thank you."

AJ's bare chest rose with laughter. "No, thank *you*."

I rose up and started untying his hands. When I finished, I handed some napkins to him and cocked my head at him. "So Mr. Machismo, is it really so bad to give up control now and again?"

"I guess not." When I pursed my lips at him, he grinned. "Okay, it's fucking amazing."

"So glad you thought so."

As he went about cleaning himself up, he kept eyeing me from time to time. "What?" I asked.

"The twisting thing and the sucking....I've never had anything like that."

I rolled my eyes and grinned in spite of myself. "You're still marveling over a blow job?"

"One like that? Fuck yeah."

"I guess I should take that as a major compliment."

He smiled and bobbed his head. "Oh yeah."

After all I'd been through with Dev's cheating, AJ's words meant more than he could ever know, especially considering I was just getting back in the game. AJ just finished rearranging his clothes when we pulled into the parking lot of his building. When Benny opened the door for us, I followed AJ out onto the pavement. While I could barely look at Benny without my cheeks flooding with embarrassment, AJ gave him a guy hug and whispered something in his ear.

Benny grinned and nodded.

With a smile, AJ then took my hand. "Come on. Let me show you my views."

Chapter Eight

AJ

As I led Mia across the foyer of my building, I cut my eyes over to her, watching as she took it all in. It was a pretty impressive place, if I said so myself. All of us guys had apartments in the city, so we could have a place to crash close to the airport and the recording studio. But Bray and Melody lived about thirty minutes south of Jake's farm, preferring the country to the city.

"Like it?" I asked Mia, as we headed for the elevator.

"It's amazing. You know, some of the doctors from St. Joe's live here."

When we got into the elevator, we weren't alone. After I slid in my key card for the penthouse, Mia ended up getting shuffled with her back against the wall of the car while I was pressed against her. Glancing over at her, a wicked thought entered my mind. Leaning over, I whispered in her ear. "You know, you deserve a little payback for that stunt you pulled in the limo. Maybe have you helpless without being bound?"

Her eyes widened as she glanced around the crowded elevator. "Don't even think about it," she warned.

Ignoring her, I angled my body so what I was about to do was hidden from view. Dipping my hand between her legs, I began to stroke her over her dress. She gasped before quickly biting down on her lip. Pressed against the back wall, she had nowhere to go and could do nothing but be at the mercy of my hand.

The elevator dinged on the Fourth floor, and a guy in a pinstriped suit, along with an older couple, got off. Even though there was more room, I didn't move. Instead, I pressed the heel of my hand against Mia's pussy while my fingers pressed harder against her clit. Her jaw clenched with the strain of keeping her moans and cries from escaping her lips. Her chest heaved, and her breath huffed out of her nose. A mixture of both pleasure and fury burned in her eyes.

I didn't turn around because people would see my khakis were tented. Watching Mia, including what I was doing to her, was so fucking hot. Her head fell back against the wall, and I knew she was getting closer to coming, and there was nothing I wanted more than to bring her to the brink.

But when the last person got off on the Twentieth floor, Mia glared up at me, her dark eyes flashing with rage. As soon as the doors closed, she shoved me away from her. "You fucking prick!"

"Don't pretend you didn't like it," I countered.

"We were in public."

"And that fact alone made you even wetter. Hell, I could feel it through your dress. You were so close to coming."

Smacking her palms against my chest, she shoved me again, sending me crashing back into the opposite wall of the elevator. Her nostrils flared before she stalked over to me. She eyed me contemptuously. "This elevator has cameras too, doesn't it?"

I gave her my smirk. "I would think so."

In a flash, both hands reached out, and I braced myself for her to hit or choke me. I wasn't even going to defend myself because I deserved it. Instead, she fisted my shirt before ripping it open, sending buttons scattering onto the floor. Her arms snaked around my neck, tugging the hair at the base of my neck. "Then let's give them a real show." Her lips came down harsh against mine, and I welcomed the warmth of her tongue in my mouth.

Grasping her by the ass, I hoisted her up to wrap her legs around my waist. I spun us around, pinning her against the wall. With one hand, Mia's fingers jerked through my hair, tugging almost painfully at the strands while the other slipped between us to stroke my dick over my pants. I groaned into her mouth, causing her to rub even harder. I pumped my hips against her hand, working the friction to my advantage. I realized if I kept it up, I was going to blow my load right there in my pants, which

wouldn't do either of us any good. Grabbing Mia's hand off my dick, I guided it between her legs. Jerking her lips from mine, Mia's wide eyes flared with desire when I used her own fingers to stroke her over her soaked panties. "Mmm," she whimpered, rocking her hips.

Watching her get herself off was hot as hell, but when the bell on the penthouse dinged our arrival, I was brought out of my sex haze. When I took my hand away, Mia cried out in protest. "Sorry, but we gotta get off, amorcito mio."

"Yeah, but that's what I was about to do," she replied with a lazy grin.

I threw back my head and laughed. "Because of you, I'm probably going to get instant wood each time I get on this fucking elevator."

Holding Mia with one hand, I grabbed my card with the other, and then staggered across the marble tile of the foyer's threshold. Once we were inside the penthouse and the elevator doors had shut, Mia's hungry lips came back to mine. I blindly made my way along to the living room. When I bumped into the couch, I eased Mia over the armrest. While her torso lay across the cushion, her lower half was elevated exactly where I needed it. As her legs dangled over the edge,

I slid the hemline of her dress up. I jerked off her panties and tossed them over my shoulder. I then relieved myself of my shirt. "Hurry AJ!" she demanded, wrapping her legs around my hips and pulling me closer.

"Patience, amorcito mio," I murmured, before digging into my back pocket for my wallet. After I pulled out the condom, I needed a free hand, so I placed it between my teeth for safe keeping. I hurriedly unbuttoned and unzipped my pants and shoved them down my hips. Tearing open the condom, I slid it on.

With one harsh thrust, I buried myself balls deep inside her. "Oh AJ," she moaned beneath me. Neither of us knew how to take it slow, so instead, I pounded into her. Grabbing her thighs, I wrapped my arms under her knees and used them for leverage to bring myself harder and deeper within her.

Once Mia came, I concentrated on my own pleasure, slamming harder and harder into her. She didn't seem to mind how rough I was. Instead, she kept right on panting and moaning with pleasure. When she came for the second time, her walls clenching against my cock caused me to come. "Mia!" I cried, before collapsing over on her.

When I could once again focus on the world around me, I found Mia was stroking wide circles across my back. I pulled away to smile at her.

She returned my smile. "Are we ever going to have sex in a bed?"

I laughed. "I say we take a quick shower and then the next time will commence in my bed."

A little crease came between her brows. "You mean, you're not ready for me to go?"

"Jesus, no. What the hell gave you that idea?"

She shrugged. "I just figured since we were done—"

Cupping her face in my hands, I said, "Mia, babe, I don't plan for us to be done until the morning...maybe tomorrow afternoon."

Her dark eyes widened. "You want me to stay the night?"

"Of course."

"I just didn't expect that."

"I'm not one of those douchebags who throws a chick out once he's done banging her. Besides morning sex happens to be one of my favorite things," I answered honestly. Even though it kinda stung, I could see why Mia would think I was a wham-bam kinda guy since I was a famous musician. It was true that I didn't bring a lot of women here. I did most of my hook-ups on the road in the bus or in hotel rooms. Off the road, I was a lot more choosey. In the past, my house had been reserved for women I was in a relationship with—who I trusted. While Mia didn't technically fit into that category, I was happy to make an opening for her. Because of her career, her family, and most of all her fiery personality, she had proven to be in a class all of her own.

Leaning forward, I kissed her intently. "So you'll stay?"

"Um, okay."

"Good. Now let's go take that shower." Taking her by the hand, I pulled her up off the couch. I pushed her hair back away from her face and gave her a long, lingering kiss—one I hoped

would show her how much I wanted her with me.

When I pulled away, I took her by the hand and started down the hall. "I really want to see your place," she protested.

"After the shower."

"Like you'll be in the mood for a grand tour then. You're already naked," she mumbled.

I laughed and smacked her ass playfully. "You know me too well."

Once we were inside the bathroom, I closed the door behind us. After I stepped over to Mia, my hands immediately went to the zipper on her dress. When it pooled in a whisper at her feet, she was left only in her bustier since I'd happily shed her of her panties back in the living room. "I'll get the water on while you get out of that thing," I said, motioning to her chest. I knew my way around a bra, but that looked way tricky.

"Okay," she whispered.

I turned on the water, letting the shower fill with steam. I stepped inside, but I left the door open. Glancing over my shoulder, I noticed Mia still stood frozen by the counter.

"Aren't you coming?"

She gave a slight nod before slipping out of the bustier. Once she was fully naked, she stepped into the shower. With her arms crooked at the elbows, her hands rested under her chin, covering her breasts. "Don't tell me you're being shy now?"

"No," she murmured.

"Then what's the problem?"

"It's just..." She closed her eyes like she was in pain. "It's the first time you've seen me fully naked."

"And it's a fucking amazing sight." When she didn't look at me, I cupped her chin in my fingers. "Hey, what's going on in that thick head of yours?"

She sighed. "Look, I'm sorry. I know this is probably my own shit I'm projecting off on you. But I kinda have a feeling about the type of girls you usually date—willowy, blonde models who are size zeroes, with perfect fake tits and don't have any cellulite."

I laughed. "Man, you really don't know me at all, do you?" Brushing her hair out her face, I stroked her cheek. "I told you back at Mama Sofia's that I like people to be real—I want the same things in the women I date too. Real figures—not some plastic stick-figure."

She stared up at me in surprise. "You're really serious, aren't you?"

"Yeah, I am." In that moment, I wanted nothing more than to hunt down her dickhead ex-fiance and beat the ever loving shit out of him. I mean, Mia was confident at her job, she didn't think twice about giving me her sassy mouth, but she was completely incapable of believing how sexy and beautiful she was. There was no way she had always felt that way. No, that asshole had done this to her—he'd not only banged some other woman and

broken Mia's heart, but he'd taken even more of her when he stripped her of her confidence.

Shaking her head slowly at me, she replied, "Just when I think all men are alike….You really are too good to be true, you know that?"

I nodded. "It's a curse really," I replied, trying to lighten the mood.

A grin curved on her lips. "Sorry for being so neurotic. This whole getting back in the game thing has my head spinning."

"How about I let you make it up to me by washing my back...and my dick?"

She laughed. "It's a deal."

Morning sunlight streaked in through my curtains. Groaning, I brought my hand to my eyes to shield them. I usually remembered to close them before I went to bed. Then I remembered what had caused me to forget. A delicious reel of images from the previous night flickered through my mind. Even though I'd been satisfied multiple times, Mia was an addicting drug, and I wanted more. Rolling over, I found the other side of the bed empty. Flipping back over, I noticed the bathroom door was wide open, so she wasn't in there. Just as I was about to get utterly pissed at Mia for bailing on me, wonderful aromas assaulted my nose.

Holy shit, she was cooking me breakfast? I sniffed the air a few times. My chest constricted when I realized that the heavenly smell was more specifically Huevos Rancheros. Mia was making me a *Mexican* breakfast. Now that was some real shit right there. I couldn't help shaking my head in disbelief. Not only was Mia a sex goddess who knew her way around a dick, but damn, if she didn't know how to cook, too. I mean, she could take care of two of the strongest appetites I had—sex and food.

Flinging back the covers, I hustled out of bed. I threw on some boxer shorts before heading down the hallway. Peeking in the kitchen, I found Mia at the stove. My deflating wood thrummed back to life at the sight of her outfitted in one of my T-shirts with only her black, lacy panties from last night.

"Morning," I said.

She jumped before whirling around. She swept the spatula to her chest. "Shit, you scared me."

"Sorry. It's just, I woke up and missed you in bed."

Mia eyed the bulge in my shorts. "Hmm, I think I know now why you were missing me."

I laughed before motioning toward the stove. "Is that really Huevos Rancheros I smell?"

"Yes, is it." She gave me a playful grin. "My, my, you look surprised that a Sicilian gal can cook something Mexican."

I laughed. "I'm shocked to see you cooking, period, least of all this."

"One of my girlfriends and first apartment mates was Mexican. I learned from her." Grabbing the orange juice out of the fridge, Mia poured two large glasses. "You know, I was kinda shocked to even find food in the house."

Sheepishly, I ran a hand through my bed hair. "Yeah, my mom takes credit for that one. She makes sure when I'm coming into town to stock the fridge and pantry."

"She likes to spoil her little boy, huh?" Mia teased. She reached out and playfully pinched my cheek.

I swatted her hand away. "She just likes to take care of me since I'm gone a lot. She doesn't get as much time with me as her other kids. I mean, Antonio's still living at home and commuting to Tech, and my sister, Cris, just lives two streets over from her."

Mia smiled. "I think it's sweet she looks after you like she does. It makes me think of something Mama Sofia would do for me."

As Mia's expression grew sad, I decided we needed a subject change. "You know, I'm really digging your attire."

With an exasperated snort, she brushed a strand of hair out of her face. "Yeah, it's a little less than I usually wear when I cook, but none of your boxers fit right." She cast a glance over her shoulder before scowling. "My ass is too big."

Sinking to my knees, I gripped her hips and turned her around. "Never, ever diss your fantabulous ass in my presence again." Along the exposed skin, I smacked one of the perfect globes before grazing it with my teeth. "Tastes as good as it looks."

"AJ!"

"Seriously, Mia, this ass is perfection—one to be proud of."

She giggled. "I didn't know I needed to start listing it as an asset."

"You should." My hands left her hips to knead both of her cheeks. "I could spend hours with it and never get tired."

"I didn't realize you were such an ass man."

"Oh, I'm equal opportunity on thighs and tits too."

Mia groaned. Wiggling around in my arms, she stared down at me. "Come on, everything is ready, and you need to eat."

"I know what I want to eat," I mused, nudging my nose at the juncture of her thighs. I flicked my tongue against the lacy, black fabric.

A little gasp escaped her lips. Then her fingers came to wrap around the strands of my hair, jerking my head up to look at her. Although her lids were hooded with desire, she demanded, "Breakfast first."

My stomach rumbled, so I pulled myself off the floor. "You drive a hard bargain."

As I made my way over to the table, she trailed behind me with our plates in hand. Just as she was about to sit down, she popped back up. "Shit, I forgot the fruit."

"It's fine without it."

"No, you need a good, balanced breakfast."

My heart tugged a little at her concern for my welfare. Even though I should have waited for her, the food looked way too tempting. After taking a large, steamy bite, I moaned in bliss.

"Damn, Mia, this is divine."

She laughed and closed the fridge. "Thank you."

I scarfed down another two bites before she returned. When Mia leaned over me to set the fruit bowl down, her dark hair swept in front of my face, sending the sweet smell of jasmine into my nose. As she pulled away, my hand accidentally grazed her breast. I knew then that I didn't want another bite of breakfast until I'd had her.

She turned to go, but I grabbed her hand, jerking her back to me. "AJ, what are you doing?"

Palming her breast through the T-shirt, I replied, "Planning to fuck you like I wanted when I first woke up this morning."

She smacked my hand away. "Jeez, Neanderthal, can't you wait until you've eaten?"

I gave her a wicked smile. "No, because I plan on having something *else* to eat first." I shoved my plate to the side. Grabbing her by the hips, I hoisted Mia up on the table in front of me.

"Oomph," she muttered, giving me a death glare. After I slid her panties off, I then propped her feet on each of the chair arms. "You are such an infuriating sex-fiend!" she huffed. When I grinned up at her, she rolled her eyes. "I went to all that trouble to make you breakfast."

"It can be reheated." I grabbed the hemline of her shirt. Glancing around, Mia bit her bottom lip. This time without saying a word, I knew she was afraid of me seeing her in the light. "You

are fucking beautiful—every single inch. You hear that loud and clear?" I growled, before jerking her shirt off. At the sight of her full, lush body in front of me, I groaned. "God, what just the sight of you does to me."

"Thank you," she murmured. It was as if she still couldn't believe it was true. How could she not believe how fucking beautiful and sexy she was? In that moment, I knew I wanted to somehow get it through her thick skull that she was a knock-out beauty in so many ways than just physically.

Glancing at the bowl of fruit, a wicked thought entered my mind. I dug out a chunk of pineapple. Cupping Mia's cheek with my hand, I brought the piece to her lips. "Eat," I commanded. Licking her lips, she eyed me before leaning in. When she bit into the pineapple, juice dribbled down her chin and trickled onto her chest. While she chewed, I swiped my tongue across her chin, sucking up the moisture. I then licked a sticky trail down her neck to suck up the remaining juice. Being that close to her breasts was too tempting, so I sucked a nipple inside my mouth.

"Mmm, AJ," she murmured, her fingers twisting through my hair.

Alternating between licking and sucking, I teased the nipple into a hardened point. I then started to Mia's other breast, but she pulled back, reaching for the fruit bowl. She brought a strawberry to my lips, and I took a bite. After I finished chewing, I sucked the other half in my mouth. I slid the uneaten part down her chest and over her stomach. Her breathing hitched when I reached the juncture of her thighs. Widening her legs, I brought my head between them. "AJ, what are you doing?" she asked in a panicked voice.

"Shh," I muttered, pushing her upper body down on the table. She angled her head to the side and gazed down at me, her brow creased.

Turning to her left thigh, I slid the strawberry against her skin. Her legs shook when I repeated my motions on her right thigh. Then I brought my mouth to her center, rubbing the strawberry against her sensitive nub. She gasped with pleasure. Going for the gold, I brought a finger up and slipped it inside her. "AJ," she moaned, raising her hips as I worked a second finger inside her. All the while, I kept rubbing her clit with the strawberry. "Oh fuck! Oh yes, I'm going to come!" she cried. Her hands flew out to grip the edge of the table momentarily before she brought them to cup her breasts. Her hips bucked up, and she started murmuring my name over and over.

When her walls finished clenching around my fingers, I withdrew from her. "You okay, amorcito mio?"

Licking her lips, she shook her head. "Take me to bed, AJ," she pleaded.

"I thought you'd never ask." I stood up, kicking the chair out from behind me. Grabbing Mia's hips, I dragged her to the edge of the table. She wrapped her legs around me, and I hoisted her up. I brought my mouth back to hers, kissing her feverishly.

When I got to the hallway, it seemed like the bedroom was miles away. I fought the urge to shove Mia up against the wall and take her right there. But she deserved better than that.

When I got into the bedroom, I gently eased her down on the mattress. Reaching around my back, she pulled me on top of her. My dick rubbed against her wet heat, causing us both to moan. "Wait, I gotta get a condom." I snatched one out of the nightstand lightning fast and was back in her arms. Mia opened her thighs to me, and I positioned myself between them before easing inside her. She felt like heaven, and I groaned in pleasure.

Instead of the pounding sex we'd had previously, this was slow, tender, and...heartfelt. It caused a whole range of emotions to ripple through me. As I kept my eyes on hers, Mia's hips rose to meet my thrusts. Her whimpers and moans made me hot as hell, but I reigned myself in. It felt too good to end it fast.

When Mia came, her arms clutched me tighter against her. Her cries echoed through the bedroom, but I loved she called my name the most. It didn't take too long before I was tensing up and coming inside her. After I was done, I didn't immediately roll off her. Instead, I let her continue swirling lazy circles with her fingers on my back while I buried my face in her neck. I inhaled her soft skin and smelled some tiny remnants of her perfume mixed with the more manly body wash I'd used on her last night in the shower. The silky strands of her hair tickled my

nose, and I rose up to kiss a trail over her neck and chin and slowly back to her mouth. I thrust my tongue inside, seeking out her warmth. After a frenzied lip-lock, my phone ringing brought me out of my post-sex haze.

"Shit," I grumbled before pulling out of her. I fumbled along the nightstand for my phone before realizing it must be in my pant pockets. I strode down the hall to find them by the couch. I had a missed call from Jake, so I called him back.

"Hey man, where are you?" Jake asked.

"Home. Why?"

"We got rehearsal at Eastman's in fifteen minutes, remember?"

Fuck, I had forgotten all about that. To celebrate our success, we were doing a show at Eastman's, the bar where we'd first come together as a band. "Yeah, I kinda forgot about that. I'll be there as soon as I can, okay?"

"You better get your ass here ASAP, douchebag."

"Bite me, ass-munch."

Jake chuckled before hanging up the phone. Out of the

corner of my eye, I spotted Mia's panties on the kitchen floor. I grabbed them and then headed down the hall. When I entered the bedroom, my bed was empty. I found Mia dressed in the bathroom and washing her face. "I figured that call meant you have to go."

I nodded. "We have rehearsal in fifteen minutes."

Eyeing my naked form, Mia grinned. "You better hurry."

"I can throw something on real quick." I closed the distance between us. "I wouldn't want to shower anyway. I wanna smell like you the rest of the day."

Turning around, she wrapped her arms around my neck. "I'd say since I used your manly smelling bath wash last night, you're just going to smell like yourself."

"And sex," I added with a smile.

She laughed. "Yes and that."

I brought my lips to hers, giving her a long, lingering kiss. When I pulled away, I cocked my head at her. "So, can I call you?"

Mia hesitated before replying, "Sure."

After another kiss, I replied, "You know if I say I'll call, I mean it, right? I'm not one of those douchebags who says that and bails."

Sadness briefly flickered in Mia's eyes. "We'll see."

"Ooh, you're challenging me, huh?" I smacked her ass playfully. "You know I love a good challenge."

Mia smiled. "Call it whatever you want."

"Just call you, right?"

She nodded. "But...only if you want." She leaned in and kissed me again, before starting for the door.

"Wait," I called. She turned around. I swung her panties around on my finger. "You forgot these."

She eyed them for a moment before glancing back at me. "Keep them to remember me by." And with a wink, she walked
out of the room.

With a grin, I shook my head. Somehow I'd managed to meet my match in every way possible. One day with her would never be enough. Hell, I doubted even a week would be enough. I knew there was no way I could let Mia get away when she could be my one and only.

Chapter Nine

Mia

When Monday morning arrived, I hopped out of bed before the alarm went off with a renewed bounce in my step. Instead of cursing at traffic, I sang along to the radio. I even managed to arrive ten minutes early to work, which caused Dee's jaw to drop.

"Well hello. Look at you Miss Thing. It's a gloomy Monday morning, but you're here early and with a smile on your face. Hmm, mmm." He snapped his fingers up and down. "Miss Mia got her groove back!"

I snickered as I bypassed him for the break-room. When I turned around from putting my purse in my locker, Dee stood in the doorway, hand on his hip. Although he had gotten every single salacious detail last night, I could tell he was eager for more.

"I'm not discussing AJ with you right now."

"Lunchtime then. I want a side of naughty with my

salad."

I laughed. "Sounds like a plan."

With several post operation patients, we were pretty slammed the rest of the morning. Of course, in between checking vitals and changing IVs, my mind couldn't help straying to AJ and our elicit weekend. Every time I did, I couldn't keep the beaming smile off my lips or the flush of warmth from filling my cheeks. When lunchtime rolled around at eleven, I made my way to the break-room. Sunday nights were always spent with my dad and the crew at Mama Sofia's, and I always brought salad back for Dee and me.

As I took out the container and something to drink from the fridge, my cell beeped in my pocket. When I pulled it out, my heartbeat broke out into a wild gallop at the name on the text. It was AJ.

The words, **Miss U,** were accompanied by a picture of him with his bottom lip poking out. When a giggle escaped my lips, I wanted to roll my eyes at my ridiculous behavior. Honestly, I'd barely been away from him twenty-four hours, and he already had too much effect on me.

My fingers furiously worked over the keyboard as I typed: **Hmm, not sure exactly which head you're missing me with.**

I grinned triumphantly as I hit send. I'm sure he was expecting some heartfelt response or a sad faced 'I miss you too'. It was just after I'd finished drizzling Italian dressing over my salad that my phone dinged again. I took a giant bite of grilled chicken before opening the text. When I did, I began to

choke.

The head of AJ's cock appeared on the screen along with the words, *He misses you even more!*

Holy shit! My shock sent me into a choking fit. I'd just recovered when my phone rang. I didn't have to guess who it was. Without even a hello, I hissed, "I cannot believe you just sent me a dick picture!"

AJ's deep chuckle echoed through my ear, warming me in places it shouldn't. "Even though you could probably make a lot of money off that, I hope you keep it to yourself."

"You have nothing to worry about on that one."

"Good idea. It makes more sense to keep it for yourself to get you through the lonely nights."

"Do you have a point? I mean, besides sexually harassing me at work."

"Yes, I do, actually. First, I wanted you to know that I did really miss you. This weekend was…off the charts amazing and fantastic."

Fighting to catch my breath, I tried to play off the intense feelings ricocheting through me. "Yes, it was nice."

AJ snorted. *"Nice?* You call multiple orgasms until you could barely walk just *nice?"*

I laughed. "Okay, okay, I agree that amazing is a better adjective. Now what's your second point?"

"I wanted to know if you were free Friday night."

"Yes, I am. Why?"

"The guys and I are playing a reunion show at the bar where we got started. I thought since you've never heard us—or me for that matter—you might want to come?"

Holy shit. He not only wanted to see me again, but he wanted to share the biggest part of his life—his music—with me. That fact alone had to mean our little weekend tryst was more than just mind-blowing sex to him. I couldn't even begin to fathom the thought that AJ Resendiz, drummer for Runaway Train, sex-on-a-stick personified with thousands of women just waiting to take care of his needs, would want to be with me again.

"Mia?" AJ questioned, through my self-deprecating tirade.

"Sorry. Oh, um, yeah, that sounds nice."

"There you go with that 'nice' word again."

I laughed. "I'm sorry. It's just you kinda caught me off guard."

"I guess it's hard to focus on anything once I've assaulted you with a cock pic before noon, huh?"

"You could say that."

"I'll remember that next time."

"Yes, save the dick pics until at least late afternoon. Evening might be best."

AJ chuckled. "I'll note that one for sure."

"Seriously though. I would love to see your band and you live in action."

"I'm glad to hear that. Our set starts at eight, and things will be pretty crazy before then. I hate to not come pick you up, but

do you think you could meet me there?"

"Sure, that'll be fine."

"Great." A long pause came on the line before AJ spoke again. After clearing his throat several times, he asked, "You think you'd wanna have dinner before then?"

The room seemed to tilt and then spin around me. He wanted to see me *before* the weekend? Surely, it was only about sex and not about getting to know me better. That had to be it. Trying to play the strictly physical card, I replied, "Guess you really are missing me bad if you can't wait until the weekend."

"Actually, I was thinking more along the lines of dinner— somewhere nice and fancy like we did before."

"Oh," I murmured.

"Being on the road so much, you enjoy when dinner doesn't come out of a box or from some seedy diner."

My heartbeat thrummed wildly in my chest. Okay, he wanted dinner and conversation, not straight sex. When I finally found my voice again, I replied, "Sure, I'd love to do dinner again. Well, as long as it's not Mama Sofia's. I mean, if we show up there again, they'll have us already engaged."

With a laugh, AJ replied, "I think that can be arranged."

"I'm off tomorrow night."

"Then tomorrow it is." At the sound of voices in the background, AJ gave a frustrated grunt. "I have to go, Mia. I'll see you tomorrow at seven?"

"Sounds good."

"Bye."

"Bye."

Long after he hung up, I sat dazed and staring at my phone. I only glanced up when Dee burst into the room. "Sorry, I'm late," he said breathlessly, as he eased himself into the chair beside me.

"It's okay. I was hungry, so I started without you."

"I see how it is."

I grinned as I passed him the bowl of grilled chicken salad. Leaning over me, Dee reached for a bottle of water from my bag. Before I could close my texts, he gasped and grabbed my phone. His dark eyes bulged. "Dayum, look who is getting sexts so early in the day!" He glanced up from the phone. "You must've made a helluva impression if he's sending you this."

I shrugged, trying to playing it off. "We were just joking around."

"This," he said, as he waved AJ's cock pic in front of me, "is nothing to joke about. You know we never, ever joke about prize pieces of flesh, and this is certainly one of them." Dee brought the phone in front of his eyes again. "And hell, he's not even hard. No wonder you're walking kinda funny today."

"I'm perfectly fine, thank you very much," I snapped.

"Mmm, mmm, he's missing you and that fabulous vajayjay of yours so soon, huh?"

I laughed. "You have such a way with words."

"I try."

We fell into silence then. After swallowing a giant bite of salad, Dee grunted. "Spill it, Mimi. What's he want?"

When I filled Dee in on AJ's call, his eyes lit up. "He's got it bad for you."

"I'm having second thoughts."

"Honey, you need to set up an appointment for a MRI cause your head needs checking for sure. There's no way in hell I could say no to that cock."

With a laugh, I playfully smacked his arm. "This is serious, Dee. I mean, getting back in the game was one thing, but a guy like AJ—a musician with a horde of women at his beck and call..." I shook my head. "I feel like I'm emotionally setting myself up to be a lamb to the slaughter."

"And then again, you could end up Mrs. AJ Resendiz."

I snorted. "Excuse me, but who needs an MRI now? I mean, you do remember this is me you're talking to, right? The girl whose history with men is the figurative equivalent of the Battle of Kennesaw Mountain."

Dee rolled his eyes. "You and your Georgia history nerdom."

Leaning forward on the table with my elbows, I cocked my head at him. "You really think that after the past nine months of my life, I'm up for this?"

"We all have our pasts and baggage, Mimi. It's our decision whether they fuck with our future."

With a defeated sigh, I rubbed my eyes. "Fine, fine. Deep down, I know you're right."

"Of course I am." When I shot him a look, he grinned. "Speaking of the future, let's talk about what hot little number you're going to wear on Friday night to get Mr. Latin Lover's gears grinding again."

Chapter Ten

AJ

Drumming my fingers on my jeans, I waited anxiously in the cramped backstage room at Eastman's Pub—the place where Runaway Train had gotten its start years ago. It was quite a different set-up from our usual concert scene, but it still felt so freakin' right to be back here. Outside in the bar, a sold out crowd awaited us, standing room only. But a packed house was the last thing on my mind. Instead, a tall, stacked brunette occupied all my thoughts—most of which were pretty X-rated.

Dinner with Mia on Tuesday night led to a 'barely make it to the bed, a path of clothes strewn up the stairs inside Mia's house' all night sexathon. The only thing that had stopped us from going at it all day Wednesday was that Mia had to go to work, which totally blew. Wednesday and Thursday night after she got off work, we skipped the dinner, went straight to screwing, and ordered in food only after we pried ourselves off each other.

I didn't want to admit it, but I was getting in fucking deep with Mia. I wanted to say it was just about the sex, but it wasn't. What we had outside of the bedroom was just as good. The shit we talked and laughed about over dinner, the way she rose to every little tease and challenge I gave her—it was fucking amazing.

When I felt a hand on my shoulder, I jerked my head up. Abby stood before me—her brow lined with concern. In Spanish, she asked, "What's up with you?"

I shrugged. Keeping our conversation private from the guys, I replied back in Spanish, "Nothing. Why?"

"You seem uncharacteristically quiet and mellow."

"Just in the zone for the show."

Abby eyed me suspiciously before Jake came up and wrapped his arms around her waist. "You guys shit talking me in Spanish?"

I laughed. "Jesus, such an egomaniac."

Jake grinned. "Always, man."

A knock sounded at the door. Jeff, Frank's temporary replacement as head roadie, opened the door. "Twenty minutes to show-time, guys."

"Thanks man," Jake replied.

"Guess we better go get our table," Lily said, rising off of Bray's lap. He smacked her ass playfully, which caused her to squeal. "Watch it, mister."

With a wink, he added, "I'd keep my eyes on you—watching only you—all night if I could."

Rhys made a gagging noise next to me. "Jesus, between the two of you and Abby and Jake, you're killing me."

"You're just jealous that your ugly mug is all sad and alone," Bray replied.

With a little swagger in his step, Rhys replied, "I won't be alone for long tonight."

"Especially if the blonde barracudas show up," Lily said, with disgust.

Rhys grinned. "I certainly hope they do." He smacked my arm. "Don't you?"

"Uh...yeah. I guess."

Rhys gave me a 'what the fuck?' look as Abby and Lily went out the door. Once they were gone, he asked, "Is your lack of enthusiasm for guaranteed ass because you're betting on Kylie being here tonight?"

Oh shit. "She's coming?" I asked in a strangled voice.

With a bob of his head, Rhys replied, "Lily's mom has the kids tonight. But I would've thought she would have let you know that via sext or some shit."

"I'm not expecting to hook-up with Kylie tonight." My gut told me if Mia and Kylie met, I was fucked and not in a good way.

Jeff sauntered back in the room. "Got Abby and Lily to their table. You guys need anything?"

Rising out of my chair, I went over to him. "Yeah man, I've got a girl waiting outside for me. She's supposed to check in at the bar. Can you bring her back here, so I can see her before the show?"

"No problem."

After Jeff shut the door behind him, a low whistle echoed through the room. I whirled around to see the guys staring at me. "What?" I snapped.

"You invited a chick to our show?" Jake asked.

"I wouldn't exactly call Mia a chick—she's more of a woman."

Rhys's eyes widened. "Holy shit, dude, you're seeing *her*?"

"I told you I was taking her out."

"Yeah, I thought for the night, but that was a week ago."

Jake and Brayden exchanged puzzled looks. "Who the fuck is Mia?" Jake questioned.

With a grin, Rhys replied, "She's the chick, er, woman...nurse I was telling you guys about who knocked the drink over on AJ and almost made him blow his load in his pants."

"Oh yeah," Brayden chuckled. "Nice one."

I shrugged. "I like her, okay?"

Jake snorted. "No shit, Sherlock. You've never invited anyone but your family to our shows before."

Rhys bobbed his head in agreement. "This is epic."

"Would you guys get off my dick about Mia please?" I growled, before collapsing on the sofa.

A knock on the door sounded, and Jeff poked his head in. "I found her."

A chorus of kissy noises echoed around the room as Mia appeared in the doorway. I shot the guys death glares before turning my attention back to her. At the sight of me, a beaming smile curved on her lips. "Hi," she said.

"Hi Mia," the guys replied in perfect sing-song unison.

She jumped and glanced over at them. "Oh, um, hi." Her startled gaze focused on the smirking faces of the guys before it came back to mine.

"Douchebags," I muttered under my breath before rising up off the couch. I closed the distance between us. Wrapping my arms around her, I smiled. "I'm glad you made it," I said, trying to tune the guys out.

"Me too."

When I brought my lips to hers, applause broke out. Without breaking the kiss, my hands rose off Mia's waist to double flip off my asshat band mates. They laughed heartily. Pulling away, I motioned to them. "I guess now is the best time to introduce you to these dickheads."

Brayden stepped forward and offered his hand to Mia. "I'm Brayden." Once they shook, he smiled and said, "You'll have to excuse our behavior. We're not used to seeing AJ with a girl."

She tilted her head thoughtfully at him. "Really? I'd think you'd be more than used to seeing him with tons of girls."

With a bob of his head, Bray replied, "Let me rephrase that. We're not used to seeing AJ quite so serious enough to bring a girl to one of our shows."

"Ah, I see." Mia shook Bray's hand. "Nice meeting you. What do you do in the band?"

"Guitar and back-up vocals."

"You write the songs, too, right?"

As Bray nodded, I eyed Mia with pride that she had remembered that little tidbit I'd told her before. Rhys stepped forward next. "I'm Rhys. We met the other day at the hospital." At the mention of the hospital, he had to bite his lip to keep from laughing.

"Ah, yes, I remember you now. You got to witness my rubdown on AJ."

He grinned at her. "Yep. Sure did."

Mia laughed. "It's nice meeting you, *again*." She then turned to Jake. "And you're Mr. Lead Singer."

He gave her his typical, smoldering grin. "That's right. Jake Slater." He shook her hand. "Can I ask you something?"

"Um, sure," Mia replied.

"Can you tell me what a beautiful and intelligent woman like you is doing with my douchebag of a band mate? I mean, he's the drummer for fuck's sake. Everyone knows the drummer is a lame-ass."

"Jake," I growled.

He held up his hands. "I had to ask." He jerked his chin up at Mia. "So?"

"I guess it would be because he has a huge dick and knows how to use it," she replied.

At Mia's response, Jake staggered back like he'd been kicked in the groin. Like Brayden and Rhys, he stared open-mouthed and wide-eyed at her. I mean, damn, I had the same fucking look on my face at her ballsy response. I knew she could give me hell, but I had no idea she would give it to the guys, too.

After a small eternity, Jake's lips curved up in a beaming smile. He turned to me. "I like this girl. She reminds me of Abby, so she's a keeper for sure."

Mia laughed. "I'm glad you think so." Stepping closer to Jake, she said, "And your statement about the drummer being a lame-ass isn't true. If you don't have a good drummer, your band's whole rhythm gets shot to shit. I haven't heard AJ play yet, but I know he has fantastic rhythm." She patted his cheek. "Just something to remember."

I fought the urge to grab Mia in a giant bear hug before taking her into the next room to screw her brains out. I'd never had a woman outside of my family stick up for me to the guys—well, except for maybe Abby. It was a hell of a feeling finding a girl like her. The women I interacted with were either so caught up in my fame, or they were absorbed with themselves and the thrill of banging or dating me. Even though she doubted herself, Mia had a lot to give to me emotionally and physically.

Jake grinned. "Yeah, I do know that about drummers. I just have to give AJ shit. I mean, he's been my best friend since we were twelve. You can ask the other guys, but he's usually on *my* ass constantly. I think he's just trying to be a gentleman tonight because you're here."

Rhys and Brayden nodded in agreement. "Total asshat," Rhys replied.

Mia laughed. "Yeah, I can see that about him."

I waved my hand to stop their ragging. "Whatever," I mumbled.

Jeff reappeared in the doorway. "Five minutes."

Jake nodded before turning to Mia. "Listen, why don't I have Jeff take you to our VIP table?" His gaze flicked over at me. "That's where Abby and Lily are. It makes sense she should sit with them."

Mia's eyes widened at the realization of who she would be with. "Um, okay. Sure."

I nodded. "Best table in the house. It's roped off from the audience and connected to the stage, so I can come over and talk to you during the show."

"Sounds good." Without hesitation, she brought her lips to mine. When she pulled back, she gave me a beaming smile. "Good luck out there."

"Thanks." When she started for the door, I smacked her ass with one of my drum sticks. She squealed and jumped. When she glared over her shoulder at me, I just winked at her.

"I'll get you for that one."

"I certainly hope so."

She grinned and shook her head before following Jeff out the door. As soon as she was gone, I braced myself for more shit from the guys. After sucking in a deep breath, I turned around to face them.

Bray shook his head. "If you're looking for a verbal smack down from me, you're not going to get it. I agree with Jake. She's a keeper for sure."

Jake snorted. "Of course you should agree with me. I'm always right."

We all groaned in unison. "Get over yourself, douchebag," I replied.

Crossing his arms over his chest, Jake added, "I'm serious. You better not fuck that one up, bro."

I grinned. "You were with her all of five minutes, and now you're all Team Mia?"

Rhys laughed. "Yep. I think I fell in love with her when she dissed your dick back at the hospital. " He slung his arm over my shoulder. "Besides, we're the Musketeers remember? 'All for one and one for all' shit? So we just wanna get on board with you cause you're totally jonesing for her."

"I'd say if she makes nice with Abby and Lily, you should marry her as soon as possible," Brayden said.

I rolled my eyes. "Jesus Christ, we've known each other a millisecond. Let's save the ball and chain shit for a while, okay?"

"You called it back in the hospital, remember?" Rhys countered.

"I was joking and caught up in the moment of some ballsy chick standing up to me," I replied.

Jake shook his head. "I was with Abby thirty-six hours when I knew she was the one. You might as well come to grips that you're in deep, man."

A foreign feeling rippled through my chest at their words. I knew I was in deep with Mia—emotionally and physically, but I didn't know if I loved her yet. Yeah, I'd teased about Mia being marriage material when she'd given me a verbal tongue lashing like no woman had before, but marriage to me was an epically sacred thing. Don't get me wrong. I'm not one of those commitment phobic douchebags who doesn't believe in monogamy—I'd had my fair share of long-term relationships before and after the band hit big. I just didn't know if I was truly ready at the moment, and at the same time, the level of what I was already feeling for Mia told me that I was already on a train running full steam ahead with her. That fact alone both excited and slightly scared the hell out of me.

Jake snickered, bringing me out of my thoughts. "Look at him. He knows he's utterly fucked, and the wheels are desperately turning in his head to try and find a way out of it."

I narrowed my eyes at him. "You're one to talk, bro. You were so fucking scared of your feelings for Abby you almost drove her away. Me, on the other hand, I know how much I like Mia, and I want to see where it goes."

"Straight to the chapel, dude," Bray replied, with a wink.

"Maybe we can have a double wedding," Jake suggested, trying not to laugh.

I raised both my hands up and flipped them off. "Fuck you, you, you and you!"

As the guys roared with laughter, Jeff poked his head in the door. He shot me an amused glance before saying, "Okay boys, it's time."

Jake grinned. "All right assholes, let's go show them how it's done."

Chapter Eleven

Mia

As I trailed behind the hulking roadie down the hallway, I couldn't help the nervous jitters that clenched my stomach. It was one thing meeting AJ's band mates. Growing up surrounded by male cousins, I always seemed to do better around guys. Women, on the other hand, were another thing, especially after my own girlfriend had run off with my fiancé. Now I was meeting the two most important Runaway Train women—Jake's fiancée and Brayden's wife, and even though I hated myself for it, I was scared shitless.

When we got to the table, they both glanced up at me. With their blonde hair and crystal blue eyes, they could have almost passed for sisters. Their questioning gazes went from me to Jeff. "Jake suggested I bring her to sit with you two. She's with AJ."

"Really?" the youngest blonde squealed, her expression lightening up instantly.

I nodded. "I'm Mia Martinelli," I said, extending my hand.

Instead of shaking my hand, she popped out of her seat like a jack-in-the-box before throwing her arms around me. "It's so nice to meet you." She pulled away to give me a beaming smile. "I'm Abby—Jake's fiancée."

Suddenly it hit me. "Oh, my God! You're in Jacob's Ladder, aren't you?"

"Yes, I am."

"I seriously love you guys—I've been a fan of your brothers for several years. I love the new album."

"Aw, thank you. That's so sweet." She motioned to the chair beside her. "Please sit down."

"Thanks."

Once I was settled, the other blonde extended her hand. "I'm Brayden's wife, Lily."

"It's very nice meeting you, too."

Abby cut her eyes over at Lily before gazing back at me. "Now I know why AJ was acting so weird earlier tonight."

"Oh he was?" I asked, trying not to let my heart do a crazy flip-flop in my chest.

With a grin, Abby replied, "Oh yeah. Very mysterious, very withdrawn...very *lovesick*, now that I think about it."

A warm rush filled my body. "I don't know about lovesick—we just started seeing each other."

"How did you guys meet?" Lily asked.

"Um, it's kinda an interesting story." By the time I

finished filling them in on the escapade in Frank's room, they were laughing hysterically.

"Now that's two of us who have met our guys unconventionally," Abby said.

"Oh really?"

Abby grinned and then proceeded to tell me about literally falling into Jake's bed. "Hmm, I think you may have my crotch drying story beat."

"I think it's a toss-up," she replied.

Lily laughed. "Regardless of who wins best story, I'm just so very thankful to see AJ is with someone like you, Mia."

My brows lifted in surprise. "Like me?"

Her cheeks tinged pink a little. "I didn't mean anything bad by it, honestly. You're absolutely gorgeous and so AJ's type. But at the same time, I can already tell that you're so...real."

Abby nodded and motioned her finger between Lily and herself. "You know, like us."

Lily using AJ's word, 'real', wasn't lost on me. All my nerves about meeting them had evaporated, and now I was just enjoying being accepted by them. I couldn't help wondering if girls who didn't get along with them probably didn't make it long with AJ or Rhys. I felt a little giddy that I seemed to be passing the test with flying colors.

We were interrupted by the house manager taking the microphone. "Good evening. I'm so glad you've all come out on this special night to welcome back our most famous house band, Runaway Train." Applause and cheering rang around the bar. "I can't thank the guys enough for being willing to come back here and play again." Glancing over his shoulder, he nodded. "So let's get this party started, huh?" Once again the applause and cheering were deafening. "So ladies and gentlemen, Runaway Train!"

Abby, Lily, and I screamed along with the other fans as the guys made their way to the stage. Once AJ settled behind the drum kit, he locked eyes with me. He grinned and winked before twirling one of his drumsticks between his fingers. Damn, I knew all about those masterful fingers. Just seeing him work his fingers like that, caused goose bumps to rise on my arms. Trying to forget my inappropriate thoughts, I smiled back. Then he launched into the opening beat of the first song while the guys' guitars followed in with him. While Jake's smooth voice, echoed through the room, I couldn't take my eyes off of AJ as he pounded out the rhythm. With his jaw set and a determined expression on his face, he was totally in the zone.

The guys played through several of their famous tracks—or at least I assumed they were their famous tracks by the audience's reaction—when Jake switched gears. "As much as we love our old stuff, we want to do some of the acoustic tracks from our new album," Jake said into the microphone. I watched as AJ left the drum set to come and sit on a stool beside Jake. Brayden and Rhys eased down on stools as well but kept their guitars.

"And here's our latest Top Forty—*Marrow and Bone*." Jake nodded his head to the guys. After he began the first line of the song, AJ joined in with Jake to harmonize. At the sound of his sultry voice, every molecule in my body shuddered to a stop. It took a moment or two for me to catch my breath. It wasn't just that he could sing—it was the way he delivered the lyrics. The song itself was one of immense love, passion, and devotion, and AJ's voice hummed with all those emotions. It touched me to the core...as well as other places.

"Damn," I murmured under my breath.

"Haven't you heard AJ sing before?" Abby asked.

My heart did a funny little skipping beat. "No," I murmured. I turned to look at her. "He's really amazing—like panty-melting amazing."

She laughed. "Yeah, I would have to agree, especially when he sings in Spanish." At my incredulous expression, she held up her hands. "Trust me, there's never been anything but friendship between AJ and me, but that still doesn't mean I don't find his singing sexy. But there's no one who truly does it for me like Jake."

After two more songs with both Brayden and AJ accompanying Jake, the guys put their guitars down and rose up from the stools. "We're going to take a quick ten minute break, and we'll be back to give you guys some more." Jake's gaze flicked over to our table. "I might even convince my fiancée to join me on stage for some of our new stuff."

"I'm going to kill him," Abby muttered, as Jake winked. She shook her head at him. "Tonight was supposed to be all about Runaway Train."

Lily shook her head. "You know how much he loves having you on stage with him." She patted Abby's back. "Besides, tonight may be about the past, but you're his future—both personally and with his music."

"I guess you're right," Abby replied. But the moment Jake appeared at her side, she smacked his arm playfully. "Okay, you get this through your thick skull right now. I'm not singing with you tonight. You're such a—" He silenced her with a kiss.

My attention was drawn away from them when AJ appeared at my side. I quickly popped out of my chair. "Oh my God, that was amazing—*you* were amazing!" I cried, throwing my arms around him. He pulled back to plant a long, lingering kiss on my lips.

"Thank you."

"I didn't know you could sing."

He shrugged modestly. "Yeah, I can carry a tune okay."

"I do declare, for once is AJ Resendiz not being an egomaniac?"

He laughed. "Fine then. I can sing the pants off anyone. Better?"

"I'd say pants *and* panties." I leaned in to whisper in his ear. "Seriously, I think you got me wet."

AJ groaned. "Don't say shit to me like that now."

"I can't help but tell you the truth." Gazing into his eyes, I said, "Will you sing me something in Spanish?"

His brows lined in confusion. "Why Spanish?"

"Abby said you sounded even sexier then, so I wanted to hear it."

"That's because she speaks Spanish and knows what I'm saying."

I shrugged. "I don't care. I still want to hear you." I lowered my voice. "I wanna see if it gets me even wetter."

He grinned at me. "Fine, amorcito mio. Tonight when I have time to spread you out beneath me, I'll sing to you in English, Spanish, or whatever the hell language it is that makes you want me to fuck your brains out. But for now, I gotta grab some water and take a piss, okay?"

I rolled my eyes. "You're so romantic."

"Hey, I stopped here first, didn't I?"

"That's true." When he started to walk away, I jerked him back to me. At his surprised expression, I kissed him. He warmed to me instantly, thrusting his tongue into my mouth. His hands came to cup my face, his thumbs rubbing along my jawline. My arms snaked around his waist, drawing him in even closer. When I rubbed myself against his crotch, he groaned into my mouth. Jerking away, he gazed down at me with lust-filled eyes. Both of our chests heaved as we fought to catch our breath. With his signature smirk, AJ asked, "Wanna join me in the bathroom for a quickie?"

"Oh so tempting, but I think I'll pass."

"But I know how public places get you hot."

I rolled my eyes. "A stinky, public bathroom screams skeevy, not sexy to me, babe."

AJ laughed. "Fine then."

"Besides, you've got way too much stamina for a bathroom quickie."

"Hmm, stroking my ego pretty hard tonight, aren't you?"

"Just stating facts." I smacked his ass playfully. "Now go take your pee break."

He gave me a mock salute and replied, "Yes, ma'am."

Once AJ disappeared down the hallway, I realized I needed to freshen up after our make-out session. "I'll be right back," I said to Abby and Lily. After I entered the restroom, I headed straight for the counter. Standing in front of the mirror, I dug in my purse for my lipstick. Two leggy blondes stumbled in the door before heading over to the stalls. Once they were shut inside, one of them moaned. "God, Jenny, did you see how fucking hot AJ looked

tonight?"

My body instantly tensed at the mention of his name. "Yeah, he's absolutely edible as always," Jenny replied.

"Too bad he's here tonight with some chick."

"With AJ, I'll doubt she'll be with him long."

A snort came from a stall. "Sounds like someone is jealous after he didn't call you back that time after you blew him in the bathroom."

"If I want him tonight, I could have him again." One of the blondes exited the stall. When she met my gaze, her eyes momentarily widened at the sight of me. Then she threw her shoulders back. "What are you looking at?" she snapped.

Even though the strong Sicilian in me wanted to grab the twiggy bitch by the shoulders and ram her head into the mirror until it cracked, I shook my head. "Nothing."

The blonde smirked at me before heading to the sink. I quickly shoved my lipstick back into my purse and blew out of the bathroom door. When I staggered back to the table, I downed my margarita in two long gulps. "Um, are you okay?" Abby asked.

"Peachy." After Abby gave me a 'who are you shitting?' look, I groaned and ran my hand through my hair. "The truth is I'm a neurotic mess."

"What happened?"

I then noticed the two blonde bitches were out of the bathroom and now were edging closer to the stage. Trying to be covert, I pointed at them. "Do you know them?"

A noise like a growl came from the back of Abby's throat,

while Lily gazed at them with disgust. "They're Sugar Magnolia sluts," Lily replied.

"Excuse me?"

"They work at Sugar Magnolia—a strip club a few blocks from here. Unfortunately, they like to spend their off nights strumming up business for the club. Then I guess you could call them bar groupies for whatever house band is performing." Lily downed the rest of her Mojito. "They also have a history with Runaway Train when the band first started here three years ago."

"Yeah, it seems the tallest one has a specific history with AJ." I twirled my finger over the salted rim of my glass. "Look, I know I just met you two, but I have to ask. How do you guys deal with it—the women?"

Abby let out a long, exaggerated sigh. "It isn't easy," she admitted. "I mean, I don't have a past, so I can't help but focus too much on Jake's and if he's going to repeat any former mistakes. At the end of the day, I just have to believe that he truly loves me enough to be faithful because he sure as hell knows it's a deal breaker between us."

When I turned to Lily, she shrugged. "You want to believe your man is committed, and he wouldn't stray. But then when you've been up all night with a teething baby, you're carrying around ten extra pounds of baby weight, and you have absolutely no desire to screw him senseless like he wants, you can't help but wonder why he doesn't just take up some slut's offer to bang him. But like Abby, Bray knows that cheating is a deal breaker, regardless of Jude and Melody. And no matter what, I know that he loves me and our kids."

"I've been through a cheating fiancé not to mention..." I quickly pinched my lips shut before I went any further. Finally, I added, "I don't know if I have it in me to deal with all this."

"That's totally understandable. But if anyone is worth trying to wade through all the bullshit for, it's AJ. He's a total sweetheart. I don't know what Jake would have done without him after his mother died," Abby said.

Lily nodded. "After knowing him for five years, I can vouch for that. He's got a heart of gold."

Deep down, I knew what they were saying was true. "Somewhere deep down beneath that cocky exterior?"

Abby laughed. "Yep, once you chip that all away, he's a keeper for sure."

I tore my gaze from them to look at AJ pounding his heart out on the drums. He glanced over at me and winked. Maybe the girls were right...maybe he really was worth fighting for.

Chapter Twelve

AJ

After I did a sizzling finale on the cymbals, Jake eased his guitar down and took up the mic. "Thanks again for coming out. We love y'all. Keep it rockin' always!" I hauled ass out of the drum kit to join him and the others to take our usual band bow. I was more ready than ever to get off the stage and get over to Mia. More importantly I was ready to get her the hell out of Eastman's and back to my place.

But Jake busted my balls when he leaned over to yell into my ear over the roar of the crowd. "Let's make a lap or two around the bar, speak to the fans, and sign some shit."

"Whatever," I grumbled.

He laughed. "Easy man, sorry for the cock block, but your dick is just gonna have to wait."

When I caught Mia's gaze, I held up a finger and mouthed, "Just a minute."

She nodded and continued talking with Abby and Lily.

Outfitted with two of our jacked up body guards, Jake and Rhys started making their way on one side of the room while Brayden and I took the other. I signed napkins, CD's, boobs— you name it while posing for pictures with fans. It took a good hour to work both sides of the room, and by the time we were finished, I was sporting some serious blue balls for Mia's amazing pussy.

Once I was free, I waved at Mia and then started making my way across the crowd to our table. Just before I reached it, Kylie bounded out and wrapped her arms in a death-like vise around my waist, molding herself against me like a second skin. "Hey stranger!" she exclaimed over the roar of the house music.

Fuuuuuuuck!!! This was so not happening. "Hey," I replied tersely, as I met Mia's questioning gaze over Kylie's shoulder. When I tried extricating myself from her, Kylie held on tight.

"You left me high and dry the other night." She gave me a seductive grin. "Wanna finish what we started?"

"I don't—" Before I could finish, Kylie's lips were on mine. I jerked away. My chest constricted in agony at the sight of Mia's face. She stared at me with wide-eyes and a quivering lower lip. Her usual tough and in-control exterior appeared crumpled, and I felt like the biggest asshole in the world.

Kylie's blonde brows rose in surprise at my reaction.

"What's the matter, baby? I didn't think you were one for playing hard to get."

"Listen, now is not a good time." As I started to pull Kylie's arms away from me, Mia bolted out of her seat, streaking towards the door as fast as she could with the packed crowd. Abandoning Kylie, I started weaving my way through the crowd. "Mia, wait!" I called.

Ignoring me, she kept fighting her way through the people. "Fuck," I muttered before I resorted manhandling people out of the way to get to her. Grabbing her by the arm, I whirled her around, forcing her to look at me. "What the hell are you doing?"

Tears sparkled in her dark eyes. "I'm sorry, AJ, but I have to go."

"Come with me," I shouted over the crowd and house music. Taking her hand, I led her through the mass of people to the backroom where we'd first met up earlier in the evening.

Once I closed the door behind us, I asked, "Is this about what just happened with Kylie?"

Mia snorted. "No dumbass, it's about the fact the drinks here suck."

I held up my hands. "Look, I'm sorry. That was a douche question. Of course, you're pissed about that. But she's just an old girlfriend of mine who thought we'd started something up again a few weeks ago. There's nothing there.

I swear."

Mia shook her head. "It's not just her. Your past seems to be everywhere. I couldn't even go to the bathroom without running into some skank who'd blown you before and had ideas she was getting her hooks into you again for a repeat performance."

I grimaced when I realized who she was talking about Lyla—one of the Sugar Magnolia girls. "Nothing would have happened with her. I'm here with you."

My words didn't appear to mean shit to Mia because her expression remained sad. "I'm sorry, AJ, but being in your world tonight was a bad idea—it just showed me how much *we're* a bad idea."

My brows furrowed in confusion. "What are you talking about?"

She closed her eyes for a few seconds before opening them again. "I know it's only been a week, but I like you. I like you a lot, okay? I don't know where this is heading, but I know that if things keep up like they are..." She drew in a ragged breath. "The bottom line is I'm not cut out for your world. I have too many of my own issues with men coupled with my insecurities to deal with your groupies."

"Dammit, Mia, I swear that Kylie and those other girls don't mean shit to me."

"But they mean a lot to me. I don't know how to deal with it. You were just supposed to be about me getting back in the game, not being tossed right back out into the same shark-infested waters as before." When I winced at her words, she reached up to cup my cheek. "I wish I could do this, but I can't." When she started to open the door, my palm landed on the wood, slamming it shut.

Desperation and anger rocketed through me. "So that's it? We're totally fucked as a potential couple just because I have a dick. That's bullshit."

"You don't understand—"

"No, I don't think *you* understand. When I'm in a relationship, I'm in it for the long haul. I have never cheated once on any of my girlfriends. Ever. I was a freakin' altar boy back in the day, and that makes me take fidelity pretty damn serious. Get it through your thick skull, Mia, I'm not Dev—I'm not going to do that to you." When Mia continued staring down at the grungy carpet, I huffed out a growl of frustration. "Look at me dammit." I reached over and cupped her face in my hands, forcing her to meet my eyes. "I mean it. I'm not Dev. Don't walk away from me just because you think I'm someone I'm not."

Pain replaced Mia's sad expression. "I wish that it was just about Dev, but there are other...bad experiences from my past that make this hard for me."

Realizing I wasn't getting anywhere with her, I decided to change up my game. With a sneer, I replied, "Where's the ball-busting, Sicilian Mia that went toe to toe with me the first time I met her? The last thing I ever would have thought is that you're a coward."

Her dark eyes narrowed at me. "How dare you call me a coward! If you knew what all I'd been through."

"We all have our shit. Quit acting like a martyr to your past."

"Fuck you!" she spat, before she reached for the doorknob. I knocked her hand away before gripping her shoulders and whirling her body around. When I molded myself against her, she struggled against me. "Stop it, AJ," she hissed.

I silenced her by bringing my mouth down hard against hers. At first, it was like kissing a brick wall, but the moment I slid my tongue against her lips, a tiny moan escaped her. Her reaction must've spooked her because she tried to jerk away. Instead, I tightened my arms around her. "Don't run away. You want this...you want *me*."

Jerking her chin up, she glared at me. "It doesn't matter what I want. Considering my past, I wanted a lot of shit that fucking wrecked me. So, let me go."

A volatile mixture of desperation and fury swelled in my chest, and I fought to keep my head on straight and not explode. I'd never met a woman like Mia, but at the same time, I knew if I let her out the door, I might not ever see her again. I was not going to let that happen—not while I was still breathing. I shook my head at her. "I'm not going anywhere, and you're sure as hell not going anywhere," I hissed against her mouth. My hands swept around her back, searching out the zipper on her dress. Once I found it, I jerked it down before pulling both of the straps on her dress down. As my hand came around her ribcage, I grazed her breast, and she sucked in a breath. Before I even touched her breast, the nipple had hardened in anticipation.

"What do you think you're doing?" she questioned breathlessly, as I continued to palm her breast.

"I'm about to fuck some sense into you," I growled, as I jerked the hem of my shirt over my head.

When she started to protest again, I took both of her hands in one of mine and pinned them above her head. Her eyes widened, not with fear, but with desire. "You like that, don't you?"

"No," she snapped, thrashing against me.

I gave a low laugh. "Oh yes, you do like it." Leaning over, I licked a trail from her chin up to her ear. A shudder rippled over her body, and I knew with every second she was warming more and more to me—giving in to what she really wanted but that her mind railed against. I nipped and licked at her mouth, grazing her bottom lip between my teeth. "How wet is your pussy right now, Mia? How bad do you want me to fuck you hard and fast up against this door?"

A whimper escaped her lips, and I could see her resolve was slowly fading. With my free hand, I pulled the front of her dress down further and eased it over her hips. It was harder than I thought one handed. After it fell to the floor, I met her gaze again. Both lust and fury burned in them. I raked my eyes over her body—her sexy black lace bra and panties caused my dick to pound against my zipper. I wanted more than anything to drive home the point of how much she really wanted me and how good we were together to her stubborn ass, but at the same time, her broken expression out in the club flashed before my eyes. I didn't want to do anything to make her hate me later on. "Tell me you don't want to do this, and I'll stop."

She stared at me, her chest rising harshly, before she slowly shook her head. "I wish I could, but I can't." She swallowed hard. "You're so fucking wrong for me, but I still want you—I want you in every way possible."

Frustration burned within me at her words. I wanted to prove to Mia that she was wrong—I was *right* for her. I dropped my hand from hers, letting her arms fall free. We stood there, staring intently at each other for a few seconds, our chests rising and falling with heavy breaths. Reaching out, I took Mia's hand and brought it to my chest, splaying her fingers over my skin. "Do you feel my heartbeat racing?"

"Yes," she whispered softly.

"That's for you and you alone."

Her dark brows rose in surprise. "You really feel that much for me?"

I nodded. "I've said it before, and I'll say it again. Don't fight it—feel it." I then slid her hand down over my abdomen and brought it over my dick. "Now do you feel that? That is fucking rock hard for you and only you. It only wants to be buried deep inside you. It didn't twitch once when Kylie was pressed against me, but all you have to do is breathe, and it's raring to go." Reaching between us, I stroked between her legs. "You're soaked for me and only for me, right?"

"Yes, AJ. Only for you," she moaned, as I worked her over the thin scrap of lace. Her head fell back against the door, and her breath came in tiny pants.

"I can do this, but I want to hear you say it." I slid one finger into her panties. "Tell me what you want, amorcitio mio."

Raising her head, she stared at me for a moment before licking her lips in anticipation. "Take me, AJ. Take me hard like we both like it."

I grinned. "I thought you'd never ask. Now undress me, Mia. Show me how much you want me." Instantly, I had a flashback of our night together in the limo when I had to prove my desire for her by touching myself and then giving over to her will. This time I was asking her submit, and it made me even harder.

Without another word, her fingers came to fumble with the button and zipper on my jeans before she undid them and slid them down. She didn't waste any time stripping off my boxers. When I stood naked before her, I jerked my chin up at her. "Now you." Mia reached around to unclasp her bra. With a teasing gleam in her eyes, she slowly slid the straps down one at a time over her arms. Then she kept one hand flat against her chest to keep her tits covered in the lacy cups. An almost caveman like grunt escaped my lips. Oh, what this woman did to me. Just when I thought I had her completely submitting to my will, she pulled a move like that. "Mia," I warned.

She gave me a mischievous grin before jerking the bra off and tossing it at me. It smacked me in the face before falling to the floor. Not trusting her to work as fast as I wanted her to, I reached out and grasped the waistband of her thong. I jerked it down her thighs. When I gazed up at her, Mia didn't shrink back being buck-naked in front of me with the harsh lights of the room bearing down on her. Instead, she wrapped her arms around my neck and brought her lips to mine. It stroked my ego that I might somehow being giving her that boost of confidence.

My hands cupped underneath her delicious ass and hoisted her up to where she could wrap her legs around my waist. With my mouth working furiously against hers, I walked us over to the couch and collapsed down onto the cushions. Mia began sliding her wet core over my dick, but I wasn't ready to be inside her yet. "Raise up," I commanded.

"Wait, what?"

A low growl came from the back of my throat before I gripped her thighs. I jerked her up to where I could bend over to thrust my tongue between her legs. I lapped and teased at her center, causing her to moan. The moment I sucked her clit into my mouth, her body shuddered. "AJ!" she cried, as both of her hands came to grip and tug the strands of my hair. I licked and suckled her outer lips before thrusting my tongue deep inside her. "Hmm, you taste fucking amazing," I murmured, my voice vibrating against her core.

"Please AJ," she begged.

"Please what, baby?"

She ground her hips against my face, trying to get more friction. "Please make me come."

"With my tongue or my fingers?"

Her chest rose and fell in heavy pants as she weighed my words. "Both. I don't care. Just make me come."

"All right, amorcitio mio." As I slid two fingers inside her, she began to rock her hips. My tongue continued sucking and licking her while my other hand slid around her body to grip and massage the globe of her ass. When her walls clenched around my fingers, she screamed my name and her fingernails left my hair to claw up my back. It hurt like hell, but it was hot as fuck.

Taking my cock in my hand, I eased her hips down over me. Her slick walls took me inch by inch until I was buried all the way inside. Gripping Mia's hips, I began working her on and off my cock. Her full breasts bounced and swayed in my face, so I reached out to suck a nipple into my mouth. "Hmm, AJ, oh fuck yes," she moaned, her hands wrapping around my neck to smother me closer to her chest. My hands left her hips to cup both her breasts. Pushing them together, I alternated between sucking both rock hard nipples. That sent Mia over the edge, and she came again. I wasn't anywhere near finishing, so I kept raising her off my dick and slamming her back down. I bucked my hips up in time. Just as I started to tighten up and feel myself about to come, Mia started to scramble off my lap. I splayed my fingers into the flesh on her hips, keeping her firmly in place. Her hand smacked against my chest. "No, AJ, you have to pull out!"

It took a moment in my sex-almost-coming haze for it to register that in the heat of the moment we'd forgotten all about condoms. "Fuck," I muttered, as I lifted Mia by the ass off of me.

Instead of flopping to the side, Mia slid between my legs onto her knees and took my cock in her hand. When I anticipated her finishing me off with a hand job, she floored the hell out of me by sliding my cock into her warm mouth. My eyes rolled back into my head as she started pumping her hand up and down my length. Just the idea of what she was doing, coupled with her actions, almost had me blowing my load. "Oh Christ, Mia," I murmured at the delicious feel of her suctioning my head. I raked my hand through the long strands of her chestnut hair, cupping the back of her neck. When I tensed up again, I arched my hips and came into her mouth. Once I finished, I gazed down at her. "Fuck girl, just when I think you can't surprise me anymore, you go and do that."

She laughed. "It was nothing."

I cupped her cheeks, rubbing my thumbs along her jawline. Man, this woman was so fucking amazing I could barely form a sentence after what she just did to me, but I needed her to know it and understand it. "Mia, that wasn't just 'nothing'. That was fucking incredible," I said gently, while gazing into her beautiful brown eyes. I cupped her cheek, rubbing my thumb along her jawline. "Sorry about forgetting the condom."

"We kinda got caught up in the moment—the very heated moment."

"Yeah, we did."

A knock at the door caused Mia to squeal and fumble for something to cover herself with. I thrust one of the enormous throw pillows at her before taking one myself. "AJ, you in there?" Jake called.

"Yeah. Give me a—"

Before I could finish, the door flew open, and Jake stepped inside. Grasping the pillow in front of my junk, I tried as best I could to shield Mia who had scrambled behind the side of the couch. When his eyes widened, I shook my head. "Thanks for waiting, douchebag."

"Sorry man." Peeking over my shoulder, he added, "And I'm really, really sorry, Mia."

"Thanks," came her muffled reply.

As we continued to stand there staring at each other, I threw up the hand not covering my dick. "Do you have a point because I'm getting a little creeped out with the peepshow?"

Jake chuckled. "Yeah, I do, and trust me, the last thing I wanna see is your naked ass." He closed the door behind him and took a tentative step forward. I glanced over my shoulder to make sure Mia was still covered. "I talked with Brayden and Rhys, and we decided to all hang out at the farm this weekend. I wanted to see if you and Mia were down for it."

My brows rose at the insinuation of Mia coming along. Jake didn't usually include any other chicks besides Lily and Abby at his house. It was sacred to him since it was where he had lived with his late mother, and he didn't want random pieces of ass dirtying that memory.

"That sounds great." I turned around and peered at Mia. "Can you get away for the weekend?"

She rolled her eyes. "Are we seriously having this conversation when I'm naked and your band mate is just a few feet away?"

"I can't think of a better time," I replied with a wink.

"You're such a cascado."

Jake cleared his throat. "For what it's worth, I'd like to have you come, Mia. It's really low-key. We'll do some grilling, hang out around the bonfire, roast marshmallows and shit. I think you'd like it. I mean, I can't totally account for your taste since you seem to be really into AJ."

Mia laughed while I scowled at Jake. "It sounds like a lot of fun. I'm supposed to work Sunday, but I'm pretty sure I can find someone to take my shift."

Clapping his hands together, Jake grinned. "Awesome. So I'll see you guys tomorrow around noon."

I nodded. "It's a date."

"Good." He eyed my pillow-clad junk. "Now put some fucking clothes on before we're never asked back here again."

With one hand, I flipped him off, and with the other, I chucked the pillow at him. Jake ducked just before it smacked him in the face. "Later, dickweed," he called as he headed out the door.

Once he was gone, I went over and locked the door, so we could get dressed without any more interruptions. When I turned back, Mia had gotten into her panties and bra with lightning quick speed. "So does coming away with me for the weekend mean we're good now?"

She giggled. "I would have thought we were good right after you, wait, what did you call it? 'Fucked some sense into me'?"

I laughed. "That's true."

Wrapping her arms around my neck, Mia kissed me gently. "Yes, I'd say we're not just good, but great. And whatever I have to do to spend more time with you, I'll do it. Including hanging out in the sticks with your band mates."

Grinning, I pulled her closer to me. "Hey, you haven't truly fucked until you've fucked in the sticks."

Mia burst out laughing. "I guess you're just going to prove it to me."

"Oh I will. That's a promise."

Chapter Thirteen

Mia

I was just throwing my makeup bag into my suitcase when the doorbell rang. Actually, it began a full on assault of lightning fast rings. Rolling my eyes, I started down the hallway. When I flung open the door, AJ stood braced against the frame grinning from ear to ear. "Miss me?"

"You personally? Yes. You being a dick by screwing around with my doorbell? No."

He laughed as he leaned in to kiss me. It was only three hours ago that I was finally able to extricate myself from him *and his bed* to go home and pack. After our backroom tryst, we'd left Eastman's together, and I'd spent the night at AJ's penthouse. It was long after three am before we were finally spent of each other and could sleep.

AJ's gaze roamed appreciatively over my ensemble of strappy sandals, khaki shorts, and a red tank top. "You look sexy as hell."

I snorted. "At ease, big boy. You just had me four hours ago—twice if I remember correctly."

"But it seems I can never get enough of you," he said in a low, throaty voice.

His words, along with the tone he used, sent warmth crisscrossing over my body. "You're such a flatterer," I teased, before smacking his arm playfully.

"It's the truth."

Although I didn't want to take his comments too literally, I couldn't help wondering if a good fuck was all I was to him. Sure, he said I was more and the mere fact I was going to Jake's farm meant something pretty big, but everything seemed to lead back to sex with AJ. Trying to lighten the seriousness of my thoughts, I added, "Well, if you play nice, I'll let you have me as much as you want tonight. How's that?"

He nodded his head. "Okay then." He peered over my shoulder. "Where's your suitcase?"

"In the bedroom."

"I'll get it for you."

"Okay. I'll feed Jack Sparrow while you get it."

AJ gave me a funny look. "Who?"

"My cat."

"You gotta be shitting me that you named your cat after a character in *Pirates of the Caribbean*."

I grinned. "I have a major crush on Johnny Depp."

AJ's nose wrinkled in disgust. "I sure as hell didn't need to know that."

Sweeping my hand to my hip, I countered, "Does that mean you won't indulge a deep seeded fantasy I have of having sex with a dude in a Jack Sparrow costume with some fierce black eyeliner?"

"Seriously?"

I laughed and shook my head. "I'm teasing you."

"Thank God. For a minute there, I was actually considering it!"

Knocking my hip playfully into his, I then motioned down the hallway. "Hurry up or we're going to be late. I don't want to make a bad impression on Jake."

"Whatever," AJ mumbled as he headed out of the living room. When he disappeared into the bedroom, I went to the kitchen and took out a bag of Whiskas. At the sound of the package crackling, Jack Sparrow came bounding into the room and hopped onto the counter.

He peered at me with his one good eye before rubbing his head up against me. "You gonna be a good boy while I'm gone?"

Flicking his tail, he gave me his usual apathetic response, but the moment I scratched behind his ears, the classic Siamese meow came from deep in his throat. All was good until AJ came around the corner, causing Jack to snap his head up and one-eye AJ suspiciously before hissing.

AJ sat my suitcase down and crossed his arms over his chest. "Hmm, looks like I'm not making nice with your pussy, huh?"

I snickered. "Testa di cazzo."

"En Ingles, por favor," he replied.

"Dickhead."

He laughed as he closed the gap between us. Jack Sparrow growled before hightailing it off the counter and skidding out of the kitchen. "What's up with his—" AJ motioned to one of his eyes.

"Oh that. He'd already lost it when I rescued him off the streets. He was living off dumpster food at St. Joe's."

"Ah, I see. Does he always act like that with strangers?"

"Just strange me. He and Dee have made friends over the year. I think he was treated badly by some men in the past." A sad smile crept on my lips. "I think that's why we get along so well."

AJ took in my words before leaning over to bestow a sweet and tender kiss on my lips. When he pulled away, he smiled. "I guess I'll just have to win him over and prove to him *and* his owner that not all men are douchebags."

"I think that would be great," I murmured. Deep down, I couldn't help but doubt AJ's sincerity or if he would really take the time and effort to prove to me he was different. I desperately wanted him to—more than anything I *needed* him to.

He nodded before grabbing my suitcase. "Come on, sexy. Your chariot awaits to take you to the great and wonderful Sticks of Bumblefuck."

I laughed. "Okay, let's go." After I got my purse and keys and threw on my sunglasses, I followed him to the door. I locked up and then we headed down the porch steps. At the sight of the gleaming silver chrome vehicle in the driveway, I raised my sunglasses onto my forehead to eye his SUV. "Nice Hummer."

"Thanks. The ride is pretty cool, too." When I glanced over at AJ, he waggled his eyebrows. "You walked right into that one."

I shoved my overnight bag at him, catching him in the gut. "Douchebag."

"Oomph," he muttered before grinning. "I'm just glad to have this bad boy back. Seems like it's been in the shop forever." He opened the passenger side door for me.

"Thank you," I replied as I climbed inside. Just before I collapsed on the seat, AJ smacked my ass. When I turned back to glare at him, he licked his lips suggestively. My response was to maturely stick out my tongue at him. He chuckled as he closed the door and made his way around the side of the Hummer.

When AJ cranked up, a Runaway Train song started playing. I cut my eyes over at him. "You were seriously listening to your own music?"

"Nope. I had it on so you could listen to my music," he replied, as he pulled out of my driveway.

"I heard it last night. Wasn't that enough?"

"I'm not convinced you're a diehard fan yet."

"I would think the fact that I'm a diehard fan of *you* and your amazing cock would cover me."

My words caused AJ to momentarily swerve on the road. When he had recovered, he glanced over at me. "I promise that I'll turn on some country for you in a little while."

I couldn't help grinning at both his reaction to my words and his compromise. "Okay, it's a plan."

Since my house was further out of Atlanta in East Cobb, I was not as far away from Jake's farm as AJ was. Even in his Hummer, his lead foot made good timing. As we got off the interstate and onto a two-lane road, our surroundings melted into an emerald blur of trees lining the road. "Wow, this really is out in the boonies."

"And we're not there yet," AJ replied with a grin.

"So you come out here a lot?"

AJ bobbed his head. "Yeah, Jake's dad and stepmom moved in next door to us when we were twelve. At first, we just got to hang out together every other weekend, but we still got tight. Then Jake started having me come out here to visit. I'd spend weeks at a time here in the summers." He turned to me with a smile. "I guess you could say our band was born up here in the boonies. We weren't more than fourteen, but Jake would play guitar, one of his cousins, Teague, would join in on bass, and then I did the drums. We became Runaway Train."

In my mind, I tried to picture a teenaged AJ pounding out the rhythm, giving his heart and soul to his garage band, or barn, performance. "How you'd get the name?"

"Jake and his emo-shit self."

"Seriously?"

AJ chuckled. "Yeah, after his parents divorced, he got really obsessed with the song *Runaway Train* by Soul Asylum. Writing songs like he does, Jake's really into deep symbolism shit. Me, I liked it because it made me think of Ozzy Osbourne's *Crazy Train*, and that was the first song I learned to play besides all the Hispanic music of my uncle's."

"When did the other guys come into the picture?"

"We met up with Brayden when we were all freshman at Georgia Tech. Teague left us high and dry to become some aeronautical engineer or some shit, so we recruited Rhys, who was doing his pre-law at Emory."

"He's the baby of the group, right?"

AJ snickered. "Yeah, he's just twenty-three. He's basically a genius—motherfucker graduated from high school at sixteen and started college right after. He comes from rich as hell, society assholes down in Savannah, so they weren't thrilled when their golden child, and only son, left school to take up with us."

"That sucks."

"*They* suck, trust me."

I cocked my head. "What did your family think of you being a musician rather than a..."

"Business Major."

"Ah, I see."

He shrugged. "They were worried about how I would make a living at first, but they didn't disown me like Rhys's parents did."

"Poor guy."

"Things are a little better between them now. My parents are pretty laid back. I mean, at the end of the day, they want my brother, sister and me to be happy. They didn't go apeshit when Antonio came out when he was so young—they supported the fact he was gay."

"Good for them."

"Yeah, they kinda flipped their lid more when Cristina got knocked up at eighteen and then eloped." He glanced over at grinned at me. "And before you ask, they were almost as pissed about her not marrying in the church as they were that she was pregnant. We're hardcore Catholics."

"So are we."

My thoughts left my own family to focus on AJ's. I couldn't help wondering what they would think of me—if they would think I was good enough for their oldest son.

"They'll love you, Mia."

I jerked my head to gaze incredulously at him. "But I—"

He smiled. "I could tell what you were thinking, and I know what the answer is. They'll love you."

"Thanks," I murmured, as I let my mind wander to whether *he* could love me.

Taking a right turn, we started down a gravel road. A swirling cloud of dust was kicked up in the Hummer's wake. We finally arrived at a sprawling, two-story farmhouse that looked like something out of a Norman Rockwell painting. The outside was white-frame with blue shutters, and it had an expansive front porch, with rocking chairs, that ran the length of the house. Flowers, of all colors and sizes, dotted the front walkway. "Oh wow...this is beautiful," I said.

"Yeah, it is, isn't it?" AJ peered through the windshield. "Sometimes after being on the road, I forget just how amazing it is—I mean, the house is over two hundred years old. When Susan, Jake's mom, bought it, she did a little renovating."

Craning my neck, I spotted a barn and some stables down the hill. From behind the barn, I could see a cloud of smoke, and I knew that must be where the bonfire was that Jake had mentioned before. "Come on, let's go meet up with the guys," AJ urged.

I'd barely gotten my door open when a giant Golden Retriever stuck its head in to lick my feet. "Well hello to you, too," I said with a smile.

AJ laughed as he turned off the car. "That would be Angel—Abby's dog—and the worst excuse for an attack dog you'll ever find."

After I hopped down, I scratched behind Angel's furry ears. "Aw, she's too sweet to be mean. Aren't you, girl?"

Angel yipped a response before running around the side of the Hummer to greet AJ. He bent down to kiss her forehead before giving her an epic rubdown. "Okay, girl. Take us down to the others." Holding out his hand, I slipped mine into AJ's.

Rolling waves of green grass swayed in the breeze as we made our way down the hill. The air was crisper and cooler up here in the mountains. As our feet crunched along the gravel, I tried not to let my anxiety of hanging out with AJ's bandmates overwhelm me. Last night when I was with Abby and Lily, I had felt so comfortable and included. It was like I fit in immediately. And as far as the guys of Runaway Train, I couldn't have asked for a better welcome. So, even though I shouldn't have felt so worried, I still felt apprehensive. When we turned the corner around the barn, Angel barked and then ran ahead of us to alert the others we were there.

With his back to us, Jake stood at a massive stainless steel grill, which was emitting some delicious meaty aromas of steak and burgers. "Yo douchenozzle, we're here," AJ called.

With a grunt, Jake laid his spatula down. "Nice to see you

finally made it, twatcake." When he turned around, I snorted at his attire. Over his shorts and faded T-shirt, Jake was outfitted in a bedazzled, black 'Kiss the Cook' apron with glittering silver lettering. He glanced down at it before meeting my amused gaze. "Abby got this for me."

"Very manly," I replied.

He grinned. "Hey, sporting this bad boy ensures I get ass."

"I heard that!" Abby shouted across the clearing.

AJ and I chuckled as Jake grinned and blew her a kiss. He then leaned over and gave me a hug. "Glad to have you with us this weekend." It was hard to believe that a guy like Jake, who appeared so cocky and full of himself most of the time, could be so sincere. He really made me feel welcome.

"Me too. Can I do something to help?"

He motioned to the picnic tables where Abby and Lily were setting up some food and drinks. "Check with the girls."

"Okay," I replied. I gave AJ a peck on the cheek before heading across the clearing. "Hi guys," I said.

Abby dropped the pack of hamburger buns she was holding and hurried around the table to hug me. "I'm so glad you came."

As I squeezed her back, I replied, "Thanks. Me too."

"I don't know if AJ told you or not, but we're setting you two up in the barn." With a wink, she added, "You know, so you can have more privacy."

My brows rose in surprise as I thought of AJ and me snuggling on hay bales as a mattress. "Um, the barn?"

Abby giggled. "I guess AJ forgot to tell you the barn is completely remodeled. It's like an apartment."

"Oh," I replied, my cheeks warming with embarrassment.

"It's really nice," Lily replied.

With a contented sigh, Abby nodded her head. "It has a lot of happy memories for me and Jake. That's for sure."

"Then thank you for letting us have it." I glanced over at Lily. "But what about you and Brayden?"

"We usually stay in the basement."

A grin played on my lips. "Let me guess. It's finished rather than being like a hole in the ground, right?"

Lily nodded. "Yes, it is."

Abby nudged Lily playfully. "I'm trying to get her to let Jake and me take the kids tonight, so she and Bray can have some alone time."

Now it was Lily's turn to blush. "Between you guys sharing your bus and then taking the kids tonight, Jake is going to start hating on me."

Abby snorted. "If he wants to stay in my good graces, he'll let us help out our friends." She waggled her blonde brows. "And that means in all ways possible."

At that moment, a tall, willowy teenage girl came striding up to the table with an apple pie in each hand. "They just finished baking," she said, as she sat them down.

"Thanks, Allison."

As I surmised the girl, I noticed she was so naturally beautiful. Her long dark hair was swept back in a ponytail, and she wore a short blue sundress. If she hadn't been so young, the insecure side of me might have been intimidated. "Mia, this is Allison, Jake's sister," Abby introduced.

"Well, half-sister in case you're wondering why we look nothing alike," Allison said with a smile. She held out her hand. "You must be AJ's girl."

My eyes widened as I pumped her hand up and down. "Um, I guess so."

"He's such a sweetheart...and a goofball."

I laughed. "Yes, he is."

"Shit, I forgot the crockpots with the baked beans," Abby grumbled. Glancing up at Allison, she said, "Will you get one of the guys to go back to the house with you to get them?"

"Sure," Allison replied. Without hesitation, she hurried across the clearing straight for Rhys, who was leaned against a tree trunk, drinking a beer. I watched as she tilted her head flirtingly while pointing to the house. He bobbed his head and sat his beer down on the grass.

"Looks like someone has a crush," I mused.

Abby's head snapped up from the table before her gaze honed in on Allison, who was walking as close as she could to Rhys up the hillside. "Maybe for her, but for him, she's just Jake's kid sister."

"Not to mention jailbait considering she's almost seventeen," Lily replied.

Shielding my eyes from the sun with my hand, I watched as Allison gave Rhys a beaming smile. "Bless her heart. That has heartbreak written all over it."

"Even if she was older, that would have broken bones written all over it," Abby remarked. She shook her head. "Jake would never, ever condone Rhys dating his baby sister."

My thoughts were suddenly interrupted when something brushed against my leg. Squealing, I jumped about a mile in the air. When I glanced down, I saw a dark-haired, dark-eyed toddler had wrapped herself around me. "Oh, um, hi," I said, hoping I hadn't just scared the shit out of her with my reaction.

She lifted her arms. "Up!" she commanded.

I stared wide-eyed over at Lily who only smiled. "Melody is so friendly. She never meets a stranger."

Stomping her tiny, pink converse covered foot, Melody repeated, "Up!"

"Okay." Anxiety rippled through me as I bent over to oblige her wishes. I had never been very maternal, and I usually was the last person on earth any of my cousins asked to babysit.

Melody's dark eyes locked on mine before she reached over to bestow a slobbery kiss on my cheek. "Thank you," I replied, shifting her awkwardly on my hip.

Her fingers came to wind through the strands of my hair. "Pwetty," she said.

"Thank you again. My Miss Melody, you sure are a talker."

Lily laughed. "We could barely get Jude talking, but we can't shut her up."

A hand came to rest on the small of my back. When I glanced over my shoulder, AJ grinned at me. "I see you're making new friends."

"I am."

Melody's face lit up like a Fourth of July sparkler. "J!" she squealed, reaching her arms out. "Get me, J!"

"Hey, my little princesa," he replied, as he took Melody from me. He kissed both of her cheeks, which were dimpled from giving him such a big smile.

I lifted my brows in surprise and turned to Lily. "Does he always act this way around the kids, or is this all just show to impress me?"

As AJ scowled at me Lily laughed. "He's actually very good with the kids. Of course, none of them were until Jude came along. They pretty much became second fathers to him."

AJ bobbed his head. "Yep, Jude was my guinea pig, and he taught me well." He snuggled Melody to his chest. "But this little chica here, she's my muñeca linda."

"En ingles, por favor?" I said with a grin.

"My pretty baby doll."

"Listen to you. Charming ladies of all ages," I replied to which AJ winked.

"Out of all the guys, she's always been enraptured by AJ. She lights up whenever he comes in the room," Lily said.

"That's cause she knows I'm the sweetest, most-handsome, best guy in the whole wide world. Right, Melly Moo?"

AJ tickled Melody's sides, causing her to giggle. Brayden strolled up hand in hand with a little boy who was the spitting image of Lily. "Hey, Mia, good to see you," he said, giving me a hug.

"Thanks. Same to you."

"This is our son, Jude." He peered down at Jude. "Say hello to Mia."

Jude thrust out his tiny hand. "Hiya Mia."

Bending over, I smiled and shook his hand. "Hi to you, too."

"Are you Uncle AJ's girlfriend?"

Shit! How the hell was I going to get out of this one? "Um..."

Brayden must have sensed my embarrassment because he reached out for Melody. "We were just going to go swing."

"Wing! Wing!" Melody screeched excitedly, as she dove into her father's arms.

Jude abandoned his father's side to tug on AJ's shirt. Pointing a small finger at me, he asked, "Is she your girlfriend?"

Undaunted, AJ replied, "Yep, she's a girl, and she's my friend." For reasons I couldn't understand, I felt a little let down by his summation of what we were. I mean, it had only been two weeks, so it wasn't like I could really claim a relationship status with him. But at the same time, I hated his answer.

Wrinkling his nose, Jude said, "Ew, girls are gross."

AJ laughed. "Give it a few years, and you'll change your mind, buddy."

Jude didn't appear too convinced as he followed Brayden across the clearing to an enormous wooden play-set. "AJ, give me a hand," Jake called from the grill.

"Be back in a minute," AJ assured.

"Okay."

As we put the finishing touches on lunch, the conversation flowed freely between Abby, Lily, and me. I was starting to enjoy their company more and more.

"So do you sing, Mia?" Abby questioned, before popping a few potato chips into her mouth.

"Oh God no. I can't carry a tune in a bucket."

Lily laughed. "That makes two of us then." She then motioned over to where Brayden was helping Jude down the slide while intermittingly pushing Melody in a harnessed swing. "Only my children appreciate my singing voice at bedtime, and that's usually only when Bray's on tour and they have to settle for me."

As I eyed the play-set, I was wondering what an engaged but childless guy like Jake was doing with one. Lily must've read my mind because she said, "He did that just for Jude and Melody so they would have a place to play when they come to visit."

"How sweet."

Lily nodded and then gave Abby a playful nudge. "And I think for future children, too."

Abby's blue eyes widened as she swallowed hard. "Oh, no, we've got to get through a wedding first. And watch your tongue. If Jake hears you say that, he'll freak out. We're not planning on kids for several years down the road." At Lily's knowing look, Abby sighed. "Okay, *Jake* isn't down for having kids for several years." Twirling the enormous diamond on her ring finger, she grinned impishly. "I'd have one tomorrow if I could."

Before I could stop myself, I blurted, "But you're so young."

Abby wrinkled her nose. "Exactly. I mean, who needs a baby when I'm a mere baby myself at twenty-two?"

"I'm sorry, I shouldn't have—"

Patting my back, Abby shook her head. "Trust me, you're not the first person to say that. My darling fiancé included."

Deepening her voice to mimic Jake, she said, "We've got all the time in the world to have kids. We need to get at least three US tours and one world tour under our belts before I knock you up."

I laughed. "Hmm, Jake sounds a lot like AJ—bossy, take charge, my way or the highway."

Abby winked. "Yeah, but isn't it fun turning the tables on them?"

With an enthusiastic jerk of my head, I replied, "Oh yes, it is." I couldn't help thinking about when I had tied him up in the limo on our first date.

AJ and Jake appeared with pans loaded with steaks, hamburgers, and ribs. As I gazed down the length of the two tables, my eyes widened at all the food. "Just wait, there won't be much left when we're done," AJ said.

"You guys can put it away, huh?"

Jake grinned. "It's not just us guys. Don't let Abby's size fool you. She's a big eater."

Abby laughed as she handed me a paper plate. "He loves giving me shit about that."

"Well, I should hate you for being able to eat so much and still stay so tiny," I teased.

"I tell her the same thing all the time," Lily replied.

Poking her bottom lip out, Abby said, "Sorry."

With a smile, I said, "You're forgiven."

"Good. Now let's eat." She waved to the others to join us

at the table. I noticed that once again Allison was at Rhys's side and managed to snag a seat beside him. After I filled my plate to the brim, AJ patted a spot on the bench, so I eased down next to him. When he scooted closer to me, I cocked a brow at him. "Would you prefer I sit in your lap?"

He grinned. "I just wanna be close to you."

Leaning over, I whispered into his ear, "Don't think you're going to be starting something with me anytime soon, Mr. Resendiz."

AJ held up his hands in surrender. "I was just trying to be affectionate."

"With you, there's always something lurking behind that affection." Lowering my voice, I added, "And it's usually a hard-on."

Choking on his hamburger, AJ snatched up his beer and downed half of it. When he recovered, he cut his eyes over at me. "Damn, girl."

"The truth hurts, doesn't it?" I questioned with a smile.

AJ chuckled before taking another bite of his hamburger. When he did, he left a glob of mustard behind. "Ugh, you're such a pig." I reached over and swiped it away with my thumb. Before I could move my hand, AJ's tongue darted out and licked the mustard off my thumb. It caused an ache to burn through my lower half. I shivered under his stare.

"Having the tables turned sucks, huh?" he questioned in a low voice.

"Oh shut up and eat your burger," I snapped.

With a wink, he brought his free hand under the table to rest on my knee. When I glanced across the table, Jake and Abby were smiling at us. I quickly focused my attention back on my plate and the conversations floating around me. It was a rowdy and raucous meal, but it felt just like being with my family at one of our weekly dinners. I felt happier than I had in a long, long time.

With our bellies full from the enormous meal and dessert, we left the picnic tables and headed over to the lounge chairs by the crackling bonfire. Before he sat down, Jake flipped the switch on the outdoor stereo system, sending music echoing around us. As I nursed a foamy beer, my head pinged back and forth between the guys' conversation—most of it was good-natured ragging on each other.

When the music switched over and Luke Bryan's *Drunk on You* belted out of the speakers, I sat up straighter in my chair. "Augh, I love this song!" I exclaimed.

"Seriously?" AJ questioned, his nose wrinkling in disgust.

I nodded. "You know I love country music, and I adore anything by Luke Bryan."

With a squeal beside me, Abby gushed, "Really? Me too. You know we met him at the CMAs." She fanned herself and giggled. "He's even hotter in person."

"Oh my God, I would die. Did you actually get to talk to him?"

Jake and AJ glanced at each other and rolled their eyes at Abby and me acting like lovesick teenage girls.

"Yeah, we did. He was so nice, too."

"I would kill to meet him."

Abby reached over and smacked my leg. "Next CMAs you're coming with me then."

"That would be awesome."

AJ grunted. "Seriously, this dude has nothing on me."

"You actually know the lyrics to this song?"

"Unfortunately yes." At my continued skepticism, he added, "You want me to put my money where my mouth is?"

Rhys groaned. "Please Mia, don't get him started."

Ignoring him, I grinned at AJ. "Come on, big boy. Give me your best shot."

"My pleasure." He sat down his beer and then rose out of his chair. He took center stage in the circle of chairs. Cocking his head to the side, he waited to start in on a line of the song. While he sang the lyrics, he mimed rolling down the windows, turning up the radio, and pouring some Crown in a cup. Abby and Allison giggled at his antics while I couldn't help smiling at him for being such a goober.

When he got to the chorus, he pointed straight at me and bellowed over the song, "Girl, you make my speakers go boom, boom—" Precisely in the moment, he whirled around to smack both of his ass cheeks on 'boom, boom'. "Dancing on the tail gate in the full moon."

"Nice," I replied as I clapped wildly.

Jake snorted contemptuously. "Don't encourage him. AJ will use any excuse to shake his ass at us."

"Don't be hatin' on my ass shaking skills. Mia's a lady who appreciates rhythm—in and out of the bedroom."

Reaching out, I grabbed him by the belt loops and jerked him closer. I leaned forward to nip with my teeth at one of AJ's butt cheeks through his shorts. "I sure as hell do."

"Easy now, you two," Jake grumbled, motioning over at Allison.

She rolled her eyes. "Oh please. I'm almost seventeen, not seven."

AJ turned around to face me. With a grin, he held out his hand. "Come on, I want to take you to see the waterfalls."

I cocked my head at him. "Is that some code word for you to get me away from the group, so you can ravish me out in the woods?"

Abby giggled. "No, there are actually some small waterfalls on the far edge of Jake's grandfather's property. They're only about twelve feet, but it's really beautiful there."

Eyeing AJ's outstretched hand, I said, "*Just* the waterfalls. No funny business that might land me with poison ivy on my ass, right?"

He pursed his lips in his signature smirk. "I'm not making any promises." When I started to protest, he held up a hand. "I can't be held accountable if you accidentally take a tumble out there and happen to roll through poison ivy."

"As long as you don't help me along in that tumble, I think we'll be fine." I then slipped my hand into his, and he pulled me out of the lawn chair.

"Have fun taking in the scenery," Abby teased.

I grinned at her before I let AJ tug me along behind him. He led me over to the barn where a Jeep and several four-wheelers were parked. Instead of going for the Jeep, he slid onto a gleaming black four-wheeler. Turning around, he then patted the sparse space behind him. "Hop on, babe."

I swept my hands to my hips. "You can't be serious."

"And why the hell not?"

"For one, you're saying that a city-boy like you actually knows how to ride one of those things, least of all drive it?"

"Yes, Mia, as hard as it is to believe, this Mexican city dweller actually knows how to drive a four-wheeler." I bit my lip to keep from laughing at his tone. Instead, I continued to look skeptically at him. AJ rolled his eyes "Listen, I've been riding them up here at Jake's since I was fourteen. But even before that, I was driving my uncle's motorcycle along the streets of Guadalajara, which trust me is a hell of a lot more dangerous than anything the backwoods can throw at you."

"Okay, okay, I stand corrected."

With a triumphant grin, AJ revved the motor to life. Hiking my leg, I slid across what was left of the seat behind him. I was practically plastered against his back. My bare thighs brushed against his.

"Hold on tight, baby," he called over the roar of the motor.

Wrapping my arms around his waist, I shouted back, "Trust me, you don't have to tell me that twice."

"You got nothin' to worry about. I wouldn't ever let you get hurt."

My heart fluttered a little at both his kind words and sincere tone. "Aren't you just a sweetheart?"

"Yep, I am." Glancing over his shoulder, he winked. "Now sit tight. I'm gonna give you the ride of your life."

I snickered in spite of myself. "Whatever."

AJ released the brake and stomped on the gas, sending us careening forward over the gravel road. A dirt storm kicked up in our wake, clouding my vision. As we gained speed, I gripped him even tighter. His rock hard abs tightened beneath my hands.

With a turn to the right, we left the gravel road and began tumbling over uneven and overgrown grass. Long before I could see it, I could hear the pounding roar of the water. I didn't realize I had been holding my breath until we reached the stream. AJ must've felt my anticipation because he shut off the engine and pointed to the right. "See," he instructed.

Shielding my eyes from the sun with my hand, I gazed to where he pointed and exhaled my anxious breath. Looming up ahead, water cascaded over three separate jagged rock formations before it pooled into a stream below.

"Like it?" AJ questioned, as I remained staring open-mouthed.

"Are you kidding me?"

He chuckled as he slid off the four-wheeler. As he helped ease me onto the ground, I replied, "I can't believe anything so beautiful is right here in the middle of Jake's property."

AJ reached out his hand for mine. "Come on, let's go explore."

Nodding my head, I slipped my palm into his. Conversation seemed to fail us as we strolled along the river bank. Our clothes rippled in a gentle breeze, while wildlife hummed and buzzed all around us. Squirrels scurried across treetops while birds cried out as they soared over our heads. I squealed and jerked AJ's hand at the sight of a doe and her fawn along the bank. But at the sight of us, they darted away back into the woods. "Did you see that? The baby was just like Bambi with spots."

AJ grinned at my enthusiasm. As I took in all the beauty surrounding me, I sighed with contentment. "I can see now why Jake loves this place so much."

"I don't know if I would call it 'love' or an obsession. It's getting harder and harder in between our breaks to get him back on the road."

"Well, it does make sense he wouldn't want to leave here. I mean, it's part of his blood. Being on the road has to be such a rootless existence that I'm guessing he's super thankful to have such a wonderful home to come back to."

He nudged me playfully. "Listen to you sounding all wise like Yoda or some shit."

I elbowed him back. *Hard.* "Please tell me you didn't just liken me to some old and wrinkly, green dude?"

"Hey, you *are* older than me."

"Keep it up, Resendiz, and I see a weekend of just you and your hand getting off."

Throwing his head back, AJ laughed heartily. "Come on now, don't get so riled up." He dropped my hand, so he could slide his arm around my waist. Drawing me to him, his warm lips nuzzled against my neck. "You know you're the sexiest cougar in the entire fucking world."

I wiggled out of his grasp and thrust a finger in front of his face. "You sir, are not redeeming yourself. I'm a measly three and half years older than you. I'd hardly call that a cougar."

"But thinking I'm your cougar cub gets me hard."

Rolling my eyes with exasperation, I huffed, "Just the wind blowing gets you hard."

AJ eyed me for a moment before roaring with laughter. His dark eyes danced with amusement as he playfully cuffed the back of my neck. "Damn, Mia, what am I going to do with you?"

"Take me down to the water," I commanded.

"With pleasure." He held out his hand again, and I slipped mine into his. We high stepped our way through the almost knee level grass towards the riverbank. When we reached it, I bent over, peering down at the gently flowing stream. In my mind, I had pictured harsh rapids flowing from the waterfalls, but this was so smooth. "Look how crystal clear that water is. You can see straight through to the bottom."

"If you think it looks amazing, you should feel it."

In a flash, I stepped out of my flip-flops and started tentatively wading into the water. As I dodged branches and other debris on the bottom, my toes squished through the silky sand. The refreshing coolness lapped against my ankles, and I sighed in renewed contentment. "It's warmer than I'd thought it would be."

"Wanna go swimming?" AJ asked from behind me.

As I glanced over my shoulder, I could see the wicked gleam burning in his eyes at the suggestion. "Hmm, we seem to have forgotten our bathing suits."

"Who says we need them?"

I shot him a coy smile. "Are you suggesting we go skinny dipping?"

"Now why would you automatically think I was insinuating a nude swim?"

"Because you're a complete and total horndog?"

AJ laughed. "Now Mia, my mind wasn't being so devious. I simply meant for us to swim in our underwear."

"Of course you did."

Playing with the hem of his shirt, AJ questioned, "So are you game?"

The heat blazing all around me, singeing my exposed skin, made the water feel even more heavenly against my ankles. I wanted nothing more than my entire body to be enveloped in the coolness. "Are you sure no one can see us out here?"

"Nope. We're too far off the beaten path."

"Okay then, I'm game."

"Fuck yeah!" he exclaimed, jerking his shirt over his head so fast I thought he'd rip the fabric.

I had barely gotten my shirt over my head when I noticed AJ was already stripped to his boxers and stood watching me intently. "This isn't a peep show, Mr. Resendiz."

"You can't fault a man for enjoying the view."

My fingers hesitated on the button of my shorts. I hated AJ seeing me naked with the lights on. With the sun beating against us and illuminating even the shady parts of the woods, he was going to see way more than I wanted.

When I continued to stall, AJ sloshed into the water,

bridging the gap between us. He walked me back to the shore before his fingers replaced mine on my shorts. As he unbuttoned them, he stared intently at me. "I know what you're thinking, so I guess I need to repeat it once again. I love every square inch of your body, including these fabulous round hips..." He trailed off as he pushed my shorts over my butt and down to my feet. On his knees, he glanced up at me. "And it bears repeating once again how much I adore and worship this ass," he said before sending a stinging smack against one of my cheeks.

My face flushed with warmth. I wanted more than anything to believe that AJ was sincere in what he said about my body, but I had too many years of self-loathing ingrained in me. With desire and admiration glimmering in his eyes, I crooked my finger, beckoning him to me. As he rose up from the ground, his gaze locked in on mine as I gave him a truly grateful smile. "Thank you, AJ."

"You're welcome," he murmured, pushing long strands of hair out of my face.

I ducked my head down to press a lingering kiss against his chest above his heart. Even under my lips, I could feel the strong beat of his heart—one that was so amazingly kind and giving. I peeked up at him through the shroud of hair covering my face. "In spite of all the joking and innuendo, you sure do know how to make a girl feel wanted."

He grinned down at me. "I'm glad you're finally realizing

how magnificent I am, both in and out of the bedroom."

At his cockiness, I sank my teeth into the skin where I had once tenderly kissed. AJ yelped and jumped back. "Mia Martinelli, did you just bite me?" He rubbed his chest while giving me a pouty face. "What a waste. I mean, it wasn't even a love bite either."

I giggled. "Yeah, well, that will teach you to make douche comments when I'm being genuine," I replied as I stepped out of my shorts.

At the sight of me in my bra and panties, AJ's expression switched over to one of pure lust. After I tossed my shorts on the bank, I wagged my finger at him. "Just swimming, remember?"

"Yeah, yeah," he grunted.

Brushing past him, I made my way deeper into the water. The further I walked into the stream, the deeper my toes sank into the squishy mud. When I realized AJ had yet to join me, I glanced over my shoulder. I spied AJ shoving his wallet back in his shorts. The blazing sun caught the gold foil wrapper, and I giggled in spite of myself. After I recovered, I called, "I would think swimming protection would include a life vest and sunscreen, not a condom."

He used his free hand to scratch the back of his neck. I could tell he was waging war with himself as to whether to bring it with him or drop it back on the pile of clothes.

Turning around in the water, I crossed my arms over my

breasts. "Do I turn you on so much that you can't imagine taking a harmless swim without us banging?"

He rolled his eyes. "There's a difference between not being able to control myself and just not wanting to, Mia. Is it that hard for you to understand that I want you twenty-four seven?"

His words sent a tingle rippling through me, but I shook my head. "Bring it here."

AJ took a few trudging steps towards me, sending water splashing around us. When I held out my hand, he reluctantly slipped the condom in it. "Thank you." When I shoved the wrapper inside one of my bra cups, AJ's mouth curved up in a smirk. "What?" I questioned with a shrug.

"I thought you were going to toss it."

"Now what a waste that would be." Stepping forward, I grabbed the waist band of his boxers, jerking him to me. "But I will make one thing clear. I get to come at least once or twice before you get to use this."

AJ grinned. "I have no problem with that."

"Good." I adjusted my bra cup, making sure the condom was held firmly in place. Once it was fixed, I continued walking into the stream until I was at chest level. "I'm going in," I said, before I dove under the water.

Kicking my arms and legs, I swam closer to the waterfall. When I resurfaced, I brushed my damp hair out of my face and wiped my eyes. Glancing around, there was no sign of

AJ.

"AJ?" I questioned. As I turned left and right in the water, desperately searching for him, my heart started to beat faster in fear.

Something brushed against me before I was jerked under by my feet. Kicking my legs, I fought against it to find my way to the surface. When AJ popped up behind me, I squealed and clutched my heart. "You shithead!" I cried, splashing his face with water.

He chuckled before wrapping his arms around me. "Did you think I'd been eaten by some river monster, and it was after you, too?"

"No, I didn't," I huffed. Pushing against his chest, I tried wiggling out of his embrace. When he kept his grip tight around me, I shook my head. "Don't think you're going to get any loving from me after you pulled that douche move."

"Aw, I'm sorry for scaring you, amorcito mio. Let me make it up to you, okay?" AJ brought his lips to mine. As he deepened the kiss, my resolve slowly faded, and I melted into him. Pulling away, he cocked his brows at me. "Forgiven?"

I smiled. "Yes, forgiven."

"Good. Let's go swim over there where our feet can touch the bottom."

"Okay." Spreading my arms out, I kicked with my feet and followed AJ's steady strokes across the water. As we got closer to the rock formations, I could see the water was growing shallower. But when I put my feet down, the water was still chin level. "I think I'm a little vertically challenged for this."

AJ laughed. "Come here. I'll help you since I got a few inches on you." He waggled his eyebrows. "In more ways than one."

I rolled my eyes as he pulled me against him. "Lame, Resendiz. Very, very lame."

"I had to go there. Now wrap your sexy legs around my waist."

"With pleasure," I replied. Grasping his shoulders, I hoisted myself up. The moment my center brushed against AJ's cock, it reared to life. I raised a brow at him. "Seriously? Isn't the water too cold?"

"Obviously not." He slid one of his hands off my hips and brought it between my legs. "Looks like we need to warm you up a little."

I gasped as he rubbed my clit. "I thought we were going to swim first."

"Can't we fuck first and swim later?" he asked earnestly.

My pleasure turned over to amusement. "You and your one track mind. You had this planned back at the bonfire, didn't you?"

"Sort of." His deft fingers brushed past my panties to slide two fingers inside me. "But I've never fucked at a waterfall before." He nipped my bottom lip, sucking it between his teeth as he began pumping his fingers even faster inside me. An amused look twinkled in his hooded eyes. "Mia, will you do the honors of taking my waterfall virginity?"

"Mmm, let me think about it." When I tightened my legs around his waist, our bodies melted together, and we both moaned into each other's mouths. He thrust his hips out, nudging his enlarged cock against my center. Filled with his fingers, I wanted even more of him, so I arched against him causing a shudder to ripple through AJ.

The teasing look he had before vanished, and one of white hot lust burned in his eyes. "I want to take you right here, right now," he rasped.

I pulled back to run my fingers through the wet strands of his dark hair. At the base of his neck, I tugged hard. "Then take me."

At my invitation, AJ enthusiastically replied by pushing hard against me. As I went spiraling backwards, I slammed my back onto the jagged rocks. I cried out in pain, rather than pleasure.

"Oh amorcito mio, I'm so, so sorry." AJ's hands went to tenderly rub up and down the stinging flesh of my back. "Here turn around and let me check on you."

I pivoted in the water to where I was facing my former nemesis, the rocks. "No cuts or scrapes, thankfully." I shivered when AJ's warm lips kissed a trail over my back. When he finished, his strong hands came to my shoulders and turned me back around. Cupping my face with his hands, he gave me a truly apologetic look. "I'm so sorry for being such a Neanderthal and manhandling you like that."

I brought one of my hands up to pat his arm. "You don't have to apologize. It was an accident. I know you would never willingly hurt me." A shudder rippled through me as a few buried memories flashed through my head.

AJ leaned over to place a chaste and tender kiss on my lips. "I couldn't live with myself if I ever hurt you intentionally."

Desperately fighting the ghosts of the past, I forced a smile to my lips. "I know that. Although you're a badass, you're a sweetheart through and through."

He scowled at me. "Thanks for making me sound like an utter pussy."

I laughed. "That's the last thing you could ever be. Besides, it's no secret that you like it rough."

"Yeah, that's true." AJ's thumb traced my lower lip. "But I feel awful."

"Would you stop wasting energy on this self-deprecating tirade and instead get your fabulous dick in me?"

His eyes widened. "Hell yeah, I can do that."

"And while you're at it, bring back the arrogant, naughty talking guy I like so much."

"My pleasure," he replied, snatching the condom out of my bra cup. While he worked on removing his boxer shorts, I reached around to unclasp my bra and then shimmied out of my panties. After I wadded them in my hands, I tossed them onto one of the higher boulders. AJ followed my lead and threw his boxers up there as well.

When he brought his gaze to mine, desire burned bright in his eyes. "Put your hands on those rocks," AJ commanded, his voice a harsh growl in my ears.

I shivered in anticipation as my trembling palms reached out for the moss-covered stones. Once I planted them as firmly as I could, I glanced over my shoulder. "Are you sure no one can see us?"

"No."

"But you said—"

AJ nudged his condom-sheathed erection against my bare bottom. His teeth grazed my earlobe before he sucked it into his mouth. My nipples tightened at the sensation, wishing he was sucking them rather than my earlobe. "Even though we're miles and miles from civilization and there's no way in hell Jake or the others would follow us, I could almost blow my load just thinking of someone seeing me fuck you out here."

A shudder rippled through me at his words. I pinned him with a hard stare. "Then what are you waiting for?"

He responded by slamming into me with one harsh thrust.

When I cried out, it echoed off the rocks around us, just like the wet slapping of our skin.

"Oh fuck, that's hot. Make that noise again," AJ murmured into my ear, as he continued thrusting in and out of me. His hands went to my waist. His fingers dug into the skin on my hips as he jerked me back and forth against him. He went deeper and deeper each time, and I felt myself easily climbing towards an orgasm. When I let my head fall back onto his shoulder, AJ leaned over to cover my lips with his. Bringing my arm back, I cupped his head with my hand, drawing him closer. His warm tongue thrust in my mouth in time with his movements inside me.

Our breathing became heavier while our moans of pleasure echoed against each other's lips. As AJ continued his harsh pounding, one of his hands left my hip to cup my breast. He tweaked and twisted the nipple with his fingers. I closed my eyes and shivered. Once my nipple had been worked to a perfect peak, his hand left my breast to entangle his fingers with my hand covering the rock. Something about the affectionate gesture in the middle of such hardcore fucking sent me reeling, and I felt my walls spasm.

"Yes, yes! Oh God, yes, AJ!" I screamed. As I came, I fisted his hair in my hands. My cries echoing off the rocks were met with AJ's satisfied grunt as he shuddered and jerked inside me. As he continued convulsing, he kept up his rabid assault on my mouth. I moaned against his lips. If he didn't stop soon, I was going to be ready for another round, and I knew we needed to get back to the others.

Breathless and drained, I pulled away. AJ's broad chest heaved as he fought to catch his breath. "Fuck me," he muttered.

I couldn't help laughing. "Yeah, I think I just did pretty thoroughly."

He grinned. "Whatever smartass. I just meant, that each time it gets more and more intense between us."

As he slid out of me, I turned around to face him, resting my hands on his shoulders. "I'm glad to hear that. I'd hate for you to be growing tired of me after two weeks."

"I don't think I could get tired of you after a fucking decade, least of all a few weeks."

His words caused a fluttering in my chest that I tried unsuccessfully to ignore. "Good." I jerked my chin up to the boulder above us. "Now why don't you be a real gentleman and go get our underwear back, huh?"

"Your wish is my command, Miss Bossy," he replied with a wink.

Chapter Fourteen

AJ

With a bounce in my step from feeling utterly and completely sexually satisfied, I led Mia up the riverbank. Reaching over, I grabbed her hand in mine and swung it back and forth. "So what's on tap for tonight?" Mia asked.

"Oh, shit gets crazy here when the sun goes down."

"Seriously?" she asked.

I nodded. "Hell yeah. I mean, we all gather around the bonfire and roast marshmallows and s'mores. It may get so off the hook that we go tip one of Jake's grandfather's cows."

When I winked at her, she grinned. "Very funny."

"So do you like G-rated parties?"

"Sure I do." She elbowed me playfully. "Especially if it means getting to spend time with you. And your friends."

The familiar ache raged in my chest at Mia's words—the one that felt like intense heartburn after a beer binge. I hadn't felt this way about a girl in a long, long time. Even though I'd thought I'd felt something for Kylie, it was nothing like what I was feeling for Mia—even though we'd barely been together two weeks. I squeezed her hand in mind and replied, "I like that."

When we got back to the four-wheeler, Mia's hand dug into one of my short pockets. I shuddered at the contact so close to my dick. "Damn babe, you already wantin' another round? You're practically insatiable," I drawled, with a pleased grin on my face.

She giggled. "Not quite, sweet cheeks. I wanna drive the four-wheeler back to Jake's."

I jerked away just as her fingers grasped the keys. "Uh-uh. Nobody drives my baby but *me*."

Cocking her head, Mia shot me an exasperated look. "Seriously? Your 'baby'?"

I swept my hands up and crossed them firmly over my chest before I bobbed my head. "You should know by now how seriously I take anything that has an engine."

Mia's disgusted expression slowly evaporated. Instead, her face took on a pleading look. She even resorted to poking out that succulent lower lip of hers. "But I haven't driven one since I was a teenager, and I would really, really love to drive your baby." She leaned in, pressing her enticing rack against me. "Come on, AJ. It would make me really happy, and I promise to show you how thankful I am later."

Oh fuck. This was totally a lost cause considering I was incapable of telling alluring females, especially this one, no. But I figured I might as well make her work a little harder for it. "How about this? Whoever makes it back to my baby first, gets to drive."

Mia's dark eyes flashed triumphantly. "Deal."

"Ready?"

"Oh yeah."

"Then go."

Just as I started to sprint away, Mia jerked her hand out of my pocket. She momentarily flashed the keys in front of my face and winked. "See ya, sucker."

I didn't even have time to recover before she started hauling ass across the gravel, literally and figuratively leaving me in her dust. "Shit!"

Peering through the cloudy air, I tried making out Mia's retreating figure. I then pushed my legs as hard as they would go. Considering I had a few inches on Mia, I was able to catch up to her fairly quickly. Out of the corner of my eye, I spotted a rolling patch of soft grass. Reaching out, I grasped her by the waist and jerked her off the road, tackling her to the ground.

"Oomph," she muttered, when we finally came to a stop after a few rolls and tumbles. Her chest heaved as those sexy black eyes of hers glared up at me, causing my dick to twitch in my pants. "What the hell were you thinking, AJ?" she huffed.

I smirked down at her. "What I'm always thinking—how to get you flat on your back underneath me." Leaning over, I brought my mouth to hers. I nibbled and sucked at her bottom lip. Her resolve began to momentarily waver. I shifted to pin her arms over her head. It put us in a position we hadn't been in before—I was straddling her.

With my thighs on each side of her hips, my weight kept her firmly underneath me. Seizing the opportunity I snatched the keys from her hand. "Ha, gotcha."

"Let me up, you ass."

"Nope. Not until I hear you say 'AJ, you are the master of the universe'." I quirked my brows before looming over her— my face mere inches from hers. "On second thought, you need to say, 'AJ, you are the master of *my* universe *and* my master orgasm donor.'"

Even though my tone was completely lighthearted, Mia's expression transformed into one of panic. Instead of squirming playfully beneath me like before, she began to thrash back and forth. Her eyes took on a wild gleam, like that of a trapped animal. And then something within her snapped. "Get off. Get off. GET OFF!" she screamed, pounding her fists against my chest so hard that she knocked the air from my lungs.

Wheezing, I stared frozen in disbelief at her erratic behavior. I remained unblinking and unmoving until she sent a stinging slap so hard across my cheek that my jaw popped. Out of my stupor, I finally rolled off her. The instant she realized she was free she leapt to her feet and began sprinting away from me. "Fuck," I groaned as I hauled up out of the grass to take after her. "Mia!"

She bypassed the four-wheeler, and instead, continued barreling down the overgrown path. "Mia, wait!" When I finally caught up with her, I reached out and grabbed her arm, causing us both to skid to a stop. I realized a second too late that it was the wrong fucking thing to do when she lunged at me, clawing and slapping my face, shoulders, and chest.

Defensively blocking her hits, I then grabbed her shoulders. "Mia, it's me, AJ." Her frenzied gaze darted around the clearing. "Look at me," I commanded. "You're safe here with me. Nothing or no one is going to hurt you. I swear."

When her eyes finally locked on mine, the sheer panic in them caused my chest to ache. But slowly that look receded. It was the pain, coupled with embarrassment, shining bright in her eyes that followed that made my stomach muscles clench like I'd taken a physical kick to the gut, rather than an emotional one.

A shaky hand went to cover her mouth as tears streaked down her cheeks. Her head shook so wildly back and forth I feared she might get whiplash. "Oh God...Oh AJ, I..."

"Look, it's—"

"I'm s-sorry. I'm s-so, so sorry," she replied, her voice choking off with her sobs.

"Baby, you have nothing to apologize about." Tentatively, I reached out to cup her cheek. When she flinched, I dropped my hand. Feeling a fucking mess of confusion and helplessness, I kicked at a few stray pebbles and waited for her to give me some sign as to what the hell I should do.

"I'm sorry. I'm sorry. I'm sorry," she kept mumbling absently.

"Mia, please don't say that."

"It's just you had me pinned down like he..." A chill ran through her body, causing her to shudder so hard that her teeth chattered.

Closing the distance between us, I ached to wrap her trembling body in my arms. "Amorcito mio, please talk to me. Tell me what I can do to help you," I begged.

Her only response was to swipe the back of her hand across her running nose while making these pitiful hiccupping sighs. I started tapping my hands nervously against my short pockets when she became still as a statue. It seemed like she stared dead ahead of us for a small eternity before she finally whispered, "I never wanted you to have to see this side of me."

This time when I reached out for her, she didn't cower

away from me. Trying to take it slow, I swept a strand of hair out of her face and smiled. "Mia, there isn't a single side of you I don't want to see. I want to know every inch of you—inside and out."

Her lip trembled like she was about to burst out crying. "Trust me, you don't want to know this." Her expression then turned sour, like she had a bad taste in her mouth. Her emotions were ricocheting so fast I could barely keep up. "Dammit, we were just supposed to have that night together—then you wouldn't have had to see me like this. It wasn't supposed to turn into me being inadequate for yet *another* guy!"

My sympathy quickly turned over to frustration, and I threw my hands up in exasperation. "Would you stop lumping me with all these assholes you've had the misfortune of knowing? That's not me, Mia. Do you see me bailing or shrinking away like some pussy? Fuck no! I'm right here, right now, wanting to know what the hell just happened so I can help you—to comfort you emotionally and physically."

She cut her eyes over at me, pinning me with a hard stare. "Yeah, I see right through your little 'knight in shining armor' routine. You think I'm broken, and by giving me a few moments of your precious time, you might be able to fix me. But trust me, you can't do shit, AJ! I'm not broken—I'm fucking shattered into a thousand jagged pieces. Pieces that will slice a perfect, pretty boy like you in two."

Although it probably wasn't the best way to handle the situation, I stepped toe to toe with her and got right in her face. "Why don't you let me be the judge of what I can or can't handle, okay?"

Crossing her arms over her chest, she scoffed at me. "Fine, you want the truth? Here it is, big boy. That freak-out I just had was because I spent almost two years with an asshole who used to beat the shit out of me."

Her words had the same effect as if she had slapped me, and I jolted back. "What?"

With a contemptuous snort, she turned away from me. "You heard me just fine, AJ."

"Jesus, Mia, I'm sorry. I had no idea." When she didn't respond, I asked, "How old were you?"

"Young and stupid," she spat.

"Just how young?"

"Twenty-one."

We fell into an uncomfortable silence. Reaching out, I gently trailed my hand down her arm. I was surprised when she didn't jerk away. I drew in a deep breath. "I know it might seem like I have the perfect life. And yeah, I'm blessed to not have any real skeletons in my past. But when someone I care about is hurting, I'm there for them. So if you want to talk about what happened, I'd like to hear it."

Her incredulous gaze snapped back to mine. "Seriously?"

I gave a quick nod of my head. "I really mean it, Mia."

She exhaled a long, agonized sigh, like one who held the weight of the world on her shoulders. Chewing her bottom lip, I could tell at any minute she was either going to come clean with me or bolt again. I extended my hand. "Come on. You can tell me about it down by the river."

Almost skittishly, Mia reached out for my hand, grasping it like it was an anchor holding her sanity together. We started making our way through the high grass back down to the riverbank. When we reached the edge, I still didn't press her for more information. Instead, I remained uncharacteristically silent, waiting for her to take the lead.

After what felt like a small eternity, she turned to me. "Even all these years later and with time spent in therapy, I still can't understand why I ever stayed with him. I wasn't the girl so desperate for her father's attention that she'd let a man abuse her. No man was, or is, a better father than Duke Martinelli." Mia shook her head. "And even though my mother bailed, I was raised by one of the strongest women I've ever known—one who taught me not to take any shit from men." A smile tugged at Mia's lips. "Trust me, when you're surrounded by Italian men, that's no easy feat."

"I think they're kinda as pig headed as Hispanic men, right?"

"You could say that," she replied. She stooped down to gather up a few pebbles along the bank. "Regardless of those two factors, there has to be some reason I completely lost my mind for eighteen months, right?"

I shrugged. "I don't think you need to blame yourself. Shit happens."

"I wish it was as easy as that." Mia chucked one of the pebbles into the stream, sending ripples along the surface. "His name is Jason. He was the second real boyfriend I ever had—the first guy I really loved....or thought I did. At first, I thought him being possessive was sweet, even sexy. He called me constantly during the day to see what I was doing, he referred to me as *his*, and he wanted to spend every waking minute with me."

Mia threw another rock into the creek, casting greater waves across the water. "But then as the months went by and we got even more serious, things changed. At first, the abuse was just emotional. All the bullshit I have about my body—that all came from him. He was able to make me feel that because of my thicker body, I was totally undesirable to any other man and that I was lucky he stayed with me at all." Mia shook her head. "But then when guys would give me attention, I was too fucking stupid to realize it or that I could have someone else— someone better. Then the guys' attention would piss Jason off. If one dared so much as looked in my direction, he would freak out and threaten to kick his ass. Then he'd accuse me of flirting or dressing like a slut. Whenever I argued with him or tried to defend myself, that's when he got violent."

As she bent over to pick up a few more pebbles, I swallowed hard, my fists clenching at my side. My heartbeat drummed in my ears at the thought of any man laying a hand on Mia. I shifted uncomfortably back and forth on my feet, desperately wanting an outlet for the rising anger I felt thrumming in my blood. "What kinda shit did he pull?" I asked in a hoarse voice.

A sigh wheezed from her chest. "At first, he would cuff the back of my head hard or shove me into walls or furniture. After a few months when I still didn't break to his commands, he resorted to backhanding me."

The world tilted and spun around me at the image that formed in my head. At the same time, I fought to catch my breath as her words had the same effect as if someone were wrenching my beating heart from my chest. "Motherfucker," I hissed.

Mia threw her head back and met my gaze. "I never, ever dreamed I'd become one of *those* women—the cowering beaten and bruised creatures I'd see on TV or in movies. And it goes without saying with Italian tempers, there were a few in my extended family who were always so damn klutzy by running into walls or falling down the stairs." Gritting her teeth, Mia threw the next stone so hard it hit the rocks across the bank. "But that became me."

"What did Duke say?"

"He didn't know," she murmured softly.

251

"But how?"

"The more violent Jason became, the more I started to retreat from my family. I was finishing up nursing school then, busy with my clinicals, so it was easy to lie." With her hands empty of stones, Mia crossed her arms over her chest, hugging herself. "But then it all fell apart around the time my cousin, Nicki, was getting married. She was like a sister to me, and as the maid of honor, I was spending a lot of time with her, which pissed Jason off. I wasn't supposed to be with anyone but him. One day we were out shopping together for wedding stuff before I had to go into work. Jason kept calling me constantly, and I could tell it was pissing Nicki off. She's the kind of girl who would answer my phone and tell Jason to go fuck himself."

"Sounds like my kind of girl."

Mia gave me a small smile. "Finally, I just turned my phone off. I was working nights, so I had to go by the house to change for my shift. Jason was waiting for me when I got home." Mia shivered violently, and I fought the urge to wrap my arms around her. "In the foyer, we had this giant, round mirror. I'd barely gotten through the front door when he came at me. I'd never seen him so enraged. Of course, he reeked of alcohol, so I don't know why I was so surprised. The next thing I knew he had grabbed the nape of my neck and shoved me with all his might into the mirror." Mia turned to me and pulled back some of her hair on the right side of her face. I'd never noticed it before, but in her hairline, there was a faint scar running from her temple, down to her ear. "My head crashed against the mirror so hard, it cracked the glass. Jason kept ramming me into it until shards fell to the floor." As she relived the horrific memories, her chest began to rise and fall with her heaving breaths.

Tentatively, I reached out to touch her shoulder. "You don't have to do this."

"No, I need to—not just for me, but for you. When it's all said and done, you need to know everything—to understand why I am the way I am with men." Tears pooled in her eyes. "More than anything, I trust you enough to be honest with you, AJ."

My heart ached for her. "I'm here, amorcito mio."

She drew in a ragged breath. "Do you remember that night when you asked me about the tattoo?"

I bobbed my head.

"You asked if I'd gotten it to cover the scars left by an accident. Well, that's partly true."

"What do you mean?"

Mia closed her eyes, letting tears trickle down her cheeks. "After the mirror shattered, Jason picked up one of the broken shards. He first brought it to my neck—told me if I ever didn't call him again, he would kill me. Then he said he wanted to leave me something physical to remind me of my mistake. It was summer, and I was wearing a tank top with spaghetti straps, which he said made me look like a whore." Opening her eyes, Mia stared out at the water. "He said he was going to cut me for every time he called me, and I ignored him." She glanced over at me. "That's where the five lines came from."

Rage burned through me, causing me to shudder from head to toe. My fists clenched involuntarily. "Give me his name. That's all I need. Not an address or a phone number. Just his name," I demanded.

"AJ," Mia protested.

"I mean it. I don't think I can rest until I track down that low-life piece of shit and take a piece out of his worthless hide for every time he hurt you."

"You don't need to do that."

"Yes, I—"

Mia held her up hand. "AJ, trust me when I say this. Jason got what was coming to him."

"What do you mean?"

She gave me a tight smile. "I'm Sicilian, remember? After my dad calmed down enough to speak and think somewhat coherently, he called some of his buddies from his old neighborhood back in Jersey."

"You're telling me that they made Jason an offer he couldn't refuse?"

"To the tune of beating him so badly he was hospitalized

in a full body cast."

"Good for your dad. Of course, I would have preferred they render him dickless as well."

Mia chuckled. "Don't think Daddy didn't contemplate having his associates take care of that."

"Hell, I admired him before, but now I admire him even more."

"Yeah, well, nobody hurts his little girl."

"I'll remember to never piss off your dad, because I sure as hell don't want to end up sleeping with the fishes."

Mia's expression lightened, and I could tell she was fighting hard not to smile. "For you, being dickless would be a fate worse than death."

Wincing, I cupped my crotch. "I gotta agree with you on that one."

This time she did smile, and I was so fucking glad to see her smiling again. It was timid—one I had never seen on her face before. Normally, she is so confident, strong. I closed the gap between us. "I'm so sorry you had to go through all that shit."

"Thank you. But I'm the one who should be sorry."

"Why?" I demanded.

"Because my past keeps fucking things up for us. I mean, I just had a major freak-out back there when you were only teasing me. As hard as I try, I can't seem to put what happened with Jason or Dev to rest." She gave me a sad smile. "You're too good for all my bullshit, AJ."

It took me a second to process her words. Why in the hell did she think I was too good for her? If anyone wasn't good enough, it was me—the goofy drummer who had never had to go through any harsh shit. "Don't apologize for shit you can't help. And you're wrong, about not being good enough. You and me...? We're good for each other." Cupping her face in my hands, I leaned in and kissed her gently. "I think you're so fucking brave to have lived through what you did."

Her brows shot up in surprise. "You really think I'm brave?"

"Hell yes, I do. I mean, you finally left that fucker."

"Yeah, but even after that awful night, it took someone who I respect very much for me to finally see the light."

"Who was it?"

"Pesh—the doctor who I did my clinical placements under. He'd suspected I was being abused for a while, kept trying to get me to talk to my family or leave Jason, but I wouldn't. That night, I was a mess when I went into work—physically and emotionally. He was the one who stitched me up. Then, he called someone to cover for us. Even though I begged and pleaded for him not to do it, he drove me straight to the restaurant. He stood beside me and held my hand while I told my dad everything from start to finish. I moved in with my dad until Jason was taken care of. I've never heard or seen him since." She shook her head. "Besides the support of my family, Pesh was there through it all. He even threatened to flunk my evaluations if I even thought of ever going back to Jason."

"Sounds like a stand-up guy to me."

A dreamy expression filled her face. "He really is."

An uneasy feeling came over at me at the way she was talking about this doctor. I couldn't help the jealousy that pinged over me that she might still be hot for this dude or worse she was somehow in love for him. Shifting on my feet, I asked the question I really didn't want to. "So were you and this Pesh guy together or something?"

Mia's eyes widened. "Oh, God no. Besides the fact he was married, we didn't feel that way about each other. I mean, I love him—as a mentor and a friend, but not in a romantic way."

My relief whooshed out of me in a long, exaggerated sigh. "I see."

"Of course I can't say the same for his brother." When I furrowed my brows in confusion, Mia replied, "It was two years after I left Jason that Pesh introduced me to his younger brother, Dev, my ex-fiancé."

I growled. "There's another asshole I'd like to rip apart."

Mia laughed. "Trust me, most of the men in my life would like to do that—including Dee. Even though Pesh is a peacemaker, I think he'd probably join in too. He was pretty livid at what his brother did, especially after what I'd been through with Jason."

We fell into an awkward silence then. The atmosphere around us felt laden down with the admission of Mia's abuse. I could tell she was still reeling—both pain and embarrassment radiated in her eyes, even though she tried to hide it. But I felt utterly and completely helpless at what to do to help her.

Finally, Mia cleared her throat. "I guess we better get back before they send out a search party, huh?"

Seeing the opportunity to lighten the mood, I grinned. "I'm pretty sure they know what we're doing out here—or what we were doing."

She made a face. "Fabulous."

"Come on," I said, holding out my hand. We made our way up the riverbank in silence. Although I wasn't saying anything, my mind was whirling with what I thought I should say or do to ease Mia's pain. When we got to the four-wheeler, I handed her back the keys. "You drive."

"I don't want this out of pity, AJ," she countered.

Damn, just when I thought she couldn't get any more stubborn, she did. "Oh Christ, that's not it at all. Okay?"

She eyed me, and the keys, for a few seconds before she snatched them out of my hand. After she sat on the seat, I slid in behind her. She cranked up as I wrapped my arms around her waist. Peeking at me over her shoulder, she grinned. "Watch it with the happy hands."

"You mean like this?" I asked, as I reached up to cup her breast with one hand while the other slipped between her legs. She squealed and slapped at my hands. I chuckled and then brought them behind me to rest on the back bar. "Better?"

She grinned. "Yes. But if it gets bumpy, I'd rather you hold on to me than fall off."

"I'd rather hold on to you, period."

"Then behave and you can."

"Yes ma'am," I replied, bringing my hands back to wrap around her waist. I nestled my head into the crook of her neck, inhaling the sweet scent of her damp hair. As we started jostling over the bumpy road, I tightened my grip around her. When we got back to the stables, loud voices and laughter echoed back to us from the fire. In the twilight, I reached out to run my fingers over her tattoo. She sucked in a deep breath. "It's in Italian, right?"

"Yes," she whispered.

"What does it say?"

"The first line says 'Ciò che non ci uccide, ci rende più forte'—'What does not kill us makes us stronger'."

I rubbed my finger along the next line. "And this?"

"'Dal buio verso la luce'—'Out of the darkness and into the light'."

When I moved to the third, she said, "'La mia famigla e il mio Dio sono il mio rifugio e la mia forza' —'My family and my God are my refuge and strength'." I slid my finger down to rub on the fourth line.

"'Essere sinceri con se stessi'—'To thine own self be true'." Peering over her shoulder, she smiled. "I minored in English, and I kinda have a thing for Shakespeare."

I returned her smiled. "You and Jake will get along great. He's obsessed."

"The next one is Shakespeare, too. 'Non è scritto nelle stelle per tenere il nostro destino, ma in noi stessi'—'It is not in the stars to hold our destiny but in ourselves'. You know, we Italian's take the stars and destiny pretty seriously."

Leaning over, I kissed along the dark lines. "It's beautiful, amorcito mio—the design itself, down to every last word."

"Thank you."

After a few seconds of silence, I got off the four-wheeler and helped Mia off. "You ready for some s'mores now?"

Mia nibbled on her lip. "Can you give me a few minutes to freshen up?" At what I imagined was my confused expression, she said, "I don't want to show up all red-faced from crying."

"Oh," I murmured with a nod. "Sure. Come on." Placing my hand in the small of her back, I led her up the hill to the barn. Grabbing my keys, I unlocked the front door and held it open for her.

Mia stepped inside and gasped. She turned around several times—her expression one of awe. "Wow, the girls weren't kidding about this place. It's amazing."

I gazed around the massive open room. "Yeah, it is. Jake's contractors did a pretty amazing job transforming it."

"Can you get my bag from the car?"

"Yeah." I motioned over to the ladder. "The master bedroom and bath is upstairs. Go on up there, and I'll bring our stuff."

"Thanks, AJ," she replied, before leaning over and pecking me on the cheek.

I hustled down to the car and back for our bags. I was out of breath by the time I got back to the barn. After I lugged her suitcase up the ladder, I found her sitting on the edge of the bed with her head in her hands.

"Mia?"

She jerked up her head up and gave me an apologetic look. "Sorry." She rose up from the bed and grabbed her bag. "I'll hurry."

"Take your time. I'm going to get out of these wet clothes."

When Mia disappeared, I went downstairs to retrieve my bag. I changed into a dry T-shirt and shorts. After I finished, I began pacing around the bedroom, waiting for Mia to come out of the bathroom. Even over the music from down at the bonfire, I heard water running and then the buzzing hum of a hair dryer. After she had been in there a long time, I fought the urge to go check on her. Finally, after what felt like a fucking eternity, she came out. My heart kick started again at the sight of her. She'd totally redone her hair and makeup, and she'd changed into a strapless, red sundress. She looked so fucking beautiful, it made my heart clench. Her dark hair tumbled in waves over her bare shoulders. Her newly applied ruby red lipstick made her plump lips all the more kissable. And needless to say, my cock surged against my zipper.

Framed in the doorway, she stared at me. We stood unmoving and unblinking as the conversations from the guys floated back up to us along with a steady thumping bass. I knew in that instant that what had been discussed down by the river had deepened our relationship, or whatever the fuck it was we had going.

When the song changed over to Bob Marley's *No Woman No Cry*, electricity crackled in the air between us. I held out my hand. "Dance with me?"

Her brows rose in surprise. "Now? Here?"

"Yes."

"Okay," she whispered. She closed the gap between us and slipped her hand into mine. I pulled her flush against me, resting my other hand on the small of her back. Closing my eyes, I took in the delicious scent of both her shampoo and her perfume. We swayed in silence to the music. When it got to the part in the song about how everything was going to be okay, I pulled away to stare into her eyes. "It really is going to be okay. You know that, right?"

Her bottom lip trembled as tears pooled in her eyes. "Even though I shouldn't, I believe you."

"Believe in me, Mia. Believe in us."

A single tear slipped down her cheek, which I caught with my thumb. "Are we an 'us', AJ?"

"I'm down for it if you are."

She shook her head. "It's only been two weeks."

I snorted. "Fuck the amount of time. I know what I'm feeling."

"But I'm confused as hell. I've never fallen this fast," she admitted.

"Me either. You know, Jake and Abby were in deep after a few days, and look at them. Brayden and Lily knew each other since they were kids, and there's grew over time. Love is still love—it doesn't have a time limit."

Her dark eyes widened at the insinuation of love. "I do think I'm falling in love with you, AJ."

As pansy as it sounds, my heartbeat accelerated at her admission. I couldn't believe this amazing woman actually wanted to give me the time of day, least of all be falling in love with me. I'd never met someone who was my match in and out of the bedroom. "Good. Cause I think I'm falling right back."

The song ended, and *Unchained Melody* began playing in its place. I could tell Jake must've put some of his mom's old mix CDs on the stereo system.

"You know, you never sang to me in Spanish last night."

"That's right. I didn't."

"Will you sing to me now?"

"This old song?"

A faint smile danced on her lips. "Please."

"Lemme see if I can remember the words," I lied. The last fucking thing I wanted to admit to Mia was that I knew the song by heart. The truth was I'd been forced by my mother and sister to watch the movie *Ghost* way too many times. If she knew that, she'd probably demand for my man-card to be revoked.

With my lips hovering over her ear, I began to sing. "O mi amor, mi cielo, yo sufro por tu adios. En mi soledad el tiempo se va tan lento si tu no estas aqui."

Mia tightened her arms around me, almost molding her body flush against mine. Closing my eyes, I focused not only on translating the lyrics, but making sure I was giving enough emotion in delivering them. I knew I was doing a pretty good job when a content little sigh came from Mia. When she braced one hand on my shoulder and used the other to draw lazy circles on my back, it was my turn to sigh. After the song drew to a close, I pulled away to peer down at her. "So how did I do?"

"Amazing," she murmured. Untangling herself from my arms, Mia started walking backwards to the bed. When her legs bumped against the mattress, she crooked her finger at me. My brows rose in surprise. "Really? Even after you just spent twenty minutes getting ready to be seen again?"

She laughed. "Yes. You proved my theory right about singing about Spanish."

At the thought of her being wet, my dick surged against the zipper of my shorts. With a groan, I pulled my shirt over my head and tossed it to the floor. "Well, you know I'm never going to argue with a chance to fuck you senseless."

When I pulled her into my arms, Mia's expression grew serious as she brought her hand to my heart. Pressing it firmly against my pec, she whispered, "Make love to me, AJ."

The touch of her fingers on my skin, along with her words, caused the beat of my heart to accelerate beneath her hand. "Anything you want, amorcito mio," I murmured, before crushing my lips against her hers. There was an urgency to it I hadn't experienced with her before. It was like we were both trying to figure out how the screwing we had done in the past switched over to lovemaking. As I deepened the kiss, Mia's hand slipped down my bare chest to the button on my shorts. Although I wanted nothing more than my dick to be freed, I knew if we were lovemaking, it was too fast. I reached between us to grab her hand. "Not yet," I whispered against her lips.

Her eyes widened, but then she nodded. I brought her

hand back to my chest, over my heart. My fingers came to intertwine in the long strands of her dark hair. It felt so silky smooth against my skin. As my tongue tangled against hers, a burning in my chest started to grow.

"Hey AJ!" Jake called from outside the barn.

"Fuck," I muttered before pulling away from Mia. Fucking cockblocker! This seriously couldn't be happening—not now. Not in the middle of our big moment. I stalked over to the window, threw it open, and stuck my head out. "What?" I growled.

Jake gave me a shit eating grin. "Get your ass down here. It's time to do Jude and Melody's bedtime song." I opened my mouth to argue, but Jake shook his head. "We always do this, man. You can fuck Mia's brains out when we're done."

I narrowed my eyes at him. "Fine, douchetard. We'll be right down. And you better hustle your ass back to the fire because I'm going to punch you for that last comment."

Jake only chuckled and started shuffling down the hillside. After I slammed the window, I turned back to Mia. "Sorry about Jake being a dick."

She crossed her arms over her chest. "It's okay. He's your band-mate and loves to give you shit."

"Unfortunately, yeah."

"So this 'bedtime song' must be pretty fucking amazing to take you out of my bed right now?"

Although I felt like an absolute pussy, warmth flooded my

cheeks. "It's hokey as shit really."

Mia's eyes brightened. "I do declare that you are blushing, AJ Resendiz."

"No, I'm not."

She grinned. "Yes, you are." On her knees, she crawled to the end of the bed and then sat back, waiting expectantly for me to explain the bedtime song.

I exhaled noisily before raking a hand through my already messed up hair. "Fine. Here it is. This one time when we were all up here hanging out, Jude was like six months old or something, and he wouldn't go to sleep. Bray and Lily were at their wits end, so Rhys, Jake, and I decided we should sing to him—*Hey Jude* to be exact. He went out like this." I snapped my fingers. "So whenever we're all together and not on the road, we sing for him and for Melody before Bray and Lily take them for their baths and shit."

Mia's hand hovered over her mouth. I didn't know whether she was going to bust out laughing or start crying. "Aw, baby, just when I think you couldn't melt my heart more, you tell me that story."

I grinned. "So does that mean you're in for us picking up where we left off when I get back?"

She laughed. "Oh yes. But you're not going alone."

"I'm not?"

"Nope, I've got to see this 'bedtime song' performance for myself."

Oh fuck. "Seriously?"

"Mmm, hmm." She hopped off the bed and came over to me. "Why do you look so pale, AJ?"

"You know exactly why."

She smiled. "And I'm loving every minute of it."

I rolled my eyes. "Come on. Let's go before Jake comes back to aggravate the hell out of me."

"Should I bring my tambourine?" she asked with all seriousness, as we headed out the door.

"Smartass," I replied, before smacking one globe of her very perfect, round ass.

Chapter Fifteen

Mia

I woke up to blinding sunlight streaming through the windows. Stretching in the bed, I glanced over at the clock on the nightstand. It was after eleven. AJ and I had slept way too late. Of course, after the bedtime singing performance, I couldn't wait to get him back to the barn. The first time we'd gone at each other like always—the ripping off clothes, heavy breathing, moaning, and skin slapping echoing through the room kinda screwing.

But then something had switched over in the both of us. The next time was slow and sweet like we had started before we were interrupted by Jake. I felt more connected to him than I ever had before, and it was both exhilarating and scary as hell. After we finished, we lay entangled in each other's arms talking and laughing until the early morning before we finally fell asleep.

AJ snored softly on his stomach on top of the sheets—his

fine, bare ass on display in the morning light. Snuggling closer to him, I ran my fingertips up and down his back. When he still didn't stir, my mind went back to last night around the bonfire as he and the guys sang to Jude and Melody. I'd been floored when after taking my seat next to Lily, Melody had scrambled out of her mother's lap and made a beeline for me. "Hold me, Mi," she'd demanded. I'd quickly picked her up and let her burrow into my arms. She'd once again wrapped her fingers around the strands of my hair.

Then, I watched in absolute amazement as the guys put on quite the cover of *Hey Jude*. I wondered what their fans would have thought about seeing them jamming around a bonfire in the middle of the sticks—Brayden on guitar and singing the lead, with AJ and Jake harmonizing. They even got us all singing on the "Nah nah nah nah nah nah" part.

Once again I glanced over my shoulder at the clock. I knew it was time we got up and moving. I leaned over and kissed AJ's cheek before lightly smacking his other one. "Wake up, sleepyhead."

"Mornin," he said, in a hoarse voice.

"Did I wear you out last night?"

He chuckled as he rubbed his eyes. "I think you did." Peeking at me through his hands, he added, "But I'm always up for another round."

I laughed. "Not happening for several reasons."

"Like what?"

"First of all, we have to be up to the house at noon for lunch, remember?" Last night before we left the bonfire, Abby had invited us to both breakfast and lunch, but then she recanted her breakfast invitation citing how AJ was not a morning person.

"A quickie would remedy that one."

I shook my head. "Second reason—we ran out of condoms, remember?"

"I bet Jake has a few left in his goodie drawer."

"What?"

Rolling over, AJ opened the top drawer on the nightstand on his side of the bed. He started rifling through the contents.

"What exactly is in there?" I asked, propping up on my elbows.

AJ continued rummaging around. "Hmm, here's a cock ring," he announced, holding it up and spinning it around on his finger.

I wrinkled my nose in disgust. "Don't even think that I'm letting you use that with me when I don't know who it's been on."

He chuckled. "Party pooper." He shuffled around some more before producing a set of handcuffs, and warming body oil. He raised his brows questioningly at me.

"The body oil, yes. The handcuffs are marginal."

"You're questioning the handcuffs when you tied me up on our first date?"

I laughed. "I remember."

He tossed the items onto the bed before returning to his quest. "Hell yeah!" he exclaimed, producing a sheet of four condoms.

I rolled my eyes. "Only you would get excited about that."

He dove over to cover me with his body. "I could give two shits about the rubbers. It's what I'm going to do to you when I'm wearing them that I'm excited about."

He reached in to kiss my neck when I stopped him by gripping his shoulders and pushing him away. "Babe, you can't start anything up right now. I don't want to disappoint Abby about lunch."

Groaning against my collarbone, AJ lifted his head. "She probably wouldn't mind if we were a little late."

"But between yesterday at the waterfalls and last night, I'm starting to wonder if I can walk."

An impish grin curved on his lips. "I like that. It totally compliments my dick."

"Of course you would. Now go get in the shower. I wanna grab something to drink first. All this sex has dehydrated me." I nipped at his bottom lip before rising out of the bed.

"Only if you promise to join me after."

"I will." When a triumphant look flashed on his face, I shook my head. "But only for a scrub down. I'm not sneaking into Jake and Abby's late for everyone to rag us about going at each other like rabbits."

He chuckled. "Whatever." He threw back the sheet and padded into the bathroom. As I eased into one of the robes from the bathroom, I heard the water turn on in the shower. I was halfway down the ladder when the doorknob on the front door rattled. It was probably Abby coming to make sure we were up and coming to lunch. I landed on the main floor just as the door blew open.

"Hey baby, I'm here," a dark-haired girl called. When her gaze met mine, I'm sure we were both wearing the same wide-eyed, open mouthed expressions of shock. In one hand, she held an overnight bag and then a key in the other. Realization of who she was crashed so hard over my head that I shuddered and drew my arms around me to stop my shaking. It was the same girl from last night—AJ's ex-girlfriend, Kylie.

"What are you doing here?" I demanded.

She pursed her glossed lips before replying, "I came to see AJ."

I felt my fingernails sharpening like claws at my side. "He's in the shower and not accepting visitors at the moment."

"Oh." She shifted on her feet. "This is kinda awkward."

"It wouldn't be if you left," I snapped. Internally I was doing a little victory dance for keeping my Sicilian strength and standing up the bitch. I hadn't been able to do the same thing with Erin—my ex-friend who cheated with Dev. I had been too emotionally crippled to ever confront her.

Her eyes widened at me. "Look, I didn't know he was with anyone. He certainly didn't tell me that last night—just that it wasn't a good time to talk. So I figured I would come up here to see him."

My heart clenched in my chest, and I found it hard to breathe. Why wouldn't AJ have told her he was with me? He had invited me to Eastman's as his date...he'd even chased after me when I tried to leave. He should have shot her down completely—not let her think there was some window of opportunity. Shaking my head, I replied, "Well, obviously he should have told you he was with me. Just like he is now."

Although she seemed to cower back a little, the look that flashed in Kylie's eyes told me she wasn't backing down completely. "Fine. I can see now is not a good time. I'll check in with AJ later." She waved the key in front of my face. "I know where to find him—I always do."

"Whatever."

Grabbing her suitcase, she then headed out the door, slamming it on her way out. "Bitch," I hissed under my breath. But with Kylie gone, my bravado suddenly depleted, and I was left shaking in the middle of the living room. My knees buckled and almost sunk onto the floor. "No, no, no,"

I murmured. This couldn't be happening to me—not again, not after all I'd been through. AJ couldn't be playing me...playing me *and* Kylie. Was he doing both of us at the same time? Leaving me and going to her or spending time with her when he wasn't with me? Was everything he'd said and done just a lie to keep me in his bed?

Just the thought of how things had changed between us yesterday sent bile rising in my throat. On trembling legs, I streaked over to the kitchen and heaved into the kitchen sink. Turning on the water, I numbly watched the puke go down the drain. The irony wasn't lost on me that my relationship, or what I thought I'd had with AJ, had just done the same thing symbolically.

After I swiped my hand across my mouth, I turned around to lean back against the sink. He was so smooth and used to having his way with all the ladies he wanted. Why would he want to get serious so soon with someone he barely knew? Especially with someone like me—my insecurities, my abuse, my fear of his cheating. My stomach churned again at the prospect, and I knew I needed to confront him. I had to hear the truth from his own lips.

A strange electricity rocketed through me when I took the first rung on the ladder. Anger replaced my hurt. What the hell had I been thinking that he was any different? That he could truly love me just for me. Dammit, in the end, he was just like Jason and Dev and all the other bastard men out there. He'd claimed he wasn't trying to play me for a little while.

Once I reached the top of the ladder, I was shaking out of rage, not fear. On my way to the bathroom, I spied the handcuffs on the bed. I snatched them up before stalking into the bathroom. Steam enveloped me, and it took me a moment to make out AJ's naked back and ass through the glass door.

He glanced over his shoulder and grinned. "Come on in, amorcito mio. The water is just right to warm you up—in more ways than one."

Fucking Bastard, I screamed in my mind. Twirling the handcuffs on my finger, I leaned back against the door frame. "So you were serious when you said you hadn't brought girls to Jake's house before?"

"That's right. Jake wouldn't allow it. Besides you're special, and I meant it." My heart shattered a little more at his words, but I kept my up with my wrath induced veneer. With a sexy grin, AJ crooked his finger at me. "Now get your sexy S&M ass in here with those handcuffs. I know you said we don't have a lot of time, but I guarantee I can make you come so hard you'll scream in under two minutes. Then, you can see how fast I can come. We'll make it a little game."

I stepped to the edge of the shower, flicking open the handcuffs. AJ opened the door for me. "So you like playing games, do you?"

"Oh hell, yes."

Reaching forward, I grasped his wet hand in mine. "You seem to play a pretty good game when it comes to ladies' hearts."

"I hope to have stolen yours," he said, with a wink.

The click of the handcuffs closing on AJ's wrist echoed through the shower stall. "No, but I'm pretty sure you broke it."

AJ's dark brows furrowed. "Mia, what's wrong?"

"You lied to me," I whispered.

"What are—"

"You just said that you never brought women here."

"I know. It's the truth."

"Hmm, that's funny because that ex of yours, the one who was all hugged up with you last night, just showed up to fuck you. Either she has your dick on GPS, or she knew to come here because you invited her." I gave him a rueful smile. "I guess juggling all your booty calls got a little confusing, huh?"

AJ's tanned features paled. He held up his free hand. "Mia, wait, I can explain—"

I shook my head furiously back and forth. "How could you do this to me? I let you in after swearing I wouldn't. I let you see the hell I'd been through..." My voice choked off. Dammit, I did *not* want to cry in front of him. "The hell I'm *still* in, and then you betray me like this?"

"I swear to God, Mia, I didn't know Kylie was coming."

"She had a fucking key, AJ!" I screamed.

"That's because she's Lily's sister. I didn't give it to her, I swear. She must've talked to Lily and realized that the guys and I were up here."

"Lily would have told her I was with you."

AJ grunted in frustration. "Maybe she just heard that the guys were all up here and decided to come. I don't know the fucking particulars, Mia. Go up and ask Lily yourself. What I do know is I sure as hell didn't invite her."

"So what, she just happened to waltz into Jake's house and steal a key?"

"She wouldn't have to. She's been up here with Lily and the kids before. She'd know where he hid it."

"You're a fucking liar!" I hissed, before clamping down the other cuff onto the shower head.

AJ's eyes widened before he jerked his hand back and forth. "Mia, what the fuck are you doing?" When I didn't respond, he cried, "You can't leave me like this!"

"Oh, I'm sure you won't have to wait long. If it's not Kylie, then some other scheduled piece of ass will show up soon, and you'll be out in a jiffy."

"Please don't do this. I'm telling you the truth."

Grabbing my makeup bag, I swept all my stuff off the counter and into the bag. Ignoring his constant pleading to uncuff him, my eyes swept around the bathroom to make sure I wasn't leaving anything. When I started out the door, his words froze me. "Mia, I...I love you. Please don't do this."

Tears blurred my eyes, causing my vision to cloud. Glancing over my shoulder at him, I gave him a sad smile. "Yeah, well, sometimes love just isn't enough."

And with that, I slammed the bathroom door.

Chapter Sixteen

AJ

I jumped with the harsh slamming of the bathroom door. Closing my eyes, I banged my head back against the tile. How the fuck had everything gone so wrong? As pissed as I was with Mia for leaving me in the situation I was in, my chest constricted at the thought that she had left me, especially over some stupid misunderstanding. With her being so erratic and quick to react, I didn't know how in the hell I could make this right. Part of me wondered if I should even bother trying. I didn't know if I could deal with having a trigger, or handcuff, happy girlfriend. But my mind kept going back to yesterday and last night and how things had changed between us. Mia had made me feel more than any woman had in the past. Could I really just walk away from that?

I grudgingly eyed my cell-phone perched on the edge of the sink before I jerked my wrist as hard as I could against the shower head. "FUCK!" I shouted, as slicing pain ricocheted through my hand. Pinching my eyes shut, I huffed several breaths in and out. There was no way in hell I was getting out of these handcuffs without help.

Out of my three band-mates, there was really only one I could call. With my free hand, I strained as I leaned over to try to grab it off the edge of the sink. Fumbling around, I finally grasped it. Dialing with my thumb, I brought it to my ear. Thankfully, Brayden answered on the second ring.

"Um, hey, it's me."

Brayden chuckled. "No shit, Sherlock. I kinda realized that with the caller ID."

"Oh yeah."

"Dude, where the hell are you and Mia? Abby's made her famous chili, and we're about to sit down for lunch in ten minutes." His voice had risen to be heard over the chattering crowd.

"Yeah, I don't think I can make lunch quite yet."

"What do you mean? Wait a sec." Rustling sounded in the background before a shriek came in my ear. "Oh no, missy. No more cookies until after lunch."

"Brayden," I pleaded.

"Sorry man, but Lily will have my ass if she realizes I let Melody eat half a bag of animal crackers on my watch. One sec. Allison, would you take her for a minute? Thanks." I heard the creak of the back-porch door. "Okay, I'm all yours."

"Listen, I need a favor, but I need you to keep this quiet."

"What's up?"

Closing my eyes, I gripped the phone tight against my ear. "I really don't want to go into this over the phone, so can you please come down here?"

"You sound really weird."

"Yeah, you would too if you were handcuffed to the fucking shower!" I snapped before I could stop myself.

A long silence came on the other end. "I'm sorry, but did you just say you were handcuffed to the shower?"

"Yeah," I growled.

"So what the hell do you need me for? Get the key from Mia and—"

"She's gone."

"What?"

I heaved a frustrated sigh. "Bray, I'm standing here buck-ass naked, shivering, and hanging by one arm from a shower head. Do you think I could explain all this shit later?"

"Okay, okay. I'll see you in a few," he replied, before hanging up.

I eased the phone back on the ledge of the sink. Then I eased back and waited. The moment the front door opened I knew I was in trouble. Brayden had pulled an uncharacteristically douche move—he wasn't alone.

As I heard the guys shuffling up the ladder to the loft, I closed my eyes and let loose with a string of f-bomb-laced expletives. When Brayden appeared in the doorway with Jake and Rhys, I shook my head. "I thought you promised not to say anything."

"Yeah, well, while I was on the phone with you, Mia came to the house looking for a car to borrow, but she was so upset, Abby wouldn't let her drive."

Jake shot me a death glare. "Thanks to your douche move, I didn't get lunch, and I'm going to have a pissed fiancée when she gets back."

I narrowed my eyes at him. "Oh, I'm so fucking sorry. Could we focus on the fact that I'm the one handcuffed to a shower right now?"

Rhys snapped a picture on his phone. When he glanced at it, he grimaced. "Dude, you didn't smile."

"When I get loose, I'm going to kick your fucking ass!" I growled.

Jake snickered. "I'd be a little nicer to him, man. If he were to leak that pic of you, it could be really bad for your rep. I mean, the cold water has totally obliterated your dick."

I lunged for him and Rhys with my free arm. They both clambered backwards out of my reach. "All right, knock it off, assholes," Brayden shouted over our scuffling.

"I'll go get the key," Jake said. While he went into the bedroom, I let my head bang back against the tile.

Brayden cleared his throat. "For what it's worth, I'm sorry."

Raising my head, I peered at him. "Thanks."

He held out a fuzzy towel, and I took it from him to start drying my face and what parts of my body I could reach with one arm.

"Man, what happened? You and Mia seemed so happy," Rhys said.

"Kylie showed up, used the hide-a-key, and ran into Mia downstairs."

Rhys winced as Brayden let out a low whistle. Jake, who had returned with the key, shook his head. "Damn, dude, that fucking blows."

"No shit," I replied as I toweled my hair a little more furiously. As Jake worked at getting me free, I turned to Brayden. "Did you know Kylie was coming?"

"She called Lily last night, and I guess Lily mentioned we were here." At my scowl, he held up his hands. "We sure as hell didn't invite her. Besides, I thought whatever was between you two was in the past."

The handcuffs snapped open, and I was no longer a shower prisoner. As I rubbed my aching wrist, I replied, "It was—it is. But for some reason, Kylie still seems to think I'm interested in a booty call."

Brayden grimaced. "She's a wonderful baby-sitter and

loves the hell out of my kids. But honestly, she makes the worst choices in life."

"Thanks a fucking lot, man," I grumbled.

"Nothing good ever comes from being a guy's booty call or fuck buddy, AJ," Jake argued. "I mean, hell, look at what happened to Abby because of Bree."

Rolling his eyes, Bray replied, "Yeah, well, Kylie is far from that level of psychotic."

Rhys exhaled noisily before pinning me with a hard stare. "True, but I told you back in Oklahoma City not to start that shit up again. Looks like you were all invested the first time, and now it's her this time."

Tilting my head, I gave him a 'what the fuck' look. "Seriously? So Kylie showing up is all my fault?"

"Well obviously you didn't shoot her down hard enough last night if she thought it was okay to come waltzing in here."

"What exactly did you say to her last night?" Brayden questioned.

I grimaced. "I just told her I had to go, and that I'd talk to her later."

"Dumbass," Rhys muttered.

I threw up my hands. "I didn't have a whole lot of time to stop and have a meaningful fucking conversation when I could see Mia freaking out and bailing."

"Regardless of how it happened, you really screwed up, dude. You should go after Mia," Brayden said.

I snapped the towel away from my face. "Are you shitting me? She handcuffed me to the shower!"

"You love her," Bray countered.

"I do not," I lied.

When I glanced over at Jake to see if he was buying my line, he gave me a sad smile. "Don't look to me for advice. I fucked up way too many times to count. Abby's a freakin' saint to love me, least of all forgive me."

While I was crumbling on the inside, I tried with everything I had to keep up my tough guy exterior. "Jesus guys, I still have my pride, and it's screaming at me not to chase after a woman who won't be reasoned with."

Jake crossed his arms over his chest. "This from the same guy who told me I had to do something epic to win Abby back."

"That was different," I mumbled.

"Because it was me? Because it wasn't your heart on the line?"

"I don't know." Pinching my eyes shut, I rubbed my forehead. "The bottom line is Mia isn't Abby—she has some real dark shit in her past."

"So what, you don't feel you're man enough to deal with all that?" Jake countered.

I snapped my eyes open to glare at him. "No, asshole. That's not it at all."

"Abby still has to deal with my shit—the women and my grief—, but she does it because she loves me." He smacked me hard on the back. "Maybe you should try to deal with Mia's shit because you love her."

When I glanced at Rhys and Brayden, they both nodded their heads. "Come on so we can eat some chili before it gets cold," Brayden suggested. With a wink, he added, "You're going to need your strength when it comes to getting Mia back."

"Fine. Lead the way," I replied. As I followed them to the ladder, I thought it was going to take a lot more than a little food fortification to give my body what it needed to prepare to battle Mia. Although after what she did, part of me was saying good riddance to her. But somehow I knew she was worth fighting for—that she was different than any other woman I'd ever been with. More than anything, I wanted to prove to her, that in spite of her past, some men would fight for what they wanted, and I was just that kind of man.

Chapter Seventeen

AJ

Four Months Later

Perched on the side of a hospital bed at Scottish Rite's Children's Healthcare, I drummed out a hard-core rhythm on the Guitar Hero drum-set. With his IV shackled hands, the teenage leukemia patient I was visiting kept right up with me during the more difficult parts. His name was Manuel, aka Manny, and when he'd heard a member of Runaway Train was visiting the oncology floor, he'd asked to meet me. So after I'd made some quick rounds, I went to his room so I could spend the most time with him. I was stoked as hell to see him sitting there in a Runaway Train T-shirt. He had been the drummer in a band until cancer had sidelined him. Even on the shitty Guitar Hero set, I could tell he had talent. But of course, I had to ride his ass a little.

"Manny, you're slacking, dude."

A grin stretched across his chalky face. "It ain't me, man.

You're the one dragging on the triplets."

"Ha! So you caught that?"

With a smirk that outrivaled mine, he replied, "You ain't got nothing on me, Ese."

I laughed. Visiting sick kids and teenagers in hospitals was one of the hardest and most rewarding parts of my job. I mean, it's a hell of a mind-tripping, ego-bend when you're the one to put a smile on the face of a kid who was bald from just going through a round of chemo. Or out of all the famous people in the world, they'd wanna hang out with you.

Today, however, was an unexpected visit to Scottish Rite. I'd been lounging on the couch with a beer in my hand, waiting to drink myself into a mindless stupor, when Abby had called me. I knew the moment I picked up the phone that she wanted a favor from me by the sugary-sweet tone of her voice. After what had happened at the farm with Mia, I'd been on her shit-list for a long time. Especially when I continued to be in her words, 'a stubborn asshole', for not reaching out to Mia.

What I had failed to tell her, or any of the guys for that matter, was that I had tried for days to call and text Mia, but she had never returned any of them. Finally the prideful side of me had said screw Mia and her stupid stubbornness. Unfortunately, my sappy-ass heart hadn't quite gotten the message.

Even though I sounded like a total pussy admitting it, the past four months had been the most miserable ones in my life. I played it off around the guys, acted like things were fine, and that I was the happiest motherfucker in the world. Whether they were truly buying it, I don't know. I mean, they had to notice I wasn't hooking up with any chicks. A few weeks after Mia left me, I took a blonde bombshell back to the bus with me. Even with all her assets and hard work, I couldn't get it up. All I could see was Mia in my mind. I ended up getting the chick off as fast as I could to get her the hell away from me. After that nightmare, I hadn't attempted to try again.

There was a part of me that felt like I needed some kind of penance for what I'd done. I mean, if it hadn't been for my past with Kylie and the other chicks, maybe Mia wouldn't have felt she couldn't be with me. Not to mention the ugly truth that I'd used a lot of women over the years. That fact was one of the reasons why I'd told Abby yes. Plus, I wanted back on her good side, so I'd agreed to come along with her and her brothers as they made a charity stop at Scottish Rite, which wasn't too far from my house.

I had a feeling there was more she wasn't telling me about why she was recruiting me, rather than Jake, but when the limo came by to pick me up, I didn't press her for any details. I figured if she wanted to talk about it, she would. I just hoped she didn't mention Mia. That was a subject I refused to talk about with anyone other than Jose Cuervo.

"Hey man, is your head in your ass or something?" Manny demanded.

"Huh?"

"You totally just screwed up. Like epically."

"Sorry." Fuck, I felt like a major asshole letting my mind wander to Mia when I should have been focusing on Manny.

"Yeah, well my problem might be that my head is in my ass, but I think yours lies in your sticks," I said.

"Ain't nothing wrong with these bad boys besides being a little banged up," he countered.

I held out mine to him. "These are for you."

His eyes widened. "Seriously?"

"Yep. But you gotta promise me you'll practice."

His head bobbed furiously. "I swear I will."

I pointed a finger at him. "You better." I took a card out of my pocket and gave it to him. "You've got my number now, so you better call me and let me know how it's going."

"Dude, I will. Thank you. That's awesome."

"Let's say the next time we jam, we do it at your house and not this shitty place?"

He laughed. "I'm down for that."

A nurse appeared before me, signaling it was time to go. "All right, Ese. I gotta hit the road. You take care of yourself, okay?"

"I will."

We gave each other the traditional guy hug, or pat on the back, before I went to meet the nurse in the doorway. I waved good-bye one last time to Manny.

"Ms. Renard and her brothers are in 305," the nurse informed me.

"Thank you," I replied.

Peering at the wall, I started counting down the numbers to 305. But then I heard Abby's sweet voice floating back to me, and I knew exactly where to find her. She had just finished singing when I reached the doorway. I wasn't too surprised to find her in the bed, snuggling with two bald, little girls who were absolutely enraptured by her and her singing. She kissed both their cheeks good-bye before rising out of the bed. As she powerwalked by me, I could see the tears pooling in her eyes. While her brothers started making their goodbyes to the girls, I left to go to Abby.

She hadn't gotten far down the hall. "Mi amor," I said softly, as I caught up to her.

"I'm okay," came her weak reply.

Side-stepping in front of her, I drew her into my arms. "Hey, it's okay to cry. This shit is hard."

Fisting the front of my shirt in her hands, she sobbed into my chest. Although I knew the little girls had gotten to her, I could tell that this was about more than just them. It most likely had to do with Susan, Jake's mom, and the grief that both she, and Jake, were still experiencing.

The sound of her brothers behind us caused her to tense in my arms. At their questioning expressions, I said, "Go on down to the limo. We'll be down in a few."

Micah nodded. "See you there."

When they were safely on the elevator, she pulled away. "Sorry about that," she sniffled.

I cupped her chin, bringing her gaze to mine. "Hey, you have nothing to apologize for. Okay? You know I'm always here for you."

After wiping her eyes, she gave a quick jerk of her head. "I know." She leaned up on her tip-toes to kiss my cheek. "I've missed you," she whispered.

Her words caused my chest to clench. "I've missed you, too."

That was all that had to be said for me to know that everything was fine between us. As we started down the hallway to the elevators, Abby slid her arm around my waist. She peered up at me and smiled. "Thanks again for coming with me today since Jake had to bail."

"Hey, I was glad to do it." When I punched the down arrow button, I kissed the top of her head. "Jake's still having a hard time with hospitals, huh?"

She nodded as we stepped onto the elevator. "I don't know how to help him, AJ."

"Just be there for him. That's all you can do."

"I will."

"You mean everything in the world to him, and he's lucky to have you and your love."

"Thanks, AJ."

I smiled at her. "No problem."

We stepped out of the hospital into the bright sunshine. Gabe, Eli, and Micah were standing outside the limo waiting on us. "Ready to head back?"

"Yep," I replied.

As I waited my turn to get inside the limo, I gazed ahead. When the realization of where we were washed over me, I felt like someone had sent a roundhouse kick straight to my gut. St. Joseph's loomed tauntingly at me from across the street. Like a sappy-ass chick, a rush of memories flooded my mind of meeting Mia for the first time.

A gentle nudge caused me to snap out of my thoughts. Abby stared up at me with a knowing smile. "Go see her," she urged.

I shook my head. "That's ancient history."

"Give me a break, AJ. You were just staring at a hospital building with a sad, lost puppy dog expression. Mia can't be history when you obviously still care for her."

"She handcuffed me to a fucking shower," I countered.

"In her mind, she had a good reason."

"Oh really?"

Abby nodded. "Regardless of whether it was a

misunderstanding or not, your past indiscretions with women came back to hurt a very vulnerable woman."

"Thank you, Dr. Phil."

Abby narrowed her eyes at me. "Watch it, Resendiz. Don't forget I know you better than you think I do. And that forty-five minute drive to Mia's house gave me a lot of time to get to know *her* and exactly how *she* was feeling."

I raked my hands through my hair. "It's too late. I didn't tell you at the time, but I did try to call and text her. She wouldn't answer."

"Maybe what you need to say should be said in person." Abby reached over to palm my cheek. "You know I love you, AJ, and I want more than anything for you to be happy. And while you may think that what happened wasn't that big a deal and Mia should have forgiven you, I disagree."

My brows shot up in surprise. "Do you?"

"Yes, I do." Abby's gaze went to the glittering diamond on her hand. "Most people would have given up on Jake—they would have never tried as hard as I did to forgive him and give him a second chance...or many chances." She then stared pointedly at me. "But then at the same time, he proved to me that in his own way he was working his ass off to show me how sorry he was and how much he truly cared for me. So maybe you need to step up and show a little more to Mia. Maybe she wants to reconcile with you, but she doesn't know how to go about trying. Maybe she needs some grand and huge gesture from you to prove that you're not like all the other assholes she's had the misfortune of being involved with."

Gabe poked his head out of the limo window. "You guys coming?"

At my hesitation, Abby patted my back. "You know a wise woman once said that fate had a funny way of intervening in our lives."

"Susan said that," I replied in a strangled voice.

"Yes, she did."

"Fuuuuccck," I groaned.

Abby laughed. "Should I take that as an 'I'll see you guys later. Thanks for letting me see the error of my ways' curse?"

"Yeah."

"What about getting home? Want me to send the limo back for you?"

I shook my head. "No, I'll hopefully be leaving with Mia...if not, I'll get a cab."

Abby reached up again on her tip-toes to kiss my cheek. After playfully ruffling my hair, she said, "Good luck."

"Thanks, mi amor. I'm going to need it."

When I stepped off the elevator onto Mia's floor, my heart started pounding so loud in my ears it drowned out all the noise around me. The stretch of hallway to the nurse's station seemed to draw on forever. As I drew closer to it, Mia's friend, Dee, stepped out a patient's room with a chart in the crook of his arm. When he saw me, I grimaced and prepared for a verbal tongue lashing.

Instead, his dark eyes lit up. "Well, well, sweet cheeks, aren't you a sight for sore eyes?"

I chuckled. "Thanks. Is Mia here?"

"She's doing some inventory in the medicine room right now." He then crooked his finger. "Come with me."

"Okay, thanks." I fell in step behind him. "Is she...?"

Glancing over his shoulder, Dee replied, "Going to bitch slap you the minute she sees you?"

Damn, he was good. Or maybe it was that he knew Mia so well. "Yeah, something like that."

Dee spun around, causing me to skid to a stop. "I'm gonna shoot straight with you, pretty boy. I wanted your balls on a skewer for a long time for what you did to Mimi."

"Dude, I tried to tell her I was sorry a million times. She wouldn't talk to me. I swear, I—"

He held up a hand to silence me, and surprisingly, I shut the fuck up. "Yeah, I didn't know that then, but she finally admitted it to me about three months ago." He took a step closer to me. "I don't really know you that well, but what I do know seems intrinsically decent despite you being a famous rock-star. I'm hoping that you've shown up here today because you miss Mia, and you want to fight for her—despite what you might have going on in your personal life."

My brows furrowed in confusion. "Wait a minute. You lost me on the personal life stuff."

He rolled his eyes. "Fine, if you wanna play coy, whatever."

"But I—"

"Look, just get in there and fight for our girl, okay?"

I resisted the urge to salute him. Instead, I nodded. "I will. I swear."

"Good." He then produced a key card from his pocket, which unlocked a door behind the nurse's station. "Go get her, tiger," he said, before smacking me on the ass.

Already on edge, I jumped out of my skin. At the same time, it felt good having Dee on my side—like I had passed some test. But like an absolute pussy, my hand shook as I opened the door. Mia stood in front of large cart filled with different medical supplies. My heart thudded against my breast bone at the sight of her. Four months later and she was even more beautiful and sexy than I remembered—even outfitted in her standard green scrubs. Her long, dark hair was swept away from her face in a twist, although a few wispy strands had escaped. She was eyeing a label on a bottle. "Dee, we're getting low on Heparin. You should call the pharmacy and order up some more units."

"It's not Dee," I said softly.

The sound of my voice caused her to jerk her head up. The bottle she was inventorying fell from her hand and smashed onto the floor.

"W-What are you doing here?" she questioned.

"I was in the neighborhood and thought I would come see you." When her brows rose in suspicion, I replied, "Oka, so maybe I was over at Scottish Rite meeting with some fans."

"Oh," she murmured.

I nervously raked my hand through my hair before taking a few tentative steps closer to Mia. "I'm just going to shoot straight with you, okay? When I was over there and saw St. Joe's, I realized how much I missed you and wanted to see you."

"You did?" she asked, her voice vibrating with emotion.

"Yeah."

The closer I got to her, the more panicked Mia appeared. "AJ, there's something I need to tell you."

"That you've missed me?" I teased, hoping to ease the tension in the air that you couldn't have sawed through with a chainsaw.

"Yes," she whispered. "But...something else."

"That you're sorry for not answering my calls and texts?" She nodded. "But most of all, you're sorry you left me naked and handcuffed to a shower."

She closed her eyes as if she was in pain. "Yes. I'm so, so sorry."

Suddenly, I couldn't get to her quick enough. Bounding around the edge of the cart, I reached out for her, but she jerked away, backing up into the wall. Fear and worry raged in her eyes, and although I was glad to see she didn't appear pissed, I couldn't help but feel something was off. When her hand flew to her abdomen as if she were shielding herself, my gaze roamed down her body to where her once baggy scrubs pulled tighter over her slightly rounded stomach—a stomach that had been noticeably flatter when we were together. It was at that moment that every molecule in my body felt like it exploded. "Holy shit," I murmured.

When I snapped my gaze back to Mia's, tears pooled in her eyes. "I'm sorry, AJ. I came to tell you—"

Even though I knew the answer, I demanded, "You're pregnant with my baby?"

"Yes," she replied as tears slid down her cheeks.

"Holy shit," I repeated. The room began spinning around me. Mia's voice sounded muffled like I was under the surface of the water. And the next thing I knew I was falling back while the world around me went dark.

Chapter Eighteen

Mia

Three Months Earlier

Staring down at the nightmarish white stick, I felt bile once again rise in my throat. "No, please no," I moaned. I gripped the sides of the marble bathroom counter to keep me from sinking to the floor. With my erratic cycles, I hadn't been on heightened alert when my period was a week or two late. But when I started creeping into the three and a half week mark, I began to panic, which caused me to swing by Walgreens on the way home from work to buy two pregnancy tests.

I was now holding positive test number two in my hand. Part of me wanted to go back to the store to see if the third test would be the charm and somehow I wouldn't be pregnant. How the hell was this possible? Just remembering how AJ and I used a condom each and every time we had sex caused a reel of erotic images of our sexcapdes to run through my mind. A flush filled my cheeks as warmth flooded my core. But then, one of those images sent me racing forward to the toilet and heaving up the contents of my stomach.

In the backroom at Eastman's, we'd been too caught up in the angry, make-up sex to remember a condom. He'd pulled out. Although my medical training taught me that not enough sperm resided in pre-come and the pull-out method was fairly effective, I couldn't help thinking that had to be the time. "Oh God," I muttered, placing my hands firmly on the edge of the toilet bowl to steady myself from passing out. Flipping down the lid, I eased down onto the toilet and like so many nights lately, I began to cry.

Just when I thought I had clawed myself out of the greatest emotional hell of my life with Mama Sofia's death and Dev's betrayal, I slammed right back down to rock bottom with what happened with AJ. After Abby brought me home, she'd waited with me until Dee could come over—I was that hysterical. I took the next two days off work and made back to back emergency appointments with my therapist.

As much as I hated to admit it, I was pretty surprised AJ tried so hard in the beginning to get me to talk to him with his many phone calls and texts. Even if I wanted to believe it was just a misunderstanding with Kylie like he claimed, I knew it wouldn't be the last time we were put into that situation. If I took him back, it would only be a matter of time before some other woman from his past, or maybe even the present, came back to haunt us—or more importantly *me*.

In the end, I wasn't like Abby and Lily—I'd been through too much heartbreak to be a strong enough woman for a rock star. And while I wanted to hate AJ, I couldn't. More than anything, I wanted to feel like I was making a sacrifice for him—I cared about him enough to know he deserved someone better, someone who wasn't emotionally crippled by their past.

The doorbell ringing brought me out of my thoughts. On shaky legs, I followed Jack Sparrow down the hallway. With trembling hands, I threw open the front door. Dee pursed his lips at me before holding up one finger. "Baby girl, this better be hella important because I just left a partially satiated marine in my bed."

"I'm sorry. You know I wouldn't have called you unless it was a matter of life and death."

Dee swept his hand to his chest. "Wait, something hasn't happened to Duke, has it?"

"No, it's nothing like that." I chewed my bottom lip, uncertain of how I was going to break the news to him.

He growled in frustration. "Well, for fuck's sake, Mimi. Spit it out!"

Unable to speak, I thrust the dreaded white stick I was

still clutching in his face. His nose wrinkled momentarily in confusion before he realized what it read. His deep brown eyes widened to the size of the salad plates at Mama Sofia's. "Holy shit, you're pregnant?"

I'd been holding the waterworks back as long as I could with him. Just hearing Dee say the word 'pregnant' caused the dam to burst, and I began sobbing hysterically.

"Hey now, don't cry. Dee's here." He stepped into the foyer and wrapped his arms around me. Although I felt comforted by his gesture, it just made me cry even harder. Dee closed the front door behind us and steered me over to the couch. "Shh, it's okay, Mimi," he crooned, rubbing wide circles across my back.

When I'd finally stop sobbing and my breath had started coming in hiccupping little pants, I pulled away to look at Dee. "I'm sorry for calling you away from the hot marine and then going psycho on you."

He kissed my cheek. "Don't you dare apologize for either of those things. You're my best friend in the whole, wide world, Mimi. When you need me, I'm here, no matter what condition you're in."

My chin trembled at his words. "Thank you," I murmured.

"You're welcome, luvie." Taking my hand in his, he squeezed it tight. "So you know I gotta ask this next question. Is it...?"

I rolled my eyes. "Of course it's AJ's."

Dee held his hands up defensively. "Well, excuse me that I don't keep a GPS device on your vagina."

His comment made the corners of my lips quirk up in spite of how awful I felt. "After all these years, you should know that if there's any action going on in my vagina, you usually know about it."

With a smirk, he replied, "Normally I would agree with you, but you just fucking blindsided me considering being pregnant is the biggest thing to hit your lady parts ever!"

A snort escaped my lips. "Only you could make jokes at a time like this."

He grinned. "That's why you need me."

"No, that's why I love you," I replied, my voice choking off with emotion.

Dee gave me a quick peck on the lips. "I love you more, baby girl." We sat in silence for a few minutes with the just the sound of Jack Sparrow's purring and my sniffling echoing through the room. "So....you're really pregnant?" He exhaled noisily. "What are you going to do about it?"

"You mean am I going to keep it, give it up, or...?"

"Or have an abortion." He cupped my chin, forcing me to look at him. "You know that you can do that, right?"

"I know I can, but..."

"But what?"

Unconsciously my hand went to rest against my abdomen. "I want this baby."

"Da fuck did you just say?" Dee asked incredulously.

Overwhelmed by my emotions, I merely bobbed my head. In a way, I was as stunned as Dee was by my admission. When I was younger, I always saw myself married with children. I knew that someday I would want a baby—I just never imagined it would be now.

Dee continued staring open-mouthed at me. "Mimi, you don't know the first thing about raising a kid."

"Thanks for the vote of confidence," I snapped, realizing just how quickly pregnancy hormones could have you expressing psycho emotions.

Dee sighed. "Seriously, besides being around your cousins, you've never even acted like you cared for children that much."

"But that doesn't mean I can't be a good mother." At his skeptical expression, I countered, "Have I ever once said I didn't want to have kids someday?"

"No, but—"

"I'm in a good place in my life to have a baby."

Crossing his arms over his chest, he countered, "Unmarried and alone?"

I huffed out a frustrated breath. "I meant, I'm twenty-eight, not eighteen. I've been to college—I have my masters. I make good money. I can support this kid."

"I'm not arguing with that, Mimi."

"Then what?" I knew if I was going to do this baby thing, I

wanted and needed Dee's support.

Dee shrugged. "I dunno. It's just hard for me to think of you with a kid."

Staring down at my hands, I thought of the one person who believed I would be a good mother. "Mama Sofia saw me with children."

"How do you know?"

"She told me a few months before she died that one day I'd be a family matriarch just like she was. That she prayed to the saints to bless me with a family." My throat burned with the sobs I tried desperately to choke down. The agony of grief once again wrapped me in its death-like vise as the hard realization that the one person I needed more than anything right now was gone.

Dee reached over to cup my cheek. "Is that why you want this baby so much? Because you're still so emotionally wrecked from Sofia's death?"

"Thanks for making me sound like a selfish nut-job," I hissed.

He groaned. "Jesus, if that test hadn't told me you were pregnant, I'd know it from the crazy mood swings."

"I'm sorry. Truly, I am. But for whatever reason, I know I want to have this baby, no matter how hard it's going to be."

Dee leaned back against the couch cushion, surmising my words. After what felt like a small eternity, he smiled. "Then, I'm happy for you."

"Really?"

"Yeah."

With a squeal, I dove over to wrap my arms around his neck. I squeezed him tight. "Thank you, Dee. You make me so, so happy."

"Ease up, baby girl. I just said I was happy for you, not that I was gonna move in and help you raise the kid. Don't even think about me changing shitty diapers."

I laughed. "I don't care about any of that."

"Bullshit. You'll change your tune and be expectin' me to stay over nights or watch the kid during the day so you can get your beauty sleep."

Raising my brows, I countered, "And you just might find yourself so in love with my little spawn that you want to spend all of your free time here."

"Mmm, hmm, we'll see about that." But his lips did curve up in a smile like he was enjoying the thought of being around my baby.

"If it's a boy, I think I'll name if after you. Derwin Martinelli has a nice ring to it, doesn't it?" I teased.

Dee shook his head. "You should be thinking about naming it after its father." He shot me a pointed look. "And just what about Mr. AJ? Where does he fit into all this?"

The happy little bubble I'd built around myself deflated at the mention of *him*. Resting my elbows on my knees, I then cradled my head in my hands. "I don't know."

"He needs to know, Mimi."

I peeked at Dee through my fingers. "I'm not sure after leaving him handcuffed to a shower that he's going to be really glad to see me or want to hear the joyous news that he knocked me up."

"You won't know until you talk to him." When I snorted contemptuously, Dee shook his head. "AJ was a lot of things, but a total uncaring bastard wasn't one of them."

Deep down, I knew he was right. AJ had too good a heart to ever be an asshole to me if I was pregnant with his child. My mind flashed back to that weekend at the farm—the way he had interacted with Jude and Melody. He was good with kids, and he would be a good father.

With a resigned sigh, I nodded. "Okay, okay, I'll get in touch with him."

"Good," Dee replied.

"But only after I'm through the first trimester."

He narrowed his eyes. "And why the fuck should you wait?"

"I've got to be six weeks along as it is. It won't hurt to wait to tell him until I know I'm not going to miscarry. That way I'll know for sure that everything is okay with the baby before I ruin his life with the news."

"Or make him the happiest man on earth," Dee countered.

"Yeah, I'm not going to hold my breath on that one."

Dee crossed his arms over his chest and huffed out a frustrated breath. "Let's call this what it really is. You're afraid of becoming your mother."

"Excuse me?"

"You're afraid that AJ is going to think you're trying to trap him into marriage just like your gold-digging mother did with Duke."

I rolled my eyes. "She may have given birth to me, but she's never been my mother. That role was Mama Sofia's."

"Admit it, Mimi."

I threw up my hands in surrender. "Fine. Yes, of course I'm worried about that. How can I not be? After ignoring his initial text and calls, I show up after not seeing or talking to him for two months to tell him news that financially, if not emotionally, binds him to me for the rest of our lives?' Yeah, call me crazy for worrying about that!"

Dee's eyes widened. "You never told me he tried to call or text you."

Shit. I had shamelessly kept that little tidbit of information to myself. Mainly because I was a bitch and knew it would make AJ appear more sympathetic to Dee. "Yeah, he did." At Dee's epically pissed pursed lips, I sighed. "He never came to see me or sent me flowers or anything. Just a few phone calls and texts. In the end, they didn't change anything about our situation."

"If it weren't for your delicate condition, I would spank you right now for being a withholding little cunt!"

Grimacing, I covered my ears. "You know I hate that word."

Dee snorted. "Which is exactly why I used it."

"Testa di cazzo," I grumbled.

"Hey, truth hurts, baby girl."

"It doesn't change anything really," I repeated, more for myself than for him.

Crossing his arms over his chest, he sighed. "Fine. But let's get this straight. I'm going to be on your ass constantly about how far along you are. The instant you hit that second trimester mark, you're going to find out where in the world AJ is, and we're going there. ASAP. Got it?"

"Yeah, I got it."

"Good."

I smiled at his smug expression. "I'm okay now if you need to get back to your marine."

"Hmm, maybe I could take him some dinner from Mama Sofia's. On the house?"

I nodded. "It would be my pleasure."

Dee rose off the couch. "Good. While I call him and see what he wants, you freshen up."

"Why?"

"Because I'm going down there with you, so you can tell Duke the joyous news."

313

My breath hitched at the thought. "You don't think I—"

"Nope. You only get one 'Get out of telling a dude I'm pregnant card' and that goes to Mr. Baby Daddy."

I laughed. "Fine then. As long as you're with me."

"Of course, I am, baby girl."

Rising off the couch, I kissed his cheek. "Thank you."

When I pulled away, he grinned. "Now that I think about it, Mr. Marine and I are going to need some Tiramisu to go along with dinner—maybe some Mia's Moose, too."

"As long as you don't plan to tell me what you're going to do sexually with that dessert, I'll be happy to get it for you."

With a wink, Dee replied, "My lips are sealed."

Chapter Nineeen

Mia

One Month Earlier

The swarming noise of women's chattering, shrieking, and giggling like idiots filled my ears. All the while the smell of sweat, cheap perfume, and beer stung my nose, making me nauseated. Somehow I found myself jostling around backstage at a Runaway Train concert. Abby and her brothers were already performing on stage. Her voice was the only soothing sound filling the air around me. "What are all these ho's doing back here?" Dee asked, as we trailed along behind some random roadie.

"I don't think I want to know," I muttered.

"Hmmph," he replied.

After my three month check-up showed everything looked good with the baby, I booked a flight to Jersey City for both myself and Dee. It made the most sense to attend Runaway Train's concert there, so we could stay with some of my dad's relatives. When it came down to actually getting to AJ, I knew there was no way in hell I was reaching out to Abby or Lily. They would try to do some major intervention. I wanted it on my terms, in the least romantic way possible, which was why I planned to ambush him at a show. In the end, I knew there was one person who would help me without asking a lot of questions, and that was Frank. He had been thrilled to hear from me. I told him I wanted to surprise AJ and the others, and he promised to keep it a secret.

He had left passes for us at the ticket office and then had the random roadie meet up with us at the gate. Now as we got closer to the inner sanctum, aka backstage, I could see Frank waiting at the top of a long hallway for us. With his usual beaming smile, he held out his arms to me. I leaned in to hug him as carefully as I could to conceal my growing bump. "You're looking good," I said as I pulled away.

"Thank you. I'm feeling good, too." He did a quick sweep of me from head to toe. "You're looking mighty fine yourself."

"Aw, thank you."

His brows lined together as he surveyed me again. "You know, there's something different about you."

I sucked in a breath and prayed he wasn't about to go for the old, 'you look like you're glowing' pregnancy cliché. "I'm seeing a nutritionist," I blurted. When Dee gave me a funny look, I added, "Lots of vitamins and organic food—that sorta thing."

"Well, even though it doesn't sound like much fun, you should totally keep doing it because you look absolutely beautiful."

"You're too sweet," I replied, shuffling my coat to cover my bump.

Frank glanced down at his watch. "I better get you back there if you want to see the guys. It won't be long before they'll be taking the stage."

When Frank opened a door on the right side of the hallway, it took everything within me not to bolt and run. After all that had happened between us, how was I going to see AJ again? The last time he'd seen me I'd been handcuffing him to a shower in a fit of jealous rage. Now I was not only going to have to face him, but also tell him I was pregnant. Dee's hand pressed against my shoulder blade and leaned in close to me. "You can do this, baby girl."

"Thanks," I whispered.

I finally stepped forward into the room on my trembling legs. People were milling around everywhere, but through the crowd, I immediately honed in on AJ. My heart did a ridiculous flip-flop as my stomach lurched into my throat.

His back was to me, and he was encircled by a group of finely dressed men and women. It was certainly a change of pace to see men in suits and women in dresses. Unblinking and unmoving, I stared at AJ—remembering exactly what my fingers felt like in his dark hair and how it felt to grip onto his broad shoulders. To my horror, one of his arms was slung around a brunette's waist while his other arm held her extended hand. As he pivoted around the group, I got a glimpse of him showing off something on her hand.

A ring.

A very sparkly diamond ring on her left hand.

The others around him were grinning, and I could read their lips saying, "Congratulations".

He was engaged.

And although I couldn't see her, I just knew the brunette had to be Kylie. Her hair color and her height were exactly the same.

I whirled around to go and ran right into Dee. His gaze wasn't on me, but instead, he was staring dumbfounded at AJ. "Oh motherfucking shit," he muttered.

"Let's go!" I cried.

When he remained rooted to the floor, I pounded his chest with one of my fists. "Move," I ordered.

"Don't you want to—"

"No, no, no! I just want to get the fuck out of here." My voice choked out with the sobs that were racking my chest. Once I got out in the hallway, I collapsed back against a wall and then the hysterics overtake me.

Dee pulled me into his strong embrace. "Mimi, you can still go talk to him."

"And ruin his life?" I hiccupped.

"It might not be true. I mean, I haven't heard anything in the news about him being serious about a girl."

I shook my head. "Their PR people kill any stories like that so they can appear more desirable to their female fans." Pulling away, I wiped the tears from my cheeks with the back of my hand. "Jesus, Dee, he had an arm around a girl sporting a fat-ass diamond. I think there is no other truth, but that he's engaged." Stormy emotions of anger, bitterness and regret raged through me. "God, I was so stupid to think he wouldn't move on. Or more importantly go back to his old girlfriend."

Dee cupped my cheek. "I'm so fucking sorry, Mimi."

"It's for the best really. He deserves to be happy."

"You could have made him happy," Dee argued.

"Not really. Not with all my baggage and shit. In the end, it would've been too much for him."

"So you're never going to tell him about the baby?"

Part of me wanted to conceal it from AJ forever. That way I wouldn't have to ever see or hear from him ever again. But deep down, I knew that could never happen. He was a famous musician who would always be thrust in my face. At the same time, I knew I couldn't deny my child its father.

I drew in a ragged breath. "I'll let the dust clear on his engagement, and then I'll call him." Dee gave me a skeptical look. "I won't be selfish and deny him the chance to be a father. I promise."

"Okay then." Dee glanced around. "Are you ready to get the hell out of here?"

"Yes. Please."

As we started down the hallway, Frank stepped in front of us. A smile stretched across his face. "Boy, I bet AJ was sure surprised to see you, huh?"

I exchanged a look with Dee. How was I supposed to play this one? "Um, he looked kinda busy, so we'll catch him after the show."

Frank's salt and pepper brows furrowed. "Oh okay."

Wagging a finger, I said, "Don't say anything. Surprise, remember?"

"Sure, sure. My lips are sealed."

"Thanks, Frank. Take care." I gave him a quick hug before grabbing Dee by the sleeve and hauling ass down the hallway before I ran into anyone else.

"You think Frank's not going to ask AJ about seeing you?"

"I'm hoping he'll forget...or that AJ just won't give a shit about me with his happily-ever-after."

"We'll see," he replied before we hustled outside of the arena and started going against the stream of fans rushing inside.

Two nights later, I was back home and at work. There hadn't been any calls from AJ, so I assumed he either didn't know I had shown up or he didn't care. I secretly hoped for the second because it made it easier to turn off the feelings I had for him. Pregnancy hormones didn't make matters easier either. I cried way more than I wanted to admit.

It was a relatively slow and quiet afternoon as Dee and I sat working on charts at the nurse's station.

"Oh hell no. You gotta be fuckin' kidding me."

Giggling, I didn't bother glancing up from my paperwork. "Don't tell me that Mr. Johnson has decided to take another nude stroll down the hall?" When Dee didn't reply, I nibbled thoughtfully on the tip of my pen. "What is it about our post-surgery male patients that make them all go a little crazy? Just for once, I'd like to see some female patient go ape-shit on her meds."

"It ain't Mr. Johnson flashing his Johnson."

"Oh?"

Raising his voice, Dee practically shrieked, "No, it's some crazy motherfucker who needs to turn his lying, cheating ass around right this instant!"

Whirling around in my chair, I couldn't believe he stood framed in the doorway, a bouquet of my favorite flowers—pink roses—draped in his arms.

"Dev," I whispered.

My hand swept over my chest, my fingers digging into the

fabric of my scrubs over my heart. After seeing AJ with a fiancée, I didn't think my ticker could take much more shock. Yet, there he was standing right in front of me as if it were only yesterday we were a couple. His black hair still fell in waves over his forehead while his chocolate brown eyes still appeared warm and inviting. Of course, there were dark circles underneath his eyes that I didn't remember being there before.

He gave me a hesitant smile. "Hey, baby."

While Dee growled, I merely cocked my brows. "*Baby*? You have the nerve after everything you put me through to show up at my work and call me 'baby'?"

Dev's broad shoulders slumped a little, and he swayed nervously on his feet. "Look, I'm sorry. I didn't mean to show up here and upset you."

"Too fucking late," I snapped.

"Can I just talk to you for a minute?" he pleaded.

"Mimi, please let me call security and have them haul his sorry ass out of here," Dee said.

I patted Dee on the shoulder. "That won't be necessary. I can handle the lying, cheating, bastard myself, thank you." Narrowing my eyes at Dev, I said, "Leave now."

"Mia, please, just give me five minutes."

For reasons I couldn't possibly understand, I rose out of my chair and motioned to the break room. "Five minutes and then you get the hell out of here, capiche?" Dev nodded before glancing nervously over at Dee as if he feared Dee was going to come barreling over to kick his ass. Instead, Dee just glowered at Dev until he disappeared into the break-room. Before I closed the door behind us, Dee wagged his finger at me. "Don't you dare say or do anything with him that will make me hurt you later."

I scowled at him. "Give me a little credit," I snapped, before I slammed the door.

Over the last year, I'd gone over in my mind many, many times how I would react to seeing or talking to Dev again. After I'd caught him and Erin going at it on my kitchen counter, I'd never spoken to him again. I'd never sought out the reasons why he had done it. I'd just cut him out of my life as best I could. Sound familiar?

Of all the scenarios of me seeing him again, most involved me going ape-shit on his ass, including nailing him in the balls repetitively. But now, I felt nothing more than slight anger, tinged with bitterness. And the fact I wasn't still harboring homicidal feelings towards him really pissed me off

Crossing my arms over my chest, I said, "You wanted to talk so talk."

"I guess you heard Erin and I broke up."

I rolled my eyes. "Yeah, I was real heartbroken for you."

"Mia—"

"I heard she cheated on you." When Dev didn't deny it, I snorted. "Hmm, the old adage of if they cheat with you, they'll cheat on you, huh?"

"I guess," he murmured.

"I would say I was surprised that she turned so quickly on you, but all the old crew knew what a cheap slut she'd always been." I shook my head at him. "But yet, rumor through the grapevine has it you wanted to marry her—someone who was a complete one eighty from me. And so soon. I mean, Jesus, we dated for three years before you gave me a ring, but with her, you were barely together five months."

Dev ran a hand through his jet black hair. "I was a fool. And as for marrying her, that was just bullshit to appease my family. They'd been on my back forever about settling down."

"With me," I spat.

"Yes, they wanted me to marry you. They loved you as much as I did." He drew in a ragged breath. "It's a lousy excuse, Mia, but the pressure to settle down and be what my family expected me to be, it broke me. That's why I let Erin get to me."

"Ah, so she made the first move."

He shrugged. "I let it happen—I let it screw up the best thing I ever had. You." He exhaled a ragged breath. "But when it all comes down to it, what does it matter who started it?"

"I don't know. It's an easier pill to swallow thinking you weren't out scoping chicks—that the new piece of ass just fell in your lap."

Dev sighed. "Things were rough between us, Mia. You know that. After your grandmother died, you shut me out. You—"

My hand flew up to silence him. "Don't you dare bring Mama Sofia's death into this! Regardless of whether I was in a fucking grief storm, you should have been there for me, standing by me and supporting me." My voice wavered, and I grimaced at giving him those emotions. "That's when I needed you most," I whispered.

"I'm sorry." He eased the bouquet of roses he still clutched onto the table. "What can I say, but that I was an immature prick who wanted all your attention? When you couldn't give it to me, I pulled an utterly selfish and despicable move by cheating on you." He took a tentative step closer to me. "Regardless of what happened, I never stopped loving you, Mia. Not one day went by when I didn't regret what I did, how I hated myself for hurting you." He drew in a ragged breath. "How I wished it was you I was making love to, not Erin."

A shudder rippled through me at his words, and I despised myself for letting my firm resolve waver. I took a step back from him. "Don't do this. Not now. It's too fucking late."

"It's never too late to right a wrong, is it?"

"You broke my heart, Dev!" I cried, my voice raising an octave, causing me to betray my emotions.

"Please," he said in a half whisper.

"Please what?" I demanded.

"Please give me another chance."

My mouth dropped open in disbelief. "You don't mean that."

"Yes, I do."

I shook my head. "You only think you want me back. Erin left you a month ago, and you're reeling about being all alone."

"No, that's not it. If it was just about being alone, I'd go out and find some new piece of ass." He pinned me with his gaze. "But I'm here right now. Putting my heart out on the line, for you."

"You got spooked about marriage and us before. You would do the same thing again."

"Not with you. If you were gracious enough to give me a second chance, it would never, ever happen."

I gave a mirthless laugh. "Yeah, well, how about this one? I'm pregnant."

Dev's serious expression turned over to shock. He blinked rapidly as he stared at me. His gaze fell on my abdomen, and for the first time, he noticed the bump beneath my baggier scrubs. "Um...wow."

"Told you. You're completely and totally spooked."

"I won't lie to you that I'm surprised. I mean, when we were together, you were never the maternal type."

"That's true, but people change."

"*Yes*, they do," he emphasized, and his meaning wasn't lost on me. When I didn't reply, he asked, "What about the father?"

I shifted my gaze to stare down at the floor. "We broke up before I found out I was pregnant."

"And he doesn't want to be in the baby's life?"

"He doesn't know yet...I don't know if he'll ever know," I admitted.

"So, then I do have a chance with you," he said softly.

I snapped my head up to glare at him. "Just because I have a kid on the way, doesn't mean I'm weak enough to take you back. I don't need the baby's father, and I sure as hell don't need you."

"But couldn't you want me?" Dev took another step closer to me. I tried ignoring how my body reacted to him being closer. Fucking pregnancy hormones! "I know you're strong enough to do all this on your own, but you don't have to. I'm here for you, Mia. I want you—with all my heart and soul."

"No."

"I'm not saying you should take me back today. Let me work hard for you—let me earn your trust back. Can't you at least let me try?"

At his words, I remembered AJ hugged up to Kylie, the diamond ring on her hand glittering in the light. Pain raged through my chest, and for a moment, I fought to breathe. Through my own stubbornness, I had fucked things up for us. There was no going back with AJ even if I wanted to. I would tell him about the baby eventually, and he would be its father. But he would never be my lover again...my boyfriend...my husband. He belonged to someone else now. And even though I knew I had loved him—that I loved him still—in the end, I'd only had two weeks with him.

I'd had three years with Dev.

Fate and destiny were two things Italians believed very strongly in. Maybe my destiny had just walked back into my life.

I took a step toward Dev. "If you think you're just going to waltz back into my life and have me fall into your waiting arms, you're fucking crazy. You want me after everything you've done, then you're going to crawl on hands and knees through broken glass to get me." I crossed my arms over my chest. "And that's without any promises of reconciliation."

He surveyed my words thoughtfully. "I'll do whatever I have to do, Mia. I swear that. And when it's all said and done, I will prove to you that I'm worthy of you."

I narrowed my eyes at him. "We'll see."

Chapter Twenty

AJ

"AJ?"

At the sound of Mia's voice, my eyelids popped open. Staring up at the tiles on the ceiling, I groaned as my head throbbed like a motherfucker.

"Are you okay?" Mia questioned softly.

My gaze spun wildly around the room. I was still in my clothes, but I was reclining in a hospital bed. "What the fuck?" I muttered.

"You're at St. Joseph's. You fainted and hit your head."

The moment my eyes locked on Mia's concerned filled brown ones it all came back to me in a rush. My gaze left her eyes to trail down her body. It froze on her swollen belly—the place where *my* child grew.

"How far along are you?" I demanded in a hoarse voice.

Licking her lips nervously, Mia replied, "Nineteen weeks."

My fists clenched involuntarily at my sides. "You're

almost five months pregnant, and the thought that I should know never crossed your mind?" I growled.

The tone of my voice caused her to jump, and remorse instantly filled me that I'd scared her. "I'm sorry, Mia. I didn't mean to say it like that."

"I know."

Wincing, I pulled myself up in the bed. "Do you have any idea what this is all like for me?"

Tears sparkled in her eyes. "I'm sorry. I never wanted to hurt you."

I barked a laugh. "I would think after handcuffing me to a shower there was some part of you that wanted me to suffer."

She shook her head. "I was angry with you then." Glancing down at the floor, she murmured, "More than anything, I was hurt."

"So because of some misunderstanding you would be so vengeful as to not tell me I had a child on the way?"

Mia jerked her head up and glared at me. "I did try to tell you. I came to your show in Jersey City."

"Wait, what?"

"It's true that I didn't tell you right away. I wanted to wait until I was sure I wasn't going to miscarry. Once I was out of danger, I got in touch with Frank." She swallowed hard. "Then when I got to the room where you all were backstage....I saw you with her."

"With who?"

"Your fiancée, Kylie," she spat.

"Whoa, whoa, what the hell are you talking about? I'm not engaged, least of all to her!"

Mia rolled her eyes. "Oh please, AJ. Aren't we passed the point of lying to each other now? I saw you with my own eyes, and Dee did too. You were all hugged up to her and flashing her engagement ring around to this group of people."

My mind spun frantically trying to process what she was talking about. And then it hit me. "Did she have dark hair?"

"Yes."

"Oh Christ," I moaned. When I swung my legs out of the bed, Mia bolted up from the chair. I held my hand up. "Wait, I can explain."

"Like you did the last time?"

"Once again, you've completely missed the mark. Her name is Andrea, and she isn't my fiancée. She's Jake's step-sister—you met their shared sister, Allison, at the farm, remember? She's marrying a suit from the label who Jake introduced her to. They'd all come down from New York for the Jersey show. I've known her since I was twelve—she's like a sister to me, so yeah, I was all hugged up to her because I was happy."

Mia paled as her hand came to cover her mouth. "Oh God..." she murmured.

I drew in a deep breath, trying to steady my fucking Merry-Go-Round emotions. "Look, I know men have fucked you over in the past so badly that you like to react first and ask questions later. That's understandable. But you can't pull that shit anymore. It's not just about me or you. There's a kid—*my* kid—to think about."

Tears welled in her eyes before streaming down her cheeks. "I know. But when I thought you were engaged, all I could think of was how if I showed up, I'd ruin your life." Staring down at her hands, she whispered, "I didn't want to be like my mother."

Even though I should've been mad as hell at her, I couldn't help reaching over to cup her face in my hands, pulling her head up to look at me. "I never would have thought you tried to trap me, Mia. And regardless of what your mother did, your dad could never think you ruined his life."

"I know."

Dee appeared in the doorway. "Looks like you came around."

"Yeah, my head hurts like hell."

"So does my back." He eyed me before snorting. "You're one heavy motherfucker."

I laughed. "Sorry man."

"Look, since AJ seems to be all right now, I think you two need to get out of here."

Mia shook her head. "But I have my patients," she protested.

"I'll cover for you."

"Dee, I can't let you do that."

He held up a hand to silence her. "This isn't up for negation, Mimi. You've put this shit off for too long. In case you missed the memo, you two have a lot to talk about, so get your asses out of here. Now."

Mia scowled at Dee as she headed for the doorway. I trailed behind her. In silence, we walked down the hall to the elevators. "Even though Dee's covering my patients, I don't want to go far. Is the hospital cafeteria okay?"

I nodded. "Sure."

The elevator dinged, and we walked in. We were the only ones on board. "So, um, have you felt okay?"

Mia made a face. "I got pretty sick around the two month mark. I'd say it was morning sickness, but since I was sick morning, afternoon and night, it was a little more than that. I had to get on an insulin pump full of vitamins to regulate me."

Great, I'd not only knocked her up, but she'd had a hard time with the pregnancy. All alone. Shifting on my feet, I stuffed my hands in my jean pockets. "Yeah, my sister, Cris, had a really horrible time with nausea and shit. I'm sorry you had to go through that."

"It's okay. I'm feeling much better now."

"You look good," I said.

"Thanks. The nausea made it hard for me to keep food down, so I haven't gained a lot of weight."

"Mia, don't do that."

"Do what?" she asked, as we stepped off the elevator.

"You know exactly what I'm talking about." As we walked into the noisy cafeteria, my hand came to rest at the small of her back. "You're beautiful no matter what size you are, so get it out of your head that being pregnant and gaining weight is going to make you unattractive or undesirable to anyone...especially me."

She stared at me for a moment, unblinking and unmoving. Finally, she murmured, "Thank you, AJ."

Grabbing my wallet out of my back pocket, I motioned to the cafeteria line. "You want something?"

"I can get it," she argued.

I rolled my eyes. "Just tell me what you fucking want, Mia."

Instead of answering me, she gave her order to the food service worker. "A grilled chicken salad with honey mustard and a Mountain Dew."

"Mountain Dew? Are you insane? You aren't supposed to have caffeine," I countered.

Mia turned to glare at me, but then her brows rose in surprise instead. I guess she didn't think I would be one to have a lot of baby knowledge. I'd picked up a lot of my knowledge from my sister and Lily. "My doctor says I can have one a day. Trust me, since I've cut out my morning coffee, you want me to have a little dose, or I'll cut someone."

I laughed. "I can totally see you doing that."

She grinned as we edged down the line. I ordered some pie and a coffee. I followed behind her with our tray as she picked out a table far away from everyone else. Once we sat down, we fell into a silence as we ate. After what seemed like a small eternity of scraping silverware and chewing, Mia glanced worriedly at me across the table. "AJ, there's something else you need to know."

"Jesus, Mia, after telling me you're pregnant, how could there be anything more shocking?"

"I-I've been talking to Dev again."

I slammed my cup of coffee down on the table, sending steaming hot liquid sloshing over the edge. "You have got to be fucking kidding me."

She jerked her head slightly. "He came to see me the night after I got in from Jersey City."

"Are you sleeping with him?" I demanded.

"I don't think it's any of your business."

"The hell it's not. You're carrying my child."

Mia's dark eyes blazed. "Oh, are you ready to tell me about every chick you've banged in the four months we've been apart."

Hunkering over the table, I spat, "You wanna a great big surprise? Well, here it is. I haven't been with anyone since you."

After blinking a few times, she stared at me in shock. "It's been four months."

I snorted. "Trust me, cariño. My dick knows exactly how long it's been."

Ducking her head, Mia refused to look at me. Instead, she pushed some of the salad on her plate. "The answer is no."

"Excuse me?"

"No, I'm not sleeping with Dev."

Relief flooded me at her revelation. "Are you dating him? I mean, what's the fucking deal?"

Mia remained silent as she chewed a piece of grilled chicken. "No, I'm not dating him. He wants a second chance. Somehow he's convinced he can work for my affection."

"Oh yeah? And just how hard is he working?"

She pinned me with a stare. "Pretty diligently."

"He doesn't care that you're carrying my kid?"

"Dev always loved and wanted children even more than I did. He says..." Mia's gaze dropped to her lap. "He says he'd be willing to raise him or her as his own."

"Over my dead fucking body," I growled.

Mia glanced up to narrow her eyes at me. "Have you really thought about this, AJ? I mean, have you really stopped to think about what a baby means for you? You actually want to be in this for the long haul? Midnight feedings, diaper duty, teething?"

Crossing my arms over my chest, I said, "It's my kid. There's no question I want—no I *will*—be in its life."

"This can't be all part of some machismo act of staking claim on what's yours."

"Don't insult the level of my love and feelings for this child—this flesh of my flesh." I drew in a deep breath before adding, "Or my feelings for you."

"And just how in the world would the baby and I fit into your lifestyle?"

I ran my hand over my face, pausing to rub the stubble along my cheeks. "I don't know right at the moment, but I'd make it work—we would make it work. Hell, Bray and Lily have two kids, and they do just fine."

"But we barely know each other."

I shrugged. "Then we'll get to know each other. You can come out on tour—"

"AJ, I have a very demanding career—one I worked very hard to get. I can't just leave it, so I can follow you around city to city on some cramped bus."

I couldn't tell if she was bullshitting me with the career thing. I mean, I knew she was serious about being a nurse, and from Frank's testimony, she was a damn good one. A part of me understood why she wouldn't want to give up her life for the rootless and crazy life of a musician, especially one who she wasn't sure she loved. Hell, I wasn't completely sold on how much I loved her—I mean, I thought I did. Regardless of the baby, I knew I cared for her more than I had any girl I'd ever been in a relationship with before. I had even gone so far as to tell Mia I loved her once—of course, I was chained to a shower head, so I wasn't sure how much she believed me or thought I was just playing her to get out.

"Do you love me even a little bit?" I questioned.

"W-What?"

"You heard me."

Mia sighed. "Don't ask me that."

"And why not?"

"Because I don't have an easy answer for it," she replied.

"For just a second, let go of the past. Focus on the two weeks we had together." I leaned forward on the table with my elbows. "It wasn't just physical, Mia."

"I know that," she whispered.

I threw my hands up in frustration and fought not to growl at her. "Then why are you fighting so fucking hard against me? Jesus, Mia, I'm sitting here trying to make this work."

Tears welled in her eyes. "I don't know why I'm fighting you. After we...broke up or whatever you want to call it, things have been so crazy." She gave a slight shake of her head. "But you don't know how much I've missed you."

My chest constricted, and I fought to breathe. "You have?" I choked out.

She gave me a sad smile. "Of course I have. I've thought of you each and every day—even before I found out about the baby. If I'm honest with you and myself, I haven't been as happy as I was when I was with you in a long, long time."

I exhaled a ragged breath. This woman was going to be the fucking death of me. I crossed my arms over my chest. "Listen Mia, I don't know what you want me to say or do. You have absolutely no reason not to trust me because I never cheated on you. I told you before that I've never been a cheater and never will, so you should know I would never do that to you. Trust me, I want to work things out with you, but you're gonna have to give a little."

Mia remained silent for some time, twisting the napkin in her lap while chewing on her bottom lip. "Next Thursday is the early gender sonogram. I would love for you to be there."

"Wow, we'll know what it is already?"

"Yes."

My mind began furiously fast-forwarding a week. "Let's see. We have a show in Philly on Wednesday night." Mia's brows rose skeptically as if she already suspected I was going to flake out on her. "But I'm already supposed to be back here on Friday, so I can leave for Mexico. But I can come back a day early."

Mia's eyes widened. "You're leaving the country?"

"Yeah, I'm going to my cousin's quinceañera. Well, all my

family is going actually. She's also my goddaughter so I wouldn't dream of missing it. Jake and Abby are coming with me to scope out some places for their wedding."

"I see," she murmured.

A thought entered my mind, and I didn't stop to question it, I just acted on it. Reaching out, I grabbed her hand in mine. "Come with me to Mexico."

"AJ, be serious."

"I'm absolutely fucking serious. The more I think about it, the more perfect it is. My parents are going to be there, so I can introduce you to everyone—let them know I'm going to be a father. And then we can spend time getting to know each other."

"I can't just up and leave for a strange country in less than a week."

"Can't or won't?" I squeezed her hand in mine. "Come on, lighten up and be a little spontaneous. It'll be good practice for life on the road."

"I can't."

"And why the hell not? I'm sure you've got to have vacation time stored up. You're not too far along to fly." At her surprised expression, I smiled. "Between Cris, and Lily, I know just enough about pregnancy and babies to be dangerous."

The corners of Mia's lips turned up, and I could tell she was fighting not to laugh. "Okay, fine, you get to the ultrasound and that will prove you want to be a part of the baby's life. Then, I'll come to Mexico with you."

Finally, I was getting somewhere with Miss Stubborn. While that fact alone made me stoked as hell, I was also pumped that in just one week, I was going to find out if I was going to be the father of a son or daughter. Finding out Mia was pregnant was intense enough, but just the thought of knowing what it would be, was even more amazing.

With a smile, I replied, "Okay then. It's a deal."

Chapter Twenty-One

AJ

I was in the Seventh ring of Hell, heading for the very fiery center. Just to be on the safe side, I had tried making my escape from Philly on Wednesday night after our show when a fucking snowstorm blew through and closed the airport for twelve hours. When flights were finally up and running, I was left with a thirty minute window to get from Hartsfield Jackson in Atlanta to Mia's doctors in North Fulton.

Bottom line: I was basically fucked.

Rhys had flown in with me since he had left his car at the airport. As I cut my eyes over at him, I shook my head. "Dude, this is a fucking Porsche. Quit driving it like a grandma."

Rhys's knuckles were white on the steering wheel. "Jesus, I'm doing ninety. Excuse me for wanting to live to see tomorrow."

"Yeah, that's all well and good, but if I'm late, I'm totally fucked with Mia. She will do the emotional equivalent of cutting my balls off and roasting them over an open flame if I miss this. That or have her Sicilian family literally do me in."

Rhys chuckled. "Listen man, you gotta calm down. Take a few cleansing breaths or some shit. I'm doing the best I can with the traffic."

As hard as I tried, I couldn't seem to take his advice to calm down. Nervous energy hummed through my body. I couldn't stop my legs from bouncing up and down in the cramped confines of the two seat convertible. I had my hands moving too as I smacked out a steady beat of our newest song *Convicted* on my jean clad thighs. As I stared down at the faded, holey pair of jeans, I grimaced. "Shit, I should have worn something nicer."

"Huh?"

Motioning to the ratty jeans and my faded button down Polo shirt, I replied, "I look like a second rate hood rat, not an expectant father."

"Daaaamn," Rhys replied.

"What?" I demanded.

He cut his gaze over from whipping in and out of lanes to pin me with a wicked smile. "Mia has got you completely and totally spinning."

"She does not."

"Oh hell yes, she does."

"This isn't just about Mia." When he continued scoffing at me, I shook my head. "This is bigger than the both of us now. I've got a kid on the way, and I gotta be the best damn father in the whole fucking world."

Rhys took one hand off the wheel to pat me reassuringly on the shoulder. "You're going to be an amazing father. I have no doubt about that."

"You really think so?"

"I know so." He turned to me and grinned. "But you may wanna start working on your language."

I grimaced. "Sh-I mean, shoot. I really do swear like a sailor."

With a laugh, Rhys replied, "You're probably okay. I mean, considering Bray is his dad and he's surrounded by us, look all the f-bombs Jude grew up with, and he's just fine."

"Yeah, that was Jude, but how quickly you forget that after da-da and ma-ma, Melody managed to say shit and damn."

"Oops, I forgot about that one."

We were making good time when one glance in the rearview mirror sent my stomach plummeting. Blue lights from an Atlanta Police Department cruiser flashed all around us. "Fuuuuuuuuck!" One peek at the clock sent me pounding my fist against the dash. "I'm screwed."

"Easy man," Rhys replied as he eased into the emergency lane. My phone vibrated in my pocket. When I snatched it out, I had a new text from Mia.

Where the hell r u? I'm at the docs, and u r not here like u promised. Appt is in 10 min!

"Shit, shit, motherfucking SHIT!" I yelled.

"What?" Rhys questioned he dug his wallet out of his pants.

"I just got a pre-rage text from Mia."

"Uh-oh."

We were interrupted by the cop knocking on the window. He appeared barely out of puberty. "License and registration please."

Rhys quickly obliged by rolling down the window and thrusting out the two cards.

Before the cop glanced at them, he asked, "You do realize you were doing ninety-five miles an hour in a seventy zone?"

"Yes sir, and I do apologize for that. I normally obey the speeding laws, but you see, my friend has a very important appointment he needs to get to. Unfortunately, to appease him, I felt it necessary to break the law," Rhys replied, oozing the charm and respectfulness he'd been raised with.

One glance at Rhys's license, and the cop exclaimed, "Holy shit!"

"Excuse me officer?"

Leaning in the open window, the cop, whose badge read Carlisle, eyed Rhys. "Are you *the* Rhys McGowan, the guitarist for Runaway Train?"

Silently, I mouthed "FUCK YEAH!" and did a mental fist pump in my seat as I saw a glimmer of hope at the end of the tunnel. I never shamelessly used my fame, but I sure as hell was going to do it today.

A million dollar grin spread across Rhys's cheeks. "Why yes, I am." Jerking his thumb at me, he replied, "And there's AJ Resendiz."

"Holy shit!" Officer Carlisle exclaimed again. His head shook back and forth so fast I thought he might lose his hat. "Dude, you guys are like my most favorite band in the world! I snuck in to Eastman's once to see you guys play."

"Really? That's awesome. We always love meeting die-hard fans, so let me shake your hand." Rhys stuck his hand through the window.

As Officer Carlisle pumped Rhys's hand up and down, he exclaimed, "Oh man, no one at the station is going to believe this!"

"You mean we're not on your dash cam?" I questioned.

He shook his head. "Nah, I've got an older cruiser, and we're still working on installing them throughout the department." He scratched the stubble on his chin. "Maybe I can have you sign something?"

The wheels in my head started spinning in overdrive. I practically leapt over into Rhys lap, so I could get closer to Officer Carlisle. "Yeah, I didn't need those balls," Rhys groaned.

"Listen man, I take full responsibility for the speeding, and I'll be happy to pay whatever ticket we need to—hell, I'll even pay double—it's just I need to get out of here ASAP!" As Officer Carlisle stared at me skeptically, I exhaled a noisy breath of frustration. "Here's the deal. I've got exactly..." I glanced at the dash and cursed under my breath. "I've got five minutes to get to the doctor's office, or I'm in deep shit."

"Dude, I'm sorry. I didn't know you're sick."

"No, it's not me. It's just if I don't get there on time my..." Shit, I didn't know exactly what to call Mia. Girlfriend? Ex-flame? Baby Mama? I cleared my throat. "It's like this. If I'm not there for the gender ultrasound for my baby, I may never have a chance to be a part of its life because its mother will emotionally cut me out of her life and then maybe even cut my balls off."

Officer Carlisle shook his head. "Dude, that's some tough shit." He shifted on his feet momentarily before nodded. "Follow me," he instructed.

As he started back to his cruiser, I glanced over at Rhys. "Think we're about to get a police escort?"

"Hell to the yeah!" he exclaimed with a grin.

Flashing blue lights commenced followed by the wail of the police siren. Officer Carlisle pulled out first and then

Rhys eased out behind him, turning on his flashers. While we started making our way down the interstate, I quickly texted Mia back to let her know I was on the way. When she didn't respond, I got a little nauseated.

"Oh fuck," Rhys groaned.

Glancing up from my phone, my heart plummeted at the sight of bumper to bumper traffic. "You have got to be shitting me!"

We came to a full stop behind Officer Carlisle's cruiser. He stepped out and then came back to the car. "Sorry man. I just heard on the radio that an eighteen wheeler jackknifed about a mile up the road."

"Damn. Damn. DAMN!" I cried. This time I beat my head, instead of my hands, against the dash.

"Stop it, AJ," Rhys demanded.

I shook my now aching head miserably and fought the urge to hang my head out the window and scream at the top of my lungs. "I'm utterly fucked, dude."

"I'm sure if you explain it to Mia, she'll—"

I snorted. "No man, you don't get it. Not only is she pregnant and a hormonal hurricane, but every single guy she's been with has let her down. It's not just about being the exception to that rule. If I screw this up, she could totally give up on me and choose that douche of an ex fiancé of hers." With shaking hands, I grabbed my phone and prepared to make the call I really, really didn't want to. But even if I dreaded calling Mia, I refused to just not show up. An excuse was better than being stood up.

"Listen, maybe you won't be too late. I mean, we're only about a half a mile down the road."

My head snapped up. "It's only that far?"

"Yeah, it's right off the road in the same medical building as my dentist. Why?"

Without a reply, I fumbled with the door handle. My shaky hands made it almost impossible to open it. Finally, it flew open, and I fell out onto the pavement. Glancing over my shoulder, I cried, "If I can't get a ride home with Mia, I'll call you, okay?"

Rhys's chocolate brown eyes widened to the size of his shiny Porsche hubcaps. "You're seriously going to run the next half mile?"

"Totally."

He shook his head slowly back and forth. "Be careful."

"Gotcha." I slammed the car door, and then started sprinting down the side of the road. I mean, the issue wasn't being in shape. After all, I usually tried to do a few miles on the treadmill at every tour stop. It was just I never quite pushed my body as hard as I was pushing it right now. The line of cars still hadn't moved when I streaked into the parking lot of the medical building. I screeched to a stop to board the elevator. Thankfully from Mia's texts I knew what floor and what suite number I needed to go to.

After the elevator dinged on the third floor, I burst through the third office door on the right, skidding to a stop on the waxed hardwood floors just inside the entrance. I lunged over to the receptionist who stood frozen with a phone's receiver in her hand. "M-Must find M-Mia," I gasped as my lungs screamed in agony. Desperate to catch my breath, I doubled over at the waist, pressing my hands against my thighs.

"AJ?"

Jerking my head up, I gazed across the full waiting room. Dodging the shocked expressions from the other women and men, I sought out Mia. Finally, I found her. She sat in a corner chair, gaping open-mouthed at me. "Hey babe," I replied lamely.

As Mia's brows shot up, the dude across from me snickered until his wife or girlfriend elbowed him in the ribs. Ignoring him, I somehow managed to pick one aching foot up and put it in front of the other to close the distance between Mia and me. It seemed like years before I collapsed down in the chair next to her.

"I can't believe you made it."

"Promised. I. Would," I wheezed, wincing at the pain in my chest. When I opened my eyes, Mia, along with the rest of the waiting room, was staring expectantly at me. "Was afraid you'd already be done."

"Well, normally I would've already been taken back, but

the ultrasound technician is stuck in some horrible traffic caused by a wreck."

I snorted thinking that I probably ran by his or her car on my way in. Mia reached over to grasp my hand in hers. "AJ, are you okay?"

"Just. Fine."

As I continued sounding like I was hacking up a lung, Mia shook her head. "No offense, but you look like hell."

I winced. "I meant to wear something nicer."

She squeezed my hand. "Oh AJ, it's not what you have on. I could care less how you're dressed."

"Really?" When she started to bob her head, I grinned and added, "You wouldn't mind if I were nude?"

Instead of admonishing me, she actually giggled. "I don't think you could have made any more of a scene nude than the way you just busted in here."

"Yeah, sorry about that."

She gave me a once over from head to toe and sighed. "I'm worried about you. Your face is beet red, you're sweating profusely, and you've just caught your breath. You look like you just ran a marathon or something."

"I sorta did."

"Huh?"

Now that I had my breath fully back, I explained about the delayed flight, the ticket, then the police escort and finally about the traffic jam that had caused me to run the last half mile to the doctor's office. Mia's hand flew to cover her mouth as her eyes widened. "Oh AJ, you went through all of that for me?"

"Of course I did."

Mia's bottom lip trembled, and I could tell she was about to let loose crying. "I, um, I need to run to the bathroom again," she said, as she rose out of her chair.

I slung both my arms over the backs of the chairs next to me. "I'll be right here waiting for you."

With a jerk of her head, she replied, "Okay, I'll be right back."

Feeling someone's hot stare on me, I glanced up from the floor and over at the middle-aged woman directly across from me. Her shaking hands held the latest copy of *Rolling Stone*— the one our kick-ass PR firm had somehow managed to get us on. She appeared to be fanning herself because she kept pulling back the cover, staring at it, and then glancing at me.

Deciding to put her out of her misery, I ran a hand through my sweat-slick hair to smooth it down before giving her my most winning smile. "Yup, it's me."

Her eyes widened in astonishment. "I-uh," she stammered.

"Nice to meet you."

"Yeah," she squeaked before burying her face back in the magazine.

Gazing around the waiting room, I surveyed the women of different ages and sizes of pregnancy, along with the ones who were there just for just routine checkups. My throat suddenly started closing up.

Holy shit. The realization that I now sat in an OB/GYN's office where I was about to learn the sex of my first child crashed over me. My legs involuntarily started bouncing up and down on their own accord. I jerked my hands off the chairs and started wringing them over and over. I fought the urge to text Bray to tell him I was having another impending fatherhood breakdown. I'd had several of those over the past week after finding out that Mia was pregnant. Bray had talked me down from the ledge each and every time. Although they'd been married at the time, Jude had been a total surprise for Bray and Lily, and one that freaked the hell out of Bray at first. I mean, we were barely twenty-two and just starting to make a name for ourselves. It was hardly the best time to start a family.

My erratic heartbeat stilled a little at the sight of Mia exiting the bathroom. Her long, dark hair cascaded down her back—she had it down just like I loved it. Her dressy top was loose fitting and red—the color that made her dark eyes pop, and she even sported red heels with her black pants. Although I knew she probably thought she was as big as a house, her baby bump still wasn't so pronounced. As she eased back down beside me, I couldn't help reaching out and rubbing her tiny tummy. She froze at my touch.

"I'm sorry," I whispered, as I started to pull away.

Mia grabbed my hand in hers and placed it back over her belly. "No, I want you to feel the baby if you want to." She smiled. "You just surprised me by wanting to, that's all."

Gently, I rubbed her stomach over her shirt. "Like I said before, I want to be a part of this child's life." I drew in a deep breath. "I want to be a part of *your* life if you'll have me."

Mia's mouth made a perfect 'O' of surprise just as the waiting room door opened. "Mia Martinelli?" a nurse questioned. Snapping her mouth shut, Mia shot out of her chair. She fumbled for my hand before dragging me along behind her.

After we left the reception area, a nurse ushered Mia over to some scales. "Let's get your weight," the she instructed. When Mia stepped on, I started to look at the digital read out. "No, don't look!" she hissed over her shoulder.

I held up my hands in mock surrender. "Okay, okay," I muttered, stepping back. Once her weight was recorded and she was off the scales, I took a few tentative steps forward, I said, "You look absolutely beautiful to me."

With a grin, the nurse patted my back. "Aren't you a sweetheart?"

"Thanks," I replied before winking at Mia. She rolled her eyes but smiled in spite of herself.

Out of nowhere, a young receptionist came bounding up to me. "Oh my God! It really is you. I almost didn't believe the other girls when they said you were here."

"Oh, um, hi," I said, extending my hand. I was in unchartered territory considering I'd never been ambushed by a fan in an OB/GYN office.

"I've never missed seeing any your shows in Atlanta. In fact, my friends and I have even driven to some in Alabama and Tennessee. I'm that big of a fan." Digging in the pockets of her scrubs, she pulled out a sharpie and thrust it at me. "I would like totally die of excitement if you would sign my boobs."

When I dared to peek at Mia, she stood with her arms crossed over her chest, giving the bimbo a death glare. "I'll be happy to sign anything *but* your boobs," I said tightly.

She pouted as she turned around and swept her hair over her shoulder. "Will you sign the back of my scrubs then?"

I gave Mia an apologetic look to which she held up her hands. "Don't mind me. I'm just here to see the gender of my unborn child. Excuse me, *our* unborn child."

Yep, I was in serious trouble. Capping the sharpie, I tossed it back at the girl. "This is really not a good time."

"Later then?" she pressed

"How about never!" Mia blared.

The nurse at Mia's side stepped forward and gently

shoved the girl back into the reception area. "Beth, please do not bother Ms. Martinelli and her guest anymore."

With an exasperated huff, Beth slumped back into her chair and whirled around to face customers. The nurse gave Mia and me an apologetic smile. "I'm so sorry about that."

"It's not your fault. I'm kinda used to it by now," I replied.

"Well, I'm certainly not," Mia hissed.

Oh great, in Mia's eyes, I had royally fucked up now. Sensing we needed a moment alone, the nurse motioned us into the ultrasound room. "You know the drill by now, Ms. Martinelli. The tech will be with you in a few minutes."

"Thank you," Mia replied.

When the door shut behind us, I inhaled a deep breath. Mia chose to ignore me. Instead, she hopped up on the table. Swinging her legs back and forth, she eyed me contemptuously. "Amorcito mio, I'm really sorry about that." I took a tentative step forward. "It's just that I'm used to interacting with fans and getting into a certain zone when I'm with them. I wouldn't have wanted to take anything away from this day for you or for me."

Mia weighed my words before reclining back on the table. The paper crinkled beneath her as she unbuttoned her pants and slid them down, tucking them under her bump. I couldn't resist stepping forward to lay my hand on her bare belly. She watched me intently, searching my face. I didn't know if she expected to me to pull a douche move and be disgusted by the sight of her stomach or what. It was still so fucking mind blowing that my kid was in there. That somehow, during our whirlwind two weeks together, we had managed to create a life.

"Mia," I pleaded. "Will you at least call me a few choice words in Italian and except my apology?"

When she finally smiled, I felt like a ton of bricks had been lifted off my chest. "Okay, I'm sorry for overreacting. I guess you couldn't help it. I mean, that chick really railroaded you."

I nodded. "I've had PR people drill it into my head never to turn away fans, so that's why I did that. I would never dream of disrespecting you and this special day."

"Thank you, AJ," Mia replied.

The door opened, and a tech in green scrubs appeared. "Hello Mia."

"Hi Karen."

"Big day today, huh?" Karen questioned, as she flopped down on her stool.

"Yeah, it is."

Karen eyed me as she picked up a bottle of some gel looking shit. "And who is this?"

"I'm AJ, the father," I replied before Mia could try to figure out what to call me.

"Nice to meet you." With a grin, Karen glanced between

us. "Regardless of what the sex is of this baby, I can guarantee with you two as parents, it's going to be attractive."

I laughed. "Thanks. We do have some good genes to bring to the table, huh?"

Mia rolled her eyes at my cockiness. "Thank you, Karen. As long as it's healthy, I'll feel extremely blessed."

"Okay then. Let's get started," Karen replied, after squiring the jelly shit on Mia's belly. Once it was covered, she picked up a wand and began running it over Mia's stomach. The instant the baby's grainy image flashed on the screen I was mesmerized. Seriously, I couldn't take my eyes off of him or her, and I fought to breathe. It was the most surreal experience of my life. Nothing compared to it—not even being on a stage in front of thousands and thousands of people. "Wow," I wheezed.

"Pretty amazing, huh?" Mia asked.

"Yeah, it's fucking intense." When Karen glanced over at me, I held up my hands. "Sorry."

She laughed. "Don't worry. I'm used to it." As she rolled around the wand, Karen pointed to an area on the screen. "There's the heartbeat."

I could hear it echoing all around me through the sound system. "Sounds strong."

"It is," Karen replied.

When I glanced down at Mia, she was smiling at me. She

squeezed my hand. Tears glimmered in her eyes. "I'm so glad you're here."

"Me too, amorcito mio. Me too." I brought her hand to my lips and kissed along her fingers.

"So are you two ready to find out what your baby is?"

Since I couldn't form words, I had to resort to nodding while Mia replied, "Yes, please."

Karen pressed harder on Mia's abdomen—the image on the screen shifted to a straight shot at what I assumed was the butt. We had a clear shot between the baby's legs.

"Looks like you are having a girl."

Tears spilled over Mia's cheeks. "Really?"

"Yes."

It took me a moment to even process the technician's words. I was going to have a daughter. An image of Melody's sweet smile formed in my mind along with her calling for Bray. I wanted to have a Daddy's Girl just like her. I could almost see a dark-haired, dark-eyed girl with pig-tails gripping my hand in her tiny one—a little girl who was a perfect mix of mine and Mia's DNA.

When I glanced at Mia, her mouth turned down in a frown. "Are you disappointed it's not a boy?"

"Are you kidding me? Our baby is going to be the first granddaughter on my side of the family—we're going to rack up some serious shit."

Mia grinned. "Only you would say that."

I smiled. "I couldn't be happier that I'm going to have a baby girl."

"I'm glad. To be honest, I really wanted it to be a girl."

"Yeah, I think it's a good idea not to unleash any AJ Juniors onto the world for a while."

With a laugh, Mia replied, "You never know. Our daughter could take after her father."

I shuddered. "God forbid."

Mia's hand came up to tenderly rub my cheek. "Don't sell yourself short, AJ. There are a lot of wonderful traits she could inherit from you."

At her sincere words, I leaned down to give her a chaste kiss on the lips. When I pulled away, confusion and affection pooled in Mia's eyes. I could tell she was still fighting with exactly how she felt about me. Once Karen finished cleaning the goop off of Mia's stomach, Mia adjusted her top and sat up on the table. "I wanted to run something by you. I kinda already picked out a girl's name, and I wanted to see if you wouldn't mind."

"Okay."

Wringing her hands, she added, "I mean, we can totally brainstorm names together. I really do want your input."

"Would you just spit it out, Mia?"

"Okay, fine. Isabella Sofia—for my grandmother."

I smiled. "It's beautiful. And my abuela's name is Isabella."

Mia's eyes widened. "Really?"

"Sounds like fate, huh?" I reached over to touch her belly. "I think Bella Resendiz has a nice ring to it."

"Me too."

I was glad to hear she wasn't going to argue with Bella having my last name. There was no way in hell my kid was going by Mia's last name or anyone else's for that matter—including that douche ex-fiance who was sniffing around.

"Here you go," Karen said, handing Mia a few snapshots and a DVD of the ultrasound.

"Thank you," Mia called as Karen left the room. She gave me one of the pictures. "In case you want to flash Bella around."

I smiled. "I'd love, too. The guys are definitely going to want to see her."

"I have to get back to work, but do you want to grab some lunch first? The crew at Mama Sofia's is anxiously awaiting the news."

I grimaced. "I can't. I've got a lot of shit to do before we leave in the morning." When Mia refused to look me in the eye, my heart clenched in my chest. All week on the phone and through texts, whenever I would mention Mexico, she would become cagey. "You are coming with me, right?"

She nibbled on her bottom lip. "I'm not sure."

At her hesitation, I clenched my jaw. "You're still not sure about me, are you?"

"That's not it."

"Yes, it is. Jesus Christ, Mia, after all I went through to get here today, you still have your doubts about my commitment to you and Bella?"

She sighed and turned away from me.

"It's never going to be enough is it?" I demanded.

"AJ, please."

Grabbing her by the shoulders, I forced her to look at me. "No matter what I do, you're always going to let the ghosts of your past fuck things up for us, aren't you?"

"No, I'm not."

"You don't want to go back to Dev—he's just a means to an end where you don't have to make a choice." I gripped her tighter. "Dammit, Mia, I want to be with you and only you. I've never cheated on you, and I've never lied to you. I've made some mistakes where we're concerned—that's the truth. But what happens between us next is all up to you."

"What do you mean?"

I dropped my hands from her shoulders. "I'm not going to let you keep playing with my feelings. I will be a father to Bella, but whether or not, I'm your boyfriend or your future husband or the man you might love, ends today. If you don't come with me to Mexico—"

Mia shook her head wildly. "Don't you dare give me an ultimatum!"

"You're leaving me with no choice. You keep saying we barely know each other. Fine then, come to Mexico with me for two weeks. Get to know me, get to know my family, get to know part of Bella's heritage. Prove to me that you're really trying."

"I am."

"It sure as hell doesn't feel that way. You're making me out to be some bad guy that I'm not. I'm just a guy who cares about you and wants more with you. You can't keep judging me for my past or my occupation." Staring into her eyes, I shook my head. "I have your ticket waiting. But I'm serious, Mia. I gotta know you're truly with me and aren't going to bail. That's not fair to me, and it won't be fair to Bella."

Tears pooled in her eyes before streaming down her cheeks. "I know. And I'm sorry, AJ. I really am."

"Yeah, well, you know where to find me. The flight leaves at two tomorrow afternoon—with or without you." I leaned over and gave her a brief kiss on the cheek before striding out of the doctor's office. Even though part of me felt like an ass for being so demanding of her, I knew I had to get my point firmly across. I didn't play games, and I wasn't going to continue playing this one with Mia. The ball was in her court, and she had to make a decision.

As I got on the elevator, I dialed Rhys. "Get your ass over here and pick me up."

"Shit dude, did things not go well?"

"Yes and no."

"Well, lucky for you, I'm just five minutes away. Traffic is still crazy as a motherfucker."

"Whatever. Just get here when you can. I gotta lot of shit to do before I leave tomorrow."

"Mia not coming with you?"

I sighed as I tugged my hand through my hair. "I don't know."

"I say you at least have time for a few beers after the day you've had."

With a chuckle, I replied, "That sounds like a plan."

Chapter Twenty-Two

Mia

The rest of the day after the ultrasound I was an emotional wreck. Before I went back to work, I had put on a happy face at Mama Sofia's where free desert was given to all the patrons in honor of Isabella—Mia's Moose of course. My dad was absolutely on cloud nine when I told him, especially about the name. Of course when he had questioned me about AJ, I had shook my head. How could I explain to him what I was feeling? How the doubts and fears of my past continued crippling me in the future with AJ? Not to mention that the one and only time AJ had actually said the words 'I love you' was when he was under emotional distress handcuffed to a shower.

I knew my dad wanted to talk to me about it—maybe even counsel me on what to do. But just like when everything was going so wrong with Jason, I hid from him. Like a total coward, I snuck out of Mama Sofia's before he could come back to my table.

In the end, I knew there was no one I could talk to about this. It was my decision, and mine alone, to make. That's what made it so fucking hard. Of course, the worst part of all was how much I loathed myself. I had become totally unrecognizable to myself, and I couldn't just blame my irrational pregnancy hormones. No, I was reaping shit I'd sown a long, long time ago. The old me wouldn't have led Dev on when I knew that I would never take him back. But there was a part of me that got some sick vindication from making him suffer.

I didn't know what was wrong with me. Deep into the core of my being, I knew I wanted to be with AJ. There was absolutely no rational reason not to give him another chance. He was the father of my daughter. I had fallen in love with him in the midst of our lust-haze. But nothing about me was rational at the moment. I kept focusing on the irrational side of things—my insecurities about AJ's career and his women, and the way I felt like I could never be good enough, or even, enough for him. Somehow I always kept coming back to my self-loathing conclusion, that he deserved someone better— although the thought of seeing him with another woman made me physically sick.

It seemed I had more time to think about it than I should have since things were slow on the floor. Somehow I had resorted to pacing around in the break room while feeling like a total nut-job.

Dee poked his head in the door. "Mimi, you have a visitor."

My heart leapt into my throat, and more than anything in the world, I hoped it was AJ. At the sight of Pesh, my former mentor and Dev's brother, standing in the doorway, the breath I'd been holding exhaled in a noisy rush of disappointment.

Pesh's beaming smile slowly receded as his gaze roamed over me. He stared at my abdomen before glancing back up at me. "Now I know why Dee called me."

His words, coupled with the emotional shit-storm of my life, caused me to burst into tears. Pesh rushed forward and pulled me into his arms. "Hey now, if I'm going to have this kind of effect on you, I'll leave."

My mirthless laugh was muffled against his chest. "No, that's not it at all. I'm kinda a mess lately."

"Well, I don't know about that, but you've certainly been busy," he mused.

I pulled away to shake my head. "I can't believe Dee called you."

"He's worried about you and the decisions you're making."

With a wince, I said, "I guess you know about Dev."

Pesh nodded. "Yes, he told me he was trying to convince you to come back to him."

"You don't sound like you think that's a good idea."

"That's because I know it's not."

My brows shot up in surprise. "What?"

Pesh exhaled a ragged sigh before resting his hands on my shoulders. "I know you and Dev were together a long time. Our family will always love you and owe you a tremendous debt for getting him back on track after those wayward years."

"Cut to the point, Pesh."

He smiled. "Dev is my baby brother, and I love him. But I know in my heart he doesn't now or will ever deserve you, Mia."

I gasped at his admission. "Seriously?"

"He's always chased after what he couldn't have, and once he got it, he wasn't satisfied. He tried for months to get me to fix you two up, but I refused."

"You never told me that."

"At the time, I didn't think you were ready to date after what had happened with Jason. Now I think it was something greater telling me to keep you apart."

I groaned. "That would have been really nice to know three years ago. It could've saved me some heartache, you know?"

Pesh grimaced. "I realize that now. It's the reason why I'm here today. This musician...what's his name?"

"AJ," I murmured.

Pesh nodded. "This AJ wants you to be with him, doesn't he?"

"I'm going to kill Dee," I muttered through gritted teeth. At the same time I wanted to throttle him, I couldn't ask for a more faithful, loving friend than Dee.

"Don't be mad at him. He loves you—just like I do. He also knows what you've been through in the last year might be clouding your judgment." Pesh's expression grew sad. "Better than anyone, I know what grief can do to you, Mia. After Jade's death, I lived a dream-like existence for the last two years. I made decisions that weren't really me—decisions that my emotional torment caused me to do. I don't want you to make the same mistakes as I did just because you lost one of the most important people in your life."

"That's very sweet of you." I then pursed my lips at him. "Does your faulty decision making have anything to do with that pregnant chick you wanted to get with?"

Pesh laughed. "Maybe a little. But wanting to be with Emma could never be deemed as a 'faulty' decision."

"You're not still after her, are you?"

"No, I'm not. We both realized we weren't right for each other—that we were in love with other people. Now we're just really good friends—like we were truly meant to be."

"What is it with you Nadeen men and being hot for women who are pregnant with other men's babies, huh?" I teased.

He shook his head. "You and Dev aren't the same thing as Emma and me—you two had a long history together." He rubbed my cheek tenderly. "Maybe it's that pregnant women have a glow about them—a beauty that burns bright from inside, like the life growing within them. You've always been beautiful, Mia. But you're truly breathtaking today."

"Thank you, but somehow I think you might be fibbing considering I have puffy eyes and a red face from crying," I scoffed.

Pesh smiled. "None of that matters. What truly matters is the heart inside the person. And I know yours has such great love within it." He gave me a pointed look. "But it doesn't truly beat for my brother, does it?"

"No, it doesn't."

With a wink, Pesh replied, "No, it follows a different drummer, doesn't it?"

"Yes, it does," I replied with an absolute certainty I hadn't had possessed before.

Taking my hand in his, he brought it to his lips. After he kissed it, he said, "Now do you have your answer?"

"Yes, I do," I whispered.

"Good. I'm glad to hear it." He pulled me into his strong embrace.

As I squeezed him tight, I said, "You're like my fairy godmother or guardian angel, you know that right? You're always swooping in to save me."

He chuckled. "I think I like being a guardian angel better than a fairy."

I laughed as I pulled away. "I think so, too."

"So you're going to go to him now?"

"As soon as I can pack my bag, I will. That's if I can actually drive home being a bundle of nerves."

Once again, Pesh took my hand. "Come on. Your fairy godmother will take you home and get you packed. Then I'll take you to AJ's."

My eyes widened. "Really?"

"Of course."

I couldn't help my bottom lip from trembling. "That's so sweet."

"Before you cry, I have my ulterior motives."

"You do?"

He nodded. "I want some advice on how to get a stubborn woman to change her mind about me. Since you're the most stubborn woman I know, I figured you could help."

I threw my head back and laughed. "I will be happy to do anything I can to help you find happiness and true love. You know that. And just who is this brainless chick who isn't giving you the time of day?"

"Her name is Megan, and she's just set in her mind about something..." He pinned me with a pointed look. "Just like you."

"Whatever," I mumbled.

Pesh took my hand. "Come on. Time is wasting for you and your prince."

By the time I got packed up and back into Pesh's Jaguar, I was a nervous wreck. For most of the time, Pesh had kept my mind occupied as we worked out a strategy for him to win the girl he was in love with, and who I could tell was also in love with him but just being stubborn as hell. Sound familiar?

As Pesh started rolling my suitcases onto the front porch, I gave a teary goodbye to Jack Sparrow. "Don't worry, Jack. Dee's going to come feed you and take care of you." He meowed in acknowledgement before nudging his head against my face. When I started out the door, my nerves began spinning in overdrive.

For the life of me, I don't know why I thought it would be good to surprise AJ, rather than call him. Showing up at his penthouse seemed so impulsive—the very thing he was trying to get me to do. I was so set in my ways of needing everything to be by the book that I figured this would prove to him, in more ways than one, that I could fit into his life. Of course, I couldn't help worrying even though AJ had given me the ultimatum, that when it finally came down to it, he would reject me. I'd pushed him too far and for too long. He would have every right to tell me it was too late for us.

As we pulled up to his building, my stomach lurched, and I fought the urge to throw-up. "Are you going to be okay?" Pesh asked.

"I hope so," I murmured faintly.

"You're awfully pale."

"I'm fine."

Pesh eyed me suspiciously one last time before turning off the car and hopping out. As I put my wobbly feet onto the pavement, he grabbed my bags from the trunk. When he rolled them over to me, he asked, "Do you want me to come inside and wait with you?"

His concern was endearing, but I knew it was time to get my big-girl panties on. "No, I'm fine. I can do this."

"Okay, if you're sure."

Slinging my purse on my arm, I wrapped my arms around Pesh's broad chest. "I can never thank you enough for this...for everything."

"You don't need to thank me. That's what friends are for."

After I pulled away, I kissed him on the cheek. "I love you."

"Love you, too."

Wagging my finger, I said, "If this Megan chick doesn't wake up soon, I'm coming to Wellstar and having a little talk with her."

Pesh grinned. "Okay, I think I'll let you."

With one last squeeze, I started into the building. Once again I realized how stupid I had been with this impulsive ambush. AJ had said he had errands. What if he wasn't home? What if I had to sit in the lobby for hours, like a crazy stalker, for him to get in?

I approached the front desk on shaky legs. "Um, can I get you to buzz AJ Resendiz's penthouse please?"

The woman eyed me suspiciously. "What's your name?"

"Mia Martinelli."

A look of recognition flashed on her face. "One moment." She picked up the phone. "Yes, Mr. Resendiz, it's Elana at the front desk. Your guest is down here."

My brows rose in surprise. Had he been expecting me? "He'll be right down," she replied, with a snooty air in her voice.

"Thank you." I hobbled over to the elevators to wait on AJ. My heartbeat thrummed wildly in my chest, and I chewed on my bottom lip until I felt blood rush into my mouth. The moment the elevator doors opened and I saw AJ, I couldn't contain my emotions anymore, and I burst into tears. His brows rose in surprise, and although I could tell he was fighting himself on whether to step forward for to comfort me or not, he held back, gripping the bar on the back of the elevator wall. It was now or never, even though we had a small audience in both the lobby and on the elevator with him.

"I'm so sorry for everything, AJ," I said through my tears. "I'm so sorry for ruining things with us by running all the time. I'm sorry I let my past with men dictate my future with you. I know you aren't Dev and you could never, ever be Jason. I'm sorry I let my insecurities about your past and who I thought you were screw up the happiness we had. Most of all, I'm sorry I was a stupid fool and didn't run straight back into your open arms when you offered them to me. You're a good man, and you'll be a great father to Bella."

Once I finished, AJ stood there staring at me for what felt like an eternity. Oh fuck. He really had changed his mind. Standing all rigid and tense, he looked pissed that I was ambushing him. The people around us stood frozen, watching and waiting right along with me. Finally, he demanded, "Does this little performance mean you're coming to Mexico?"

"Yes, I really want to go. If you still want me," I hiccupped.

A grin spread on his lips as he pushed off the wall of the elevator and stepped outside to meet me. "I could never stop wanting you, amorcito mio. Even with all your damn stubbornness and freaky, exaggerated shit that goes through your mind, all I want is you."

I shook my head furiously. "But I don't know why. You deserve so much better than me. Someone who isn't consumed by their past or can't embrace your profession. I don't know if I can ever prove to you how good *you* are to *me*— how good you *are* for me."

AJ cocked his head at me. "Are you done?"

"Yes. Why?"

"Because I want you to shut the fuck up so I can kiss you."

Throwing myself into his arms, I wrapped my arms tight around his neck, drawing myself flush against him. As he slid his arms around my waist, my lips sought out his. Applause echoed around us, causing me to jerk away. As I stared wildly around the lobby, one woman asked, "Are they filming a movie or something?"

AJ and I both laughed. "Come on. Let's get you upstairs." Glancing over my shoulder, he saw my waiting suitcases. "You were really serious about coming, huh?"

"Yes, I was."

"I'm glad," he replied as he got my bags. Thankfully, we were alone on the elevator ride up to the penthouse. But the moment the doors shut behind us, I had an elicit flashback to the last time I was in this elevator with him. Heat flooded my cheeks, and I fought the urge to fan myself.

"Having a sexy flashback of us?" he questioned with a smirk.

"Not at all. The pregnancy hormones give me hot flashes," I lied.

AJ laughed. "Bullshit, Mia."

I rolled my eyes. "Okay, fine. Yes, I was thinking about us."

He eased closer to me. At the gleam in his eyes, I backed away from him as far as I could until I bumped against the elevator wall. "Don't even think about it," I warned.

"Let me guess, you think when we get upstairs we should be talking and doing more repairing of our 'broken relationship'?"

I bobbed my head wildly up and down. "Yes, we have a lot to talk about."

"True. But all I want to do is fuck you senseless."

I laughed at his honesty. "I would've figured as much."

He closed the gap between us like a hunter stalking its prey. "The question is do you want to fuck me senseless?"

I sighed. "Wanting you physically has never been an issue for me, AJ," I answered honestly.

"It's just the emotional part, huh?"

"Yes. But I'm working on that. I promise," I whispered.

The elevator dinged our arrival at his penthouse. After AJ took out his card, he pinned me with a stare. "So you *do* want me to fuck you senseless?"

I licked my lips. "Yes, more than anything."

"Good." AJ motioned for me to go on inside. After I stepped into the foyer, he followed me inside with my bags. He didn't even stop in the living room. Instead, he continued rolling them down the hall, and I simply trailed along behind him. Once we got inside the bedroom, he closed the door behind us. I eyed him, waiting to see what his next move would be. I was pretty sure it involved getting me naked and flat on my back.

After he abandoned my luggage, he sat down on the bed and crooked his finger at me. With a smile, I walked slowly across the bedroom towards him. "I know in the elevator you said you wanted to fuck me senseless, but I was wondering if we could meet in the middle."

"What does that mean?" he asked.

I wedged myself between his thighs before bringing my arms around his neck. I ran my fingers through the jet black strands of his hair before leaning over to kiss him gently. His warm mouth opened, and I darted my tongue out to dance along his. When he groaned into my mouth, I felt moisture pooling between my thighs. "I've missed you," I murmured against his lips.

"I've missed you, too," he replied, his hands sliding around to cup the cheeks of my ass.

I eased back to stare into his eyes that were already hooded with desire. "Will you make love to me, AJ?"

A lazy smile slunk on his face. "Of course I will. You know, you're the first woman I've ever given up control for."

I sucked his bottom lip into my mouth before flicking my tongue over it. My teeth grazed it lightly before I pulled away. "I feel honored—I truly do."

AJ's fingers left my ass and went to the hem of my sweater. Rising up off the bed, he lifted it over my head. After he undid my pants, I slid them down my thighs. I tried shaking off the ghosts of the past as I stood before him in only my bra and panties. Of course this time, I really did have more weight not only in my stomach, but in my breasts, hips and thighs.

AJ's gaze left mine to trail down to my extended belly for a moment before reaching out to brush his fingers over my bump. It tickled a bit, and I shivered. "So I guess we're having a mutt, huh?" he questioned.

My eyes widened before I smacked his arm. "Don't you dare call Bella a mutt!"

AJ laughed. "I just meant she's going to be mixed, that's all. A bit of Mexican and a bit of Sicilian."

I cocked my brows at him. "Mixed sounds way better than mutt."

"She'll be multilingual for sure."

"That's true."

AJ slid back on the bed and crossed his legs Indian style before grasping my hips. He pulled me over to where I rose up to straddle his lap. He pushed us back further on the bed. Staring intently at my mouth, he brought his hand up to brush his thumb over my lips. "Come se dice en Italiano?"

"Labbra."

"Mmm, they're labios in Spanish."

My index finger came to circle his mouth. "And this?"

"Boca," he replied before his tongue darted out to lick my finger.

"It's the same in Italian, except we Sicilians say vucca, too."

His brows quirked up. "We're not so different, are we?"

"No, we're not."

AJ's hands slid slowly down my neck, pausing for his fingers to tease along my clavicle before they dipped down and cupped my breasts. "And these?" he questioned with a squeeze.

"Seni."

A smile slunk on his lips. "Another one we have in common. But their senos in Spanish. Or pechos." He tugged on the straps of my bra and pulled down the cups to expose my breasts. "And these?" His fingers tweaked my hardening nipples.

I sucked in a breath before replying, "Capezzolos."

"En Español son pezónes."

"I see." He leaned over to suck one of my nipples into his mouth. His tongue flicked at the pebbled bud, and my hands went to rake through his hair. "Mmm, la bocca mi fa bagnato."

"En Ingles por favor," he replied, before he blew air across my puckering nipple.

"Your mouth makes me wet."

"I'm glad to hear that. Cause you're making me hard as a fucking rock.

"So what is this called then?" I asked, as I cupped the bulge in his boxers.

"Maestro de tu universo," he murmured against my breast.

Gripping his hair with one hand, I jerked his head up to meet my gaze. "I don't think so, egomaniac."

AJ grinned. "Fine. It's a pene or verga."

"Same in Italiano...it can also be cazzo in Sicilian."

"I know it wants to be in *this*," he said, cupping me between my thighs over my panties.

I giggled. "That would be a vagina...or for you since you're crude, it would be pussy, and that's figa."

"Cueva en español." As his fingers slipped inside to rub over the wetness he'd caused, he murmured, "Tu coño me vuelve loco."

"I have a crazy pussy?" I teased breathlessly.

Amusement danced in his eyes. "No smartass, your pussy drives me crazy."

I laughed. "Right back at ya," I said, before working him harder over his boxers.

AJ's mouth met mine in a frenzied kiss. Our tongues swirled against each other as our fingers worked to free one another of each other's underwear. After I tugged AJ's boxers over his hips, he pushed me up on my knees to pull my panties down my thighs. Easing me onto my back, he then slid them down my legs and tossed them over his shoulder. He kicked out of his boxers before his body hovered over mine.

Even though this was about making love, I'd already had enough foreplay. "I want you inside me, AJ," I pleaded.

Turning me onto my side, AJ spooned up beside me. Gripping under my knee, he lifted my leg up and then guided himself inside me. With one thrust, he filled me, and I cried out. His warm lips nuzzled my neck while his hand slid around my ribcage to cup my breast. "Oh baby, you and that sound. Do it again."

He pulled out of me all the way before easing slowly and deliciously back inside again. This time, I whimpered. The next time he pulled out, he slammed back into me, and I did cry out. "Fuck," AJ murmured.

His movements inside me became almost like a piece of music he might play. They varied between fast and hard and then soft and slow. I felt so in tune with him and so reconnected. He must have felt the same way because we came together. Even though it was early in the evening, he snuggled closer to me. His hand slipped around my waist to rub my belly. Even after he stopped, he kept his hand pressed against my stomach. It wasn't long before he was snoring softly against my neck. As I began to drift off, I tried once and for all to put the ghosts of my past to rest, hoping, more than knowing, that everything was finally right for me when it came to AJ.

Chapter Twenty-Three

Mia

Peering out the window of AJ's uncle's car, I took in the surroundings of Guadalajara. While AJ sat up front rattling along in Spanish to his Tio Diego, Abby was smooshed between me and Jake in the backseat. Rather than a hotel, we were staying with AJ's abuela who had a house in the heart of the city. From what I gathered, she had a soft spot for AJ like Mama Sofia had had for me. While I was thrilled to be staying with her and meeting all of AJ's family, I was a little intimidated by the fact that Abuela didn't speak English.

Turning to Abby, I asked, "So what do I do to not look like the out-of-place gringa?"

She giggled. "Just kiss both their cheeks and say 'mucho gusto'."

I nodded. "Okay, I think I can do that."

"And I promise to let you know if anyone is talking smack about you. Okay?"

I laughed. "Yes. Please do."

We turned onto a street with houses in rows pressed so tight together they even shared a retaining wall, rather than the townhouse approach I was used to back in the states. Since the house was practically on the street, we pulled into small garage. The moment I stepped out of the car, I was ambushed by AJ's relatives.

"This is my mom, Mari," AJ introduced, patting a woman with a shoulder-length bob haircut. With a curvy frame, she was a lot shorter than AJ, and I assumed he'd gotten his height from his father.

Mari's arms were immediately around me, squeezing me tight. "Oh Mia, it's such a pleasure to meet you."

"It's a pleasure meeting you, too. AJ has told me so much about you." With a smile, I added, "Especially about how you like to spoil him."

She laughed as she pulled away. "Yes, I've probably set him up to be utterly taken care of by you." She wagged a finger. "But don't you dare let him get away with that," she instructed.

AJ snorted. "Yeah, I don't think that will be a problem."

Mari and I laughed. "No, I don't think so either."

A tall man, who could have been an older version of AJ, stepped forward. He gave me a warm smile as he offered me his hand. "I'm Joaquin."

"Nice to meet you."

Before I could say anything else, a handsome, muscular guy stepped in front of me. "Mucho gusto," I began. But when I leaned in to kiss his cheeks, he jerked me to him and then proceeded to lay one on me. I squeaked against his lips before pushing my hands against his chest. When I stumbled back, the guy grinned at me and winked.

AJ huffed a frustrated breath beside me. "And that would be my dickhead brother, Antonio."

Relief momentarily flooded me that this was AJ's gay brother and not some overly amorous relative who had ideas of girlfriend swapping. "Uh, nice to meet you."

"Admit it, Mia. I'm a better kisser than this douchebag." When I widened my eyes, he laughed. "Just teasing you." He then leaned in to bestow a chaste kiss on my cheek. "It's a pleasure meeting the mother of my future niece."

I gave him a sincere smile. "Thank you."

He then grabbed AJ in a bear hug. "Glad to see you, big brother."

AJ grunted. "I just saw you yesterday when I came by the house, twatcake," he huffed. But I noticed he did squeeze Antonio tight.

"Where's Cris?" AJ asked.

With a roll of his eyes, Antonio replied, "Miss Cristina took the kids up the street to the market for some sweets."

AJ's brows furrowed. "You mean Abuela didn't make a cake?"

Antonio grinned. "Of course she did. It's just Cris's kids are too Americanized from having a gringo for a father." He jerked his chin up at me. "Just like your daughter will probably turn her nose up at most of our food."

I laughed. "Well, in her defense, she has been fed the majority of Italian food the last four and a half months."

"Is she going to be back for lunch? I really wanted Mia to meet everyone."

"I think she and the gringo mentioned taking the monsters to the zoo."

I grinned at Antonio's summation of his nephews, Jase and Luke. AJ had told me the five and seven year olds were a handful. I also knew from some comments AJ had made that Cris was the most Americanized of her family. I could tell he didn't like how she distanced herself from her roots.

"Alejandro!" a voice called, cutting through the noise of who I assumed to be AJ's aunts, uncles, and cousins behind us.

We whirled around to see a petite, elderly woman, with her flowing white hair tucked back in a bun, coming toward us. She wore a multi-colored housedress. When she got to him, AJ bent down so she could bestow two kisses on his cheeks. "Mijo," she cried, before wrapping her arms around him. He rubbed her back and kissed the top of her grey head. All the while he spoke softly to her in Spanish. An aching burn rippled through my chest at the sweet sight before me as my mind went to Mama Sofia. It was times like these when I saw true maternal love at its finest, I realized just how much I dearly missed Mama Sofia. It was hard not becoming teary watching AJ with his abuela.

When Abuela pulled away, her gaze immediately honed in on me. I shifted nervously on my feet as she stared at me, sizing me up. "Abuela, ella es mi novia, Mia." He turned to me and smiled. "This is my grandmother, Isabella."

Trying to break the tension, I stepped forward. "Mucho gusto," I said, before kissing both her cheeks. I gave her a quick hug. After I pulled away, I said to AJ, "She knows she's part of the reason why we're naming the baby, Isabella, right?"

He nodded and then translated to her. With a nod of her head, she then began rattling away in Spanish to AJ. When she was finished, she moved on to speak to Abby, who began conversing fluently with her in Spanish.

"What did she say?" I whispered.

"That you're a gold-digger, and I should run away while I still can." He shook his head. "She wonders if Bella is even mine."

My eyes widened in horror while my hand came over my mouth. "Oh my God!"

AJ busted out laughing. "Jesus, Mia, would you get a grip? I told you no one in my family would ever think badly of you."

"You stronzo!" I cried, smacking his arm.

"Easy killer," he teased.

"So what did she really say?"

"That you were very beautiful, and that she could see you had a good soul and a loving heart."

I gasped. "She really said that about my soul and heart—like my anema e core?"

AJ smiled. "Yes, she did."

"I can't believe it. It's like fate."

Leaning down, AJ bestowed a tender kiss on my lips. "I would say the same thing."

The telephone rang, and Abuela went to answer it. "Come on guys, I'll show you where we're sleeping."

We followed AJ down the hallway to the bedrooms. He stopped at the first door on the right. "So you and Abby will be in here," AJ said to me, before pointing into the room with a queen sized bed.

As he sat down my suitcase, Jake, Abby, and I all exchanged an open-mouthed, wide-eyed look of shock before turning to AJ. "Wait, what?" Jake demanded.

AJ grimaced. "My abuela, she's hardcore, man. I mean, serious on the old-school catholic stuff." He jerked his thumb to the silver crucifix over the door and then motioned to the one over the bed. "So needless to say there's no sleeping together when you're not married."

"That's understandable," Abby replied, sitting down her bag.

Jake's brows shot up so far they disappeared into his hairline. "Oh hell no, my dick doesn't understand that shit at all!"

AJ stood toe to toe with Jake. "You think I like it any better than you do? Mia and I just got back together yesterday after my four months of fucking blue-balls celibacy. But when we're in my abuela's house, we respect her and her rules. Got it, Ese?"

After staring him down for a moment, Jake finally nodded. "Yeah man, I hear ya. Sorry for being an asshole."

Abby threw her arm over my shoulder. "I look forward to snuggling with you, Mia."

Knowing it would drive the guys wild to tease them, I nodded. "I really like to spoon. Hope you don't mind since it's so hot down here, I have my really skimpy pajamas."

Biting on her lip to keep from laughing, Abby nodded. "Oh totally. I'll probably just go with a tank top and panties, if that's okay with you."

"It's fine. I'm not modest at all. You can go naked if you want."

When we turned to look at the guys, drool practically oozed onto their chins. We couldn't hold back our laughter any longer. "Gotcha," we said in unison.

AJ rolled his eyes and wiped his mouth. "So not funny."

Abuela poked her head in the bedroom. "Alejandro, conmiga arriba."

"Si, Abuela."

Abby grinned at AJ before reaching over to ruffle his hair. "Look at you being all 'yes ma'am' to your grandmother."

He shook his head. "Hey, nothing pisses her off more than bad manners. Let's go upstairs. We can check out where Jake and I will be sleeping. Then we'll have lunch on the rooftop."

After we left my and Abby's room, we followed AJ down the hallway to a door leading outside. The steps up to the rooftop consisted of a circular, wrought iron staircase. When we got to the top, I gasped. The entire top of the roof was actually like a floor, and it had gold tiles with mosaics of colors swirled into them. The walls were decorated with Mexican art and porcelain. A fence ran the length of the top. The air was cooler, and you could see for miles in the distances over the roofs. "Wow, this is amazing."

AJ grinned. "Even though the views would have been better from the bedroom up here, Abuela didn't like the idea of you on these stairs too much." His hand reached out to graze my belly.

My heart swelled with her concern. "Really?"

"Yeah."

"That's sweet."

He leaned in for a quick kiss before taking me by the hand

and leading me over to the table. His parents, along with the rest of his family, were already seated. "Right here, Mia," Antonio suggested patting the seat next to him.

Instead of giving his brother shit, AJ eased me down next to Antonio and then squeezed in beside me. Abby and Jake found places at the head of the table. My eyes widened at all the food while my stomach growled with hunger pains.

After piling on some tamales and beans and rice, I glanced down at the plate that Antonio passed me. "What's this?" I asked AJ.

He grimaced. "Cow tongue."

My eyes widened. "T-Tongue?"

"It's kinda a delicacy. They know how much I love it."

Even though I was starving, just the mention of tongue, along with the sight and smell of it, caused my stomach to turn. Fearing I would throw up, I clamped my hand over my mouth. I almost knocked my chair over as I stumbled out of it before racing into the bedroom off the roof. Glancing wildly around, I searched for the bathroom. Finally, I saw it and raced inside, slamming the door behind me. When I got to the toilet, I heaved just twice before my stomach started to settle. I had just finished gargling some mouthwash I'd dug out from under the sink when a gentle knock came at the door. "Mia?" AJ questioned.

After I spit, I swiped my mouth and then reached over to unlock the door. He ducked his head in, his brow creased with worry. "You okay?"

"My stomach is fine, but I'm mortified that I just did that in front of your family. God, what a nice impression."

"Aw, amorcito mio, they don't give a shit about that. You're pregnant—shit's gonna bother you more than normal."

I grinned up at him. "I gotta say that pregnant or not, that tongue woulda freaked the hell outta me."

AJ laughed. "So you're telling me you Sicilians don't eat weird shit?"

"Yeah, I'm sure they do back in the old country, but not in Atlanta."

When my stomach rumbled between us, AJ grinned. "Come on, let's get out of here."

"Would they be really offended if I went to lie down instead of being at the tongue table?"

AJ shook his head. "No, I mean, let's really get out of here. I'm getting my Baby Mama some American food."

"But I don't want—"

AJ silenced me by bringing his lips to mine. When he pulled away, he cupped my cheeks in his hands. "Quit worrying about pissing off my family. They love you just for having my baby."

I crossed my arms over my chest. "Your illegitimate baby."

"Hey, we can always legitimize her while we're down here."

"If that's a proposal, you need to step up your game."

AJ laughed. "Come on, let's go."

When we stepped back onto the roof, everyone's gaze honed in on me. I tried not to blush and cower behind AJ. He held up a hand. "She's fine. I'm going to take her for some fresh air."

His mom nodded and then translated for his relatives. "Sorry," I said.

She smiled. "Don't worry about it, honey. It happens to all of us. Just feel better."

"Thank you."

I let AJ lead me over to the stairs. Once we were back on the main floor, he grabbed a set of keys off the hook. I followed him out the front door as he popped the lock on one of the cars on the street. After we buckled up, he floored the engine, and we pealed out of the spot.

"Um, are you insane?" I asked as we flew around the narrow streets.

"Sorry, amorcito mio, but this is how we drive down here."

"And I thought Atlanta was bad," I muttered as I cringed.

At the sight of the Golden Arches a few minutes down the road, I gasped in pleasure. "You guys have McDonalds?"

AJ chuckled. "Contrary to popular opinion, this isn't some third world country. We even have a Wal-Mart."

"Everywhere has a Wally World."

"Whatever," AJ replied as he eased up to the drive thru.

I longingly eyed the burgers and fries on the menu. Still worried about gaining too much weight and being undesirable to AJ, I knew I shouldn't get anything really fattening. With regret, I said, "I'll have the chicken salad.

AJ rolled his eyes and ordered us both double cheeseburger meals and fries. He had them add an apple pie as well. "What was that about?" I demanded as he began to pull forward.

"That's about you and your neurotic weight shit." He cut his eyes over to me. "I want you to eat what you want to eat."

I snorted. "Fine. When I get as big as Shamu—"

"I'll love every inch of you," AJ countered, with a determined look in his dark eyes.

My heart melted at his words, even though it was hard to believe him. "Whatever," I mumbled, but I did lean over and kiss him. After we got the food, he pulled the car into a parking space and left it running. After he handed me my burger, I hurriedly unwrapped it and shoved in a bite. "Augh, this is terrible for me, but so fucking good," I murmured through my mouthful.

AJ laughed. "I'm just glad to see you're eating for you and Bella."

"Hey, as long as you don't give me tongue, I'll be fine."

"We'll get you some 'Mia friendly food' later at the local market."

After wiping my mouth with my napkin, I planted a kiss on AJ's cheek. "My hero."

"You're welcome."

When we were finished, AJ tossed the trash bag in the back seat and cranked up the car. "Come on, let me show you my city."

"But what about your family? Won't they be mad at me for keeping you gone so long?"

He shook his head. "Once I tell them you wanted nothing more than to learn everything you could about your second home, Guadalajara, you'll be putty in their hands."

I laughed. "If you say so."

"We have two weeks with my family, Mia. Stop worrying."

"Okay," I said with a smile.

Once we got to the historic downtown part, we abandoned the car in a parking deck, and AJ began his tour on foot. At the sight of an empty horse drawn carriage on the street corner, a thought popped into my mind. After everything we had been through, we needed a little romance, and what could be more romantic than a carriage ride?

"Can we do this?"

AJ eyed the white and pink carriage with disdain. I guess the fact the overhanging had pink fringe didn't help matters. "Seriously?"

"Please."

"I'm going to look like a fucking pansy tourist in that thing."

I poked my bottom lip out. "Do it for me and Bella."

He snorted. "Like she gives two shits about a Pepto Bismol covered carriage ride." But even as he was arguing, he was getting his wallet out. He stepped forward and spoke to the driver. Taking my hand, he helped me inside before hopping in to sit beside me. On the back of the carriage, there were two heart-shaped cut-outs for windows. I nestled closer to him before jerking my head back. "Oh, look. It's all romantic."

AJ shifted in his seat. "Let's not mention romantic shit, okay?"

My anxiety at his comment kicked into overdrive. "But I thought we could use a little romance."

He grinned. "I'm all for romance, but considering I won't get to have sex with you as long as we're at Abuela's, I think we need to nix anything that might make me even more sexually frustrated."

Relief flooded me at his real reason for shooting down my romantic vibe. As I gazed out the carriage, I peered at the surroundings. "Then I think we better find a hotel that we can duck into from time to time."

He arched his eyebrows in surprise. "Really?"

"Mmm, hmm. Pregnancy makes you really horny—or at least it has me."

He laughed. "Let me guess. You need a stud like me to take care of your needs?"

"Yes, I do."

"Fuck yeah," he muttered before kissing me on the lips. Considering we kept making out, I didn't see much of the ride before AJ called the driver to stop and let us get out in the city center. AJ helped me down, and then proceeded to give me an official tour, including historical information.

As I gazed around at the architecture, I said, "This is really beautiful—it reminds me a little of Italy."

"A lot of the design is in the similar neoclassic style."

An imposing cathedral caught my eye. "Wow, that is breathtaking."

"That's the Catedral de Guadalajara or Catedral de la Asunción de María Santísima."

"I want to go to mass there."

"Sure, we can come back any day you want."

"Thank you."

He nudged me playfully. "You'll make a big impression on Abuela waning to go to mass."

"Really?"

"Yep. She goes every day. Usually to a smaller church close to the house."

A tug pulled at my heart. "She sounds just like Mama Sofia. She went every day, too. She'd give me such grief when I only made it on Sunday." I smiled at the memory.

As if sensing my grief, AJ wrapped an arm around my waist. "Speaking your Italian heritage, I bet you'd like the Degollado Theater." He motioned across the plaza.

"Yes, I do," I murmured as my gaze took in the intricate details of the building that looked somewhat like a replica of the Parthenon. "Do they have operas?"

He winced. "You like opera, huh?"

I grinned. "I'm Italian. The great tenors are a part of my heritage."

"Yeah, they do. Maybe we'll go one night we're here."

My brows rose in surprise. "You in a tux?"

"Hell yeah."

"Very tempting, Resendiz. Very, very tempting."

He laughed. "I'll have my Tio Diego to get us some tickets."

"That would be very sweet of him."

"I can't wait to introduce you to him at the Quinceañera."

"I look forward to it." Deep down, my feelings betrayed the enthusiasm in my voice. Although I was used to a huge family, it was a little overwhelming meeting all of AJ's, especially since most of them here didn't speak English. So far, even with the language barrier, they'd all been so nice and welcoming. It made me grateful that Bella would have so many people to love her.

We strolled along the streets, taking in the sights and sounds, until AJ came to a building that looked like a giant warehouse. "What's this place?"

"San Juan De Dios—a shopper's paradise."

"Ooh, yes, please."

AJ groaned. "I knew you would want to go in there."

"I'll make it quick, I promise. I'm getting tired anyway."

"Okay." As we stepped inside, AJ said, "Actually I need to make a stop while we're here too." He then steered me toward a jewelry counter, which caused my throat to close up. Surely, after what I had said in the bathroom he wasn't bringing me to look at rings. This trip was about taking it slow and getting to know each other. He must've noticed my stricken expression because he chuckled. "Easy girl. I'm just here to pick up a present for my goddaughter. I thought with you being a chick, you might be able to help me out."

"Oh," I replied, before the breath I'd been holding was exhaled in relief. As we surveyed the contents inside the glass case, I peppered AJ with questions about his goddaughter's likes and dislikes. Surprisingly, he knew more than I thought he would, and once he told me her favorite color was purple, I picked out a bracelet and earring set.

"Damn, you have expensive taste," AJ muttered, as he jerked his wallet out his pocket.

"Come on, your goddaughter only has a Quinceañera once." I nudged his arm. "Besides, you're a famous musician. You don't want to come off as cheap, do you?"

"No," he replied, as he took his change. After we waited for them to gift-wrap the boxes, we started making our way through the stalls of clothing and blankets. "I think I'll get a sombrero for my dad."

AJ snickered. "Yeah, I can see him styling that at Mama Sofia's."

"That's the point," I replied with a grin.

When I bought some other small souvenirs for Dee, Shannon, and some of my cousins, AJ insisted he pay for them. When he started to take the packages from me, I held them back. "I think I can carry a few bags in my 'delicate condition'."

He shook his head. "It's not about you being pregnant. It's a customary thing here in Mexico." When I opened my mouth to protest, he replied, "Get your feminist panties out of a twist, Mia, and let me do something chivalrous, okay?"

"Fine," I grumbled, before handing over the bags.

We were on our way out when AJ stopped at a barrel of jewelry. He fished something out and paid the lady. He then took my hand in his and slid a black, metal bracelet on my arm. I glanced down at it before shooting him a look. "You're kidding me, right?"

"What? It's a Saint's bracelet."

"Duh, I know what it is. I'm Catholic too, remember?"

"Then what's the problem?"

I shrugged. "They're kinda hokey now because Bella wears one of them in the *Twilight* movie."

"I don't give a shit what they wore in some sparkly vampire movie. They're for protection." AJ brought his hand to my stomach. "I pray for the saints to watch over you and Bella. If anything, wear it to humor me, okay?"

I fought to catch my breath at his words. Even though we were in a crowded market, I'd never felt more connected to AJ in my life. "Okay, I will," I whispered.

"Ready to head back?"

I nodded in reply. As we started back to the car, I stared down at my bracelet. From time to time, I let my fingers graze over the saint's pictures.

"Wait just a sec, okay?"

Before I could ask him what he was doing, AJ had crossed the parking lot to where a woman and her son sat. Shielding my eyes from the blazing sun, I saw the sign in her hand. Although it was in Spanish, I knew it must be asking for help. AJ reached in his pocket and took out a wad of money. She smiled and ducked her head at his gesture. The boy, who couldn't have been more than seven, pointed at AJ's head. I saw AJ grin before he took off the Braves baseball cap he'd been sporting since we left Atlanta. He placed it on the boy's head, which caused him to beam with pleasure.

And in that moment of AJ's kindness—when there was no

paparazzi or fans to impress—I knew what a truly decent and honorable man he was. But more than anything, I knew how much I truly loved him and wanted to be with him. In that moment any doubt I had about him or about us instantly evaporated.

As he walked up to me, his smiled faded, and concern lined his brow. "Amorcito mio, why are you crying?"

"What you just did..." I said between my hiccupping cries.

"Oh that. Yeah, I—" I silenced him by throwing my arms around his neck and pressing myself tight against him. "Hey, hey, what's this?"

I pulled away to stare into his eyes. "I love what you just did—for the mother and for the boy. I love that you pray for me and Bella. I love that you won't give up on me, and you keep pushing me to see beyond my past. I love that as hard as I try to make you just like all the other men out there, you keep proving me wrong. I love that you wanted to bring me here to meet your family..." My lip quivered harder. "I even love that you got me fatty American food to eat."

AJ smiled. "You're welcome." With his thumb, he brushed away some of the tears streaming down my cheeks. "I do all those things because I love you. You know that right?"

"I do." I leaned over and brought my lips to his. When he tried to deepen the kiss, I eased back. "I love you, too," I murmured against his lips.

AJ's closed eyes popped open. "What did you say?"

I laughed. "I said, I love you, too." At his expression of disbelief, I cupped his face in my hands. "I know without a shadow of a doubt that I love you." Tears continued to spill from my eyes onto his shirt. "You're my anema e core."

AJ's lips were warm and tender against mine. When he pulled away, he tugged my bottom lip between his teeth for a second. "You make me really happy, you know that?"

He sank down to where he was on eye-level with my belly. "You hear that, Bella? Your stubborn-ass mom finally told your old man she loves him."

"We gotta work on your mouth before she gets here." He grinned up at me before pressing a tender kiss on my stomach. I brought my hands up to cup his cheeks. As the beads on my Saint's bracelet caught the sunlight, I knew I was truly blessed.

Chapter Twenty-Four

AJ

"Oh my God, that was amazing!" Mia exclaimed as we excited the Degollado Theater. Since I begged to differ, I kept my lips pinched shut. I'd almost dozed off twice. Okay, so maybe I did fall asleep since Mia elbowed me because I was snoring. I'd even drooled a little on her arm. Thankfully, she was so fucking stoked to be seeing her favorite opera, *La Bohème*, that she could have cared less about what I was doing.

But I still felt like an ass because tonight was all part of a very strategic romantic plan. It had started off this morning with a Mariachi band serenade. When she and Abby had staggered out onto the rooftop at six am to find a full ensemble of musicians and singers belting our anthem of *Guadalajara*, she had stared wide-eyed and open-mouthed at me like I had totally lost my mind. To me, the Mariachi band was an obvious choice. I mean, Guadalajara is where

Mariachi originated. But I guess Mia felt a little ridiculous in her pajama pants and bed hair in front of a bunch of strange men in glittering suits.

But that all changed when I led her out to the chair waiting for her in the center of the roof. Then I took my place among the singers. I'd been practicing secretly for days while she was spending time with my family. In perfect Spanish, I began singing *Aneme e Core* to her. As the sun began to rise over the city, tears glistened in her eyes as I knelt before her and took her hands in mine.

When I finished the song, she dove into my arms, smothering my face with kisses before bringing her lips to mine. "I love you so much," she murmured against my mouth.

"I love you, too."

The band stayed on, and while they sang *Amorcito Mio*, Mia and I danced together. That's when I surprised her with tickets to the opera. She had squealed with delight and squeezed me harder. When everyone had started heading back to bed, I kept Mia out on the rooftop. Pressed into an alcove where no one could see us, I'd spun her around, pressed her palms against the wall, and then jerked her pajama pants down. The more I pumped furiously into her, the more vocal she got.

Even though I didn't give a shit if Jake heard us in the bedroom, I didn't want the neighbors or worst of all Abuela to hear. I covered Mia's mouth with my hand. "You make me so fucking hot with those sounds, but someone is going to catch us," I whispered into her ear. She bobbed her head, and almost made me blow my load by flicking her tongue against my hand in time with my thrusts. When she came, she bit down onto my fingers. I followed quickly after her.

Now everything was going according to the plan I had in my mind. Well, except for the fact I found opera boring as hell and with a full stomach from our romantic dinner, I had made an ass of myself falling asleep.

Staring up at the starry sky, Mia gasped. "Look at the moon, AJ!" she exclaimed.

As I peeked up at the rounded, full moon, I shrugged. "What about it?"

Spinning around, Mia practically glowed with happiness. "It's a bella luna just like in *Moonstruck*, my most favorite movie ever. And we just went to the same opera in the movie, too."

Since I had no idea what the hell she was talking about, I merely smiled and took her hand. "Let's go there," I motioned to what looked like a carousel without the animals. It was perfect not just because it looked incredibly romantic all lit-up in glittering, white lights with an excellent view of the city. But to me, a Merry-Go-Round was so symbolic of mine and Mia's relationship so far.

"Okay," she replied with a dreamy smile. Somehow she

had managed to find the sexiest maternity evening dress I'd ever seen. It was black satin that hugged her curves. My favorite was the plunging neckline that showed off her expanding tits. The back of the dress hung low, exposing more of her delicious skin. When she had stepped out of the bedroom wearing it, I had to hold myself back not to rush forward and bang her in the hallway.

After leading her up the stairs, I was stoked to find no one else inside. "This is so beautiful." She pressed herself against me. "Thank you for today, AJ. Everything has been so amazing on this trip. Your family has been as wonderful as you described them. I feel as though they have accepted me with open arms. I hate that we have to leave in a few days."

I nuzzled my head into the crook of her neck. "You're welcome. And, of course they love you. How could they not? But we'll come back. I promise."

"Good." She ran her fingers through my hair. "God, I love you so very much," she murmured.

Just those words caused my perfect plan to get shot to hell. "Marry me," I blurted, my voice vibrating against her neck.

She jerked away and stared incredulously into my eyes. "What?"

"You heard me."

"Yes, but I'm pretty sure a statement like that bears repeating."

I grinned. "You're not a traditionalist, but if you'd like, I'll get down on one knee."

"You can't be serious."

"Dead serious."

Mia's brows crinkled. "But we barely know each other."

I shrugged. "How much does any couple actually know each other when it comes down to it? Sure, I might've only known you five months—"

"Which four of those we were apart," she countered.

"But I still know I want to spend the rest of my life with you." My hand came to rest on her stomach. "Besides, you're carrying my daughter."

Staring up at the twinkling lights, Mia gave a sad sigh. "I don't want to get married just because of Isabella. That's what happened with my parents. I never want you to resent me or come to view me as 'the chick who trapped you with a kid'."

I shook my head furiously from side to side. "I could never think of you like that. Hell Mia, if anything, I'm the one that's trapping you. I chased your stubborn ass down until you finally decided to give us a real chance."

"You say that now, but who knows what might happen in the future?"

"Don't you want to marry me?" My voice had taken on a wounded tone.

Mia turned to bring her hands to my face, cupping my

cheeks. "That's not it at all. Any woman would be honored to marry you. This is about me and all my hang-ups. All this seems too good to be true—*you* seem too good to be true. I'm waiting for the other shoe to drop where I wake up to realize this isn't real."

I couldn't fight the anger building within me at her response. "Dammit Mia, how many times do I have to prove that punishing me for your past isn't fair?"

With a wince, she replied, "I don't know...And I'm sorry. I truly am."

"You know the four months I spent apart from you were miserable. Before you, I thought I'd been in love with other women before. When they left me, I was desolate. But it was nothing compared to what I experienced after you left. I was fucking obliterated."

"So was I," she admitted.

I threw up my hands. "Then what the fuck else is there to say? We're miserable when we're apart and happy when we're together."

Tears pooled in her eyes, and I shook my head. "No more bullshit about how I'm too good to put up with all your hang-ups and blah, blah, blah. Just marry me. You can't worry about the future—we're not even promised tomorrow. Just here and now. When I see Bray and Lily together and Jake and Abby, I'm envious of what they have. I want that with you and only you."

Tears spilled over Mia's cheeks, but she didn't bother wiping them away. "Oh AJ," she murmured.

I pulled her into my arms before taking her face in my hands. "It's been a whirlwind, but I know that I love you. I think I loved you from the moment you tied me up in the limo. I'd never had a woman challenge me like you did."

"You really want to marry me?"

"I sure as hell do."

She laughed and swiped the tears from her cheeks. "Then where's the ring?"

"I'm so glad you finally asked." Reaching into my pocket, I pulled out a small, velvet box. When I cracked it open, a sob choked off in Mia's throat. The tears flowed so freely she had to blink several times.

"That's Mama Sophia's ring," she whispered.

I nodded. "The base is. I had them reset it in platinum, and then I added the other diamonds."

"But how did you—"

"Your dad sent it to me." I smiled. "Along with his permission to marry you."

Mia staggered back, and I had to grab her shoulders to steady her. "When? How?"

"I had Duke give the ring to Rhys to bring when he flew down today. And then I asked him everything when we skyped a day or two after we got here." I winked at her while my mind went back to the day I'd called Duke to ask him if I could marry Mia. I'd been such a nervous pussy I had been shaking when I did it. I mean, the man had every right to take my balls for knocking up his daughter. That in itself was scary enough, but this motherfucker was a former NFL football player with friendly ties to people associated with the mob. I was ready to shit my pants or go into Witness Protection by the time he answered the phone. But he'd surprised the hell out of me, though, by breaking down and crying like a pansy himself.

I gripped Mia's chin in my fingers, tipping her head up to look at me. "He was more than happy to give us his blessing, not just so Bella could be legitimate. But because he wanted his baby girl to be happy."

A sob echoed through Mia's chest before she really let loose with the tears. "Oh AJ," she murmured.

I took the ring from the box before taking her hand in mine. "Emiliana Sofia Martinelli, you are the most stubborn and infuriating woman I've ever met. Even though you drive me crazy and sometimes I want to bang my head against a fucking wall when you're being difficult, there's no one else in the world I want to spend the rest of my life with."

She laughed at my words. "Thank you...I think." As I knelt down before her, she stroked my cheek with her hand. "Alejandro Joaquin Resendiz, they broke the mold after they made you. Every stereotype I had about men, you managed to break, and I thank God for that. I've given you such an uphill battle, but you always came back for more. I never thought I could love again or be loved, but you proved me so very wrong." She stooped over to bring her lips to mine. "Thank you for loving me."

"It's my pleasure, amorcito mio. To me, you're perfect." I kissed her again before I slid the ring on her finger. She held it up to examine it against the twinkling lights.

"This is so beautiful."

"A beautiful ring for my beautiful girl."

"Thank you, AJ. Thank you for everything." She smiled down at me. Grabbing me by the lapels of my tux, she pulled me up off my knees. "Remember our first day in the carriage when I said we needed to get a hotel room?"

A smirk slunk on my face. "Yeah, I remember."

"Tonight I want to make love to my fiancé, and we know it isn't happening at your abuela's."

"I couldn't agree more. No sneaking around tonight or roof-top quickies for my future wife." I ran my thumb over her lips. "I want to spread you out on the bed beneath me, so I can make love to you nice and slow."

A shiver rippled through her. "Let's go now."

I chuckled. "Okay, come on."

Chapter Twenty-Five

Mia

Five Months Later

On aching, swollen feet, I tagged along behind AJ to our third Grammys after party of the evening. Even though I was dead tired and wanted nothing more to crawl into bed, I didn't dare go back to the hotel room to crash. AJ was on such an adrenaline high since it had been a huge day for Runaway Train, and I wanted to be along for the ride as his supportive fiancée.

Earlier in the afternoon, I'd felt like I was Cinderella in a fantasy land. Outfitted in a glittering red maternity gown that AJ proclaimed to be sexy as hell, I'd sat in the third row of the Staples Center surrounded by A-list musicians. We'd started off flying high when Abby and the boys of Jacob's Ladder had won the Grammy for Best Country Duo/Group. Then later I shed tears of elation and pride when Jake and Abby won Song of the Year, especially knowing how it had been written about Jake's late mother. When it came time to announce the Best Pop Duo/Group performance, I held AJ's hand as he nervously tapped his leg. He'd been on edge all afternoon, but he could barely contain himself in his seat now.

When they had announced Runaway Train as the winner, I thought he would keel over with a heart attack from the excitement. Watching him take the stage with the guys had me grinning until my cheeks hurt and clapping until my palms were red and stinging. Brayden had been shoved in front of the mic to do the thank yous, and he did an amazing job. In the end, the guys racked up Best Pop Album as well.

Once the ceremony had ended, we'd been shuffled back into the limo we'd arrived in to start making our way to the after parties. I became immediately star struck at the label party when I saw who all was milling around. Even as the fiancée of a famous musician, it was still hard to believe this was now my life. Bella got in to the festivities as well as the later it got, the more she kicked the crap out of me.

After dancing for hours, we'd just left the Chateau Marmont hotel for a smaller party when AJ eyed me in the limo. "Do you think you need to go back to the hotel?"

"No why?"

"You look a little tired."

Cocking my head at him, I asked, "Is that a nice way of saying I look like shit?"

He laughed. "Is that the pregnancy hormones talking?"

"No, it isn't. Besides, Bella is having fun. She's kicking up a storm."

AJ's hand came to rest on my enormous belly. "Man, she's really going at it, huh?"

I grinned. "Yeah, she is."

"Well, if you're sure."

I leaned over to kiss him. "I wouldn't miss one minute of this amazing night with you."

AJ brought his hands up to stroke my face. "I love you, Mia."

"I love you more."

Once we got inside the hotel, AJ and the others got drinks while I made my way to the hors d'oeuvres. Bella usually went on a kicking frenzy when she was hungry, so I was trying to appease her. Not only were ribs hurting from her exertions, but my back was as well.

I'd just finished my plate when AJ held out his hand. "Wanna dance again?" Even though I would have preferred sitting at the table and staying off my ballooning feet, I smiled at him and slid my hand into his. Halfway through the second song, I knew I'd made a mistake. The dull ache that had been building throughout my lower back and into my abdomen grew more intense.

With a gasp, I pulled away from AJ. "I think I need to sit this one out," I shouted over the thumping bass of the music and roaring of the crowd.

AJ's dark brows knitted together as he brought his hand to my abdomen. "Are you all right?"

Forcing a smile to my lips, I bobbed my head. "I just need to sit down and get some air." When he started to lead me off the dance floor, I pressed a palm against his chest. "No, this is your night. I can make it to a table just fine." He opened his mouth to protest, but I pressed my lips to his to silence him. "I'm fine." I motioned toward the crowd of people who were waiting to talk to him. "Go, have fun."

"Okay. Love you."

As I weaved in and out the throng of people, I thought I would never make it outside to the veranda. People milled around, mainly smoking, but it wasn't nearly as crowded as inside. My heels clicked down the tile as I tried to get away from the clouds of smoke. I sighed with relief when I found an empty chair tucked into an alcove. But after I got off my feet and took in a few deep breaths, pain still radiated through my lower back and abdomen.

"Mia?"

I glanced up to see Brayden standing before me. When he realized it really was me, he quickly extinguished the cigarette he'd been smoking. "Sorry about that."

"It's okay."

"What are you doing out here by yourself?"

"I just needed some air."

He dug a pack of gum out of his pockets and offered me a piece. When I declined, he popped three pieces in his mouth. He gave me a sheepish grin. "Would you do me a huge favor and not tell Lily I was out here smoking? You know, considering I allegedly quit three months ago."

I laughed. "I'll make you a deal. I won't tell Lily about the smoking if you won't tell AJ that he was right, and I really shouldn't have tagged along to all the parties tonight. The ceremony was enough."

Brayden crossed his arms over his chest and cocked his head suspiciously at me. "What do you mean?"

I sighed. "I'm tired, that's all."

"Mia," he implored.

"Fine. I'm having some...pains."

Brayden knelt at my side—his expression clouded with worry. "What kind of pains?"

"It's nothing. Seriously. It's just my back and feet." When he pursed his lips at me, I caved. "I started cramping out on the dance floor. But I'm sure I just overdid it tonight, and I need some rest. If I sit here a little longer and put my feet up, I'll be fine."

"I'm going to get AJ," Brayden said, popping up from the ground.

I grabbed his sleeve and jerked him back. "No, please don't do that."

"Mia, as a husband, trust me when I say that when your wife is pregnant and in pain, you want to know it. To AJ, you're more than his fiancée—you're already his wife"

"But this is the most amazing night of AJ's life—one he has worked so hard for. He's been on cloud nine all day, and I want him to savor each and every moment. I can't bear to ruin one second of it by causing him unnecessary worry as the nagging fiancée."

"He needs to know, and I'm going to tell him."

"Not if I get to him first!" I countered. When I shot out of my seat, all hell broke loose below my waist. A twisting, wrenching pain ricocheted through me, and I moaned.

"Mia?" Just as Brayden stepped over to me, my water broke with such a force that it splashed down my legs and onto the top of Brayden's shoes before spreading on the floor.

As Brayden and I gazed down at the puddle we stood in, my hand flew to cover my mouth. "Oh God, I can't believe that just happened. All that 'what to expect' crap doesn't quite prepare you for Splash Mountain." When I dared to look up at Brayden, I shook my head. "I'm so, so sorry about your shoes."

He laughed. "Mia, honey, I could give two shits about my shoes right now. I'm a little more concerned about the fact you're in labor."

"Oh damn," I muttered.

"We need to get you to the hospital."

Tears stung my eyes. "Now I'm really going to ruin AJ's night."

As I sniffled, Brayden's hand came to cup my cheek. "Mia, I promise you when it comes down to it, awards and parties won't mean shit when he holds Isabella in his arms for the first time. Nothing will ever compare to that moment when he sees the life he helped create."

My lip trembled at his sweet words. "Thank you."

He smiled. "You're welcome. Now why don't you just sit back down here while I go find AJ, and then we'll get you to the limo."

"Yeah, that should be—" My voice choked off as pain ripped through my abdomen like a steam locomotive charging through it. I doubled over and cried out. Around me, I could hear Brayden talking furiously to someone, but I couldn't make out his words through the agonizing pain. It seemed to go on forever before it finally let up.

"Mia!" AJ cried.

I glanced up to see him tearing down the veranda—his face ashen with worry. When he got to me, he wrapped me in his arms. "Amorcito mio, it's okay. I'm here now."

Before I could stop myself, tears stung my eyes. "Oh AJ, I'm so sorry about going into labor tonight."

His eyes widened. "Don't you dare say that! You and Bella are my world."

Another pain rippled through me, and I cried out. "Come on. We gotta get you to the limo." AJ wrapped one arm around my waist while the other he used to push us through the crowd. Brayden started ahead of us, shoving people out of the way to clear a path. By the time we got outside, Jake, Abby, Lily, and Rhys were pacing beside the limo.

"Oh my God, Mia," Abby cried, rushing up to me.

"I'm okay...I'm just in labor."

"And we're going to get you to the hospital ASAP," Lily replied.

"No, no, you guys need to stay and have fun," I protested.

Jake grinned and shook his head. "I think there's a new party to go to—'Miss Bella's Introduction to the World Party'."

I laughed. "Yeah, it's going to be a rocking one for sure."

"All right, enough talking. You need to get inside the limo. Now," AJ commanded.

"Eesh, so bossy," I muttered before I dipped inside. AJ threw his tux jacket across the seat. Just as I sat down, another pain gripped me. AJ immediately appeared at my side and grabbed hold of my hand.

When I finally came out of my pain haze, I saw that Abby and Jake had ducked inside as well. "That was intense," I croaked.

"I'm so sorry," AJ murmured, kissing my cheek.

I was adjusting myself on the seat when the limo driver appeared at the door.

"Why aren't we moving?" Jake asked.

His face paled. "We seem to be having engine problems."

"Excuse me?" I demanded through gritted teeth.

"It won't start."

"You gotta be fucking kidding me!" AJ exclaimed.

Jake shook his head. "Maybe we can borrow someone else's car or limo?"

The limo driver shook his head. "I just called the paramedics on dispatch. They were right around the corner, and they should be here any minute."

"Shit," I muttered as another terrible contraction ricocheted through me. Looking back, I realized all the pains I'd had yesterday and today weren't just the usual pregnancy pains or Braxton Hicks. Even though I was a Cardiac nurse, how the hell could I not have realized the signs that I was in labor?

I gripped AJ's hand tight as I rode the agonizing wave of pain. When it finally subsided, I relaxed. But it was at that moment that I felt something had shifted below my waist. "Um, this is probably totally in my imagination, but it feels like she's coming out already."

Abby peered down at her phone. "Your contractions are coming faster and faster together. Do you want me to..." She glanced between AJ and Jake before looking back at me. "You know, check on things...down there?"

"Yeah, it probably wouldn't hurt. I mean, between the two of us, we probably have just enough nursing training to be dangerous when it comes to labor and delivery."

When Abby reached to ease up my dress, Jake threw up his hands defensively. "Wait, I'm sorry, but I have to get the hell out of here," he said, before ducking out of door. I caught a glimpse of Rhys pacing outside with Brayden and Lily before Jake closed the door.

Abby gently reached under my dress to remove my soaked panties. She tossed them to the side, and then pushed the hemline up. "Oh my God!" she screeched.

"What?" AJ and I demanded in unison.

"You were right. Bella's head...it's like...right there."

"Oh, shit, I've already crowned?"

"Whoa, what the hell is crowning?" AJ questioned.

"Didn't you read any of the baby books I gave you?"

A sheepish look entered his face. "I skimmed some of them. Those birthing pictures were way intense."

"Well for your information, crowning means it's time to push."

He shook his head wildly back and forth. "But you can't push yet. The paramedics aren't here. Can't you just hold it in?"

The death glare that both Abby and I shot him caused him to shrink back into the seat. He held up his hands defensively. "Sorry, that was a really stupid question." He swallowed hard. "Okay, then what do we do?"

I opened my mouth but was interrupted by the wail of an ambulance's siren. At AJ's horror stricken face, I squeezed his hand. "It's okay now. The EMT's will know what to do."

Just as they knocked on the window, another pain seized me—this time it felt like a giant's hands were squeezing my abdomen. I couldn't help but pinch my eyes shut and push, regardless of whether the paramedics were there or not. Voices echoed around me, but all I could do was focus on the contractions as they came harder and faster.

AJ

As I crouched down at Mia's side in the back of the limo, the irony of the situation wasn't lost on me. We'd come together sexually as a couple for the first time on a limo floor and now our daughter was going to be born in one. Mia was advancing so fast that the EMT's refused to move her.

When I'd dared to protest that maybe having a baby in a limo wasn't the best idea, they had ignored me. Instead they'd jerked up Mia's dress even further and widened her legs for the delivery. Shit was getting epically real, and I wasn't sure I could handle it.

But when I got my first sight of Bella's crowned head, it

was like a lightning bolt zapped me. Even from my vantage point, I could see she had a head full of jet black hair. Something about seeing that tiny head sent wonder and instant adoration rippling through me. This was *my* baby girl. I no longer gave a shit that we were having her in a limo and not a sterile delivery room. All I cared about was that my daughter— mi niña—was about to be born.

While I whispered soft words of reassurance in Mia's ear, she huffed and puffed out breaths of air as her face contorted in pain. I hated that she had to do this shit without any good drugs. The entire time she was pregnant she had never once advocated for natural childbirth—she'd even refused those classes where they teach you to breathe because she knew she wanted drugs. But now she was being denied that all because of me, and her stupid honor as my loyal fiancée to tag along with me to my Grammy party shit.

An electricity crackled in the air as one of the paramedics began moving faster between Mia's legs. A flurry of activity was going on below her waist, but I focused on her. I held her gaze as she rode the waves of pain, and then finally I resorted to singing Spanish into her ear. I knew she'd always said that Spanish turned her on and that was the last thing she was thinking about now, but I figured it might be a little soothing. It seemed to help a little.

And then almost like magic, one minute Bella wasn't there, and the next she appeared, bloodied and wailing in the paramedic's hands. Tears stung my eyes at the sight of her, and I didn't bother trying to hide them.

As the EMT suctioned Bella's nose and mouth, Mia squeezed my hand. "Is she okay?" she questioned.

The EMT smiled. "Looks fine—great, actually, considering everything. Of course, they'll check her over at the hospital." Turning to me, he asked, "Would you like to cut the cord?"

"Sure," I replied, taking the scissors from him. Once Bella was freed from Mia, the EMT wrapped her in a blanket and handed her to me. "Sir, I'm going to get you to hang on to the baby while we get your wife ready for transfer to the hospital."

Unable to correct him on our marital status, I merely bobbed my head. I couldn't have spoken if I had wanted to. I was too enthralled by the tiny bundle in my arms. Even though she was still a little bloody and messy from delivery, Bella was the most breathtakingly beautiful thing I'd ever seen in my life, next to her mother that is. Her lungs seemed to be working just fine because she was wailing her head off, her tiny features scrunched in anger. "Welcome to the world, my love," I murmured in Spanish.

At the sound of my voice, she cut off her screams before popping her eyes open to stare up at me. "Holy shit," I muttered before shaking my head. "Great, now I'm already cursing in front of you. You'll have to cut your old man some slack, okay?" She continued eye-balling me like I was the greatest mystery in her new world. The truth was she was the greatest mystery in mine—the greatest treasure I could ever possess.

The EMT's hand on my shoulder brought me out of my trance. "Okay, I need you to step outside with the baby, so my partner can get the stretcher for your wife."

When I eased out of the limo, I found a throng of people had gathered around both the limo and the ambulance. Thankfully, our EMT's partner, along with the police, had worked at erecting sheets up to block the view of any bystanders or paparazzi.

Through the faces, I caught sight of Jake and the others standing to the side of the ambulance. Walking as carefully as I could, I made my way over to them. "Hey," I said lamely.

Jake snickered. "Dude, you like you've just come back from war. I thought it was Mia birthing the kid, not you."

"Shut up, douchebag." I glanced down at Bella before looking back at him. "Seeing her born, holding her in my arms—it's the most fucking intense thing I've ever experienced." At the f-bomb, I winced. "Great, she's been here less than ten minutes, and I've cussed twice."

Abby smiled as she leaned down to kiss the top of Bella's head. "There are worse things you could do besides cuss in front of her. You're obviously doing something right because she seems very comfortable."

"I guess you're right." My attention was drawn over my shoulder where the rattling wheels of Mia's stretcher came screeching up to the open ambulance door. Although she was pale and sweaty, Mia had never looked more beautiful to me. She gave a smile to the others before she was loaded into the ambulance.

"See you at the hospital, okay?" Abby called.

"Okay," Mia replied.

"Congrats Big Daddy," Jake said, before slapping me on the back.

"Thank you." I smiled before turning to hand Bella to the EMT. I didn't trust myself to climb inside with her in my arms. I hopped in and then slid across the bench. The EMT had handed Bella to Mia, and she was cradling her in her arms with tears streaming down her cheeks. When she glanced up at me, she smiled. "Thank you."

"For making you have a baby in the back of a limo?"

She shook her head. "Thank you for giving me everything I hadn't realized I had ever wanted."

I leaned over and kissed her. "I feel the same way."

Chapter Twenty-Six

Mia

Blinking my eyes, I tried remembering where I was. The antiseptic smell of a hospital assaulted my nose, and for a minute, I thought I was back on the Cardiac Care floor at St. Joe's. But if I was on a shift, what the hell was I doing in bed? When I shifted slightly, a wave of pure exhaustion rippled through my body along with an ache between my legs so strong it felt like a Buick had driven straight through it.

And then it hit me. I'd given birth to my Bella. A replay of the night's evens came crashing over me. Oh God, I'd given birth in the back of a limousine outside of a Grammys after party. What could be more bizarre? I could only imagine by now the story and pictures had been leaked, sending the media into a frenzy.

My ears perked up at the sound of singing. Turning my head on my pillow, I followed the sound to where AJ sat in a rocker with Isabella in his arms. I remembered that once we'd gotten to the hospital, they had taken her from me. After weighing and measuring her, she'd been given back to feed. Once she finished and left my arms again, exhaustion had set in, and I'd fallen asleep.

Now that I'd woken from my mini-coma, I saw that Bella had been cleaned up, dressed in a onesie, and outfitted with a tiny cap with an enormous pink bow on her head. As he rocked back and forth, AJ softly sang to her in Spanish. With wide-eyes, she stared up at him, occasionally flailing her tiny hands or flicking out her tongue. The expression of pure love and wonderment on AJ's face as he stared down at his daughter caused my heart to still and then restart.

When I caught AJ's gaze, he smiled at me before glancing back down at Isabella. "Looks like Mommy is finally awake."

"Have I been out long?" I questioned, as I tried pushing myself up in the bed.

"About three hours."

My brows popped up in surprise. "Really?"

He nodded. "You needed it though."

"I guess so." With a groan, I wiped my eyes. "I feel like I've been hit by a bus."

"I would imagine so. You just gave birth, for Christ's sake."

"In the back of a limo, no less."

Instead of making a jab at our situation, he gave me a sincere smile. "Even though it wasn't here in the hospital like we would have wanted, it was still the most amazing experience of my life."

Tears pooled in my eyes from his words and the depth of emotion with which he said them. "It was, wasn't it?"

He nodded as he took Bella's fist in his fingers. "You know, I thought I loved her before, but now that she's here, it's incredible."

Sniffling, I reached for a tissue on the bedside table. "I love you for loving her so much, AJ. But most of all, I love you for being the man that you are."

"I love you too, amorcito mio."

I wanted to kiss him—to wrap my arms around him and not let go—but I was too tired. I couldn't stifle my yawn. AJ smiled. "You just rest, amorcito mio. I've got Bella all taken care of. Well, until she needs some boob time again."

"Whatever," I murmured, with a grin.

When AJ started humming to Bella again, I giggled. "You know, you're setting me up for failure singing to her like that. What will we do when you're out on the road, and she's stuck with tone deaf me?"

AJ grinned. "Maybe I can go to the studio and lay down some tracks for you to play when I'm gone."

"That sounds like a good idea." I motioned to the bassinet. "You should lay her down for a little while. I know you have to be tired, too."

"I'm fine," he murmured.

"But remember how the baby books all said that we'll spoil her if we hold her too much?"

"Yeah, well, fuck Dr. Spock and those other asshats."

"AJ!"

"Sorry. I know I need to watch my language around her." His blazing black eyes met mine. "Besides, I thought we both agreed not to listen to those books and raise her in our own way."

"Yes, I know, but—"

He exhaled a painful sigh. "I just want to do this as long as I can, Mia. I mean, we'll be leaving for the East Coast tour in two weeks." He bit his bottom lip like he was trying not to cry, but the tears welled in his eyes anyway. "I already feel this choking panic that I need to memorize every detail of her face, her hands, and body before I have to go so long without seeing her."

"We'll Skype together every night, and I'll text you pictures every day," I protested, softly.

He gave a quick jerk of his head. "It isn't the same thing as holding her in my arms, cuddling her close to my heart, and smelling her sweet, little baby scent." He pinned me with a glare. "And don't you dare say something to lighten the mood like 'well, you won't be thinking she smells so sweet at the next diaper change'!"

"I wasn't going to," I murmured. After all the issues we'd had, the only argument AJ and I had experienced in our last five months together was my decision not to come out on the road with him once Bella was born. It wasn't that I didn't want to be with him—I just wanted Bella to have the comfort and safety of a nursery not on wheels. There was also my job to contend with, which even though AJ thought it was absurd, I wanted to go back to nursing in a few months. It wasn't about the fact we didn't need the money—it was the need within me to help and heal people.

But as I watched the tears drip off of AJ's cheeks and onto Bella's blanket, some of Mama Sofia's words echoed through my mind. "Marriage is all about compromise, Emiliana. It's give and take, but in the end, it's always going to be the woman giving more because she's the soul and heart of her man and her family. And when it comes to being a mother, there is nothing that you won't sacrifice to ensure the happiness and health of your child." The more those words rolled through my mind, the more I realized what I had to do. "AJ," I said.

"Yeah?" he questioned, not taking his eyes off of Bella.

"I don't want you to have to be separated from Bella or from me."

He jerked his gaze over to mine. "What are you saying?"

"I'm saying I'll go on the road with you—if you'd still like that."

"Like it? I'd fucking love it!" He leapt out of the rocking chair and came to my side. With Bella nestled in one arm, he leaned over the rails of the bed with the other. He gave me a lingering kiss that warmed my heart. When he pulled away, his brows furrowed. "You're really willing to quit your job and live a chaotic life on a cramped bus just for me?"

"Not just for you." I kissed the top of Bella's capped head. "For her, too." I smiled at AJ. "Like her mom, she's blessed with an amazingly, loving father, and she shouldn't be deprived of one second with him."

"Oh God, you make me so happy," he said, bringing his lips back to mine.

"I feel the same way about you." And in the middle of a very idyllic, very romantic kiss, Bella let out a wail that I could only classify, as 'I want milk, and I want it now!' Pulling away, I rubbed AJ's cheek tenderly before taking Bella in my arms. I didn't know how I became so blessed, but I was certainly grateful.

After all, a year ago during the darkest times of my life, I would have never thought it was possible to be experiencing the happiness I was now. I wouldn't have dreamed there could be a man like AJ—one who was so wonderful, so sweet and caring, so generous both in and outside of the bedroom. Most of all, one who was my true soul-mate that Mama Sofia had always said would one day come along. Instead, I would still be believing the many lies my ex's from my battered and broken past had told me.

But when I least deserved it and after being so stubborn, I

had found acceptance of myself, the love of a lifetime, and a family of my own.

Epilogue

AJ

One Year Later

As I stood at the doorway leading to the altar of Christ the King cathedral, I fidgeted nervously back and forth on my feet. At the same time, my fingers tapped out a beat on the black pants of my tux. The intensely sweet aroma from all the floral arrangements stung my nose, while my ears rung from the sound of the enormous pipe organ blasting out the pre-wedding ceremony music.

Wrapping an arm around my shoulder, Jake said, "You know, we can still run if you want?"

I snorted. "Yeah right. You want a mob of angry Sicilians after us?"

Jake laughed. "Nah, I'm good."

"Besides, there's nothing more I want to do than marry Mia."

"I know, man. I just had to tease you." He glanced down

at the platinum band on his left hand and shook his head. "Who would have thought you and I would be shackled with balls and chains at the ripe old age of twenty-six?"

"Not me. That's for damn sure," I replied, with a smile. I jerked my chin up towards Rhys. "Now we just gotta get him someone, and we'll all be old married dudes."

Rhys shook his head wildly back and forth. "Screw that dude. I'm not getting married until I'm thirty."

I rolled my eyes. "Yeah, I said the same thing."

"I said forty," Jake said.

With a shrug, Rhys said, "Well, it ain't happening for me anytime soon. Got it?"

"Whatever," Jake, Brayden and I all said in unison.

We were interrupted by the wedding coordinator. "It's time."

While my heart leapt into my throat with nerves, I clapped my hands together as if anxiously ready to get this show on the road. It wasn't that I was nervous about marrying Mia—I'd totally been the chick in the relationship by being ready to get married immediately. Hell, I would have married her in Mexico right after I proposed. But she had wanted to wait to give us time to settle in to being engaged, to our new life on the road, and most importantly, to having Bella before we tied the knot. In the end, it made the most sense because she wanted the dream wedding she'd once planned years ago with that douchebag Dev.

Between my touring schedule and a newborn, it had taken a little longer to get the wedding planned and executed.

With a confident smile at my groomsmen, I said, "Okay, let's do this."

My first step out into the crowd was one of total confidence. As Best-Man, Antonio followed behind me, then Jake, Brayden, and Rhys. My Tio David was part of the crew and my father, as well as some of my cousins. We were a full house of attendants with both Mia and I having nine attendants...each.

The organ started up the chords of *Canon in D* for the bridesmaids to enter. The large double doors at the back of the church swung open, and a chorus of 'aww's'! rang through the cathedral at Bella's appearance. Toddling as best she could up the aisle, she looked like a living and breathing doll in her frilly white dress and lavender ribbons in her short, dark hair. She had turned one only a few weeks before, but she had been walking since she was just ten months old, much to mine and Mia's dismay of chasing her everywhere.

Holding her hand, Melody wore a matching white dress with lavender sash. Even though Melody was almost three, both she and Bella were loaded guns on whether they would actually execute their duties as flower girls. While Melody gripped her basket tight in her hands while occasionally tossing a few lavender petals onto the floor, Bella was completely oblivious to the petals in her basket. Instead, she was enjoying the attention of everyone she passed. Her tiny hand waved and blew kisses to people. Man, she was a little ham, just like her old man.

When she got half-way up the aisle, she saw me at the top of the altar. Her face brightened, and her chubby cheeks stretched into a wide grin, showing off the bottom and top teeth she'd cut. "Dada!" she shrieked, before dropping her basket and barreling towards me. Laughter rang around us at her outburst.

"No Bella!" Melody shouted.

I didn't bother telling her to stop. Instead, I squatted down and held out my arms for her. She dove into them, bestowing kisses on my cheeks. From the way she was acting, you would have thought she hadn't seen me in months, rather than a few hours.

"Look at you, mi bella princesa, mi niña hermosa," I said, kissing her cheeks.

Bella tilted her head and gave me a teasing little smile that outrivaled my signature smirk. Yeah, she'd inherited a big dose of my cockiness. She was a downright flirt when it came to the guys and getting what she wanted from them. Just like me, Jake and Rhys were wrapped around her tiny finger. People already loved to tell me that I was in for nothing but trouble when she got to be a teenager. Jesus, I didn't even want to think of that. I'd probably end up in jail for throttling some horny twatcake.

"Now, go to Abuela," I instructed, motioning to the front bench where my mother held out her arms. Bella's tiny brown brows furrowed while her lips turned down in a pout. "Go on. She has Cheerios for you in her bag."

"Hmm," she murmured, before I put her back down. If there was one thing she was addicted to, it was Cheerios. Thankfully, she made a bee-line for my mom who was waving the zip-lock bag at her. I had just retaken my place at the head of the altar when the organ began the introduction to *Ave Maria*, for Mia's entrance. I gave a quick smile to the girls...and Dee, who was Mia's Honor Attendant or Dude of Honor or some shit. I glanced back at the guys who all grinned back at me.

When the doors opened revealing Mia and Duke, my heart shuddered to a stop. It felt like an eternity before it started beating normally again. I had never seen her so fucking radiant. Her long, dark hair fell in waves over her bare shoulders. A glittering tiara sat on top of her head, holding her veil in place. Her strapless dress showed off just enough of her fabulous rack to get the lower half of me up and running.

As she approached me at the altar, tears sparkled in her eyes. "Hey, don't cry, amorcito mio," I whispered.

She shook her head. "Don't worry. They're happy tears. I promise."

"They better be."

"Who gives this woman in marriage?" the priest asked.

"I do," Duke replied. Taking Mia in his arms, he hugged her tight. As he pulled away, he kissed Mia's cheek tenderly before turning back to me. He held out his hand, and I shook it firmly. "Good luck, son."

"Thank you."

He gave Mia a final kiss before taking his seat on the first pew. "Dearly beloved we are gathered here today..." the priest began, but I tuned him out. With my heart beating so wildly I thought it might explode out of my chest, all I could do was stare at Mia. Until that moment, I hadn't truly realized that there had been a hole in my heart—one that only Mia's love could seem to fill. She and her love confounded me, humbled me, and so completely astounded me. I knew I was one lucky bastard.

Mia

I pressed myself flush against AJ, my husband of four hours, and swayed to the music under the twinkling ballroom lights. Besides the birth of Bella, today, my wedding day, had been the most amazing day of my life from start, and now, to almost finish. After the ceremony, we had left the church for my dream reception venue—The Egyptian

Ballroom at the Fox Theater. Since we were comprised of two ethnicities known for partying, we had been going full force since seven o'clock.

I'd cut the massive seven tiered cake and smashed some onto AJ's face while he'd managed to accidentally drop a piece down the front of my dress to be recovered by his tongue. I'd thrown my bouquet into Allison's eager arms, only to have Dee teasingly snatch it away. Then AJ had used his teeth to extricate the garter off of my leg to throw at Rhys.

We'd spent the rest of the night dancing in each other's arms. There was truly no better feeling. Our first dance as man and wife had been to *Anema e Core*, which was soon followed by *Amorcito Mio*. I'd barely eaten any of the massive spread of food or had some of the free-flowing alcohol. All I wanted was AJ—the man of my dreams and thankfully my reality as well.

Suddenly, in the middle of a romantic love song, my Spidey mommy senses perked up, alerting me that something was wrong with Bella. Sure enough, Mari started across the floor with a wailing Bella in her arms. The moment she saw AJ and me, she stretched out her arms and kicked her legs.

"I was going to take this little girl on across the street to the hotel to bed, but I got halfway out of the ballroom when she started screaming for her mama and dada."

"Come here, mi amor," AJ crooned, taking Bella from Mari.

Snubbing back her tears, Bella rubbed her red eyes with her tiny fists. I leaned over to kiss her wet cheek. "It's way past your bedtime, sweetheart. Go on with Abuela. Mommy and Daddy will see you in the morning."

AJ nudged me. "Surely she can stay a little while longer and dance with us? I mean, how many times do her parents get married?" he questioned, with amusement twinkling in his eyes.

With a grin, I shook my head. "You are spoiling her rotten. It's no fun playing bad cop all the time, AJ."

"Actually, that could be really fun for us to play in the bedroom."

Considering his mother was still standing right there, I smacked his arm. "Fine. She can stay. But when she starts screaming again, I'm walking away, and you can deal with her." I hugged Mari, before she started off the floor and back to her table.

AJ wrapped his free arm around me to where Bella was cocooned between us. She rested her head against his shoulder. He jerked his chin up at the band leader who nodded. When the opening notes to *Unchained Melody* came on, I smiled and pressed myself closer against AJ. I remembered the first time we had danced to this song, and he had sung to me in Spanish. This time he began singing to both me *and* Bella. By the time the song ended, she was fast asleep.

"I'll go put her down," I said.

"Nah, let's make our exit."

"It's only midnight, AJ."

"So?"

I laughed. "It would be considered poor form since Italian and Mexican couples do not leave the reception until at least two in the morning."

He snorted. "As long as the booze keeps flowing, the food keeps coming, and the music keeps playing, they'll be fine. Besides, we did the whole cake cutting/bouquet throwing shit." He leaned down to nuzzle my neck. Whispering into my ear, he said, "I'm ready to consummate our marriage, aren't you?"

"Yes," I murmured. His words in my ear started up a thrum of desire within me—one only AJ could do.

"Good. So let's get the fuck out of here."

AJ waved to our remaining guests and motioned down at Bella's sleeping form, as if she excused us for making a run for it. Mari rose out of her chair and came with us since Bella would be sleeping in her and Joaquin's suite tonight. We were leaving for Mexico in the morning—this time when we spent a few days with Abuela, we would be sleeping together. Then it was on to a resort in Puerto Vallarta while Bella stayed behind with Abuela.

Joined by two hulking body guards, we made our way

outside onto Peachtree Street. There were only a few straggling paparazzi wanting to get a picture of us. A year ago we'd given them quite the story with Bella's limo birth. As flashbulbs went off all around us, AJ quickly handed Bella to me and then took off his tux jacket. He wrapped it around my shoulders so Bella would be shielded from the flashes of the photographers.

We hustled across the street to the Georgian Terrace. When we got to her floor, Mari took Bella from me. Thankfully, she was still sleeping soundly. I think the day's events had completely worn her out. Before she stepped off the elevator, Mari turned to me with a smile. "Today was so very beautiful. We're so happy you're officially a part of our family now, Mia."

I smiled. "Thank you. I am, too."

She gave me a quick hug before heading off to her room. AJ and I continued on up to one of the bridal suites. "So, did you buy something sexy to wear for me tonight?"

Even though I had one entire bag of my luggage full of naughty items from my lingerie shower, I shook my head. "What would be the point? You'd get hard if I was wearing a flannel gown."

AJ threw his head back and laughed. "True. But I'd still like to see you in some lace and garters."

I wrapped my arms around his neck. "Then, I think that can be arranged."

When we got into our hotel room, I made a beeline for my suitcase. I pulled out a racy, white number that Abby had given me. I grinned at AJ who was tearing out of his tux so fast I thought he would rip it. Turning around, I glanced over my shoulder at him. "Unzip me, please."

He groaned. "If I do that, I might not be able to stop."

"If you don't, I'm never getting out of this massive dress."

"Fine, fine." He then worked the zipper down for me.

Cupping the front of my dress, I winked at him. "Be back in a minute."

"Make it a second."

I slipped into the bathroom and began making fast work of getting out of the fancy crinoline and the intricate bustier. I had just finished adjusting my garters when AJ stepped into the bathroom. "Wait, I'm not—"

My words dried up at the sight of him twirling a set of handcuffs around his finger. He jerked his chin up at the massive grotto shower with a gleaming silver showerhead. "I think it's time for a little payback, Mrs. Resendiz."

With a squeal, I tried to escape him, but he was too fast. I was locked into his tight embrace. He smiled down at me with such love in his eyes. "You know, I loved you even after you handcuffed me to that damn shower at Jake's."

"I loved you when I did it...and even after, too."

His lips crushed against mine with a mixture of both lust and love, and I knew I was in for a night I'd never forget.

About the Author

Katie Ashley is the New York Times, USA Today, and Amazon Best-Selling author of The Proposition. She lives outside of Atlanta, Georgia with her two very spoiled dogs and one outnumbered cat. She has a slight obsession with Pinterest, The Golden Girls, Harry Potter, Shakespeare, Supernatural, Designing Women, and Scooby-Doo.

She spent 11 1/2 years educating the Youth of America aka teaching MS and HS English until she left to write full time in December 2012.

She also writes Young Adult fiction under the name Krista Ashe.

Made in the USA
Middletown, DE
29 June 2016